Praise for

A Midnight Dance

"*A Midnight Dance* is a fun, spicy historical romp that's sure to delight! A lovely twist on Cinderella . . . [A] deliciously dark hero and a heroine who's more than a match for him!"

—Jennifer Ashley, *New York Times* and *USA Today* bestselling author

"Wickedly passionate . . . [A] sensual treat."

—Sylvia Day, national bestselling author

"Lila Dipasqua's 'Fiery Tale' version of Cinderella sets the classic story ablaze . . . with a passionate, resourceful Cinderella and a wild and dashing Prince Charming." —Anna Campbell, award-winning author

The Princess in His Bed

"Lila DiPasqua's lushly erotic writing is sophisticated, sensuous, and deeply romantic. If you love historical romance, this is an author to watch!" —Elizabeth Hoyt, *New York Times* bestselling author

Awakened by a Kiss

"The most luscious, sexy take on classic fairy tales I've ever read! The three heroes are delicious!"

—Cheryl Holt, *New York Times* bestselling author

"An erotically charged retelling of classic stories. Steamy yet sweet, DiPasqua expertly melds emotionally charged erotica with fantasy, love, and hope, leaving no doubt as to the happily-ever-after. These are not your ...

... ing author

"Lila DiPasc ... th mirth, passion, and ... ce Junkies*

"A sinfully e ... ters that's sure to please." —*Lovin' Me Some Romance*

Berkley Sensation titles by Lila DiPasqua

A Midnight Dance

Lila DiPasqua

BERKLEY SENSATION, NEW YORK

THE BERKLEY PUBLISHING GROUP
Published by the Penguin Group
Penguin Group (USA) Inc.
375 Hudson Street, New York, New York 10014, USA
Penguin Group (Canada), 90 Eglinton Avenue East, Suite 700, Toronto, Ontario M4P 2Y3, Canada
(a division of Pearson Penguin Canada Inc.)
Penguin Books Ltd., 80 Strand, London WC2R 0RL, England
Penguin Group Ireland, 25 St. Stephen's Green, Dublin 2, Ireland (a division of Penguin Books Ltd.)
Penguin Group (Australia), 250 Camberwell Road, Camberwell, Victoria 3124, Australia
(a division of Pearson Australia Group Pty. Ltd.)
Penguin Books India Pvt. Ltd., 11 Community Centre, Panchsheel Park, New Delhi—110 017, India
Penguin Group (NZ), 67 Apollo Drive, Rosedale, Auckland 0632, New Zealand
(a division of Pearson New Zealand Ltd.)
Penguin Books (South Africa) (Pty.) Ltd., 24 Sturdee Avenue, Rosebank, Johannesburg 2196,
South Africa

Penguin Books Ltd., Registered Offices: 80 Strand, London WC2R 0RL, England

This book is an original publication of The Berkley Publishing Group.

Cover illustration by Jim Griffin.
Cover design by George Long.
Interior text design by Laura K. Corless.

PRINTING HISTORY
Berkley Sensation trade paperback edition / August 2011

Library of Congress Cataloging-in-Publication Data

DiPasqua, Lila.
A midnight dance / Lila DiPasqua.—Berkley Sensation trade paperback ed.
p. cm.
ISBN 978-0-425-24198-1
1. Fairy tales—Adaptations. I. Title.
PS3604.I625M53 2011
813'.6—dc22

2011014129

PRINTED IN THE UNITED STATES OF AMERICA

10 9 8 7 6 5 4 3 2 1

To my grandmother, Lila DiPasqua.
I'm proud to be named after this amazing lady.
She was a woman with great strength and sharp wit.
The heroine in this book in many ways mirrors her.
Had she been in Sabine Laurent's shoes, she would have demonstrated the same loyalty, love, and courage.

To my grandfather, Nicola DiPasqua—a decorated soldier, known for his bravery, strength, and kindness, and the greatest grandpa ever.
Birthdays aren't the same without having you there to share my cake with.
Thank you both for being my guardian angels, aligning the heavens, and making this book possible.

To my parents and brother, because you're the best.

And to Carm, Julia, Christian, and Olivia for making my life complete.

A Historical Tidbit

Long before Hans Christian Andersen and the Brothers Grimm, there was a French writer by the name of Charles Perrault. He was the author of *The Tales of Mother Goose*, and started the beloved genre of fairy tales. He lived in seventeenth-century France during the reign of the Sun King, Louis XIV. Louis was a lusty king. His glittering court was as salacious as it was elegant.

During this most wicked time period, Perrault wrote stories that have delighted people for centuries: *Sleeping Beauty*, *Little Red Riding Hood*, *Puss in Boots*, and *Bluebeard*—to name a few.

The following is based on his most famous fairy tale of all . . . *Cinderella*.

Happy Reading!

Lila

Prologue

May 1650—Paris

"I have a plan!" Isabelle Laurent announced the moment she yanked Sabine inside the costume room at their father's grand theater and slammed the door shut.

Elaborate costumes and colorful plumes, wigs, and props for the latest comedy, *The Foolish Wives*, filled the space. The very play that could be heard faintly, the actors' voices seeping into the silence.

Sabine frowned. "What plan? What are we doing here?" Her ire was stirred. Mischief shone in her twin's eyes. Sabine wanted no part of her sister's scheme. Whatever it was. The play was almost over, and she wanted to spend the remaining time watching her dark-haired prince from behind the stage. The only place Father allowed them to be when at his comedies.

Unseen and out of the way.

Her Dark Prince was in attendance tonight. And it was all because of her lucky new shoes. Covered entirely in glass beading, Isabelle referred to them as "the glass slippers." The last three times Sabine wore them, her Dark Prince had attended the play, her father's theater drawing royalty and aristocracy alike.

Though he wasn't really a prince, he was the firstborn son of the powerful and prominent Marquis de Blainville.

Jules de Moutier. He was nineteen.

And without a doubt, the finest male she'd ever seen in *all* her fifteen years. *And oh how exceptional he looked . . .* Tall. Beautiful. With dark hair. Mesmerizing dark eyes. And when he smiled or laughed—a rich masculine sound that was music to her ears—he had the most attractive dimples near his mouth that made her heart melt.

Always the center of attention, he had such commanding presence, drawing all eyes in the room to him. But he never noticed her. Never glanced her way. Not with so many silly females vying for his attention, all but giddy when they captured it.

Oh, but he'd definitely notice her next year, when she'd be introduced to society. And Sabine already knew what she'd wear—a golden-colored gown.

And of course, her lucky glass slippers.

She was counting the days. Had dreamed of their meeting at the ball. Their dance. The moment he'd declare his affections. And their first kiss. She was going to give him his best kiss ever! Better than any of the females she'd seen him kiss on those heart-sinking occasions, when he thought he wasn't being observed.

She could barely stand the wait.

"I'm leaving." Sabine turned, anxious to get back to Jules.

"Fine. Go. I'll get close to the handsome Moutier brothers all on my own."

That stopped Sabine dead in her tracks. Isabelle had a *tendre* for Jules's younger brother, Luc. And a rash, impetuous nature. She adored her sister, loved her with all her heart. They couldn't be any closer even though they were as different physically as they were in spirit.

"How are you going to do that?" She couldn't stop herself from asking, despite being much more levelheaded and less adventuresome.

Isabelle smiled. "I'm going to slip out that door." She pointed to the one at the opposite end of the room. "And run up the alley to the front of the theater. The audience is about to leave and I'm going to brush past Luc."

Sabine's mouth fell agape. "You're not!"

Isabelle was now grinning. "I am."

"Father will be furious."

"Only if he finds out. You can stay, or you can come with me." Isabelle blew her a kiss and bolted out the door.

Sabine remained indecisive for all of two heartbeats before she tore out of the room and was on her sister's heels, the thought of getting close to Jules quickening her steps. As she raced up the darkened alley, Isabelle's laugh drifted back to her on the warm summer breeze, inspiring her own. Sabine emerged onto the main street near the front entrance of the theater. Her foot slid out from under her, her bottom colliding hard with the cobblestone road; a sharp pain shot up her spine and made her wince.

The roar of laughter from the crowd exiting her father's theater assailed her ears. Her left palm stung. Her derrière ached. And she blinked back the tears, mortified by the spectacle she'd just made of herself. Chin-down, she was too afraid to look up. Afraid that in the crowd she'd see her Dark Prince, or rather, see him laughing at her.

Isabelle was at her side in an instant, falling to her knees and throwing a consoling arm around her shoulder. "Sabine . . ."

A pair of black polished boots appeared next to her just then. She looked up. Her heart flip-flopped.

It was *he*. The handsomest man in the realm. Her dark-haired prince. He lowered himself down on his haunches.

"Are you all right?" he asked, his voice caressing over her. She was lost in the vision he made, his most kissable mouth voicing words of concern for *her*.

She blinked.

He frowned slightly. "Is she mute?" he asked Isabelle.

"No, my lord. She can speak." Her sister pinched her back.

Sabine flinched. "I—I am fine. Thank you."

Then it happened. He smiled. At *her*! And what a glorious smile it was.

"You lost your slipper," he said. Picking up her fallen shoe, he gently clasped her ankle and slipped it back on her foot. She forgot to breathe.

He rose, and to her amazement, he held out his hand. Isabelle pinched her harder. Sabine jerked and quickly placed her hand in his. It was warm, strong, and felt so right. She knew he'd held the hand of many beauties from the finest families in the noble class, but at that moment his hand was all hers. His attention was hers. His melting smile was only for her.

She rose with his help, ignoring the pain in her backside.

"Do be careful." Then he leaned in. The world shifted beneath her feet. Her breath lodged in her throat. "You have beautiful hair," he whispered in her ear, and with a wink he walked away, enveloped back into the throng that had been waiting for him.

"Oh, Sabine . . ." Isabelle stepped up behind her and, hugged her around the waist. Resting her chin on Sabine's shoulder, she said, "Can you believe what just happened?"

Her hand and ankle still tingled where he'd touched her. The glass slippers had more than worked their magic this night. And she knew right there and then, down to her very marrow, that the next time they'd meet, there would be more magic to come . . .

1

Once upon a time there was a woman whose life was in cinders. Her story has been retold many ways, many times, throughout the realm. Throughout time. Her family's wealth was gone, as were their elegant home, their prestigious theater, and her lovely gowns. They were as lost to her as her girlhood dream of marrying a man she'd loved from afar. A man who was well beyond her reach.

A man she'd dubbed her Dark Prince, for he was tall, dark, and oh so handsome.

But her opinion of him had soured. No longer did she believe in a happily ever after.

Yet one night, at the stroke of midnight, the stars aligned.

Destiny stepped in.

And she came face-to-face with her Dark Prince. But she didn't arrive before him as she'd dreamed all those years ago. She was not in a golden-colored gown, but in humble attire, not in a gilded carriage, but in a rickety cart, as worthless as a pumpkin, driven by two men, as meek as mice . . . carrying wine mixed with a special potion . . .

August 1658—Just past the stroke of midnight . . .

This was sheer madness.

But what choice did she have?

Sabine Laurent struggled to maintain a brave façade before her two younger cousins.

The flickering flames of the campfire ahead drew closer and closer as her cousin Gerard drove their cart through the darkened forest. Her heart thundering in her ears, she could barely hear the crunching of twigs and leaves beneath the wooden wheels.

Robert, Gerard's younger brother, sat silently in the back with the flagons of wine, the very air around them thick with tension and trepidation.

"Sabine, what if this goes terribly wrong?" Gerard whispered, his tone laced with dread.

That was the very question tormenting her. She prayed she wasn't leading them to their deaths. But then, if they didn't have the funds they owed in two weeks, they were all dead anyway. Not just the three of them, but the balance of her family, who were at home, thankfully unaware of what she was about to do. Unaware that at the marketplace, mere hours ago, she'd stumbled upon the very miracle they needed.

"You will call me Elise. Not Sabine. All will be well if we do not deviate from the plan," she managed to say firmly, her tone belying her mounting fear. For the first time since her father's death last month, there was a glimmer of hope. A way to clear their debts and spare their lives.

A means to more than restore her family's fortune.

A means to search for Isabelle . . . Her throat tightened instantly. She missed her sister more than she could allow herself to feel. The pain was too excruciating to bear.

Isabelle was her other half. Her heart and soul now empty without her.

Sabine took in a quiet breath and steeled her courage.

Just ahead, in the heavily guarded camp, there was a wealth in silver.

And by God, she was going to steal it.

She couldn't—wouldn't—have anything else taken from her. Or lose anyone else she loved. Her losses in the last eight years had been too many. And too great.

Fate had *finally* shone in their favor. That morning she'd chanced upon the most incredible conversation between two thieves-of-the-sea. Clearly, the two degenerates thought that in a town filled with ignorant French peasants, so far from the Italian border, it was safe to discuss in Italian their latest captured prize from Spanish ships and the route they were taking to rendezvous with more men of their ilk.

But Sabine had understood every astounding word.

There were many things she blamed her father for. There were many reasons she still harbored bitterness toward him, even after his death, but the education he'd provided his twin daughters with was better than what most women of the upper class received.

Male laughter erupted from the camp. Sabine jumped.

Stay calm. You can do this. You can.

She was no stranger to the theater. Her late father was the prominent playwright Paul Laurent. She'd been raised around actors and knew how to put on a convincing performance. As children, she and Isabelle used to write their own plays and perform them for the servants. Acting was in her blood. She could play any role.

Even the role of a whore.

Sabine adjusted her neckline a fraction lower, her fingers fidgety, the coarse material a sharp contrast to the sumptuous gowns she'd once owned. Her wealthy middle-class family had had social standing once. A magnificent townhouse in one of the most prestigious areas in Paris. A bright future.

Now their future was bleak—that is, if they didn't get hold of that ever-nearing treasure.

"What will we do if we cannot get them to drink the tainted wine?" Gerard pressed. "What will *you* do if, when alone with their leader, he wishes to sample you before the drink?"

Another round of laughter rushed up at her from between the trees and shrubs. Tightening her jaw, Sabine stared straight ahead at the camp with cold resolve.

She'd come to terms with exactly what she'd do. Though she'd never admit it to her cousins, she was prepared to make the ultimate sacrifice and let the scoundrel have her body. She'd detach herself from the act, numb herself to it—just as she'd numbed herself against the loss of her sister these last five years—and acquiesce.

Whatever it took to succeed, that's what she'd do.

She couldn't enter a situation like this and not be resigned to the very real possibility that he'd have her before she'd get him to down the wine.

"They could murder you, Sabine. All of us. But not before they rape you. Repeatedly," Gerard added.

Dear God, she didn't need this. His words were only shredding her courage.

"Leave Sabine alone, Gerard," Robert defended. "If—If she says it's going to work, I believe her." Sweet Robert, just sixteen, trusted in her. Her family had always looked to "sensible Sabine" to fix matters. There was nothing "sensible" about this plan. But desperate people were forced to do desperate things. It sickened her that this was all she could come up with to save them from the consequences they faced.

"If we don't pay the taxes we owe the Crown, they could arrest us and throw us into debtors' prison," she said tightly. "You've heard the stories. You know what happens to women confined in cells with all-male guards. They are raped. *Repeatedly.* And let's not forget the conditions of the prison. Disease is rampant within its walls. I doubt we'd all survive the incarceration. And if they decide instead to cast us off our land, we'll starve. One by one. There will be no escaping it. Hunger is still widespread. The realm has yet to recover from the ravages of the *Fronde*." The *Fronde*—the civil uprising incited by a group of ambitious noblemen—had almost dethroned their young King and thrown the country into chaos. Five years since the end of the unrest, and still the realm reeled.

If only there had never been an uprising.

If only her father hadn't sunk them further into debt once they were forced to move out of the city to their country home. If only he hadn't sent Isabelle away. She'd still have her sister. Then she wouldn't be so hollow inside.

"But, Sabine . . . this plan . . ." Gerard's voice trailed off.

Why did he insist on arguing with her? He knew the reality they faced.

"Gerard, if you"—twisting around, she looked back at Robert—"either of you have a better plan, speak of it now."

Robert lowered his eyes.

"Well?" she pressed, demanding a response.

"I've no other plan," Robert murmured. "Though I wish I did."

So did she. Sabine turned her attention to Gerard.

"What about you, Gerard? Have you something better to suggest?" In the moonlight, she could make out his profile as he stared straight ahead.

His face was taut and he swallowed hard before he said softly, "No."

"Then we'll proceed with my plan." Good God. She was really going to go through with this.

She was going to have to face a camp full of men, convince them that a woman who was still a virgin was an experienced harlot, and persuade their leader to purchase her services. It was the only way to enter the camp. Once inside, she and her cousins would have to make sure every man ingested at least some of their tainted wine.

Heaven help them. *This plan is beyond mad . . .*

She readjusted the neckline of her dress, desperate to distract herself from the terror twisting in her belly.

This is going to work out in our favor because it has to.

"A King's ransom in silver is just ahead. Our plan will work. Be brave." It amazed her how courageous she sounded while her very entrails quivered and quaked, unsure exactly whom she was trying to reassure more—them or herself.

"Well, well, what have we here?" The voice came out of nowhere.

Her heart lurched.

A dark-haired burly man had appeared from the thicket with several large intimidating friends. He scratched his scruffy chin and grinned. It was mirthless and menacing.

She met Gerard's gaze. The fright in his eyes was unmistakable. Her courage faltered.

"Go on," she whispered, forcing the words out. There was no turning back now.

These men didn't look as though they'd let them simply drive on past.

Gerard glanced at the men and gave her one last look. Holding his gaze, she silently pleaded for him to proceed before her courage completely gave out, her bottled-up fright so barely contained.

Finally, he cleared his throat and got down from the cart.

"Sir, we're hungry and your cooking fire drew us. Spare us some food and we'll provide you with wine to wash it down." Gerard sounded so convincing, it elated her. All those times she and Isabelle used to force him to act in their plays had rubbed off on him.

The brute chuckled, his comrades joining in.

Slowly he unsheathed his sword. The ominous blade gleamed in the moonlight. Sabine's stomach dropped. He placed the tip to Gerard's chest in proximity to his heart. Her cousin stiffened. A scream lodged in her throat. *Dear God . . .*

"We don't share," the brute said, "unless it's the woman you're offering." The roar of male laughter assailed her ears. Every pair of eyes from the unruly bunch was fixed on her in lewd assessment.

"Wh-Who is the leader among you?" Gerard asked. "I w-w-will offer the woman to him and *only* him in exchange for food."

"*Jésus-Christ*, Fabrice, put the sword down before he pisses his breeches." A tall thinner man with blond hair approached.

With a muttered curse, Fabrice reluctantly lowered the blade.

"Who are you?" the blond man asked Gerard. "State your business here in these woods truthfully, or I'll have Fabrice finish what he started."

Gerard looked up at her, his reluctance to continue clearly readable on his face. She nodded to him to proceed. *Courage, now.* The blond man didn't seem as frightening as his friends.

Gerard looked at the ground. Taking in an audible breath, he released it slowly before he was able to speak again. "We've been traveling all day and are hungry," he wove his tale. "We offer some wine to your men—and the woman *only* to your leader—in exchange for food."

"Why only him?" Fabrice lamented.

"Silence!" the blond man snapped. He then looked up at her and said, "Step down and come closer."

Sabine clenched her teeth to keep them from chattering. The moment her feet touched the ground, she was relieved her knees didn't buckle beneath her.

She approached the blond man on shaky limbs, managing to conceal her disquiet.

He looked over her upturned face, then down her body with a dispassionately critical eye. She held in her outrage. Never in her life had she been so crudely assessed. But then, a whore wouldn't mind the preview.

And that is how you must act.

"Turn around," he demanded.

Sabine turned slowly, allowing him time to assess her backside, fighting down the humiliation with purposeful resolve. *This is all part of the role.*

When at last she faced him again, he said, "Good. Wait here. I'll speak to the commander and suggest your deal to him."

* * *

"*Merde*, Raymond, have you lost your fucking mind?" Jules Thomas de Moutier snarled. Members of his crew who'd been sitting around the fire immediately rose and cleared the area, noting his escalating ire. "You allowed someone close to the camp when we hold our biggest capture to date?"

The rest of the men stood guard around the perimeter of the camp. Too many desperate peasants would risk death for what he had in his covered carts.

Raymond shook his blond head. "They're harmless—a woman and two men, no, more like boys, merely looking for food. Take a look at the woman. You will like what you see," he implored.

"I don't care what she looks like. *Jésus-Christ*, I've more important things on my mind."

Five years. Five horrific years he'd spent privateering, preying on Spanish ships and ports during the realm's ongoing war with Spain. And finally he'd accumulated enough wealth.

With this latest prize he could repurchase his family's lands. Or at least part of them. By God, he'd repurchase parcel by parcel if he had to, until he'd reclaimed everything that had belonged to his family.

Everything that had been wrongly stripped from them.

Everything that was rightfully theirs.

Once he had enough land, respectability would follow. Enough time had passed since his family's disgrace. He prayed that he could convince someone to talk. Someone out there knew the truth about who'd so treacherously doomed his father.

And why.

"My lord, as a loyal servant to your family for many years, to you, personally, during your time in the King's Navy, I know how difficult it has been for you since your father's death. But—"

"*Death*, Raymond? He didn't simply *die*." Jules couldn't keep the venom from his tone. "He was falsely convicted and executed for treason." Why the bloody hell was Raymond bringing up the subject? He knew better. The mere mention of his father's tragic end immediately hurled him into a volatile mood. Just about anything set him off now. He barely recognized the man he'd become over the last five years. Angry. Bitter. The man he once was, was gone, along with his birthright. His family's honor.

His beloved father.

"Be that as it may," Raymond said. "What I do *not* understand, my lord, is this celibate lifestyle you've adopted. How many times have we come ashore and you have allowed the men to sate themselves? Many. How often have you indulged yourself? Rarely. You've always had your share of beautiful women, some all but begging for any sexual favors you were willing to bestow upon them."

Unwanted memories of his past sexual exploits flooded his mind. His body tightened, a physical reminder that his latest stint of celibacy had been lengthy.

"Raymond," he said, his voice low, edged with fury, "are you trying to torment me this night?"

"Of course not! I'm trying to alleviate some of your torment."

His torment wasn't going to be alleviated by thinking about those days when he'd had it all—when he was heir of the Marquis de Blainville. A distinguished officer in the King's Navy. And had his choice of women wherever he went, indulging in carnal diversions—his favorite vice—when he wasn't occupied with his naval duties.

In his absences from home, he never imagined anyone would fabricate lies—that his father had been in league with those who'd tried to overthrow the King during the *Fronde*. Or that he and his brother, Luc, would be stripped of their nobility, their lands, tossed out of the Navy, and forced to feed themselves by captaining privateer ships for Simon Boulenger, the captain of the realm's unofficial fleet.

He hated what he'd been reduced to, what had been done to his family's name. Not a friend to be found in the cursed lot of his peers.

And now Raymond wanted him to *purchase sex*. This added a different dimension to his humiliation. A humbling example of how far he'd fallen for a man who had always been offered carnal pleasures in abundance *for free*.

It was damned difficult for his pride to bear.

And so he took to abstaining until he reached a point where he could stand it no longer; then and only then did he allow himself a brief fuck, the women utterly forgettable. In fact, in the last five years, he couldn't remember a single one of their faces.

He'd sooner take his cock in hand than pay this camp follower for sex.

Jules placed his hands on his hips and gazed at the crackling fire. "Get rid of her. All of them. I'm not interested." His life was on the verge of changing at last. As soon as he delivered this latest capture to Boulenger, he'd take his share of the bounty and walk away from privateering for good.

"No," Raymond answered defiantly for the first time ever.

Jules's gaze shot to his servant. "*What did you say?*"

Raymond swallowed. "It—It is out of regard for you that I decline. To speak frankly, my lord, it has been difficult to watch your self-induced suffering with these long periods of abstinence." He shifted his weight, nervously. "Did—Did I mention her fair coloring? It is the very type you have always preferred . . ."

Jules crossed his arms over his chest, wrestling with his ire.

"M-May I be frank again, my lord?"

"Well, of course, Raymond," he responded tightly. "There seems to be no stopping you tonight."

"This latest capture is significant. It would be beneficial if you had a clear mind. Knowing you as I do, you're ready to leap out of your very skin."

Jules tamped down his resentment. He knew Raymond's words were true, but he'd be damned if he was going to admit it.

"My lord, she is attractive, blond, and *here*. It is something you need."

Jules's patience finally snapped. He stalked up to Raymond and growled in his ear. "What I *need* is my life back, not a fuck in the forest."

2

Robert began to mutter a prayer.

"Stop that!" Gerard whispered forcefully, immediately silencing his younger brother.

Sabine ignored them, trying to peer between the trees in the distance, her attention focused on what she could see of the camp—more particularly, the "commander." The blond man was speaking to someone, but she couldn't see to whom.

Fabrice and another man remained a short distance away, keeping guard and preventing them from getting any closer.

It was then that the blond man stepped back, revealing the commander to Sabine.

Her breath caught.

It couldn't be . . . Sabine stared harder. *No. It only looked like him. It couldn't actually be . . .*

She watched intently as the dark-haired man stalked away from the blond man, disappearing behind the trees then reemerging near Fabrice and the other guard.

Robert gasped. "It's the Marquis de Blainville's son!"

Stunned, Sabine stared at the unmistakable sight of Jules de Moutier. He was in profile talking to the blond man once more. And he seemed angry.

Sabine tore her gaze away and looked at the ground, trying to control her breathing. Good God. She couldn't believe it!

"You—You said they were thieves, Sabine," Robert whispered. "We cannot steal from a *noble*."

"Quiet, Robert!" Gerard snapped. "He is an *ex*-noble. His family was stripped of everything when the Marquis was convicted as a traitor. Their lands reverted to the Crown. That's why we owe taxes to the King and not him or his family. He is *nothing*."

Not true.

Jules de Moutier had had too much impact on her life to be dismissed as nothing.

Memories of watching him arrive at the theater, always surrounded by men and women who hung on his every word, were still vivid in Sabine's mind.

Sinfully beautiful, his potent appeal—that knee-weakening smile and those fathomless eyes—had had her utterly enthralled. Heart, body, and soul.

Yet that was all before the mighty Moutier family had brought about her family's ruin.

Except for his occasional irritating invasion into her dreams, she hadn't seen him in eight years.

You're going to have to entice Jules de Moutier into purchasing your sexual favors. Incredulous, she reeled.

Her eyes were drawn back to him standing in the distance.

He wore a white shirt and black breeches. His hair was longer than the last time she'd seen him; his shoulders were broader, too. He looked more muscled, stronger. Gone were all signs of his boyish charms. With his confident manner, his tall powerful body, he exuded authority on a whole new level. He was every bit a man, with an edge of danger. And even more devastating to behold. Her stomach fluttered wildly.

The unexpected physical response ignited her ire.

She wasn't the same foolish girl who used to drain inkwells writing stories with Isabelle about the two gorgeous Moutier brothers, and how the men would fall madly in love with them and whisk them off to their castles. Back then she'd had more romantic, utterly unrealistic dreams of Jules than she could count.

She'd been naïve about how corrupt the Moutier family was.

Until the *Fronde*, when traitorous families like the Moutiers had thrown the realm into turmoil for five years. And driven so many into financial despair.

Her father had lost their theater because of the *Fronde* and soon after sold their country estate, land that had belonged to her family for generations, to the powerful Moutiers, obliging them to pay taxes to Jules's family just so they could continue to live in their deteriorating château—when her family had never been governed by any lord before.

Taxes that were raised at whim.

His family had inflicted incredible hardship on hers.

After all these years, after everything that had transpired, it galled her that she trembled just being in his presence.

And now her former infatuation was the leader of these scoundrels. It shouldn't surprise her. Further proof of his unsavory character.

"If he recognizes us, we are dead. What do we do, Sabine?" Robert asked.

Sabine looked at Robert's young face. He and his brother had rarely attended her father's plays. He actually believed Jules had noticed him the handful of times he'd ridden past while traveling to and from the Moutiers' neighboring country estate.

"He won't recognize us," she assured him. He'd always looked right through her at the theater. And the incident with the slipper had been significant only to her. He'd never remember it. "He wouldn't know us from other lowly commoners. We are going to proceed as planned." They were going to steal the silver. *From a Moutier.*

Oh, this was going to be sweet.

She'd show him as much mercy as his family had shown to hers.

Sabine marched up to him and his men, her cousins quick on her heels.

"Good evening," she said with a smile.

He turned his head, his gorgeous dark eyes locking with hers. A thrill shivered down her spine. She held her smile, irked by yet another physical response he effortlessly inspired.

"Good evening," he said.

Say something provocative.

" 'Tis a beautiful night. The stars are bright. A perfect eve for one's delight. No?"

Jules and the blond man exchanged curious glances. A few of the men chuckled. Mentally she cringed.

Whores did *not* recite poetry.

Not even bad poetry.

You'll cease behaving like a fool, and start behaving like a prostitute. She wasn't completely ignorant on the matter. Far too curious for their own good, she and Isabelle had often spied upon the patrons at the theater. She'd overheard sexually explicit conversations between lovers in dark corners, and between whores and their customers in the alley outside.

Focus.

Sabine clasped her hands behind her back and pulled her shoulders back a little, a casual pose that also helped emphasize her breasts—and she needed all the help she could get there.

She was delighted when his gaze dropped to her breasts, knowing they were more visible with her top fastenings undone.

"What say you, my handsome lord? Shall we dismiss these gentlemen?"

He studied her for a moment. She forced herself to stand still and not fidget under the weight of his scrutiny. He crossed his arms and tilted his head to one side. "Have we met before?"

One of her cousins choked on a cough. His response unbalanced her briefly.

She pushed back the apprehension. "I think not. You would be one man a woman wouldn't easily forget. And I"—she paused for dramatic effect—"leave a *lasting* impression."

Male hoots filled the air.

She was pleased with herself. And the double entendre. She would leave a lasting impression on him. Just not one he'd like.

Jules simply arched an eyebrow. "What is your name?"

"Elise."

"Well, Elise, about your offer, I wish to—"

Sensing the impending rejection, she stepped closer to him, suddenly enveloped by his scent—rugged, masculine, and all too appealing. She tried to ignore it.

"To accept?" she prompted.

He frowned and rested his hands on his hips. "That wasn't what I was going to say."

"What a shame. I think you should reconsider."

"And why is that?"

"Because I'm willing to wager you give a woman a tumble as good as you look."

Again, male hoots rippled through the small group of his men.

"Commander, she is hot for you!" one guard said.

"If you don't want her, I'll take her," Fabrice suggested.

Her stomach clenched. *God help her if he gave her away to the others*. It was something she had to prevent at all cost.

Ignoring his men and her compliment, his expression remained unchanged. "That doesn't give me reason to have you."

"Ah, but you see, your appeal inspires me." She rose up onto the balls of her feet and leaned close to his ear. His proximity sent her nerve endings into a frenzy. In as sultry a whisper as she could muster, she said, "I am well worth your time when I am . . . fully inspired."

She dropped back down onto her heels and looked into his eyes. Arousal flared in their dark depths, sending a hot jolt through her system. She fought against it, refusing to let these annoying physical responses distract her. By God, she would best him. And exact a little bit of revenge on a Moutier, to boot. She'd be the victor.

She had to be.

Sabine forced herself to stare into those disarming eyes, wishing she could curb the calamity he incited inside her. "Oh, what I intend to do to you . . . will make it impossible for you to *ever* forget me." Her smile was genuine.

More male hoots erupted.

A smile twitched at the corners of his lips, despite the heated interest that burned in his eyes. "Really? Do tell, Elise. What are your intentions?"

Boldly, she moved her gaze down his sculpted body, a provocative appraisal, playing her role, buying herself time to think of an appropriate response. It was then she saw the unmistakable bulge in his breeches. Her pulse leaped.

She, a sexual novice, had done *that* to *him*—a seasoned rake?

A surge of much-needed confidence filled her. She moved her gaze slowly, suggestively, back up his body, using the time to steady herself against the fresh wave of heat that shot through her blood. She shouldn't be reacting this way toward him. She understood just what kind of man he was.

By the time she met his gaze again, she'd returned a firm smile to her face. "It would seem that I have sufficiently raised your . . . *interest.* You can send me away and ponder whether you made the right choice during this long, warm night . . . here alone in your camp . . . *of all men.* Or you can sample what I offer and find out firsthand what I intend." She tilted her head coquettishly. "What say you?"

Sabine held her breath and waited for his response.

3

No doubt about it. Jules had definitely gone without sex for too long if this woman's odd attempts to entice him were actually having an effect.

His cock was as stiff as a spike.

He'd had every intention of sending her away. Yet the longer he spent taking in her petite appealing form, her delicate curves, the longer he inhaled the sweet forest scent emanating from her hair, the more his head and his cock were at odds.

Dieu, he most definitely liked her pale-colored hair.

Illuminated by the night's silvery light, it was the color of starlight and moonbeams. Twined into a thick braid, resting on her bare shoulder, it looked silky soft. He was gripped by a powerful urge to untie the bit of ribbon that held it bound and drive his fingers into it. He wanted to tilt her head back with a sensual tug of her pretty hair and feast from the column of her slender neck down to those perfect perky tits she wanted him to notice.

Merde. He was actually lusting after a *prostitute.*

One who looked like an enchanted creature from the Fae. He

could easily envision her lying naked for his pleasure, basking in the light of the moon, like a forest nymph. All his for the taking.

He couldn't believe it, but for the first time in a very long time, he found himself actually desiring the woman. Not just the release.

Better still, he was affecting her, too. Each time she neared, he sensed her arousal. Even in the night's light, he could tell she was flushed. A glance at her graceful neck told him that her pulse raced. And her pretty nipples, ones he was dying to taste, were pressed ever so enticingly against her chemise, begging for his attention. Reactions that were peculiar for a common whore. Yet extremely tantalizing.

For a woman of her trade, it was odd to find one who looked so fresh and lush instead of dulled and jaded. It meant she was either a lusty little piece who'd prove to be a spirited sex partner, or new at her craft.

"Sir?" The elder of the two young men with her spoke up. "The woman for you, some burgundy for you and your men, in exchange for food—and perhaps a few coins. What say you? Do we have a bargain?"

Jules glanced briefly at the young man then returned his attention to his tempting forest fairy. He saw apprehension flash in her eyes for just an instant. That, too, struck him as peculiar.

All right. He'd ask a few questions to allay the niggling doubts that were nibbling at the fringes of his mind, and if she answered them to his satisfaction, he'd have her, and indulge in some much-needed sexual oblivion.

Jules reached for her braid and lifted it off her shoulder, letting its silky weight rest on his palm. Her eyes widened ever so slightly.

Holding her gaze and the braid, he stroked down along the satiny hair—purposely brushing his knuckles lightly against her soft skin—languorously making his way down to the scrap of material tied in a bow that rested so enticingly on her breast. She made the faintest sound. So soft, in fact, he wasn't certain he'd heard it at all.

He leaned in toward her ear and said, "Elise, you've not had a lot of experience whoring, have you?"

Then he pulled back and looked into her eyes, half expecting to see her falter, hoping desperately she wouldn't. To his delight, she was sporting her usual smile. "I have enough experience to make certain you will be well pleased. Rest assured."

Good answer. Next question.

He caressed his thumb over the velvety braid. "Who are these men with you?"

"No one of importance. Simply traveling companions. For protection."

"Are they forcing you to do this?"

"No," she said without a moment's hesitation. "I do what I want"—she cocked a delicate brow—"and I want *you*."

A smile tugged at the corners of his mouth. By the smug look in her eyes, he could tell she was convinced she'd have him at her mercy. He was a born leader. He'd always been naturally dominant, in and out of bed. He planned to have this beautiful, spirited woman completely undone and at *his* mercy.

Oh, this was going to be sweet.

He hadn't had good sex in too damn long.

He released her braid. "Raymond?"

"Yes?" He heard the smile in Raymond's voice. Normally it would have irked him, but in his ardent state, he didn't care a whit.

"Have a private spot prepared for Elise and me."

"Immediately, Commander." Raymond turned and ordered one of the men to do his bidding.

"Martin," Jules said.

The young man stepped forward from the group. "Commander?"

"Escort Elise and her companions into the camp and provide them with some food."

"Yes, Commander."

Jules turned to her and said, "I'll be with you shortly."

Her smile grew. "I will follow your man," she said obligingly. "But at the moment, I find my hunger for you supersedes my appetite for food. I'd rather devour you." She gave him a saucy wink.

He found himself fighting back another smile, despite the hungry twitch of his cock, his every rakish instinct telling him that they were going to be a perfect sexual match. "I look forward to it, Elise."

Once everyone had left, Jules turned to Raymond. "Watch the young men."

"Of course, my lord. They will be guarded the entire time." Raymond was still smiling.

"And about the burgundy they offer, anyone who drinks a drop forfeits his share of the bounty. I'll not have any of the men drunk while we possess our capture. Besides, their insistence about the burgundy being part of the bargain gives me pause." Aside from a handful of people, Jules trusted no one. No matter how harmless they seemed. Not since his world had fallen apart. Not when his silver treasure was going to change his life.

His appealing little blond camp follower was there to serve only one purpose. Once the sexual encounter was over, she and her friends would be turned out. With their wine.

"As you will. No one will drink the wine. And, my lord, you are most welcome." Raymond's smile broadened.

Jules slanted him a look. "Don't be so smug, Raymond, simply because you did well tonight in convincing me to see the girl for myself."

"We're quite fortunate that such a fetching and fiery woman came along. Enjoy her—as I'm sure you will—and do take your time."

Jules smiled. "I plan to."

This was going to be a night neither of them would forget.

* * *

Clutching the wineskin and wooden goblets she'd retrieved from her cart, Sabine followed Jules's man Martin to a small clearing.

The spot was private. Secluded. Blankets had been laid out on the soft forest floor.

Martin walked over to add more kindling to the fire. Its lambent flames immediately increased.

"The commander will be with you momentarily," Martin said and left.

Grateful for the solitude, she took a moment to settle her nerves. They'd made it into the camp. *Everything is going well.* Her cousins were eating and would soon be providing the men with the burgundy. Barely touching her food, her stomach in knots, she was glad to be away from them. The horror her cousins had felt with every salacious comment she'd uttered to Jules had been palpable.

Spotting a fallen tree near the edge of the blankets, she walked over to it and knelt down. She placed the wooden goblets on the log and poured the wine. Her friend Agnes, an apothecary of extraordinary skill, had advised her that one goblet of the burgundy would be enough to affect a full-grown man. But what about a man Jules's size? Should she have him drink two cups?

One thing was certain: She had to get him to down the burgundy before he touched her again. The feel of his caress against her skin had all but buckled her knees. The way her body reacted to him was beyond maddening. And utterly unsettling.

Footsteps approached.

Drawing in a quiet breath, she let it out slowly and turned around, a smile fixed on her face.

Jules stood ten feet away, silently watching her, firelight and moonlight illuminating his masculine beauty.

Without a doubt, the man was pure male perfection . . . Did he have to look *that* good?

The corner of his attractive mouth lifted in a slight smile. "Shall we begin?" he said, his tone so sinfully sensuous.

She gulped quietly. "Of course." Sabine looked away and picked up the goblets off the log.

Turning to face him again, she was in time to see him pull his shirt over his head and toss it casually onto the blanket.

Her mouth fell agape.

There before her was a feast for the eyes. Unable to help herself, she devoured every beautiful dip and ripple on his strong chest and muscled abdomen.

Gracious God . . .

"Elise?"

She felt her cheeks grow hot. Her whole body warmed, yet she couldn't tear her eyes away from his stunning physique.

"Huh?"

He hooked his thumbs into the waistband of his breeches. "We are going to have to be physically closer in order to have sex, no?" She heard amusement in his tone.

She jerked her gaze up to his and quickly clamped her gaping mouth shut. Giving herself a stern chastising, she forced herself to smile.

"Oh. Yes. Forgive me. I was simply admiring you." Did she sound pathetic or provocative? *Get up and go to him.* Why didn't her legs move?

With a lopsided grin, he approached her, his heated gaze fixing her to the spot.

He sat down before her on the fallen tree. His riveting half-naked body was so close, his handsome face so near. *Stop gawking! You'll make him suspicious. He'll think you're inexperienced.*

"Why don't we drink?" she quickly suggested and held out one of the goblets to him. If he took anything else off, she'd expire on the spot. As it was, her heart was trying to burst out of her chest.

To her joy, he took the goblet. His other hand reached out and grasped her braid.

Good Lord, not the braid again . . .

Quietly, he studied it, his thumb caressing it as he had before. Her insides danced.

"The burgundy is quite good," she prompted.

"Undo the braid."

Her heart lurched. Sabine managed to maintain her smile. "The braid?" she repeated like an idiot. There was nothing wrong with her hearing.

He took her goblet out of her hand and set it down beside him on the tree trunk. "Yes. The braid."

She looked at her goblet—an arm's length away—then back at him. Thankfully, he still held his goblet. He was watching her. Waiting for her to comply.

It's simply a braid. She could definitely do that.

"As you wish," she said, amazed at how calm she sounded while on the brink of discomposure. Untying the worn ribbon, she unbraided her hair for him.

"Run your fingers through it," he ordered. There was such hot desire in his eyes. It was intoxicating. And it amazed her. She still couldn't believe he wanted her. Or that he was even looking at her when in the past she'd been practically invisible to him. How many times had she craved a glance. His touch. His kiss. That was so long ago, a different time, before his kith and kin turned the world black.

Threading her fingers in her hair, she complied with his request. Her blond hair swooshed back down, hanging loosely.

Taking one of her tresses, he brought the lock to his cheek and stroked it along his jaw. "You have beautiful hair," he said.

His words unbalanced her. That was the very same thing he'd said to her the night she'd slipped and lost her slipper. Only this time there was such a carnal quality to his words, her sex tightened in response.

"Thank you. So do you." *So do you? What sort of imbecilic response is that?*

This would have been so much easier if he'd become potbellied, bald, and had bad teeth.

Anxious to get this over with, she decided to move things along.

Daringly, she dipped her finger into his goblet. Intending to put a drop on his lips, she said, "Would you like to try the wine?"

He caught her wrist before she touched him, his action surprising her.

Moving his goblet closer to her mouth, he released her wrist and said, "Ladies first."

Oh, God. Remain calm. Don't overreact.

"You are most kind," she responded, recovering quickly, though her heart rhythm did not. She took hold of the goblet, her fingers inadvertently brushing his. Did he notice they trembled?

Her nerves and the extreme situation were clearly distorting her reactions to him. Nothing more. If she kept her head, maintained some semblance of control over herself, she'd prevail.

Looking down at the wine, she searched for direction. She wasn't about to drink any of it. This was difficult enough without some of the drugged wine in her system. What could she do? *Stay in character.* That was the answer. The key to success. She was playing the part of a whore, a seducer, an enticer.

She would entice him to drink even if that meant she had to delve deeper into her role. An idea came to her.

"Would you be so kind as to assist me—may I have your hand, please?" She held her hand out, waiting and praying he'd comply. There was curiosity in his eyes. And after what seemed an eternity, he placed his hand in hers. Carnal awareness crackled in the air between them. She could tell he felt it, too. The expression on his face had changed from desire to a feral hunger. It inflamed her further. A mortifying moisture pooled between her legs.

Her insides in havoc, Sabine glanced down at his hand in hers. It was strong, his fingers long, warm. She liked the feel of his skin. A little too much for her own good.

She couldn't allow herself to forget how his family had preyed on hers, overtaxing, overburdening. Living off their misery. She didn't feel sorry for what had become of him. Had he inherited his father's title and lands, there was no reason to believe he'd have cared a whit about the suffering of those who lived on his lands any more than his father had. He deserved his fall from "grace."

And he deserved what he had coming to him once she was through.

Knowing his palm would hold too much of the burgundy, she rotated his hand, tipped the goblet, and let a few drops land on the inside of his wrist.

Hesitating a moment to let most of the droplets run off, Sabine bent her head and pressed her lips to his skin.

The instant her mouth touched him, her senses were swamped by a heady rush. Her eyes fluttered shut. She forced them open, trying to recover her wits, yet she couldn't resist brushing her mouth lightly across his wrist. He made a sound from deep inside his throat. It reverberated in her feminine core.

Overcome by the warmth and texture of his skin, she lingered a moment longer, then kissed his wrist. The urge to kiss him again gripped her fiercely. It took a moment to shake loose of its hold.

She pulled away slowly and met his gaze, her breathing sharper than before. And there was a pulsing between her legs that throbbed in time with the heavy thuds of her heart.

If she hadn't been so shaken, she would have been elated. She'd successfully avoided the tainted wine. But it had come at a price. The most private part of her body was now rioting and aching for relief.

She scrambled to find her voice. "The burgundy has never tasted finer," she somehow managed to say. "You should try it." She held the goblet out to him.

"Perhaps I should," he responded. Relived, she almost wept when he took it from her hand.

Holding her gaze, he moved the goblet toward her then dripped a drop onto her bare shoulder. The wine was startlingly cool against her heated skin.

He leaned in.

Knowing he was going to press his mouth against her body, she braced herself for the thrill of it. The droplet had rolled down her arm before his lips finally grazed over her shoulder. She closed her eyes. The light flick of his tongue against her skin drew a moan from her throat.

He pulled back, his mouth mere inches from hers, his breaths mingling with her own. "I'm not certain I like your wine. Perhaps I should try it again?"

She blinked. Unable to command her voice, she gave him a delayed nod.

The barest smile played across his mouth. He opened the top fastening on her bodice. Her eyes widened. And then he opened the next. *Dear God.*

Then another fastening.

And another.

Think of something! What could she say to stop him? She couldn't reveal her duplicity. She couldn't—*Oh!* Her opened bodice slipped off, revealing her chemise.

Amid her heightened distress, she felt a ludicrous pang of embarrassment. Her chemise, although clean, was old and worn. Not fancy or pretty like the undergarments she'd once owned. Like the ones worn by his former mistresses.

She looked away, unable to look into his eyes, trying desperately to think of a way to regain control of the unraveling situation.

He lowered her chemise to her waist. She swallowed down her protest, her upper body exposed, her breasts veiled by her hair.

He brushed her tresses aside, revealing her to the summer night and his gaze.

"Elise . . ." he said.

Unable to read much into his utterance, she cast him a sidelong glance, expecting to find him assessing her. Yet by his expression he seemed to be marveling at her instead.

His hand caressed the outside curve of her breast. She gasped at the jolt of erotic sensation. It drew his gaze back up to her face.

Then it happened. He gave her one of his full knee-weakening smiles. Gorgeous dimples and all.

"You're exquisite. With the nipples of Venus," he said. "I wonder if they taste as good as they look." Dipping the tip of his finger into the wine, he placed a drop near her racing heart and watched with fascination as it ran down toward her nipple. She was frozen. Expectant of what he might do. Unable to stop it from happening.

The moment the droplet dripped off the tip of her breast, he slipped his arm around her waist, lowered his head, and sucked her nipple into his hot mouth. She cried out, and flung her arms around him, the pleasure so keen she all but swooned. Squeezing her eyes shut, she pressed her cheek against his dark hair. Each luscious pull of his mouth contracted her sex, deep delicious pulses that vibrated to her clit.

She couldn't catch her breath. Not when he continued to ply her with skillful sucks, licks, bites. The sensations radiating from her breast were melting her mind.

She'd kept herself numb for so long. Yet the pleasure flooding through her was so intense, there was no containing it. Or controlling it.

His mouth burned a path to her other breast and repeated the exquisite torture. Her head fell back. Her lips parted in a silent cry, and she held on, lost to the hunger.

He had her arching and moaning, her breaths dragging up and down her throat.

He stopped suddenly. Sabine whimpered at the cessation. Dazed and panting, she snapped her eyes open, her body frantically clamoring for more.

She was shaky and ravenous, her sex slick with her own juices.

He was smiling again.

"You have very sensitive breasts. I like that." He tossed the goblet with its contents behind him onto the ground, dropped to his knees in front of her, and pulled her up tightly against him. She felt the solid bulge in his breeches.

He bent his head, his hair brushing her cheek. "We don't need wine," he murmured in her ear. "The carnal heat between us is intoxicating enough."

Before she could react, she found herself flat on her back staring up at him. He'd straddled her, his knees on either side of hers, and was bent over her, his palms near her head. She was caged in. All his potent male attention was focused on her.

She squirmed. She couldn't pull back. Nor could she cool down her overheated body. Yet she couldn't surrender herself.

Not to *him*.

A devilish smile formed on his handsome face. "Beautiful forest fairy, you're all mine."

4

With her moon-kissed hair spread out on his blankets, her soft skin a pale glow, and those luscious breasts rising and falling with each accelerated breath she took, she looked less like a whore. More like an angel.

And even better than Jules had imagined.

Though he knew there was a strong carnal connection between them, he never expected that the mere brush of her lips against his wrist would leave him burning. *Jésus-Christ.* He wanted to fuck her so badly, his sac ached. He could barely hold on to the load of come, the engorged head of his cock already moist with pre-come.

And he reveled in it.

In this fierce desire she inspired. In the intense reactions she elicited from his body. It was unbelievable.

And oh so delectably *real.*

Her lips were slightly parted, and he was stunned by how starved he was for their taste.

He couldn't recall the last time he'd indulged in a long hot kiss. It used to be an integral part of the pleasure in any sexual encounter. Yet somewhere along the way he'd lost interest in the simple intimate act. It had no place in the kind of detached colorless sex he now had.

But sex wasn't going to be detached or colorless with her. With this woman, the last thing he wanted to engage in was a cold fast fuck.

Resisting the lure of her mouth for the moment, he brushed a pretty blond tress off her cheek, then let his fingers trail lightly down the side of her lovely face and along the slender column of her neck. She closed her eyes, and arched to him. She couldn't hold back a moan.

He smiled.

He grazed his fingertips across her breast and over her pebbled nipple, enjoying the sound of her excited gasp. He liked how highly responsive she was to him. How genuine her desire was. How undone she'd become when he'd tasted her nipples.

He couldn't wait to taste those ultrasensitive tips again.

In fact, he couldn't wait to discover all the hot spots on her pretty little form that would drive her wild. He wanted her completely lost to the lust they incited in each other.

He wanted pure unbridled abandon.

He wanted to fuck her the way no man ever had before.

Jules lowered his head and brushed his mouth over the sensitive spot below her delicate ear. She made the most sensuous sound. His eager prick thickened further, reaching painful proportions. He was so bloody hard, his cock felt heavy as lead.

The anticipation of sinking his length into her soft silky sex, sensing it would be just as highly sensitive as the rest of her, was delicious.

She'd said he'd be well pleased. And he was.

This was far better than any purchased sexual encounter he'd ever had.

He sat back on his heels. "Look at me, Elise."

Opening her eyes, she met his gaze. She had a delightful desire-dazed look in her eyes.

"I want you to forget we have an arrangement. Tonight is about mutual pleasure. You're going to hold nothing back." He placed his hands on her thighs and began sliding her skirts up her legs. "And I am going to make you come harder than you've ever come before. But first, you're going to take these off and show me all of your beautiful body."

She looked shocked. It was understandable. His offer to pleasure a common whore was far from commonplace. Yet one he was serious about. Before they were through, he was going to rock her sweet form with a powerful release. Or three.

* * *

Clearly, Sabine's ears weren't working any better than the rest of her body parts. Had she heard him say *mutual pleasure*? He wanted her naked? *Totally?* It took everything she had not to cover up her breasts. Now he was suggesting that *all* of her attire be removed?

Didn't prostitutes simply raise their skirts? Why was it necessary to have her completely unclothed?

She was so frenzied inside, she simply stared up at him. If she didn't think of something soon, Jules de Moutier was going to relieve her of her virginity. It didn't help that the tormenting ache between her legs worsened the higher up he pushed her skirts. She wanted to take his bounty, make him suffer, yet he was torturing her in the most sublime way. The words "NO!" and "YES!" were screaming at her from different parts of her body with equal ferocity.

His hands moved over her *caleçons* and stopped to rest on her hips. Heat from his palms radiated through the cloth of her drawers. Her fever spiked. Making quick work of the ties, he slid the *caleçons* down her legs, the cloth lightly grazing along her sensitized skin.

Her breaths short and shallow, Sabine tried not to make any telling moves that would give her away, like squeezing her thighs closed, knowing a whore wouldn't do that. Her amorous experience totaled three kisses on three different occasions from Leon de Vittry, Baron de Lor, an admirer of her father's plays. Leon had never so much as stirred her. She hated it that Jules was having such a disastrous impact on her senses.

He paused to take in the sight of her sex. A slow perusal.

"Very pretty . . ." he murmured, then with a few fluid movements, he'd spread her legs and was suddenly kneeling between them. Her heart lurched. "You've got a lovely little clit, begging for attention."

Oh, God . . . At the mention of that part of her anatomy, a hot pulse quivered through her core. Before she could shore up her defenses, he leaned over her, his weight on one palm near her shoulder, and stroked his other hand over the curls at the apex of her legs. She caught her gasp before it escaped her throat. His hand slipped within the folds of her slick sex and gently massaged her needy flesh. Not enough to alleviate the torment. Just enough to fuel the fire. She bit down on her lip to keep from moaning out loud. It took everything she had not to arch into his enticing palm and grind against it.

A slight smile lifted the corner of his sinfully perfect mouth. "You're so wet, you're soaking my hand." The situation was far worse than that. The throbbing between her legs was unbearable, his hand so very close to that spot that was causing her such distress.

But he was avoiding the pulsing bud.

Glancing away, she gazed blindly out into the dark forest, looking for anything that would distract her from those skillful strokes on her sex.

"Elise . . ."

She dragged her gaze back to him.

"You want to come for me, don't you?"

Oh, she wasn't about to admit to that, under any circumstances.

He'd lowered his body down beside her as his hand continued

to work her sex without missing a single perfect stroke. His chest rested partially on top of her, his skin feeling warm and wonderful against her own.

His words, his scent, the feel of his body against hers, and the fierce pulsing between her legs were eroding her sanity.

Did he have to make this feel so good? How did whores do this? Didn't they remain unaffected and simply put on a performance?

"You're holding back your reactions to me," he gently admonished, amusement in his eyes. "There will be no professional distance tonight. I want your eyes on me, and I want to hear every sultry sound you make, without censor." He stroked her clit. This time a sound erupted from her.

His smile broadened. "That's it. Just like that . . . There is no reason to hold back or moderate yourself in any way. I want you to do whatever comes naturally."

Whatever comes naturally? This was in no way natural for her!

"Forget everything . . . There is no one else in this forest. Just us." He brushed his lips along her jaw and down her neck. "Beautiful Elise," he whispered against her skin. "I'm going to enjoy fucking you." His fingers grazed over her aching nub once more.

Hot excitement shot up her spine. She cried out and threw her arms around him. Burying her face in his neck, she fought to steady herself under his sensuous attack. He pinched her clit lightly. Another cry shot up her throat; pleasure shuddered through her. He was creating sensations like none she'd ever known.

What was the point in fighting this any longer? She couldn't curb her hunger for him. She wasn't about to reveal her duplicity. Or back out. When she'd embarked on this plan, she'd known the risks.

Besides, she wasn't Sabine. She was *Elise*. Elise could indulge in a carnal encounter with him—without qualms. She had no grievances against Jules de Moutier. She could allow herself to explore this delicious act, steal some pleasure, then steal the silver. Elise could do as she wanted—things Sabine would never do—and at the moment she wanted to taste his skin again.

Without another thought, she skimmed her lips along his neck to his ear, stopping just below it to gently draw on him. His groan was thrilling.

He pinned her to the forest floor under him. She couldn't miss the hard bulge pressing against her belly. Resting his weight on his elbows, he looked down at her. "Oh, no you don't. You're going to come for me, first." He dipped his head and lightly bit her earlobe. She lost her breath. Lifting his head, he met her gaze, one of his stomach-fluttering smiles forming on his face. "What's your pleasure? Name it. I'm game to oblige. And I am difficult to shock, I assure you. Tell me what you want me to do to you."

Urgency pounded in her veins. Her gaze fell to his mouth. His most alluring mouth. Just the sensation of his lips on her neck had felt too much like heaven. Oh, there was something she most definitely wanted him to do. Long ago, she'd filled pages in her journal imagining what it would feel like.

"Kiss me," she had Elise say.

She saw surprise flash in his eyes. She'd managed to shock him after all. The request for a kiss wasn't something a man usually heard from a strumpet, she supposed. But at the moment, she didn't care.

To her delight, he lowered his mouth. Parting her lips, she tipped her chin up. He stopped short, barely touching her lips.

"Where?" he whispered into her mouth.

Where? He was truly beginning to frustrate her. She had a strong urge to simply grab his ears and haul his mouth down onto hers.

"My lips." Was it not obvious?

"Mmmm, I see." He brushed his lips ever so lightly over hers. Instantly she lifted her head off the blankets, seeking more contact with his mouth. He pulled back ever so slightly, keeping his lips close, but still didn't give her the kiss she craved. He was going to be sporting a serious bruise soon!

"Where else do you want me to kiss you?" *Where else?* "Tell me," he coaxed while his mouth continued to hover over hers.

Why couldn't he just get on with this?

"My neck," she offered. Once the words were out of her mouth, she was flooded with a warm rush.

"And?"

"And?"

"Where else?"

How many more places did he need her to mention? How many more places did a man kiss a woman? Maddeningly, it was clear he wasn't going to proceed until he was satisfied by her answer.

"And . . ." There *was* another place that came to mind where she wanted him to kiss her. Again. "My . . . breasts." Never in her life had she uttered such a brazen request. But then again, she wasn't Sabine at the moment, was she?

He pulled back enough to look into her eyes. Dimples adorned his gorgeous smile. "Anyplace else?"

Good Lord. Enough! "No. For now, the list will suffice. I'll give you further instructions later."

His brows shot up. He burst into laughter. "Elise, you are delightful." He lowered his head and gave her the lightest kiss. Pure bliss vaulted inside her. "Beautiful," a slightly deeper kiss, "fiery," a longer kiss, "and wonderfully impatient. My favorite combination in a woman. Let's get to work on your list."

* * *

Jules had her mouth in an instant, muting her gasp, driving his tongue past her parted lips. Of all the pleasures she could have selected when he'd given her carte blanche, she asked for *a kiss*. He found that strangely touching and, coming from her alluring mouth, utterly erotic. Capturing her face between his hands, he angled her head for better access to the soft recesses of her mouth. It took all of two frantic beats of his heart for the kiss to become hot, demanding, unleashing the pent-up desire he had for her. Kissing her mouth was heaven on earth. A taste of paradise. He couldn't stop the bliss that groaned up his throat.

Jésus-Christ, how he'd missed this.

This was perfect spine-melting passion.

She kissed him with equal fervor, matching every hungry stroke of his tongue. He could feel her melting in his arms, surrendering to the raw desire, helpless against it, and he wanted to howl at the sheer pleasure it gave him. The small sultry sounds emanating from her throat incited him further. His cock seeped more spunk. Yet at the height of passion, when the fire burned white-hot, when all he could think about was driving his prick into her dewy cunt, he became aware of her hand at the nape of his neck gently caressing him there.

The tender, unusual gesture surprised him.

He broke the kiss and looked down at her, their breathing labored. Her eyes were darkened with passion and he wasn't certain she was even aware she was touching his neck this way.

Breathlessly, she said, "Don't—"

"Don't?"

"Stop." She lifted her head, seeking his mouth. "Work on the list . . ."

He couldn't help chuckling, her responses adorably novel. *Dieu*, he'd smiled and laughed more with her during their brief acquaintance than he had in the last five years.

"How is this?" he said and trailed his mouth down her neck, moving across her skin, toward her breasts. A soft mew escaped her and she arched to him. A delicious untamed reaction.

A blatant invitation to suck those pretty nipples again.

One no man would refuse.

He slid his body lower, wrapped an arm around her tightly, and rolled with her onto his back, pulling her soft form on top of him—her nipple dropping into his ready mouth. He sucked. She gasped and jerked, her palms slamming down onto the blankets on either side of his head. But he held her securely in place, not allowing her to pull away from the sudden spike of erotic sensations. He sucked, laved, and lightly bit her tender teat—enjoying the arousing sounds she made, the restless wiggle of her soft derrière. And the glorious friction against his engorged cock.

Bending his knees, he kept her legs spread apart and grazed a hand over the seam of her bottom, following its sweet curve until his fingers slipped into her juicy folds. He sank a finger into the slit of her sex with one fluid glide. Her bottom flexed. His groan eclipsed her soft cry.

A single digit was all he had buried in her hot wet core, yet it was so tightly clasped, it was mind-numbing. His cock twitched eagerly.

A warning flitted through his mind, and quickly burned away. He lightly pumped his finger in her. Her sheath twitched convulsively. He was so fucking hard, his cock unbearably full, yet he couldn't pull his hand away from her snug wet sex. Releasing her nipple from his mouth, he gazed up at her. Her eyes were closed, her delicate brows drawn together, and her hair was down around them like a silvery veil.

"You've got the sweetest cunt, Elise."

A small sound escaped her lips on a pant, but she didn't open her eyes, enthralled by the sensations in her sheath as he pushed and pulled his finger with measured strokes. He wasn't sure she even heard him.

He plunged his free hand between their bodies and captured her clit. She whimpered loudly and ground herself against him. He was fingering her, her juices dripping down his thrusting finger onto his hand, driving him to the edge of his control. He'd barely stroked her clit twice when she lurched at the sheer force of her release and came with a long hard cry, her body straining against him, her orgasm taking them both by surprise.

He refused to stop, his hand still working her soaked sex, milking more pleasure from her body until her little shivers and shudders, until those decadent spasms of her vaginal walls, completely ebbed.

Only when she was slumped on top of him, boneless, dragging air in and out of her lungs, did he withdraw his finger and ease her onto her back, pinning her beneath him. She buried her face in his shoulder, her warm breaths caressing his chest. Her pale tresses tickling his chin.

"It's been a long time since a man made you come, hasn't it?" he said in her ear. She came so quickly.

She kept her face in his shoulder. "You could say that," she mumbled against him.

He was on his knees between her thighs in an instant. Reaching down, he undid his breeches in haste. "We're going to remedy that and make up for lost time. This time, I'm going to make you come with my cock." He couldn't wait any longer. He had to possess that snug heat right *now*.

She looked so good naked in the moonlight—it made his mouth water.

Freeing his prick from its confines, he grasped his cock and squeezed it to combat the throbbing, his cock feeling thicker and heavier than it ever had before.

Her gaze was riveted on his erect shaft protruding from his open breeches. She bit her lip, her earlier confidence faltering.

"You're . . . um . . ." she began, looking flustered. "Rather, your . . . generous size . . . Have any of your past lovers experienced . . ." She looked uneasy. "Discomfort?"

A smile pulled at the corners of his mouth once more. He was large, but he knew just how to use his girth and length to pleasure women.

Jules lowered himself slowly onto her soft form.

"I'm not going to hurt you."

She was so slick, he anticipated an easy thrust would see him buried to his balls. "This is about mutual pleasure, remember?" He wedged the head of his cock at her entrance. He had every intention of entering her with a slow downstroke, feeding her his length inch by inch, savoring every moment of his possession, but with his cock at the entrance to paradise, with the overpowering allure of his beautiful forest fairy and his self-imposed celibacy all decimating his resolve, he thrust in all at once.

She recoiled with a painful cry.

"Jésus-Christ!" he hissed out from between clenched teeth. A *virgin.*

Her face was turned. Her eyes were squeezed shut, refusing to look at him.

Balanced on his forearms, he was practically shaking with the effort it took to hold still. The pressure around his cock was magnificent, his prick pulsing within the confines of her sex. She had the tightest, most glorious sheath he'd ever known.

Good Lord . . . There was no way he had the strength to pull away from her now. He was past the point of no return.

He withdrew slightly. The drag against the sensitive underside of his shaft tore a groan from his throat. Pleasure exploded through his senses. He filled her with one solid stroke. She made a strangled sound at the back of her throat that sounded less like pain. More like pleasure. A mimic of his own sound of rapture.

His possession was complete. He felt her body relax and she drew her arms around him again, enveloping him further. He couldn't stop thrusting. The friction was sublime. Dear God, he'd never been inside a woman who felt this good. He gave her long deep luscious strokes of his cock, quickly picking up the tempo, until he was fucking her with complete abandon, with powerful plunges, his angle making perfect contact with her sensitized clit.

The sensuous sounds she made inflamed him further.

He drove into her faster. Harder. Her body now rising up to meet him on his every downstroke, sucking him in deeply each time.

Her inner muscles fluttered and contracted. He knew she was about to come. He braced himself for it, aching to spew everything he had. The most exquisite torture he'd ever known.

She surged her hips upward, her cry filling his ears. Delicious uncontrollable little spasms quivered through her core, sending spellbinding sensations coursing along his cock, and hurling him into orgasm. He reared just in time; come shot from his prick onto the blanket, powerful jolting eruptions, each a burst of ecstasy, a deeply draining rush. Until his muscles melted.

Until he'd purged his prick dry.

It took a few moments before he could muster the strength to roll off her. The lassitude that had seeped into his muscles quickly dissipated, her lies igniting a fury he was all too prone to nowadays.

Merde! How did a virgin convince him she was a whore? *Because you wanted her so badly, you ignored the signs. Everything. Just so you could have her. Merde! Merde!* He was livid at her for tricking him. And at himself for letting her.

She may have been untried, but she was not entirely innocent. She'd put on a performance, with the intention to deceive. Clearly, she was up to something. But what? Why the deception? What did she hope to gain?

He bolted upright.

Jésus-Christ, an ambush!

He scanned the trees and shrubs, looking for men lurking, waiting to attack. No. If it had been an ambush to gain his treasure, it would have occurred by now—*before* he'd had her, not afterward.

He shot her a look. Her face was turned away, her alluring form open to his view. She hadn't moved. The question "*Why?*" bellowed in his head.

* * *

Sabine reeled. In her wildest dreams she'd never imagined the physical act of copulation could be this powerful. Could leave her this shaken. She was so undone. Emotions clashed within her. She felt good. She felt vulnerable. She felt angry.

She felt the sting of tears.

She was *not* going to cry. Not in front of him. She hadn't cried in years, not since the day Isabelle left. She hadn't even cried when she'd been told the news of Isabelle's death a year later. That day she froze inside, numbed herself to the pain of it all. Since then she'd battled daily between what her head told her and what her heart felt—that Isabelle was alive.

It left her unbalanced, bewildered. Lost. Just as she felt now. How pathetic was she?

She couldn't accept her sister's demise. She couldn't remain detached, even remotely, in her enemy's arms. And she hadn't fooled Jules into believing she was sexually experienced either.

He'd realized the truth.

Sabine sat up and slipped her chemise back on, her hands shaky.

He jerked her chin up, startling her. He was down on his haunches, clearly furious. "You lied to me," he growled. "Why did you pretend you were experienced? What game are you playing?"

Her own emotions erupted. She shoved his hand away. "Game? This is no game." She shot to her feet. Turning away from him, she took a few steps, needing space and time to collect herself. Needing to shut him out and the devastating effect he'd had on her.

She pulled on her skirt, becoming frustrated with her fumbling fingers as they bumbled with the fastenings.

Collect yourself!

From the way he was behaving, she was going to have to provide answers. She was going to have to think of something believable that would satisfy him—at a time when she felt too unraveled to think clearly. She'd already paid a price for her plan with her lost innocence.

She couldn't let him cast her out now.

He grasped her arm and spun her around to face him. "Why. Did. You. Do. This?"

She laughed and blinked away more tears she refused to shed. Being Elise was exhausting. Consuming. And she was beginning to despise her.

"*Why?*" she repeated. "Are you that much of a fool? Why would any woman profess to be a whore and enter a men's camp if not because she was *desperate*."

"My patience is running out. Speak plainly!" he barked. "And your words this time had better be *the absolute truth*."

The stone-cold look in his eyes sent a shiver of dread through her. Fury was coming off him in waves. She found herself mourning the loss of his smile, his heated looks. And she hated it that she did. She felt defeated. She'd lost the battle. Yet she had no choice but to fight on.

She still had to steal his captured prize.

But Jules de Moutier was not a man to be trifled with. This former officer of the King's Navy was a veteran in battle, skilled at weapons, with a small army of armed men at hand under his command.

She had only her two younger cousins and desperation arming her.

"I didn't wish to deceive you. I didn't think you would want me if you knew I was a . . . virgin."

"You are correct there! Who are you?"

Lying was much like acting. You had to put on a believable performance. And the most convincing lies incorporated as much of the truth as you could allow.

"My name is Elise Marquette." The false name slipped past her lips. "I couldn't have you turn me away. I'm desperate for funds. What else was there for me to do?"

Mistrust was clearly readable in his eyes. "You have the wine. You could have sold it for coin," he said tightly.

He'd cornered her. What she was about to admit to was a risky tactic to take, but she was out of options. He didn't look as though he'd let her skirt around the subject of the wine. God help them . . . "I couldn't. The—The wine is . . . tainted."

"You *poisoned* the wine?" he roared.

"No!" Her heart was slamming in her chest. "Not poisoned.

I swear! It's drugged. To induce sleep. We were going to take coins from you and your men. We wouldn't have taken everything. We would have left you some." She was oh so careful not to let on that she knew of the captured wealth on hand.

"So you came here to steal." His expression was fierce. "Why let me fuck you? Because you couldn't get me to drink the wine beforehand?"

She crossed her arms, feeling chilled by his anger. Once again she found herself longing for his previous warm manner. "I'll admit I didn't come here with the intention of participating in any sort of . . . intimate act with you, but then . . ." Her next words caught in her throat.

"But then *what*?" he snapped.

She forced the words out—words that spoke too much of the truth for her liking. "But then . . . you touched me . . . kissed me . . ." She wanted to say no more. Each day she went through the motions of living, unable to mourn her sister. Simply surviving, more dead than alive. She'd forgotten how to feel. She didn't even want to. Yet this man—of all men—had inflamed her senses and jolted her body to life with such startling intensity, she still trembled in the aftermath. She'd rather cut out her own tongue than have to admit to *him*, "I didn't want you to stop." How she wished that was a lie.

"Really." His voice was bland.

"Yes, really!" His skepticism was wounding when it shouldn't be at all. How ironic that she had to convince him of something she wanted to deny.

It took everything she had not to give up this mad scheme and run. But she didn't have that luxury. "You . . . overwhelmed me." Sadly that, too, was the truth.

He placed his hands on his hips. "Why didn't you sell the wine before you 'tainted' it?"

"We tried to do that at the market. The realm is in financial chaos, in case you haven't noticed. We had no takers. I've been traveling for some time. I'd only met the young men I'm with today.

The wine was theirs. The idea to do this was mine. I convinced them to barter some wine for some sleeping powders. They did just that, mixed it into the wine, and we devised a plan."

His jaw tightened. Tensed, she wondered if he could hear the pounding of her heart.

"Why did you select us?" he asked.

"You were the first group of men we came upon who looked as though you had some coin to spare."

His brows shot up. "You walked into a camp of men you knew *nothing* about?"

"Yes."

"*Merde*. Woman, are you mad?"

"No. Just utterly desperate. And out of choices. I had nothing to lose."

"Except your innocence and your life."

She gave a harsh laugh. "Why worry about my innocence if I am dead? And dead is what I'll be without coin. Most of my family is gone. My home is gone because I didn't have the money to pay our lord his taxes. What choice did I have?"

He studied her in silence. Her insides in frenzy, she prayed he believed her.

His eyes narrowed. "Those men you are with, did they know you were a virgin?"

"No!" She was intent on protecting her cousins, for she could see his ire rising once more.

"Did you lead them to believe you were sexually experienced?"

"I told them nothing about myself. They're practically boys. Like me, they only resorted to this because they're trying to survive. What would you do if you were in our desperate situation?"

He didn't answer her, and his expression was unreadable.

He needs more convincing.

She quickly added, "This has been a night of firsts. I've never stolen or tried to steal before. I swear it. And I've never experienced . . . the things I experienced with you tonight. What happened between us was not a ruse. It was . . ." She looked away, unable to look in his eyes as she said, "Bliss." How she wished that were a lie, too.

Still he remained silent.

It unnerved her. She forced her gaze back to his. His dark eyes gave nothing away.

She hadn't come this far to lose the silver treasure. She wouldn't. Couldn't. She had to convince him to keep her with him—near the silver.

She pressed on. "I'm traveling to the town of Maillard. It's but a three-day ride. I have a cousin there who is a schoolmaster. He's the only family I have left." There was no cousin in Maillard. She'd purposely selected the town because she knew it was en route to his point of rendezvous. "Send the young men away, if you wish. But let me stay with you. *Please* . . . take me to Maillard. Take me to my cousin." That would give her three days to find an opportunity to find his capture. And seize it.

More maddening silence.

Why didn't he respond? If only she could decipher his thoughts.

"Look at me." She opened her arms theatrically. "I am no threat to a man like you."

His tactile gaze moved down her body then back up and met her eyes. He stepped closer and cupped her face in his warm palm. Her nerve endings sparked to life. "You want to stay with me, do you?" His thumb lightly brushed her cheek.

"Yes," she said, a little too breathless.

"Why should I believe you? Why should I believe anything you say?" His touch was distracting.

"There are many in my situation in the realm. Why are my words so difficult to believe? I've confessed the truth about the wine, about my original motives. I'm simply a woman in dire straits. A woman who . . ." The truth caught in her throat. *Say it!* "Who found unexpected pleasure in a stranger's arms. Couldn't you tell there was nothing false about how your touch affected me?"

"Your passion wasn't a lie," he conceded. His sensuous voice stroked over her like a caress. His hand continued to cradle her cheek, with tender appeal.

"May I stay with you, then? Will you escort me to Maillard?" She had such an overwhelming urge to put her arms around him and lean against his strong body. And it astounded her. She never leaned on anyone. Ever. Everyone always leaned on *her.*

She kept her arms at her sides, by force of will, but she couldn't stop her gaze from drifting to his mouth. A mouth that was all too perfect in too many ways.

The more he touched her, the longer he remained close, the more she craved both. He was drawing her back under his influence, and she was having a difficult time locating the will to fight it. She had no understanding of the unbreakable attraction she had to this man.

Though it wasn't going stop her from doing what she had to do.

She'd either find a way to master it, or submit to it. *Whatever it takes . . .* She was a survivor. And ultimately the victor in this charade.

"Please, I would very much like to stay with you," she said.

"Really." His tone was far too bland for her liking. "Is that all you want, Elise?"

She gazed into his eyes. So darkly sensual. Far too stirring.

Whatever it takes . . . Say the words. If you don't, he could assign one of his men to escort you to Maillard, sending you away from the camp and the silver. "I'd like you . . . to show me more of the same kind of bliss you showed me tonight." When this was over, she'd force herself to forget this night and all the shocking things Elise had done and was about to do.

Jules slipped his arm around her waist and drew her against him. A wave of pleasure crested over her. He dipped his head. "Is that so?" he whispered near her mouth.

She couldn't speak, not when his lips were so close to her own. Not when she urgently wanted him to kiss her.

His mouth came down on hers. She closed her eyes. Her womb

clenched. Enthralled by his taste, she could feel her passion mounting. She pressed herself against his solid muscled form, feeling herself pulled into a dream she'd had once. And lost.

He pulled away, and stepped back. She slammed back into reality.

She was left missing the contact, mournful of the brevity of his kiss. And grappling with the usual discomposure he caused with but the briefest physical contact.

He had his head down, his long strong fingers at work refastening his breeches.

"Well?" she nudged, tamping down the carnal craving he'd stirred. "What is your answer?"

He looked up at her, his task completed. Snagging his shirt off the blankets, he threw it on and cocked a brow.

"You wish to know if I'll let you stay and be your lover for the next three days until we reach Maillard?"

"Yes," she answered.

He stepped close to her again. "That depends."

"On what?"

"On what your friends have to say, and what stories *they* give." Her stomach dropped.

He stalked away.

5

Sabine raced after Jules. Her knees almost buckled when she saw him march past the brute Fabrice, yanking his sword from his scabbard without breaking his stride. Idly standing guard, the brute's head snapped up in surprise.

Jules stopped before Gerard and Robert, seated near the fire.

"Get up," he ordered, sword in hand.

Her cousins leaped to their feet, both clutching wineskins.

The murmuring around them died. Like predators closing in on their prey, the men who'd been sitting around the campfire rose and neared their leader, surrounding Gerard and Robert.

Robert looked around at the circle of men entrapping them, bewilderment and fear etched in his expression. Gerard's gaze shot to her. His eyes widened, the shock on his face arresting her steps. It was then she realized her hair was unbraided and mussed. Her appearance disheveled and telling.

Gerard's horror contorted his face. "Dear God . . . You didn't . . ." His words trailed off. He remained frozen, staring at her.

She had to briefly look away, unable to stand the pleading in his eyes as he silently begged for the reassurance that she hadn't resorted to giving herself to Jules. When she found the courage to return his gaze, she saw devastation in their depths. It tortured her to see it, to see the hint of—tears. Her throat tightened. She'd run out without any thought about her appearance for her cousins' sake.

Seemingly oblivious to Jules's threatening presence, Gerard's expression told her he thought the price she'd paid was too great. How could she ever explain to him the pleasure she'd found in Jules's arms? She couldn't even explain it to herself.

Jules moved to Gerard's side and laid his sword across her cousin's throat.

Terror slammed into her.

"You've been found out." Jules spoke in the deadliest tone. "I should run you through here and now for your little scheme." He glanced at Robert. "Both of you." Jules's body was rigid, his muscles tight with restrained rage.

Gerard finally dragged his gaze to Jules. Never in her life had she seen that much contempt in her cousin's eyes. His nostrils were flared, his breathing quickening. He looked ready to kill Jules.

She had to do something. Fast. She broke through the circle of men.

"This is completely unnecessary!" she protested. "Put down the sword."

"S-um-Elise?" Robert spoke up. His eyes were round with fright. "Wh-What did you tell him?" His terror was torturous.

With a knot in her throat, she had to swallow before she could speak. "I told him everything." In her rattled state, she'd completely mishandled it all.

"E-Everything?" Robert asked, alarmed.

"Commander?" Raymond approached. "What is amiss?"

"We have criminals in our midst," Jules growled.

"Criminals?" Raymond gave her cousins a sweeping glance. "These half-starved boys and this woman?"

"They came armed, Raymond." Jules leaned closer to Gerard. "Why don't you tell us about *the wine*?"

Gerard stared straight ahead, his eyes were cold and angry.

"I've already told you about the wine, *and* about our plan to steal some coin," Sabine interjected. "What more do you need to know?"

"You *what*?" Robert choked out.

"Mademoiselle, you'll not speak another word," Jules decreed. "Do you understand!"

"You wish me to remain silent and watch you terrorize these helpless boys?" she shot back.

"Helpless boys? I think *thieves* best describes what they are. And I intend to find out how much of a liar *you are*. You either remain silent, or you will be removed from this conversation entirely." Jules tossed Raymond a look.

Raymond grasped her elbow. She yelped in surprise when he yanked her away from Jules's side.

"Don't!" Gerard cried out to Raymond, but Jules pressed the blade firmer against his throat.

"You are the one who bargained her," Jules said to Gerard. "And you're going to answer my questions. Is that clear?" Each word was firmly dealt, dripping with implied threat.

Gerard shot Jules a murderous glare.

"ANSWER!" Jules bellowed. She jumped.

"Yessss," Gerard hissed out from between clenched teeth, never breaking his hate-filled gaze.

A muscle twitched in Gerard's cheek. He curled his hand into a fist as though he were going to lay a blow. For the love of God, he had a sword to his throat! What was he thinking? They were unarmed, outnumbered, and Gerard was facing a man who was considerably larger, not to mention highly skilled in swords and pistols.

"How well do you know this woman?" Jules asked.

The questioning had begun. Her heart rapped violently against her ribs. She prayed her cousin would answer Jules's questions to his satisfaction and not do anything foolish for the sake of her honor.

"Not well at all, it would seem." Gerard's anger simmered in his words. "For I cannot imagine why she would tell *you* anything."

"Careful with your words and your tone," Jules warned. "When did you meet Elise?"

Dear God. She couldn't believe her ears. Jules's choice of words was perfect! She yanked her arm free from Raymond's grasp.

"Answer his question *precisely* now. Everything will be all right," she told Gerard, hoping he would understand her meaning, for if he answered how long he'd known *Elise*, all *would* be all right.

Gerard looked at her and swallowed. A bead of sweat appeared on his brow. "I . . . I met Elise . . . today."

Oh, yes!

"Why did you try to steal from *us*?"

"Why not?"

"Did you know she was an innocent?"

Gerard clenched his teeth. "*Was*? As in, *no longer*?"

"Answer the question!"

"I told you, I only met her today."

"And you didn't know she was a *virgin*? You couldn't tell?"

Gerard glared at Jules. "Could *you*?"

* * *

A fresh wave of hot rage shot through Jules. He tightened his jaw and pressed the blade of his sword against the young man's throat in a way that forced him up onto the balls of his feet.

"Are you trying to provoke me?" Jules snarled, every fiber of his being fiercely urging him to vent his rage. Why *should* he restrain it?

Why should he show any mercy to someone who wanted to deceive and rob him?

"Stop!" Elise ran and faced him. "No more!"

The look of fright in her eyes sent a sobering jolt through him.

It was then he noticed the younger one had tears streaming down his cheeks, quietly praying, and the one before him, despite his best efforts to hide it, visibly shook.

Jésus-Christ, what was he doing?

He'd never raised a weapon outside of battle, and couldn't remember ever losing his temper before five years ago.

Now, any sort of duplicity sent him into a full fury.

The two young males before him were nothing more than—as Raymond had described—half-starved boys.

Having to resort to doing the unimaginable in order to survive.

Lord knows he'd had to do the same. While he was nothing more than a *commoner*—his stomach clenched—he'd been forced to resort to, God help him, *privateering* for his country rather than serving his nation in the King's distinguished Navy. The only thing that got him through each miserable day was his dream of returning honor to his family's name, reclaiming his life, and exacting revenge on those who'd had a hand in stealing so much from him.

His dream rested in the captured Spanish silver in the carts nearby. He was overly protective of it.

He was overly sensitive to trickery.

His gaze returned to Elise. She watched him warily.

"Has he not answered your questions to your satisfaction?" she asked. "Have we not proven we've nothing left to hide?"

Taking a deep breath, he let it out slowly, then lowered his sword. "Martin. Xavier."

The two men approached.

"Take the flagons of wine off their cart."

With a nod, the men walked away to do his bidding.

The two young men before him were watching him, leery, waiting for his next order.

"Are—Are we free to go?" the younger one asked.

"In a moment," Jules advised. "The wine stays here."

The two boys glanced over at Martin and Xavier as they removed the wine from their cart.

"Oh, of course. You keep it!" the younger one offered, sounding relieved. He wiped his tears off his cheeks with a quick swipe of his hand. "And thank you. Thank you for not killing us." He gave him a nervous smile.

The older simply looked down at his feet.

Jules squeezed the hilt of his sword. He wanted silence while he wrestled down the emotions still simmering inside him. If anyone had attempted thievery on board one of his ships, the punishment would have been severe. But they were not part of his crew. Even so, that didn't mean he could simply let this go.

His eyes were drawn back to Elise. She watched the men unloading her cart. Even in her disheveled state there was no denying it—she was beautiful. *Three days and two nights in her company . . .* Should he agree? His body roared, "YES!" *Merde.* His knees were still weak from the intensity of his orgasm.

He couldn't believe he'd had such incredible sex with this sexual novice. Having an inexperienced woman had never appealed to him before. The only virgin he'd expected ever to have was his wife—one day, after he'd regained his nobility and could marry in the class of his birth. The woman who would give him heirs, and would have the title "Marquise de Blainville," and the esteem that would come with it.

Elise met his gaze and returned it, unflinching. The urge to reach out and pull her near was as powerful as his urge to initiate her into further carnal delights. She was so genuinely sensual and passionate.

And someone who'd attempted to deceive you.

His decision to take her to Maillard would be dependent on the wine.

Jules tore his eyes away from her and cast his gaze at his own covered carts nearby. *Jésus-Christ.* If she'd succeeded with her plan, she'd have discovered the wealth he had at hand.

"Commander, the wine has been removed," Martin advised.

Glancing at the thwarted thieves, he sensed their apprehension. She'd said the wine was drugged. What if it had been indeed poisoned? What if the plan had been to kill them all? Desperate people resorted to desperate measures. He couldn't allow his lust to cloud his thinking.

That's what had landed him in this mess to begin with.

He didn't want to believe she'd be a part of such a heinous scheme. But he wouldn't just let them walk away without knowing for certain just how dark a deed they'd plotted.

"You are free to go," he said, noting the instant relief on their faces, "*after* one of you drinks a goblet of your wine. Raymond, pour their burgundy."

Raymond stepped forward. Stooping, he picked up one of the fallen wineskins and a wooden goblet from the ground.

A stillness fell upon the camp, the crackling of the fire mingling with the sound of pouring wine. The tension from the young men and Elise was palpable.

Raymond held out a full goblet.

"Well?" Jules asked. "Which of you will volunteer?"

The three would-be thieves looked among themselves.

"I will," Elise announced and reached out her hand.

Jules's heart lurched. He caught her wrist, stopping her from grasping the goblet. "No. Not you." Deep inside, he was immensely pleased. She wouldn't have been willing to drink the wine if she knew it was poisoned. She'd told him the truth.

He believed her story.

"Why not?" she asked.

"Because they might have lied to you and purchased poisonous powder instead,"

She frowned. "That's nonsense. The wine is drugged. Not poisoned. I believe them."

"I don't. It will have to be one of them who drinks it."

He was keenly aware of her wrist in his hand, and fought back the impulse to caress the inside of her wrist in light, sensuous circles with his thumb. Touching her inspired a number of salacious thoughts, all of which involved leading her back to their secluded spot, stripping off her clothing, and taking her slowly.

Jules released her wrist and focused on the two males before him. "My patience is thinning," he warned.

They exchanged looks once more. Then the younger, a lanky boy with dark hair and eyes, stepped forward, clearly surprising the others, and took the goblet from Raymond's hand.

"I will drink it," he said and took a sip. "There. You see? It's not poisoned." He smiled.

Jules tamped down his annoyance with the cheeky youth. "What is your name?"

"Robert, sir."

"Well, Robert, that's not enough. *Down all of it.*"

"Is that really necessary?" Elise asked. "If he'd poisoned it, would he have offered to drink it?"

"I'm willing to be lenient about petty theft. But not about attempted *mass* murder. If he is willing to drink the entire goblet, then they are free to go."

Jules leveled Robert with the full weight of his regard. "Finish it."

Robert cast his accomplices an uneasy look. "If I drink it all, I'll simply fall asleep, correct?"

"Yes, you'll wake up in a few hours," the other male said.

Elise nodded. "You'll be fine, Robert."

Appearing assured, his smile returned. He lifted his goblet. "Well then, here's to all of you, and to a good night's rest." He downed the wine.

Jules waited and watched for any ill-effects. Silent moments slipped by. He looked at Raymond. Raymond simply raised a brow.

"Go," Jules ordered the young men, satisfied, wanting them out of his sight. "If I ever catch you near my camp again, you'll rue the day."

"We won't ever bother you again," Robert promised and walked toward their cart, still moving with a normal gait.

Jules gave his men a nod, dismissing them. They began to disperse, resuming their previous activities, but Raymond remained by his side.

It was then Jules noticed that the older male thief was still fixed to his spot. With a defiant tilt of his head, he glared at Jules.

Jules stabbed the tip of his sword into the earth between his boots and held the hilt with both hands. He narrowed his eyes. "You have something you wish to say to me?"

"Yes. I do," he said. "I *will* see you again."

Jules could feel ire prickling his skin, growing rapidly irritated by the young man's insolence and his stupidity. "Oh? Where?"

"In hell."

"Gerard!" Elise exclaimed.

Jules pulled his sword out of the ground. Gripping the hilt fiercely in his right hand, he took a step toward the brash youth. "And what makes you think you'll see *me* there?"

Gerard glanced at Elise. "After what you and I have done to this woman tonight, our souls will be damned."

Jules tightened his jaw. "Now you are contrite? Where was your conscience when you were trying to *sell her*? You've got to be the greatest of fools to linger in my presence a moment longer than necessary. Unless"—Jules raised his sword to Gerard's throat—"you wish to appear before your Maker for your Judgment *now*."

"No!" Elise's hand shot out. She shoved at Gerard's chest. "Go! Get on the cart. Leave *now*."

"My pleasure," Gerard said between gritted teeth. "Let's go."

"I am staying."

"*Pardon?*" Gerard looked aghast.

"I am staying with him." She moved closer to Jules. "If you'll allow me to?" Her comely face was turned upward, awaiting his answer. "Will you take me to my cousin in Maillard?"

"Your *WHAT*?" Gerard spat out. "Are you mad? You are not staying with him! Or them." He pointed to Jules's men around the campfire.

Jules grabbed him by the throat. "*Gerard*, is it?" Gerard's eyes widened in horrified astonishment, as his throat was in the clench of Jules's grip, his toes barely touching the earth. "You are leaving. *Now.*" He easily tossed him back, sending him stumbling backward, coughing.

Jules turned to his loyal servant. "Raymond, have them escorted from the camp."

"Immediately, Commander. What about the woman?"

Jules met her gaze. She stood quietly beside him, her eyes silently beseeching him.

"She's going with us to Maillard." She slipped a hand in his and smiled. Her delicate hand felt warm and right in his. A perfect fit. Just as their bodies had been.

Within moments, Gerard was being dragged to his cart.

"S-Elise!" Gerard called out. "You cannot stay alone with these men! I'll not leave you here!"

"You don't dictate to me. I'll be fine," she said, her body now rigid.

Jules concurred. She was better off with him. He couldn't bring himself to place her back in the hands of the two she'd arrived with. Boys or no, what if they became desperate enough to attempt this scheme again? He was shocked by just how abhorrent the notion was to him.

"You'll not be fine! You'll be carnal amusement for him and his lot!" Gerard shouted back, struggling against the man hauling him to the cart.

Jules swore. How dare he suggest Elise would be treated worse than he'd treated her. "I'm going to teach him a lesson once and for all . . ." He took a step toward Gerard.

She jumped in his path and shoved her hands against his chest. "Don't!" He glanced down at her, not in the least bit dissuaded from his intended action.

* * *

Sabine flung her arms around his waist and buried her face in his shoulder. "Please," was all that escaped her throat.

She clung to Jules, her bravado fragmenting. The accumulation of all she'd been through tonight was beginning to take its toll on her. She looked up into his eyes. "He's young. They both are, and they are perhaps a tad smitten with me, as well. Don't punish him. Please. There's been enough misery and suffering. Let me speak to him. I'll make them leave promptly without you needing to do a thing." The lies flowed out of her with ease.

She'd do anything, say anything, that would keep Jules from hurting Gerard.

Jules looked at her skeptically. "I don't know about that . . ." There was mistrust in his tone.

"I wish them gone. Not hurt. Surely you're no longer concerned about *them*? Or me?" She wanted her cousins safe—away from the camp. Then she wouldn't have to worry about them. They wouldn't be at risk or suffer because of her mistakes. Sweet Robert, who always smiled and jested even when there was nothing to smile or jest about, had been drugged because of her. It didn't escape her notice that he was conspicuously silent.

She heard one of her cousins howl in pain. She spun around. Robert was in the grips of slumber, in the cart, just as she'd suspected. Another man held Gerard's arms securely behind his back as he dragged Gerard, kicking and thrashing, back to the cart. Fabrice approached and slammed his fist into Gerard's jaw, his head snapping to the left.

"Stop!" she screamed. Frantically she turned to Jules. "Make them stop, please!"

He stared over her head at Gerard and his men. "Fool. None of this would be happening if he'd left quietly."

"Allow me a brief moment. I will talk some sense into him."

His gaze fell to hers, his scrutiny unnerving. As he pondered her request, she prayed she'd been convincing enough to allay his fears.

"Only because I want them out of my camp now, I'll allow a *brief* moment. Say your good-byes."

* * *

Sabine could sense Jules and his men watching them from a short distance away.

"Don't do this, Sabine. *Please* come home," Gerard pleaded in a hushed whisper. There was already a bruise on his jaw.

"If I don't do this, there will be no home."

"I forbid this." Gerard growled. "You are *not* staying."

"You'll cease your arguing this instant. I have only a brief moment. Listen well. You'll take Robert and go. Jules is going to start to wonder at your protests for a woman you have only known *one day*. Your behavior is putting us all at risk," she chastised.

"Maillard is three days away. I refuse to leave you alone with him for three days!" Gerard raised his voice to an earnest whisper. "Especially after what he's done—"

"Enough." What she and Jules had done wasn't something she'd discuss with her cousins. Or anyone. She pierced Gerard with a fierce look. "We have no choice."

She knew she couldn't show any weakness or he might not leave.

"The town of Delatour is about a day's ride," she said. "If you travel through the night, you will arrive there by midday tomorrow. I should reach there by late afternoon. The innkeeper,

Joseph, and his wife, Anne, are indebted to our Agnes. Her tonic healed Anne's stomach ailments. You know what Agnes put in the wine. Gather the ingredients. I will get Jules and his men to stop at the inn for the evening meal. Their *tainted* meal. Tell Joseph we'll share the wealth. He'll have enough to purchase a hundred inns."

From the corner of her eye she saw Jules approaching. He stopped behind her. "That is sufficient time to say farewell," he announced. Though he wasn't actually touching her body, she was strongly aware of his closeness. Of his beautiful muscled form. It caused her heart to quicken and a warmth to unfurl in her belly. To Gerard he said, "Go. Now. You won't be asked again."

Gerard looked at her. She stood firm, despite the frenzy building inside her. Reluctantly, he turned and walked toward their cart. She swallowed down her panic as the reality of the moment hit her hard. They were actually *leaving*. Soon she was going to be alone with these men. With Jules de Moutier.

The man she'd asked to be her lover.

She watched Gerard climb up onto the cart. With a last look, he drove the cart away with Robert sprawled out unconscious in the back, moving farther and farther from her.

She clenched her teeth to keep from calling out, "Don't go!" She hated it that she was alone. That without Isabelle, she did everything alone.

How she hated it that her father had taken Isabelle from her and sent her to work at one of the Moutiers' châteaus for Charles de Moutier, Jules's father.

Even if she could interrogate Jules about what had happened to her sister, it would be a waste of time. He was never at the country estate while her sister was employed there.

He'd never care what happened to a servant anyway.

Jules slipped his arm around her waist and pulled her back against his solid form. "Elise," he murmured in her ear. She turned her head to look at him over her shoulder. Her insides fluttered. Her traitorous body was bent on siding with the enemy.

"Now that we have settled the matter of your request to be escorted to Maillard, I look forward to moving on to your other request."

6

The night air had cooled.

Sabine sat on fresh blankets near a small crackling fire. Back in the very spot where she'd given herself to Jules, awaiting his return. Tall oaks surrounding the clearing loomed over her, the rustling of leaves as the wind brushed past abrading her taut nerves, keeping her on edge.

She wrapped her arms around her legs and gazed up at the stars twinkling in the blackened sky. Though it was a serene sight to behold, she didn't derive any tranquility from it. How could she? He'd be back at any moment, and the man had the devil's touch. He'd made her scream in ecstasy. Scream. *Her.* She was practical. Levelheaded.

She could quash any emotion, control every reaction—except when he neared. Or when he touched her.

Enough.

She wasn't going to torture herself about it. She did what had to be done. It hadn't meant a thing. The only memory she'd allow herself to retain was how she'd bested him and how she'd made him pay—in a small way—for all the misery he and his family had inflicted. He, like his father, was a traitor to the Crown. The ruin of the realm. They'd put their ambitions above all else.

She'd do the same in turn.

She rested her forehead on her knees and looked up the moment she heard footsteps.

Jules approached her, all muscle and sinew. With the slightest touch of arrogance to his stride that bespoke his exalted bloodlines. The light breeze that whispered through the forest pressed his shirt against his chest, allowing her to make out the sculpted lines of his chest.

It was unjust that this man should be this physically appealing.

He was fashioned into such mouth-watering perfection.

Jules lowered himself onto his haunches before her, the firelight giving his handsome face a warm hue. "Are you all right?"

His question took her by surprise. It was the very same question he'd asked her long ago, when she believed him to be a different kind of man. Why would he care if someone of her social class was all right when he'd proven to be indifferent to the suffering of those beneath his elevated birth?

"I'm fine. Thank you."

"We need to talk." He slipped his hand under her chin. "What you attempted tonight was bold. There aren't many men, much less women, who would have tried what you tried."

She kept silent, unsure where he was going with this.

"I do admire your courage, Elise. But I'll not tolerate any more deceit. Or any trouble. You'll do as you're told. Always. Is that understood?"

"Yes." She disliked his authority over her. She'd had enough of the Moutier authority to last several lifetimes.

"Good. Now lie back."

She stiffened. Just like that? No kisses or caresses as he'd done before? As if she needed it. Just having him near caused a quickening low in her belly.

Jules cocked a brow, waiting for her compliance. *You're supposed to want this. It's what you asked for, you fool.*

Sabine lay back, her mind working as fast as her heart.

For the second time that night, his hands were sliding her skirts up. She could perhaps feign a malady to keep him at bay. Nothing too severe, or he might cast her out.

"About your obvious intentions . . . I . . . well, I mean to say . . ." she began.

His hands slipped between her thighs. She gasped, her sex already feeling slick. Slowly, he eased her legs apart. A lopsided smile appeared on his mouth. "Jules."

"Pardon?"

"I think we're intimate enough for you to call me Jules. Now, relax. I'm trying to make you more comfortable."

This was supposed to make her more comfortable? Did he jest? It didn't relax her. It incited every fiber of her being.

He reached toward the pail of water someone had placed near the fire.

"J-Jules . . . I'm afraid I'm not feeling—OH!" She jerked when she felt a cool wet cloth against her inner thigh.

"Easy. Allow me to wash this off."

"Wash what off?" She sat up immediately and saw a light stain on the linen cloth in his hand. *Blood.* Alarm shot through her. "I'm bleeding?"

Dropping the cloth back in the water, he placed his hands on her shoulders and gently pressed her back down. "You're fine. It's normal. There is a bit on your thigh. Nothing more."

Dear God, how could she have forgotten what happens when a maidenhead breaks?

Lightly, he passed the linen against the inside of her leg again. What he was doing was so unexpected, so astounding, it completely threw her off balance. Jules de Moutier, indifferent to the plight of the lower classes, was bathing her—with tender care.

She turned her face away, looking into the darkness, uncertain what to make of the consideration he was showing her.

He moved the cool cloth against her sex—the gentlest touch—gliding along the folds. She bit down on her lip. The linen repeatedly grazed over her sensitive sex, sending luscious sensations swirling through her body, tightening her nipples. She was fighting a losing battle; retaining control over herself was futile. He was decimating her resolve in delicious degrees. She couldn't hold back the soft moan that slipped past her lips.

"Does this hurt?" he asked.

Keeping her head averted, she said, "No," fully aware of how breathless she sounded.

Dipping the cloth in the pail, he pressed the damp linen more firmly against her sex. She closed her eyes. Every stroke of the cool cloth made her body hotter. Made her clit pulse harder. *The only thing I want from him is his silver*, she tried telling herself, a weak effort to do what she usually did—disconnect. But all it took was another light brush of the cloth against her greedy flesh for her body to contradict the notion.

"Are you sore, Elise?"

"*No . . .*" No, wait. She should have answered yes.

Turning her head, she met his gaze. He was smiling.

Her face grew hot. She sat up and pushed her skirts back down. "I think we've finished the bath, no?"

Still smiling. "I was finished a long time ago. I was simply enjoying your reactions."

She was thankful for the darkness, for she was certain her blush reached all the way down to her toes.

He tossed the cloth into the pail. "Where are you from?"

Mentally she groaned. She was too tired, her senses too overwrought. The last thing she felt like doing was weaving more lies. "A town, far away."

"What is this faraway town called?"

"What is it called? Oh, my town is called . . . Fillon. It's to the south."

"I've never heard of Fillon."

That is because I made it up. She gave him a shrug.

"Where are your personal effects, Elise? You've only the clothes on your back. Don't you own *anything*?"

She glanced down at her attire. "Oh. My things . . ." She scrambled for a believable explanation. "I didn't have many. What little I had . . . was stolen two days ago."

He silently studied her in that unnerving way he had. "How long have you been traveling?"

Hadn't she given him this information already? Was he testing her? "Two weeks?" she answered, hoping it sounded plausible.

"Alone?"

"Well, no, the King escorted me part of the way, but then His Majesty had to return to the palace." She frowned. "Of course *alone*."

"*Merde.* You are beyond reckless. What would you have done if you'd encountered a band of criminals? What is one woman alone going to do against a group of men?"

Just wait and see . . .

"I've told you, I couldn't stay where I was. My lord is of the belief that paying his taxes takes precedence over my well-being. Besides, I can take care of myself. I have been doing so for a long time."

"Yes. It would seem you're quite a resourceful woman. You put on a commanding performance as a whore. Since no man has ever had you before tonight, tell me, how did you manage it?"

"I . . . um . . ." *Think. Think!* "In our town we had a widow who took in unwed men and widowers. I overheard her at times . . ." Many towns had such women. It was a believable tale.

Once again, she found herself under his silent scrutiny.

Once again, she prayed he didn't see through her ruse.

He reached out and tucked her hair behind her ear, leaving a tingling on her skin in its wake. "Far too venturesome . . . And desirable." Capturing her chin and her undivided attention, he lowered his head and brushed his mouth against hers. Her lips parted for him. "My forest fairy . . . so highly arousable. We are going to have a memorable time together between here and Maillard, aren't we?"

"Yes . . ." But not in the way he thought.

He crushed his mouth to hers, and drove his tongue past her lips, kissing her with mind-spinning intensity. Inebriating her instantly with his taste. A rush of arousal flooded her body, her nipples straining hard for his attention. All right. She'd allow him to give Elise a kiss or two. Then she'd come down with a malady, put on a convincing performance, and reject him. The next thing she knew her fingers were tangled in his soft hair, and she was returning each kiss, her tongue matching his, stroke for stroke.

He stopped abruptly.

Stunned, her eyes snapped open. She realized he'd pressed her back onto the blankets and was stretched out partially on top of her.

"Why did you stop?" Mentally she cringed at her question and the slight desperation in her tone.

"Because we aren't going to have sex."

"We aren't?"

"No." Rolling onto his side, he propped himself up on his elbow and played with a lock of her hair between his fingers. "I rode you hard. Too hard for a virgin." He ran the lock of her hair lightly down her throat. "But starting tomorrow, you're all mine."

He wasn't going to take advantage of the situation?

She should be elated. He was solving her dilemma for her—at least for tonight—yet he left her wanting. Unsated passion hummed through her veins.

He sat up, grabbed the folded blanket near his feet, and covered them both as he lay back down.

Nudging her onto her side, he pulled her tightly against his front, her bottom cradled in his groin. She couldn't miss the bulge in his breeches, his hard generous sex pressing against her lower back. Her sex responded with a warm gush.

It took everything she had not to wriggle against him. The urge to create any type of friction between their bodies was so great.

His strong arms wrapped around her. "Good night, Elise."

She closed her eyes, but not because of fatigue. Thanks to him, her body was fully awake, a tormenting need rioting inside her.

How, by all that was holy, was she to sleep like this?

"Good night," she murmured.

What poetic justice this was. She'd been intent on denying him, yet he'd denied her. And made her want him, nonetheless. Worse, she'd have to sleep with his muscled body curled around her.

One more day. That's all that stood between her and the silver. Well, actually, that wasn't all. There was also a camp full of men. And their leader—the most sinfully seductive rake ever to grace the King's court.

* * *

The first thing Jules became aware of upon rising out of sleep was the cool temperature. His arms and chest were chilled. Eyes closed, he reached for the blanket only to find none anywhere on his body. Softly, he cursed and opened his eyes.

The day's first light had only just appeared. The trees overhead were still darkened in shadow, looking blackened against the cloudless indigo sky.

Lying on his back, Jules scrubbed a hand over his face. *Dieu*, he was cold. Looking around, he easily solved the mystery of his missing blanket.

It was to his left, wrapped around the woman next to him. Warmly cocooned within it, she lay on her side deep in slumber, her hands tucked beneath her cheek, the few flaxen tresses spilling out of the blanket looking as silky as he knew they felt.

His pretty forest fairy.

Propping himself up on his elbow, he took in her lovely face in the dim early morning light. Memories of her naked form, her sweet tits and the firm grip of her wet sex around his buried cock heated his blood. Currents of delicious lust coursed through his body. He couldn't believe she still held his interest the next morning. Or how much he was looking forward to having her again. Nothing would give him more pleasure than broadening her sexual repertoire.

She was deliciously hot-blooded. All this pent-up passion just waiting to be released. All his for the unleashing. The mere thought made his heart race. He shifted to accommodate his erection.

He hadn't had the pleasure of seducing a woman in a very long time. And he had a slow, sensuous seduction in mind for her. He'd have her very hot and very wet before he'd finally rock her beautiful body with another hot orgasm.

Jules slid close to her and pressed against her warm form. It hadn't escaped his notice that being with her leavened his mood. The bitterness that enveloped his soul seemed to recede just enough for him to catch glimpses of his old self.

"Elise," he said softly into her sleeping face. "You *are* a little thief. You've stolen the blanket."

She rolled over onto her other side, her shapely derrière now snug against his straining prick. "More sleep . . ." she murmured, clearly not inclined to awaken just yet.

A smile tugged at his lips.

It took everything he had not to unwrap her, wake her with long languorous kisses, and sink his hard cock into her moist heat. Was there a finer way to start the day than having a beautiful, sensuous woman?

Jules ran a lock of her soft hair between his fingers. Regrettably, since it was daybreak, he had to leave her side. A matter of utmost importance required his attention.

He sat up.

The cloudless sky promised a sunny day. He couldn't wait to

discover the color of her eyes and see her edible little form in the sunlight.

"My lord?"

Jules looked up and saw Raymond, ever loyal and discreet, standing with his back to him at the tree line of the clearing.

With a sigh, Jules rose and walked over to him. Sensing his approach, Raymond held out a fresh shirt.

Jules took the article of clothing. "Thank you. You may face me." He quickly donned it, consciously aware of the chill in the air again now that he was away from Elise.

"Of course, my lord." Raymond turned around. He handed Jules his baldric and rapier. "I hope you had a good night's rest."

He hadn't, really. With the blond forest fairy near, he'd been hard most of the night. It was the first time he'd been alone with a desirable, passionate female and not acted on the powerful urges she inspired. But then it was his first time deflowering a virgin.

Jules slipped on the baldric then sheathed his sword. "Is Simon here?"

"Yes, the captain and his party have only just arrived."

Simon Boulenger was the French Crown's most successful privateer and the captain of its privateer fleet. A second-rate supplement to the King's Navy during the realm's ongoing war with Spain, the privateer fleet attacked Spanish treasure ships returning from New Spain, weighted with precious metals. The two men, of similar age, had developed a friendship.

Jules owed Simon his life.

After his family's disgrace, it was Simon who'd entrusted the command of two of his ships, one to him and the other to his brother, Luc, at a time when it seemed no one in the entire realm would have anything to do with a Moutier. Thanks to Simon, Jules had a purpose, and a means to regain the wealth he'd lost.

He and Luc had worked independently, utilizing their naval skills with a vengeance, and had amassed a small fortune between them.

"Excellent," Jules said. "Then let's complete this transaction once and for all and hand over the silver."

"What about the woman, my lord?"

Jules glanced at her bundled form. After the delivery to Simon, Jules was going to meet Luc in the town after Maillard, and finally work to reclaim his life. But first, he was going to spend some decadent days and nights with the lovely Elise Marquette. After five long years, could it be that his luck was finally improving?

"Let her sleep. By the time she awakens, Simon will have his silver and be gone. We can then leave for Maillard."

7

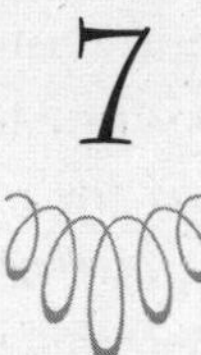

Simon Boulenger smiled as he surveyed the men transferring the chests of silver to his carts. "Well done. You keep this up, Jules, and I may allow you to do this indefinitely."

The hell he would.

His hands on his hips, Jules scowled. He hated privateering. Hated it that his naval and battle skills were no longer required or welcomed in the King's official Navy. "You know this is only temporary."

Simon didn't understand. He'd always been a commoner. He may have risen from his humble beginnings as the son of a fisherman to command a small fleet of privateer ships, but he'd no idea what it was like to have everything he identified with taken from him.

Jules had lost everything that made him who he was. His entire world had imploded on him.

He had no patience left. He wanted his life back. He wanted it now.

"With your skills, you and your brother are welcome to

continue as long as you wish," Simon said. "After I deliver the King's share of this capture to the Superintendent of Finance and attend to a few matters, I'll be returning to Marguerite."

"With more peasants in tow?" Jules's tone was dry. The island of Marguerite was located in the West Indies. Jules had been there many times during his employ with Simon, to attack Spanish ships and ports located there. Among the many islands, some still independent kingdoms and pirate domains, Simon and his men had laid claim to Marguerite. Over time, it had developed into a private settlement. At first it was simply a safe haven for those who worked and fought under Simon's command, and their families. However, little by little, Simon brought over peasants, giving them employ in the cane fields, allowing them—according to Simon—to escape the oppression they faced here. He didn't treat them as indentured servants, as many of the island governors in the area did, but gave them fair wages and decent accommodations.

Jules held his tongue out of courtesy, even though he didn't agree with Simon's practice of pulling tenants away from their lords and out of the realm. Nobles depended on the income from their tenants, and these peasants benefited from the protection of their lords while living on their land. To upset this balance wasn't good for the stability of the nation. And the realm had been through enough upheaval.

"Of course," Simon responded with a smile. "I'm trying to save as many of my kind from your kind as I can. You know there is plenty of room for you on Marguerite."

Although Marguerite had been built up over the last eight years and was indeed a comfortable settlement, Jules's life, his future, rested right here.

Before Jules could decline the offer, he saw the look on Simon's face change as he stared at something past Jules's shoulder, distinct male interest entering his eyes.

Without glancing behind him, Jules had a strong feeling he knew exactly what, or rather whom, Simon was looking at.

Jules turned around. Elise stood a few feet away. Her eyes were wide and fixed to the commotion around the carts.

Ensnared by the vision she made, Jules took in her pale blond hair, sensuously tousled, her comely face, and delicate body—all gloriously illuminated by the bright early morning sunlight. *Jésus-Christ.* She looked just as good as she had drenched in moonlight.

He approached her.

She looked up at him, delicate brows drawn together. Her eyes, the same color as Spanish silver, were utterly entrancing. He felt his prick stir.

He formed a smile. "Good morning."

"Who are all these men? What's happening?" Her eyes franticly scanned about.

She looked positively distraught.

He glanced over his shoulder at the men moving the chests from one cart to the other. He had no idea why such a sight would cause her such distress. He supposed the men looked menacing, especially to a petite woman, but last night she'd boldly walked into a camp of men she knew nothing about and attempted to steal while pretending to be a whore. She had more than her share of courage and fortitude. Why was she so nervous?

Slipping his fingers beneath her chin, he tilted it up, gaining her attention. Her skin was so warm and silky. "Everything is fine. There is nothing to be concerned about. The men will be gone soon."

"Why are they here? What are they doing to the . . . things in your carts?"

Before Jules could fabricate some sort of explanation, Simon sauntered up.

"Well, who have we here?" Simon's smile grew, his regard fixed on Elise—a little too intently for Jules's liking. The fact that he noticed or even cared how Simon looked at her surprised him.

Simon waited for an introduction, then rolled his eyes. "Mademoiselle." He reached out and took hold of Elise's hand. "I'm told he"—Simon nodded at Jules—"has manners, but to date, I've seen no sign of them. I'm Simon Boulenger. Who might you be?"

"This is Elise Marquette," Jules answered for her. The foreign emotion twisting in his gut was disconcerting and utterly absurd. So was his desire to rip Simon's hand off Elise. One good fuck and he was reacting like this?

"Elise Marquette," Simon repeated. "Lovely name. *Enchanté.*" He kissed Elise's hand.

Jules gritted his teeth and had to look away.

"Tell me, Elise," he heard Simon say, "are there other women in this forest as beautiful as you?"

"Why don't you go search for one?" Jules suggested. "I believe there is a cliff in that direction." He pointed left.

Simon shook his head, feigning dismay. "Ungracious, isn't he? If he is this rude to you, mademoiselle, you need only advise me, and I'll set him straight."

Sabine had no idea who the attractive man holding her hand was, nor did she care.

They're taking the silver!

Jules and his friend were both tall men. She wanted them to move so she could better see what was happening. So she could think of a way to stop them from taking the chests. She couldn't lose the silver.

She just couldn't.

"Elise?" The sound of Jules's voice captured her attention. The stranger had released her hand, and Jules was now cupping her cheek. She didn't need the distraction of his touch. She needed to think of something.

"Are you all right?" he asked. "You're flushed."

No! She wasn't all right! "I'm fine. Just a bit of a headache."

Afraid Jules would force her to return to their private clearing, away from what was happening in the camp, she rushed around the two men to a fallen tree near the ashes of the campfire and sat down.

Surreptitiously, she watched what the men were doing from behind the veil of her hair while she massaged her temples, pretending to knead away the ache.

Stop. Stop taking the silver away!

Suddenly her view was obstructed by Jules's body. He was down on his haunches before her, studying her silently. Further unnerving her.

"Are you certain it is only a headache that ails you?" he asked.

She had to collect herself. He was no fool. And he was questioning her behavior. She was making him suspicious.

Tucking her hair behind her ear, she formed a smile. "I'm sorry. I realize I'm behaving foolishly. I woke up, and you were gone. Then I came here and saw all these men . . . I was simply taken by surprise and I overreacted. I don't like surprises." She glanced past his shoulder to the men near the carts. "In my experience, they've never been a good thing." This wasn't supposed to happen. The rendezvous wasn't supposed to occur for another four days!

How had she gotten it wrong?

"My headache is only slight. I'll be fine. I'll sit here and cause you no trouble. I promise."

She'd no idea what he was thinking as he observed her. He had an uncanny way of masking his thoughts, of making his expression difficult to decipher.

"You didn't eat last night," he finally said. "How long has it been since you've had a meal?"

She didn't want his concern. She wanted him to move.

"Yesterday. Noon." Unfortunately it was true, but she wasn't hungry. Not with the knots in her stomach. The silver was *leaving*. How was she going to stop it?

Jules gave a signal to Raymond. Raymond walked up, handed Jules a goblet, then left.

"Here," Jules offered it to her.

She took the goblet.

"Drink it," he ordered. "It's burgundy. We carry the untainted kind."

She smiled, albeit weakly, at his jest and took a sip, not wishing to argue. "It's good. Thank you." She held the goblet out to him. *Go away!* He was too distracting.

"Finish it, *chère*. It fortifies the blood," he said. Raymond returned then with pieces of bread in a bowl. Jules took a piece and dipped it into her goblet. "I'm told this is His Majesty's favorite way to break the fast each morning. Bread dipped in diluted burgundy. But of course, you know this, having traveled with him," he teased and brought the wine-soaked bread to her lips.

She had no choice. She took a bite and forced herself to chew with a frozen smile even though her stomach balked at the thought of food.

His usual sensuous smile tilted the corner of his mouth. He placed the bowl on her lap. "I'll leave you to your morning meal. We'll be leaving for Maillard soon."

He rose and walked away, toward the group of men.

Thank God. Now at least she could think without his scrutiny. Or his presence clouding her mind. The silver couldn't leave. Not without her. She'd not gone through all this for *nothing*.

Helplessly she watched, sickened by the fact that one of Jules's carts was now empty.

Feeling someone watching her, she glanced to her left and noticed Raymond observing her a few feet away. Fear fisted in her belly. Had the horror she felt inside reflected in her eyes? About ten years Jules's senior, Raymond appeared to be a perceptive man. His hazel eyes looked sharp. And he was loyal to his commander. He wouldn't hesitate to report any peculiar behavior to Jules.

Carefully schooling her features, she offered him a small smile, dunked another piece of bread into the wine, and placed it in her mouth.

Somehow she forced her gaze to the bowl of bread on her lap, focusing on her meal instead of the goings-on near the carts.

What was she going to do now?

* * *

Three chests of silver.

By the time Sabine had finished forcing the food down her throat, the men had removed the chests from Jules's last cart and were now loading provisions onto it. From her furtive glances, she was sure there were three chests still on one of Jules's carts.

Three chests of silver would be enough to live like royalty. An immense fortune. Her family would be safe. They'd want for nothing. She'd have everything she once had.

Except Isabelle.

With her 'Sabelle, she'd feel whole again. And alive.

All she had left of her sister were memories she couldn't bring herself to dwell upon, the stories they'd written together, and Isabelle's precious journals. She'd left the journals behind when she'd gone to work at one of the Moutiers' country mansions. She'd asked Sabine to hold on to the journals for her, promising she'd return one day, for she'd never abandon Sabine or her treasured journals for good.

But seemingly, she had.

Logic told her that after all these years, if Isabelle was alive, she'd have contacted her.

Yet something inside her undermined logic. And it stemmed from the special bond she and her twin shared. If Isabelle *was* dead, shouldn't she feel it?

Why didn't it *feel* as though she was dead?

Was it wishful thinking? A desperate longing? Or was the feeling right?

With the silver, she could hire an army to search for Isabelle. To hunt down every former servant the Moutiers had, and question them about her sister. About what happened the day of the fire.

Raymond approached.

She put down her bowl, giving him her full attention. He had a cloth folded over his arm.

"Mademoiselle, please follow me," he said, and walked away.

Sabine's stomach dropped. He was heading out of the camp. She didn't want to leave. She wanted to stay near the silver. Where she could watch it. Guard over it. Make certain it didn't go away. Glancing at Jules, she noted he was still involved in conversation with some of his men.

Raymond stopped some distance away, turned, and waited.

What on earth did he want? Couldn't he leave her be? If she balked in any way, she'd raise suspicions. And that was something she couldn't risk.

She rose. Her legs didn't feel as shaky as they had when first she awoke. But worry over the chests of silver—her chests of silver—still gnawed at her.

As she followed Raymond out of the camp, she watched the cart with the treasure out of the corner of her eye. Some of the men were placing canvas bags and pottery flagons onto it. Her flagons were nowhere in sight. Likely they'd been emptied and destroyed.

She walked with Raymond along a narrow tree-lined path until they reached the river's edge. He placed the linen sheet he had draped over his arm down on a rock and held out a cake of soap.

"You may refresh yourself before we leave."

She took the soap. "Thank you."

Then he held out the old ribbon she used to tie her braid. There was only one place he could have retrieved that: the spot where she'd succumbed to Jules's sexual allure. Her cheeks heated. Murmuring another thanks, she took it from him.

He gave her a nod, turned, and walked away.

Sabine looked around. She was alone.

Eager to return to the silver, she stepped closer to the edge of the river, knelt down on the grass, and scooped up water. She splashed it over on her face and began bathing as best she could without removing her clothing, all the while fighting back the memory of Jules bathing her. It had taken a considerable amount of time to fall asleep afterward. The man had left her feverish and frustrated.

Grabbing the linen, she dried her face and arms.

Last eve, when sleep wouldn't take hold, her mind raced, and she came up with a way to get Jules to stop at the inn in Delatour. She'd use her request to be lovers to her advantage. She was going to seduce him into it—later that day.

Sabine combed her fingers though her hair, braided it, and secured it with the ribbon.

Yesterday she'd entered the camp without knowing what she'd be facing. Today she knew what she had to do. And who was standing between her and the treasure.

She didn't have things in her life that made her happy anymore, but rescuing her family, and taking wealth from a Moutier, was going to feel wonderful.

Drawing in a fortifying breath, she let it out slowly, rose, and turned around.

"Hello, *chère*," Jules said. She jumped back. He'd startled her so badly, her heart hammered.

"You're rather nervous this morning." From his tone and his look, she didn't know if he was trying to tease her again or if he was insinuating something. She swallowed down a spurt of fear. She *was* behaving like a lunatic this morning. And she was going to cease before all was lost.

"You startled me. I was bathing . . . I thought I was alone. I didn't hear you. I didn't know you were skulking around."

He lifted a brow. "Skulking around?" A smile lifted the corner of his mouth. He slipped his hand under her chin. "I don't need to skulk. I've already seen your sweet form, Elise. And last night I was inside you. I think we can dispense with modesty." Memories of how good he'd felt inside her, how good he'd tasted, flooded her mind, causing a wave of hot tingles to shimmer over her nerve endings. How did she respond to *that*? Her gaze fell to his mouth before she forced it back up to his eyes.

"I'm finished my bath" was what tumbled out. *Brilliant answer, Sabine.* Mentally she groaned at the awkward utterance.

He tilted her chin up a notch, bringing her lips a fraction closer to his. "Really?" His thumb lightly stroked her cheek. "What a shame."

She felt a quickening in her core. He wasn't going to make this easy, was he? That now-familiar heat was spreading through her body. The very same heat that had kept her awake and needy in his arms last night.

He'd said she was passionate. Perhaps that was it. Her physical reactions, these base needs, stemmed solely from her deprived existence. A passionate woman long denied. Clearly she was even lonelier than she realized. These physical responses had nothing to do with him at all. A small voice inside her balked at the notion.

She silenced the voice, intent on moving matters along. "Are we leaving now?" She'd managed to keep her tone light, belying the havoc inside her.

"After I've had a bath." With his gaze fixed on her, he moved his hands to the fastenings on his breeches, untying them.

Good Lord. Her senses were already awakened and highly attuned to him. And she was still agitated and on edge over the silver treasure she'd almost lost this morning. This was the last thing she needed.

She'd hoped to somehow reach Delatour and avoid another carnal encounter between them. Yet as she watched, mesmerized at the male perfection disrobing before her, her body railed in protest over the plan.

He pulled off his shirt and tossed it casually onto the grass. Sunlight warmed his strong shoulders, his chiseled chest. A long time ago, when she'd dubbed him her "Dark Prince," she'd thought him to be as majestic as a mythical god. At the moment, every sublime inch of him was. She had the powerful urge to run her hands over his skin, wanting to feel all those beautiful dips and ripples beneath her fingers. Moving her gaze down his body, she caught sight of his erect cock boldly protruding from his breeches. A particular part of his anatomy he knew how to use with mastery.

Her sex clenched hungrily.

Sabine forced her gaze away. "I'll leave you to your bath and return to the camp." She stepped around him, eager to distance herself and snap the spell. He caught her wrist, halting her in her tracks. Placing his hands on her shoulders, he applied a firm pressure. She sank down onto a rock she wasn't even aware was there, her gaze dropping immediately to her lap. A more neutral sight.

"Stay," he insisted and straightened. "Unless . . ."

"Unless what?" She kept her eyes averted, nervously plucking at a thread on her skirts, keenly aware of the pulsing between her legs that was worsening by the moment—his proximity the root cause.

"Unless you feel you cannot resist me and might ravish me. In which case, I forbid you to leave." She heard the smile in his tone.

He was toying with her.

Sabine bristled—at herself for her weakness toward him, and at him for his conceit. He knew his own appeal and his potent effect on women. At the theater, he'd moved about with his disarming smile and a casual confidence that bespoke it. He knew how to work females into a frenzy of need. If there was a man on this earth who could incite a woman to ravish him—he was that man.

She shot him a look, her nose almost colliding with the tip of his generous sex jutting from his open breeches. She squeaked in surprise, jerking her chin down, looking away. A purely reflexive response. She dropped her forehead into her palm, mortified, wanting to kick herself for her laughable reaction. It wasn't as if she hadn't seen his shaft before. What was her problem? Her problem was that she hadn't gotten so close to that part of his anatomy as to risk losing an eye.

Jules de Moutier was used to women who were more sophisticated about such things. *If he thinks you're silly, he'll become disinterested and cast you out.*

Dear God, he had to think her a complete idiot.

"Elise." Did she hear a restrained laughter in his tone? The thought only heightened her embarrassment. Warm strong fingers wrapped around her wrist. He pulled her hand away from her face.

He'd lowered himself onto his haunches before her. The crest of his sex came into view once again. Good God. *Will you stop looking at him there?*

She yanked her gaze back to his face.

* * *

Jules fought to keep a straight face, amused by her antics. Her cheeks were pink, warmed by her adorable blush. She was so many different types of women. The alluring camp follower. The damsel in distress. The bashful ingénue. And he wanted to fuck them all. It was so damned enticing seeing her teeter between her passionate nature and her inhibitions.

"There's nothing to be embarrassed about. And it's more than permissible to look," he said, brushing an errant wisp of blond hair from her brow. "It's what lovers do—look, touch, taste." Her eyes had darkened and her nipples pressed hard against the inside of her chemise. All blatant signs of desire. And keen interest. Last night she'd asked him to be her lover. First, he'd coax away all her virginal shyness.

Then he'd have her complete surrender. Unabashed.

He couldn't wait for the day to unfold.

The sun wouldn't set before he'd have her again.

8

"Did you enjoy your bath, my lord?" Raymond asked as Jules approached.

The camp had quieted. Simon and his men were gone, and most of Jules's men had left with him. Five men remained—five of Jules's largest, most trusted and skilled swordsmen—not to mention one cart full of provisions with three chests of silver concealed beneath them.

Jules's attention was drawn to Elise. She was seated on a fallen tree on the opposite side of the camp, watching the men as some readied the horses, while others made a last check to ensure all items on the cart were secured.

She observed the activity around her looking innocent enough, he supposed. *But still* . . . There was a slight stiffness in the way she sat that bespoke some inner agitation.

"Your bath, my lord. Was it enjoyable?" Raymond asked once more.

"Hmm? Yes, the bath . . ." Jules kept his gaze fixed on Elise. "It was fine."

He'd bathed while she sat on the shore. In fact, it had been a most enjoyable game—to catch her watching him bathe. He'd sensed it each time her curiosity had drawn her gaze to him. But with this intuitiveness he seemed to have where she was concerned, he could also sense her agitation—the very same agitation that had plagued her all morning. An agitation she was trying to hide.

Her unease was beginning to give him pause. Was this simply nervous excitement over their arrangement? Or was it something more?

"I thought you would have taken longer, my lord, especially with the lovely lady so near."

Jules took one last look at his blond forest fairy before he pulled his gaze away from her.

"Raymond, do you think she's behaving oddly?"

"Oddly? What do you mean?"

"She's been jumpy all morning."

Raymond shrugged. "She is a woman alone in the company of men she is relatively unacquainted with. I would think it would be natural for her to feel some unease."

"I don't think that's it. The woman is virtually fearless. Yet she appears out of sorts."

Raymond smiled. "That probably has something to do with you, my lord."

Jules frowned. "How so?"

"The lady is taken with you. I've seen the way she looks at you and she doesn't quite know how to behave around you. She is not as experienced as your usual paramours. She did, after all, yield her innocence to you last eve. I don't believe her behavior is out of the ordinary given how novel the situation is for her."

"Perhaps . . ." Jules glanced at Elise once more as he mulled over Raymond's words. They didn't sit right with him. "She certainly looks like a peasant in those clothes, but . . . she doesn't speak like one."

"Didn't you say her cousin was a schoolmaster? Obviously, she comes from a family with some education. She may even know how to read and write a little. It would certainly explain her finer speech."

"It would," Jules conceded.

"If I may offer an observation, my lord?"

"Of course."

"Since the lady's arrival, I've seen you behave more like—well, the way you used to be before . . . everything happened. The woman is beautiful. You find her company pleasing. Allow yourself to simply enjoy her. Experienced or not, the lady has no objections to you doing so."

Raymond was right. He was letting his general distrust play with his imagination, and he wasn't going to allow his time with Elise to be marred by his ever-suspicious mind. *Dieu*, what possible concern could he have? That she'd steal his silver? The notion was laughable. Even if she knew the contents of the chests—which was impossible—she wasn't much of a thief. Last night proved that.

She met his gaze and offered him a small smile. Hair so pale, a face so fine, and a womanly form made for a man's pleasure, that inspired an assortment of sexual fantasies. Ones he intended to fulfill. A sweet temptress who was drawn to him, drawn to sex. And all his for the next three days.

He shoved aside his niggling doubts.

There was no time like the present to stoke the delectable fire between them.

* * *

Sabine was so tense, she was ready to scream. Normally she wasn't prone to female hysterics, but Jules de Moutier was unsettling her on so many disquieting levels.

She wanted to cover her face with her hands and groan her

frustration, but he was watching her from across the camp and his men were nearby. It took all the acting skill she possessed just to maintain any level of composure.

Bad enough he rattled her confidence every time he neared, but having him bathe close by—in all his naked glory—had been devastating to her inner peace. The devil that he was, he'd caught her every time she'd stolen a glance. And smiled.

Once he even winked at her.

The river and all the surrounding land had once belonged to Jules's family. Rivers and forests were for the exclusive use of the lord of the land—though the lower class did their share of poaching and trespassing. It was one of the many laws imposed by the upper class. Including the Moutiers.

Yet despite the land being confiscated by the Crown, Jules had waded into the river as if it still belonged to him. He may have lost his social standing at court because of the *Fronde*, but clearly not his aristocratic sense of entitlement.

His bathing in the river was proof of that.

Despite having been practically born with a quill in hand, she doubted she could adequately describe just how incredible he'd looked, his muscled body wet, water droplets running down his skin.

Deep in conversation with Raymond, Jules ran a hand through his wet hair. There he was in all his male beauty. Sure to provoke sinful thoughts in the most pious nun.

Couldn't he have a hump?

She forced her gaze away, reminding herself that he wasn't the perfect prince she'd once believed him to be. He was a *Frondeur*. A traitor.

And he and his kind had cost her her world.

He's also been surprisingly kind, shown unexpected concern, and offered his protection until Maillard, a voice whispered though her. Fiercely, she quashed it. Stealing the silver was paramount. Necessary. Just.

The bit of consideration he showed didn't come close to repaying what he'd cost her.

Jules was approaching now, a smile upon his lips. By tomorrow, he'd no longer be smiling. Not after she'd taken every last piece of his silver and was nowhere to be found.

She stood up and returned his smile.

"It is time to go," he said.

"Of course. I'm ready."

The sun wouldn't set before she had his treasure.

She and her family were going to be wealthy. Rich beyond their wildest dreams.

Oh, this was going to be so very good.

She walked with him to the men on horseback and moved directly to the cart, noting there was a spot beside the driver for her.

"I'm afraid not," he said.

She turned and gave him a questioning look.

Jules patted his horse. "You'll ride with me."

* * *

Oh, this was so very bad.

His hand was near her breast. Just below it actually, but it may as well have been caressing it for all the torment his hot motionless hand was creating.

Sabine tried to focus on the passing trees, the birds overhead, the sounds of the snapping twigs beneath the horses' hooves, anything but the arousal simmering inside her, her sex moistening by the moment.

The cart carrying her future on it was just ahead. So was the small group of Jules's men on horseback. Having lost all track of time, she was unsure how many hours they'd been traveling.

It felt like days.

Jules's hand moved across her ribs, his thumb grazing the

underside of her breast. Her nipples tightened against her chemise. She closed her eyes, trying to steel herself against the seductive sensation. Trying not to think about the sublime torment he'd put her nipples through last night. She had to reach Delatour without giving in to this. Another sexual encounter with this potent man and she might lose her mind.

She wanted to shift her body but didn't dare. The bulge in his breeches was pressed against her bottom. Any movement would rub him intimately. Knowing he wanted her was wreaking havoc inside her. From the moment she'd first laid eyes on him years ago, he'd always had a stirring effect on her, but on meeting him again, now as grown woman, her reactions to him were far more carnal.

"Your heart is racing," he said near her ear.

"Is it?"

"Just relax. I won't bite . . . *yet.*"

She glanced over her shoulder at him. Smiling, his eyes shone with wicked promise and a look that told her he knew she was coming undone.

Knocking him from the horse would be wrong, wouldn't it?

Opting instead for a more appropriate response, given that she did, after all, ask him to be her lover, she forced herself to relax against him and said, "I'm afraid I'm not used to this." *What an understatement.*

"You're not used to what, *chère*? Being aroused?"

Her face grew warm.

Softly, he said, "Tell me what the desire is doing to you." The darkly seductive quality of his voice only inflamed her further.

"You—You want me to . . . describe it?" Did he actually expect her to voice the reactions he was eliciting from her body? "I'm not certain I can do that."

"Try."

She gazed back at him speechless.

"Shall I go first?" he asked. "Shall I tell you how you make me feel?"

Good Lord, no. "I . . . well . . . I suppose . . ."

"I feel," he murmured low, "like stopping this horse . . ." He halted the horse.

She looked around and noticed the men beginning to dismount. The only man to glance their way was Raymond. He gave Jules a nod in response to some silent command and turned away.

Before she could comment, Jules brought his mouth close to her ear once more. "I feel like taking you into the forest, stripping off your clothes, and fucking you . . . for hours." Her heart missed a beat. "You want to come, don't you, Elise? You're going to take my cock in . . . slowly . . . nice and deep."

Hot excitement roared through her. Think about the Greek alphabet. Anything! But not what he just said.

"But before that, I'm going to taste you, most especially that very sensitive pretty little clit of yours."

Alpha . . . Beta . . . What was the next one? She couldn't think or catch her breath. That very part of her anatomy he referred to was pulsing as wildly as her heart.

"Are you imagining it, Elise? Can you imagine what it will feel like when I taste you there? When I draw your clit into my mouth, and suck, and lick . . ." She squeezed her knees together to combat the throbbing between her legs. "I'll build the pleasure until it's so keen, until you can't take it any longer, until a strong climax shudders through your body and you come against my mouth. Can you imagine it, Elise?"

No, don't imagine it! He couldn't be serious. No one would do something so . . . shocking, surely.

"Answer me," he said softly.

"Men don't do that. I think you're jesting."

He pulled back. A purely male grin formed on his handsome face. "I promise, you'll enjoy it, as much as you enjoy having your breasts kissed and fondled."

Her nipples were so hard. The yearning to have his mouth on them, his hands on her body, was beyond fierce.

He nuzzled her neck. "You're blushing, Elise." His warm breath tickled her skin, sending tiny tingles down her spine. "Once you're grown accustomed to receiving pleasure, inhibitions fall away. When that happens, you'll be hungry for my cock in your mouth and eager to return the pleasure."

Another wave of arousal slammed into her. She fisted her skirts. This she'd seen before; whores in the alleyway outside the theater performed this service on their customers. She'd always thought it was a distasteful act. Until now. Instead of being appalled by his words, they heightened her hunger for him.

"I think we should dismount," she suggested. Anything to put some space between them and give her a chance to sober up from his seduction.

He met her gaze. "I agree."

Dismounting, he reached up and helped her down. Her legs felt shaky. Grasping her hand, he immediately strode toward the trees.

Oh, God. They were heading into the forest. What had she done?

He pulled her along past his men, who were busy pulling items from the cart.

"Raymond!" Jules barked without breaking his stride. "Where?"

"Straight ahead, Commander."

She was all but running to keep up with him as he walked briskly through the trees until they came upon a clearing. A picnic had been set up, no doubt by Raymond. A blanket and basket were set out.

They were secluded in the woods, with a giant rock nearby that rose almost to Jules's height. He pressed her back against it.

Bracing his palms against the large stone on either side of her head, he hemmed her in. He had the most decadent look in his dark eyes. "You asked me to be your lover. To experience sexual pleasures. Tell me you want me to claim your pretty cunt any way I want." He was so sinfully delicious. It was astounding just how appealing she found his wicked words. She swallowed.

Focus on the plan. His interest was crucial for its success. She was going to put on yet another performance. The most important ever.

Sabine relaxed her shoulders. "Yes . . . I want that."

He leaned in. His mouth was oh so close to her own. "What do you want? Let me hear you say it," he prompted and lowered his head. His mouth was on that sensitive spot below her ear, slowly moving down her neck.

A moan escaped from her throat, her breaths already short and shallow. She was so hungry for a taste of his mouth. "I . . . want you to . . ." He nipped at her earlobe. Her words died on a gasp. Her arms at her sides, she realized she was digging her fingers into the stone. It took everything she had not to throw her arms around his neck and beg him to take her then and there. *You are jeopardizing the plot. Concentrate!*

But then he cupped her breast, and over the fabric of her chemise, stroked his thumb over her distended nipple. Her knees almost buckled. "Jules, I want you to . . . do all the things you described. But what I want more than anything is to—" She could barely speak while he teased her nipple and kissed her neck, the most luscious sensations swamping her.

"To what?" he said against her skin.

"To experience them with you . . . on a bed."

He lifted his head. "A bed? Where do you see a bed?"

"Is there no place you can take me where we could have a bed to ourselves?"

After several tension-filled moments, he said, "There is an inn in the next town, Delatour."

She could barely contain a shout of joy. "There is? How wonderful. How long would it take to reach there?"

"A few hours. Not long."

She gave him a big smile and threw her arms around his waist. "Will you take me to the inn in Delatour and show me carnal pleasures?" None of this would come to pass. She ignored the pang of regret that whispered through her. Her body burned for him, but there was something greater at stake here than her physical gratification.

He gave a nod. “We’ll stop at Delatour.”

She’d done it! “Thank you.” She beamed, then stepped away and moved toward the food basket.

He caught her arm. “But we’ll begin the carnal pleasures now.”

9

Jules yanked Sabine up against him. She flattened her hands against his chest.

Her sense of triumph dissolved.

As did her smile.

"But . . . the inn. The bed. Wouldn't it be good to wait?" She was too aware of the length of his body against hers. And the raw desire still streaming through her blood.

"It will be good here," he wickedly promised, untying the ribbon securing her hair and tossing it onto the blanket. "We'll have a bed. Later. I'll have you again at the inn." His fingers unraveled her braid. "I'm afraid patience isn't one of my strengths. I don't like to wait for what I want." He brushed her hair behind her shoulder, captured her distended nipple between his fingers through the cloth of her chemise and lightly pinched. She gasped and fisted his shirt. He held the tender tip firmly, letting the pressure build into scintillating throbs. Her breathing spiked. "These pretty nipples are hard, wanting to be sucked. And we both know you're warmed and wet. You don't want to wait any more than I do." He leaned in. "You want to be taken right now, don't you?" he murmured in her ear.

Gently, he tugged and twisted her nipple with devastating finesse, sending a continuous stream of stunning sensations through her system. The only response she could muster was a whimper.

Just when she thought she'd cornered him, he'd cornered her once more. There was no way out. She was too far into this scheme to quit.

He lifted his head and met her gaze, clearly wanting a response.

Damn him and damn the way he made her blood burn.

She cleared her throat and ceded. "Yes," she said on a pant. *Ah, but now you're free to enjoy him.* The thought had such staggering appeal.

He gave her one of his stomach-fluttering smiles, dimples and all. "Yes, what?"

"Yes . . . I want you to . . . take me now." She wanted it so badly, it hurt.

He trapped her face between his strong hands and claimed her mouth in a hot hungry kiss. It sent her up in flames. An attack on her weakening defenses. She parted her lips, desperate for more. He didn't disappoint and thrust his tongue into her mouth.

He had the most delicious taste. He gave the most dizzying kisses. The wild impulses he inspired were dazzling. She was spinning out of reality and into a world of dreams—a magic only he could weave. Gripping his shoulders, all she could do was hold on for the ride. He stripped away her clothing, every brush of his fingers against her skin sublime. She ached to be filled by him. The initial discomfort she'd experienced the last time was a small price to pay for the blinding pleasure that followed.

"Undress me," he growled against her mouth. Trembling, she realized she was down to her chemise and *caleçons*, yet couldn't muster shock.

Not when her mind was focused on seeing his beautiful body again—the lure of touching him beckoning and beguiling her.

Fumbling, she managed to slip his doublet off his broad shoulders, down his arms, and onto the ground near the heels of his boots.

His hands slid down her back, over her derrière, and slipped beneath her knee-length chemise. Cupping her bottom, he lifted her up to her toes and ground her against his erection. A groan of pleasure escaped them both.

He set her back down. "Continue. Don't stop now." His breaths were quick and shallow, matching her own.

She grasped his shirt but couldn't free it from his breeches. Impatient, he pulled off the article and tossed it to the ground, then grasped her wrists and placed her hands on his bare chest.

"Touch me. I want to feel your hands on me."

Oh . . . yes . . . Years ago she'd longed for it and had imagined it at least a thousand times in her most private dreams.

Slowly, she ran her hands down his muscled chest, savoring the feel of his skin, the ripples of his abdomen. His skin was warm. So inviting. He closed his eyes, sucked in a ragged breath, and let it out in a forceful rush.

His every heated response elated her. Incited her. Moisture seeped from her sex. He swore. "Take this off." He grabbed the hem of her chemise and removed it with a yank.

His heated gaze moved over her body, his tactile regard like a hot caress over her skin. He reached out and cupped her breast. She braced herself for the jolt of pleasure coming her way. He stroked his thumb over her nipple. She couldn't stop the mewl that escaped from her lips.

"They look even better in the sunlight," he told her. "You have such pretty nipples . . ." His thumb drew lazy circles around the tormented tip. "And best of all"—his voice dropped low—"they're so very sensitive."

Before she could ready herself, he hauled her to him, swooped in, and sucked her nipple into his hot mouth. A cry erupted from her lungs. She threw her arms around his shoulders and arched hard against him.

He gently bit and sucked the sensitized peak. She moaned, her fingers tangling in his hair, holding him close. This was exquisite torture, each hungry pull of his mouth causing her sheath to clench.

He turned his attention to her other breast and created the same heated havoc, her nipple at the mercy of his skillful mouth, plying her senses with each rasp of his tongue and suckling sensation. Shaking, she squeezed her eyes shut, unsure how much longer her legs would hold her weight.

The moment his fingers yanked on the ties on her drawers, her *caleçons* slipped down her legs and fell to her feet.

He picked her up in his arms as if she weighed nothing and set her down on the blanket, his actions surprising her. Towering over her, he stripped off the remainder of his clothing. His heated regard holding her riveted, she pulled in her knees, wrapped her arms around her legs, and watched.

He stood before her, completely unclothed and at ease. His rigid shaft snared her attention.

She looked away, her confidence faltering.

* * *

Jules knelt down in front of her and sat back on his haunches. He knew what she was thinking.

"There'll be no pain this time," he reassured her, not wanting anything to interfere with the sexual abandon she'd been experiencing. She stirred such intense carnal hunger, it was difficult to remember her lack of sexual experience.

The blush on her cheeks only made her silver eyes more vivid. She tightened her arms around her legs. "I want you to kiss me again."

Now there was a request no man would turn down. "I'm going

to kiss you, Elise." Every last inch of her edible form. "Everywhere." Pulling her arms loose from her legs, he pressed a kiss to the inside of her wrist. Then, wrapping his fingers around her ankles, he lifted her feet one at a time and placed them on either side of his thighs.

Though she was deliciously aroused, she stiffened slightly, her knees still together. Inexperience and inhibitions getting in the way. He wrestled to control his fever for her. *Dieu*, he couldn't believe how strongly he wanted this woman.

He settled his hands on her bent knees. "Spread your legs," he coaxed.

She bit down on her lush lower lip, pausing a moment, before she relaxed her legs enough for him to ease her knees apart.

"That's it. A little wider," he urged until her knees spread to his liking. "Good. Just like that."

She sat very still, her long flaxen locks cascading over her back and arms. He devoured the sight before him, watching as her sweet breasts rose and fell with each quick breath, her pert ultrasensitive nipples looking so tempting, begging to be sucked again. He took in her smooth belly, and the dark blond curls between her legs, taking his time to linger on her clit, so swollen with need.

And her glistening sex. Pink, trickling with desire.

Ripe for the taking.

Lust licked up his spine. The memory of slipping between those pouty folds, sinking into her, made his cock throb; a spurt of precome leaked from his prick. For as long as he lived, he'd never forget the delicious feel of her tight sex.

He scored his finger down her wet slit. She gasped and jerked.

"You are beautiful," he said. "Every part of you."

He rose to his knees, urged her onto her back, and balancing on one hand, leaned over her. His other hand on her sex, he lightly fingered her, keeping her keen, avoiding her clit. Not letting her come. She gave an impatient little squirm.

"You're so wet. You've no idea what that does to me."

Softly panting, she glanced down at his cock. "I believe I have some idea. Some things are *hard* to miss."

He laughed. Despite her innocence, he loved it that she couldn't stop herself from looking at his prick each time the opportunity presented itself. "You're learning quickly." He lowered his body, partially covering hers. She quickly slipped her arms around him.

He gave her clit a light flick. Her hips jerked and she moaned her approval. "More?"

"Yes! *More* . . ." She pulled him down for a kiss. "Too much talking," she said against his mouth. "Not enough kissing."

He smiled, then took command of the kiss, turning her famished kisses into ones that were languorous and lush. She was delightfully different from any woman he'd ever known. He was accustomed to dictating in and out of the boudoir. Looking to please him and maintain his interest, the women always deferred to his demands during sex. Elise had a will of her own, and spoke her mind when she felt the need. It was novel. And from her, appealing.

He eased two fingers inside her slick core, slid them out, and then glided three fingers back in, gently stretching her, muffling her mews with his mouth.

He pumped them in and out of her, adding a fourth finger, listening to her whimpers, noting the random jutting of her hips as she encouraged him on—her clench around his fingers making his heart hammer harder.

"Does that hurt?" He knew from her reactions it didn't, but he wanted to hear her admit it.

She buried her face in his neck. "*No* . . . I want . . . I need . . ."

"I know what you need, beautiful Elise." *Jésus-Christ*, he needed a release just as bloody badly.

Pulling his fingers out, he reached up and grasped her wrists, pinned them down onto the blankets, giving her a fast hard kiss before he moved his ravenous mouth down her neck, to her breasts.

Pausing long enough to bite and suck, lick and tease those luscious pink teats, he relished every shudder and sensual sound he wrung out of her. She arched to him, urging him to linger.

But he had another destination in mind.

He released her wrists and trailed his mouth lower—down her belly, to the top of one velvety thigh, before heading toward her soft wet sex. Realizing his intent, she tensed. He granted no quarter, shoving her legs wide apart with one quick movement. He lowered his mouth and licked her slick slit.

She lurched and gasped.

Holding fast, he ran his tongue up to her clit, then sucked it into his mouth. She cried out with a sharp jerk of her hips, but he easily held her in place and began to feast, sucking on her in a steady rhythm. His aching sac was full, his cock hard and heavy, straining to its limits, yet he wouldn't relent, crushing his prick into the blankets to stave off his climax. She tasted so good, so perfect, he couldn't stop.

She wiggled and writhed, her fragmented sentences and incoherent words mingling with the sound of his heart pounding in his ears.

She made a sound at the back of her throat. Then there was a shift. He felt it the moment it happened. With a soft whimper, she thrust herself hard against his mouth, unable to control the urge and surrendering completely to his erotic kiss. If he had the strength to pull away, he would have shouted in triumph. Her surrender was as sweet as her taste. He laved her unresisting flesh, her legs trembling near his shoulders. She moaned and mewed, helpless against her own need. Her body tensed. And close to her climax. So close. He celebrated his imminent victory with a final hard suck.

* * *

Sabine screamed, ecstasy flooding through her core in hot pulses, her sex contracting wildly with each delicious spasm. He lightly licked her, unrelenting, until the muscle-melting contractions ebbed. And her body was boneless.

Her leaden legs were spread out, his mouth laving her dewy folds, yet all she could do was lie there, panting, her heart still pounding.

He kissed her thigh, then around her navel. Sabine closed her eyes, reeling in the aftermath, light tremors quivering through her body. He drew on her nipple. Her eyes flew open with a sharp gasp.

"You are delicious," he said.

She got a glimpse of the dark hunger in his eyes before he kissed her mouth. Her taste on her tongue was shocking, but she had no time to react; he wedged his shaft against her opening. She stiffened the moment the crest of his cock slipped inside her.

"Easy. I'm not going to hurt you." Slowly accommodating his girth and length, her body gave way to the downward pressure of his cock. He was filling her. So completely. So sublimely. A delectable inch at a time.

Looking away, she bit her lip, struggling to steel herself. She was far too shaken from their last round of carnal play. She needed more time to shore up her defenses before she'd be ready to face another shattering experience with him.

"Don't, *chère*. You're tensing and holding your breath. Put your arms around me. Just breathe."

She closed her eyes and wrapped her arms around him. He kissed her, skillfully easing more deeply into her. Penetrating her defenses farther in the most glorious way.

"*Jésus-Christ*, you feel so good . . ." *Oh, so did he.*

A soft alarming emotion whispered through her. A voice told her this felt right. Panicked, she suddenly needed—wanted—the physical pain to distract and distance herself from the intimacy, from the tender feelings welling inside her.

She surged her hips and sheathed him. He growled. She answered with a gasp. The voluptuous sense of fullness and the lack of pain from his possession hit her hard. So, too, did a stunning flare of arousal.

"I like your eagerness," he said. "As much as I like your hot, tight—" She had his mouth in an instant, unable to listen to his sensual voice or the shocking things he said. It was mortifying, but they had the most unsettling effect on her libido.

"Take me hard and fast," she pleaded against his lips. Maybe, by some miracle, if he was quick, she wouldn't have the time to lose herself to him again.

"When you have all of me," he murmured against her lips.

She pulled her mouth away. *"Pardon?"*

He gripped her hips and drove into her with a final solid thrust, sinking in even deeper than before. Her cry of shock and pleasure was eclipsed by the sound of satisfaction that erupted from deep within his chest. His mouth was on hers, his tongue filling her mouth. Lodged deep inside, his shaft filled her sex. She felt utterly possessed.

His hips remained motionless. The bud between her legs ached anew. She writhed, impatient. It was inexplicable but his stillness stoked the flames of desire hotter.

He withdrew halfway then glided back in deep. "Does it feel good?" She moaned.

Her breathing was accelerating. He wanted to talk *now*?

The yearnings became more insistent with every wild beat of her heart. He was as gripped in arousal as she. Why his procrastination? "More. Please . . ."

"More? You mean this?" Once again he withdrew, but this time he rammed her with luscious intensity. A whimper tore from her throat, her vaginal walls left quivering in the aftermath.

"Yes. That. More of that," she heard herself say, having no idea who this wanton creature possessing her body was. But she couldn't dwell upon it. She wanted him so fiercely.

"You'll have more. I will ride you hard and fast." She squirmed in anticipation, her beaded nipples pressing against his strong chest. "But first you are going to tell me how it feels to have my cock inside you."

Oh, God, he wouldn't relent!

"It feels . . ." She searched her mind for the right word. "You feel . . ."

"What?" He licked the sensitive spot below her ear, then bit her earlobe.

She closed her eyes briefly and swallowed. "So good. Incredible."

"It is about to feel even better." He gave her a searing kiss and drove in deep and hard. She moaned her delight against his mouth. Finally he began to move his hips.

The magnificent friction from each driving thrust of his thick length melted any remnants of her resolve. Her fingers tangled in his hair. And she returned his kiss with equal ferocity, wanting more. Everything he had.

He filled her again and again, taking away the emptiness. She wanted him to stay inside her. To keep her enraptured so that she'd never have to return to reality again.

Moving her hips, she met his thrusts, matching his rhythm.

"That's it," he said against her mouth. "That's good. Don't stop."

She couldn't stop any more than she could pluck the sun from the sky. The force of each thrust shook her body. Her inner muscles contracted. He groaned.

"Come for me," he rasped. "I can feel how close you are." *Oh, yes!* It was just beyond her reach. She had to have it. Or die. He was using all the strength in his powerful body to drive each thrust inside her. Every slam against her womb left her wanting more. Craving more of this. Craving more of him.

"More . . ." she pleaded, half delirious.

He grabbed her hips and shifted his angle. A shock of pleasure shot through her body.

Rapture exploded inside her. His name screamed in her head, or maybe from her mouth, her body uncontrollably clutching and releasing his thrusting sex.

He gave a sharp grunt and continued to plunge, his chest rising and falling with labored breaths. Abruptly, he jerked himself out. Eyes shut, a deep sound of pleasure rumbled from his chest as he spent himself between their bodies. In the grips of his release, the muscles in his neck and strong arms corded. He'd never looked more beautiful.

Transfixed, all she could do was stare as the image was branded into her memory.

His body finally relaxed. His weight on his elbows, he lowered his head and rested his forehead on hers.

Her body still shaky, she tightened her arms around him and held him, basking in a sense of peace the likes of which she'd never known. Sabine closed her eyes and allowed herself to enjoy his scent, the feel of him against her. Luxuriating in the quiet soul-nourishing moment.

The world with its injustices seemed far away. Reasons that divided them blurred. He felt more like her Dark Prince and less like her enemy.

Lifting his head, he gazed down at her. A slow smile formed on his lips, drawing a smile from her. When he gave a soft chuckle, it moved her to one as well. For the first time in years, she felt so light she could fly.

He brushed his lips against hers, his warm rapid breaths mixing with her own. "Beautiful forest fairy . . ." he whispered into her mouth, then ran his tongue along her lower lip. Tingles sped down her spine. "That was so very good."

His words pleased her far more than they should. "Too good . . ." *Pure bliss . . .*

He kissed the corner of her mouth. "No such thing." She heard the smile in his voice.

Pressing languorous kisses along the side of her neck, he trailed a warm path up to her ear and back down to the curve of her shoulder. Softly she moaned. She was thoroughly sated, her muscles delightfully lax, yet he could still elicit heated reactions from her.

What woman could remain—*Oh!* He nipped her earlobe—unstirred by this man when he'd set his sights on her as the object of his desire?

"They should warn women about you in the *Gazette* . . ." she said breathlessly.

He lifted his head. "The *Gazette*? The Paris paper? How do you know about the *Gazette*?"

She froze. Her heart gave a hard thud before it began to pound. If her wits hadn't been so sluggish, she wouldn't have made such a blunder.

"I . . . I . . . heard about it. From my cousin. Th-The one in Maillard. He's been to Paris." She forced herself to maintain his gaze. For the first time, she found herself hating to lie to him.

"Have *you* been to Paris?" he asked.

"Me? No. You?"

He rolled off her and sat up. She felt bereft immediately. He picked up a cloth near the basket. "Yes. I have," he said tightly. His family's city mansion, Hôtel de Moutier, had been his primary residence. It, too, had been stripped from him upon his family's disgrace.

Clearly, the mention of Paris caused him distress. Had the last five years been as difficult for him as they had been for her? Sabine arrested her thoughts. She couldn't dwell on him this way.

No matter what, she still had to do what she had to do. Besides, the last thing she wanted was to shatter this moment with painful thoughts. She'd found an unexpected moment of contentment. And she wanted to linger in it awhile longer.

It was the first time she'd experienced any kind of happiness in a long time.

It was the first time she'd experienced any kind of happiness without Isabelle being a part of it.

He moved onto his side. Propping himself up on his elbow, he schooled his features as he attempted to hide his true feelings from her, and wiped her thigh clean.

"Tell me about Fillon," he said.

"Fillon?"

He stopped wiping and lifted a brow. "Yes. Your *town*?"

"Oh! My town, Fillon. Of course. What do you wish to know?"

He gave himself a quick wipe and tossed the cloth away. "Tell me about your family there."

She stiffened. At the mention of the word "family," her heart constricted; Isabelle's name echoed in its empty chambers. "I've already told you, I'm alone." This wasn't a subject she wanted to discuss. Especially with him.

"Easy, it's all right." Clearly he'd noted her sudden distress. Capturing her chin, he gave her a soft unhurried kiss she felt all the way down to her toes. "I thought to make this less of an impersonal encounter by learning more about you. But if you wish to keep it impersonal, you don't have to answer—"

"Impersonal encounter?" That sounded cold and unappealing. And what they'd experienced together had been anything but.

"Yes. An impersonal encounter. The sharing of bodies and nothing else."

The description bothered her. And she didn't know why it should.

"Do you have something to hide? Something you don't want me to know?"

She sat up. "I've nothing to hide." For her numerous lies, she was overdue for a lightning bolt.

"Good. Then tell me about the people in your town."

She plucked at a thread on the blanket. "They didn't like us."

"Really?" His brows shot up. "Why not?"

"They thought we were . . ."

"What?"

"Odd." That was mildly put. Why on earth was she telling him any of this? When she'd told him so many lies, why tell him the truth about her life?

"Odd? How so?"

"My family was . . . well . . . different. They enjoyed entertainment. A certain type that the townspeople frowned upon." Sabine lay down on her side to face him, tucking her hands under her cheek. "They were rather a rigid lot." Though her father never cared a whit what the townspeople thought, they were all made to feel like outcasts. She and her father and Isabelle, and members from her father's troupe—his longtime mistress, Louise; her two daughters, Josette and Pauline; Vincent; and Olivier—weren't well received. The townspeople's true feelings toward those from the city, in particular actors, were unmasked once they no longer owned their own land and were in financial ruin.

Jules brushed one of her locks off her shoulder. "What sort of entertainment did your family enjoy?"

She propped herself up onto her elbow. He didn't recognize her. And there was no way he'd ever find her again. She decided it was safe to reveal a bit more. "We would invent tales and act them out. A sort of mock theater, you could say."

"Really?" he said with interest. "How often?"

"All the time. It would leaven the days." A way to stay connected with an old life they once knew in Paris.

Jules was genuinely surprised. She was anything but ordinary. And by far the most interesting and exciting woman he'd met in a long time. "Whom did you perform for?"

She ducked her chin in the most adorable manner. "Well, no one would come to watch. So, we performed for . . ."

"Yes?" he said anxious for her answer, unable to guess at her next words.

"The chickens."

He burst into laughter.

She joined in.

The sound of her laugh was as delicate and appealing as the rest of her. He was enjoying himself immensely.

"Of course, they weren't a very quiet audience," she related.

"No." He couldn't help chuckling again. "I don't suppose they were."

"I told you, we were odd." She gave him one of her pretty blushes.

"I find your eccentricity charming."

Her smile faded. "You do?"

He leaned in. "I do." Lightly, he kissed her mouth.

To his delight, she slipped her fingers into his hair and deepened the kiss. He parted his lips, a silent demand for her to slip her tongue inside his mouth. Pleased that she complied in an instant, lavishing his tongue with soft swirling caresses.

His cock swelled to life. *Jésus*, he could make no sense of it. Having fucked his way through the French court, he'd always favored women with a certain social standing who were experienced in recreational sex. The last woman on earth he ever imagined would capture his carnal interest would be a virgin of inferior birth. And yet he wanted her again—eager for another mind-bending sexual experience with her.

She pressed more firmly against his mouth, her kiss becoming more impatient, her tongue no longer as playful, more urgent. He ran his hand over the sweet curve of her hip and down her thigh. A shiver of excitement rippled through her. He liked how sensual she was. In fact, he liked everything about her. He even liked the way she caressed the nape of his neck during sex. He didn't know what to make of it, but no matter how heated she became, she'd tenderly stroked him there each time.

And he was never certain whether she was aware she was even doing it.

Normally he wouldn't have changed his travel plans, but the thought of having her on a bed, fucking her to ecstasy and back, was too much to turn down.

Breaking the kiss, he rose. "Delatour awaits. As does our bed."

10

"That is Delatour," Jules said in her ear, tightening his arm around her waist ever so slightly.

Just ahead was the stone wall that surrounded the market town.

Sabine's stomach clenched.

The men slowed the horses as they neared its entrance. Only about two hundred feet of dirt road separated them from the town.

During the journey he'd repeatedly dropped hot kisses on her shoulder and neck, melting her insides a little with each one. In fact, throughout the day he'd been devilishly charming.

A day that had been the most incredible one she'd ever had.

Sublime carnal encounters aside, she'd lain with him afterward talking, enjoying an easy rapport. Before leaving for Delatour, she'd bathed with him in the river. He was the first man she'd ever bathed with. He was her first for many things, and she'd been unable to keep from touching him, tasting his mouth. It was exhilarating. Around him she was different, somehow transformed. He made her feel beautiful. Desirable. And even worse—happy.

He'd been altogether perfect.

As perfect as she'd once imagined her Dark Prince to be. He wasn't supposed to be like this *now*.

She had every confidence her cousins had set their plan in motion at the inn.

Only now it no longer felt right to do to him what she had planned.

In fact, it felt very wrong.

She was practically choking on the turmoil inside her.

The sky reflected her disquiet. Gray clouds loomed overhead, blocking out the late-day sun. It only served to elevate her sense of gloom and dread.

"Our bed nears." He smiled. The appeal of those three words, the promise of luscious pleasures, tormented her further. There'd be no further intimate encounters.

She was about to drug him and steal from him.

After what they'd shared together, in the end, he'd despise her. And she had no idea why the notion bothered her as much as it did.

You have no choice. It was that simple. Yet it wasn't.

He brushed his thumb along the curve of her breast. A soft gasp shot up her throat, sensations spiking from his touch to every sensitized nerve ending in her body. He was making this so difficult for her. He'd purposely fanned the fire inside her all afternoon during the ride to Delatour, inflaming her senses to a fiery pitch, in anticipation of their arrival at the inn.

"Your heart is racing again. Does this mean you're anxious to reach the inn?" He repeated his caress. Pleasure rippled through her.

Stay focused. She had to start distancing herself from him.

Think of the huge debt. What she had left of her family. *Think of Isabelle.*

Sabine covered his hand and gently squeezed it, needing to still those decadent strokes. Mustering a small smile, she looked over her shoulder. "Yes. I'm most anxious." *That was mildly put.* She'd never felt more inner torment in her life.

Horses' hooves clattered over cobblestones.

She snapped her head around.

Delatour. They were inside the wall. The sight was like a fist to her belly. Jules led their party through the town. Lined with three-story white-and-timber buildings, its busy streets were noisy. Chaotic.

She felt swallowed up in the confusion. Heated haggling between merchants and customers, the incessant clucking of chickens, the shouts and laughter of children as they darted about assailed her ears. Carts rattled by. People moved past. The clamor and bustle escalated her distress.

It was all too loud for her frayed nerves.

A number of onlookers cast curious glances their way—their focus was Jules. It was then Sabine realized he was keeping to the middle of the road—just as any Aristo would—forcing others to either side. Only the upper class rode down the center of the street, and they were the only ones permitted to walk under the protective canopy like jetties that jutted from the buildings. The rest of the population had to occupy the other spaces that put them at risk for a dousing from the chamber pots emptied out of the windows above.

From the corner of her eye, she could see that he gazed straight ahead and didn't seem to notice the stares. His repeated defiance of society's mores surprised her. He rode on, acting as if he were still privileged.

Jules negotiated a right turn. There it was. Located at the end of the road, made of gray stone, it stood three floors high—the inn.

A fresh wave of uncertainty hit her hard. She fought to reassert her resolve.

This is no time for a crisis of conscience!

Jules stopped the horse and dismounted.

He reached up to help her down. The moment her feet touched

the ground, he slipped his fingers beneath her chin and tilted it up. He pressed his warm mouth to hers, instantly kindling a seemingly insatiable need for him. His scent, his taste filled her senses and for a moment quelled her agitation. Unable to resist the seductive pull of his kiss, she parted her lips for him, encouraging him into her mouth—uninhibited at the public display. But he lifted his head, denying her time to bask in the splendor of his mouth.

"Wait here," he said with a wink.

Somehow she stopped herself from dragging him back for one last kiss.

With her heart in her throat, she simply nodded and watched him walk away, leading his horse toward his men. They stood in a group near the cart and horses in front of the inn.

It was then she noticed Raymond was missing.

Sabine looked about, yet couldn't spot Jules's loyal servant. He was never far from Jules's side.

Where was he? He had to partake in the tainted meal her cousins had prepared. Good Lord, she couldn't take one more complication.

Speaking to his men, Jules didn't appear concerned about Raymond's disappearance.

She watched the early evening breeze caressed his dark hair, his tall strong body, blowing his linen shirt against his sculpted chest. He looked princely.

He looked so good, it hurt.

She pulled her gaze away.

This was the stuff her father's comedies and tragedies were about. A woman finds a modicum of bliss in the arms of her enemy, only to have to destroy it by her own hand. Ironic. Tragic.

Pathetic.

She kicked a small stone on the ground, all too aware of the knot in her throat. Had fate not intervened, she'd have never known this incomparable experience with him. She wouldn't have stood any more of a chance to be with him than those women on the streets today.

Footsteps approached.

She looked up just as Jules reached her side. With one of his devastating smiles, he linked his fingers with hers, and bringing the back of her hand to his lips, he pressed a kiss to it. "Ready?"

Briefly glancing past him, she saw the men, cart, and horses heading to the stables at the side of the inn. She gazed back into his deep dark eyes and had to swallow before she could say, "Yes."

He led her inside.

It took a moment for her eyes to adjust to the dimness of the room. There were a number of wooden tables and chairs with a few patrons seated at them. A stone hearth was to their left.

"*Good evening.* Welcome!" the female voice behind them said.

Sabine stiffened. *That voice sounded too much like* . . . She turned. Her heart lost a beat.

Beneath the familiar matronly dress from their chests of costumes, her hair powdered to look older and her slim body padded to appear fuller, was *Louise*, her father's longtime mistress and star actress from his troupe.

What on earth was she doing here?

It was impossible for her cousins to have reached home and returned with her in time.

Jules frowned. "Where is the owner?"

Dear God, he knew Joseph.

Louise's years on the stage shone through as she held her perfect unwavering smile. "Why, you know my cousin Joseph? How delightful! Come have a seat. I'll have my husband bring you and your lady something to drink."

Husband?

"Did I hear you mention me, *chérie*?" Vincent, Louise's older brother, also from her father's former troupe, approached. He, too, was dressed to appear older than his years.

Was her *entire* family here? Where were her cousins?

Just then she took a closer look at the people seated at the tables. She all but groaned out loud. Clearly, Robert was no longer under the influence of the tainted wine. He was at one of the far tables—dressed as a woman—with Gerard, who looked old enough to be his, *or her*, father.

What were they thinking, sitting out here in the open?

If Jules were to recognize them . . .

"Why yes," Louise said to Vincent. "This lovely couple has just arrived. What can I get for you, sir?" she asked Jules, her tone most cordial.

"The owner." It was an unmistakable command, distinctly weighted with authority.

Louise's eyes immediately filled with tears. She pulled out a handkerchief from her bodice and dabbed her cheeks as two teardrops gently rolled down her face on cue. "I would love nothing more than to do that, but alas, I cannot." She lowered her head, muffling a soft sob with the handkerchief. Vincent, seasoned actor that he was, placed a consoling arm around his "wife's" shoulders while looking every bit as stricken as she.

"Please forgive my wife's emotional state. I'm afraid Joseph's dear wife, Anne, has become ill," Vincent explained. "Joseph has taken her to an apothecary who saved her life once before. We are quite concerned about her. We pray the woman can help her."

Louise pulled away from Vincent and composed herself. "Yes." She dried her cheeks. "It was lucky we were here visiting when she became ill."

"She'll be fine." Another familiar voice came from across the room. Sabine shot her gaze to the left and briefly closed her eyes.

Oh, Lord. Agnes, too?

"I've heard incredible things about that apothecary. She *is* gifted," Agnes said as she approached. Stopping in front of Jules, she grinned up at him.

Agnes was no actress. She was an apothecary, the very one

who'd helped Sabine by tainting the wine, and yet another member of her blended eclectic family. Agnes rarely held her tongue when her short temper flared. How was she to put on a believable performance?

Sabine peeked up at Jules. He looked serious. Too serious. Frantically she searched for recognition in his eyes, praying there would be none. Her father had had only one strict rule: She and Isabelle were to be invisible whenever they were at the theater. However, Jules had seen Louise and Vincent perform many times. She hoped for once his aristocratic attitude worked in their favor—that his inherent disinterest in the lower class would keep him from looking too closely at the "couple" before him.

"Your names are?" he asked. She couldn't read much into those three curt words.

"Oh! What terrible manners. My apologies," said Vincent. "I'm Gilbert and this is my wife, Bernadette."

Louise walked over to Agnes and placed her arm around the older woman's shoulders. "This is my sister, Claire."

Since Jules wouldn't know Agnes, she didn't need a disguise. Nor did she need to sport that ridiculous grin affixed to her face. She was trying too hard, overcompensating for her dislike of nobles—including all Moutiers.

Instead of appearing genial, she looked daft.

"Really?" Jules responded, glancing at Agnes and her imbecilic expression. "I'm afraid I don't see a family resemblance."

Agnes opened her mouth to respond. Louise gave her a quick squeeze, cutting off her words by saying, "We had different fathers. Claire's father died tragically young. Our mother remarried my father."

Agnes shot a disapproving look, clearly displeased at being silenced. Especially by Louise. She had very little patience for Louise's grandstanding ways.

Agnes had very little patience. Period.

Afraid she'd begin bickering, Sabine cleared her throat.

The distraction worked. Agnes turned her hazel eyes on Sabine. Her idiotic grin returned.

"Oh, sir, my compliments! Your lady is *lovely*," Agnes exclaimed with a tad too much exuberance. "*So* lovely! Let me take a closer look." Agnes walked up to Sabine, then scrutinized her from head to toe.

What on earth was she doing?

"She has lovely features, as I'm sure you've noticed," Agnes said. "But I fear she's a bit"—she clamped her hands on Sabine's hips—"thin. Some of my mutton will do the trick. We'll have these hips and breasts filled out and then you'll have something to hold on to!"

Sabine felt heat rush to her face.

If God was looking to punish her, she preferred the lightning bolt to this.

Louise pulled Agnes back. "Please forgive my sister," she said to Jules. Lowering her voice to a loud whisper, she added, "She hasn't been the same since her fall last winter." Louise tapped her temple.

Agnes crossed her arms over her ample bosom. "Fall . . . *humph* . . . I do have *my hearing*," she shot back. "And my memory works just fine. Trust me, I will remember that comment later."

"Easy, now," Vincent said. "Claire is right about hips and breasts." He gave Jules a wolfish grin. "Sir, I ask you, is there anything finer than the curve of a woman's hips? Or a perfect plump breast? Heaven, no?"

What were the chances that the floor would give way and her family would fall through?

Jules placed a hand on her elbow; his touch immediately made her insides flutter. "You seem to have done a good job maintaining the inn." To his credit, he chose to ignore the mortifying comments of her absurd lot before him. She wanted to kiss him for that.

"Why, thank you." Louise was quick to take the praise. "We've maintained it to impeccable standards, for Joseph and dear Anne."

Jules glanced around. Sabine held her breath, feverishly hoping that he didn't recognize Robert and Gerard. "It's very quiet. Not normal for this inn."

"Well, yes, it is a bit quiet . . ." Vincent agreed. Sabine sensed that somehow they'd managed to clear out the inn.

"Then I'm certain there's no problem with room selections. I'll take the largest room on the second floor. The one at the end of the hall," Jules advised, and began escorting Sabine toward the stairs.

"Wait!" Louise exclaimed and rushed to them. Fixing a smile back on her face, she said, "Why not sit down for some nourishment, and then proceed upstairs to the room you desire?"

He paused at the foot of the stairs. "I think not. We will have our meal in our room."

"But your lady, lovely as she is, looks quite tired. Perhaps a small rest and some food first . . . then you won't have to be *interrupted* with your meal."

The door opened, grabbing Sabine's attention. Raymond entered the inn.

"I'll be right back," Jules said to her, ignoring Louise, and stalked toward Raymond.

Louise linked arms with Sabine. "Allow me to escort you to a chair," she said loudly, for Jules's benefit. They began to walk.

"What are you doing here?" Sabine whispered.

"Agnes, in a rare moment of good sense, confessed that she'd tainted wine for you and what you intended to do with it. Fearing for your safety, we rushed to find you. Fortunately, when we reached Delatour, we happened to see Gerard and Robert. Gerard filled in the rest."

Louise continued with a tight smile on her face. "Although I do approve of stealing from the Aristo—after what the Moutiers have done, he deserves what we're about to do to him—you haven't exactly handled this well. I can't believe you gave yourself to him. Sans a maidenhead, it will take a greater dowry to marry you off. How could you do this, Sabine? I swore to your father on his deathbed I would take care of you, and you do something like this."

Livid, Sabine stopped dead in her tracks and cast a quick glance at Jules. He and Raymond were engrossed in conversation. "No one in this family has come up with a solution to our dire situation. So I took the matter into my own hands, as I've been forced to do so many times before. I'm trying to keep us alive. A fortune in silver sits in the stables with five of Jules's men. I've managed to come this far. On my own. And I'll see this through to its successful conclusion." The knots in her stomach had tightened with each word. "Further, my body is my own. What I choose to do with it is none of your concern. Neither is it your responsibility to 'marry me off.' " Marriage was the last thing on her mind.

There had only been one man she'd ever thought to marry.

And he was across the room. About to be drugged and robbed.

"Don't be ridiculous. We'll use the funds to purchase a new life for ourselves, and for dowries . . . especially for Josette and Pauline. Oh, and they need new gowns . . . a whole new wardrobe, in fact. My poor girls have been in rags long enough. As have I."

At the mention of Louise's spoiled daughters, her ire spiked. She was not her father. She didn't need to placate and indulge them the way he had, simply to keep his mistress happy and from leaving his troupe. Pauline and Josette were not his children and yet they, together with Louise, had done their share of draining Sabine's family's funds dry. Sabine had allowed them to remain after her father's death because her conscience wouldn't permit her to toss them out.

Knowing what would befall them if she did.

But she hadn't done all this just so Louise and her daughters could attain status and new gowns.

The wealth wasn't Louise's to spend.

"I'll decide how the silver is spent. After the debts are cleared, I'm searching for Isabelle."

"Oh, Lord. Not this again. Isabelle is gone—"

"Stop. I'll not hear talk of her being dead." Perhaps it was because of Jules and old memories he stirred, but the feeling that Isabelle was still alive was stronger than ever.

"Sabine, sooner or later you're going to have to accept the truth. It's been five years—"

"I *will* find her. With the silver, I'll have plenty of wealth to search." She knew it sounded mad. They knew where Isabelle had been buried.

She hadn't been able to bring herself to visit the humble grave. Too many conflicting thoughts and emotions paralyzed her.

"This is no place to discuss this," Louise said, casting a furtive glance at Jules. "We are putting an end to this scheme. Quickly." She urged Sabine down onto a chair. "Tell him you're tired and hungry. Encourage him to eat here and not upstairs, where he seeks to satisfy *other* appetites. Whatever he orders will be sufficiently laced. His men will meet a similar fate." Louise's smile turned genuine. "This is all very sweet, indeed."

"Enough. He approaches," Sabine said, relieved to silence Louise.

Sabine watched as he moved toward her, his movements confident and sinfully riveting.

She'd shared Louise's contempt. Her perfect Dark Prince, the Aristo she'd been so smitten by, had over time turned into a soulless villain. And now he was her lover. It was becoming increasingly difficult to define her feelings toward him.

Jules held out his hand and helped her to her feet. "Come." That single word held such wicked promise. It left her feeling warmed and wet.

"The mutton is ready right now," Louise said.

"I detest mutton. And I like the lady the way she is. She doesn't need any." His endearing compliment wrapped around her heart. Jules leaned in and near her ear he said, "For the next hour, I'll make you forget about food and fatigue. Afterward, I'll have a meal fit for royalty brought to us." He pulled back. The devilish look in his eyes caused her insides to dance. "What say you? Do we stay down here and dine? Or do we proceed upstairs?"

Vincent and Agnes moved closer to Louise. They awaited Sabine's reply.

If she chose to dine with him here, their laced meal would soon see Jules unconscious. This ordeal would finally be over. Proceeding upstairs would only prolong the inevitable. *An hour alone with him* . . . That would only make matters worse. No?

Feeling her family's gaze bearing down on her, aware they were confident of what responsible, *sensible Sabine's* answer would be, her decision suddenly became clear.

She smiled into his handsome face. "Why would I want food, when I can have you?" she said.

He grinned.

Her family's jaws dropped.

Jules placed her hand on the crook of his arm and escorted her toward the stairs.

"But—But . . . are you certain you wouldn't rather eat *here*?" Louise asked, her tone tinged with a measure of alarm.

"Quite certain," Sabine responded coolly. Without a backward glance, she kept walking. She couldn't stop smiling. For once she wasn't self-sacrificing. She was doing something solely for her. What she wanted to do, and what she wanted more than anything was to enjoy him one final time.

Why hasten back to reality when she could linger awhile longer in the realm of dreams?

11

The moment Jules closed the door and removed his baldric, she launched herself at him and flung her arms around his neck.

Unprepared, his back hit the wall. He grunted on impact. She sealed her lips to his and devoured his mouth, starved for his taste. He trapped her face between his hands, angled her head, and possessed her mouth, kissing her with inebriating intensity, making her sex leak and ache. Each tantalizing stroke of his tongue spiked her fever. Her clit pulsed harder. He was more potent than any of Agnes's aphrodisiacs could ever be.

She had an hour to enjoy her Dark Prince, to lose herself in the fantasy, and nothing was going to distract her from that.

Not even her meddling family.

She'd locked herself in a prison of numbness and hadn't realized how badly she needed to escape until he'd touched her.

Blindly, she reached for the closure on his breeches, desperate to touch his skin, to run her hands over his solid chest and muscled abdomen. Her shaky hands fumbled. Just as she was about to tear them open, he spun her around and shoved her hard against the wall. Her gasp was muted by his mouth.

Gripping her hips, he lifted her and wrapped her legs around his waist.

His hands were on her bottom. The hard bulge in his breeches was now pressed against her needy sex. He rolled his hips, grinding himself slowly against her private flesh. She whimpered, her head falling back against the wall, overwhelmed by the physical yearnings coursing through her blood. She'd never felt so out of control. So consumed with desire.

"Tell me what you want." His voice stroked her overstimulated nerve endings. "Let me hear you say it."

What she wanted . . . She wanted to forget and pretend. She was a great pretender. She pretended she held out hope for a better day. She pretended to have strength and the desire to carry on as one misery-filled year without Isabelle bled into the next. And at this very moment, she pretended he was her Dark Prince. That she was his. And the past had never happened.

Refusing to delve into the error of her actions and thoughts, she cupped his face. "I want you to make the world go away," she said against his mouth, "just as you did before. Take me. *Hurry.*"

Smiling, he stroked his solid shaft against her sex again, drawing a moan from her. "Pretty forest fairy, I'm going to show you how to prolong the pleasure. How to savor it." He kissed along her jaw to that spine-tingling spot just under her ear. "There's no need to hurry."

Prolong? She closed her eyes. She could barely form words, her heart as erratic as her breathing. "There's no time for that . . . I want to do this . . . twice . . . and after that . . . once more. We only have an hour . . ."

His soft laugh tickled her neck. "We have all night. Not to mention the next few days together."

Her heart sank. *No, they didn't.* She turned his face to hers and had his mouth again. Like a moth to the flame, she couldn't resist its enticing heat and wriggled against his hard cock.

"Jules," she said between kisses, "we can proceed slower, as long as you define 'slower' as 'quick and soon.' "

That drew another chuckle. "Patience . . . I know you want to come, and you will . . . in due time."

* * *

Jules could tell she didn't care for the words "in due time" or "patience." Her heels were delightfully digging into the small of his back and her soft derrière was wiggling in his hands, as she tried to rub her clit against his cock. Unable to contain the urge. Famished for the friction.

Jésus-Christ, he loved how fiery she was.

She was determined to hasten matters along. He was determined to thwart her efforts. A sexual contest of wills. How delicious was that?

"Your nipples are hard, begging for attention." He didn't need to see them to know. "They need to be sucked, don't they?" That stilled her.

Panting, her cheeks pink, she shivered and gave him a shaky nod.

He fought back his smile. She loved having her luscious tits fondled. Loved it even more when he had one of those ultrasensitive teats in his mouth.

"Open your bodice and offer them to me."

In an instant, she was yanking at her clothing, opening, shoving, pulling her chemise down under her breasts.

Her pretty pebbled tips made his mouth water. He gave each one a soft suck, enjoying the sharp arching of her body and her little mew.

"Is your pretty cunt wet, Elise?"

"Open your breeches and find out."

A chuckle rumbled from his chest. There were so many things he liked about her. He liked her company. He liked how she'd brought sexual pleasure back into his life. Hell, he'd enjoyed every moment of his time with her. She was adorably bold, beautiful, and bright. Though he knew he'd never see her again after they parted, the notion left him with an uncommon sense of regret.

Holding her bottom with one hand, he slipped his free hand between their bodies and under her skirts. "You're not getting my cock just yet." Before she could protest, he fed two fingers past the slit of her drawers and into her tight wet core.

She sucked in a breath. Her hands squeezed his shoulders. Her sex was soaked, hot, so soft . . . and deliciously clenched around his fingers. His hard cock twitched with anticipation. His heart hammered harder. Holding back a load of come, his sac felt full and heavy.

Curling his buried fingers, he rubbed that sweet spot inside her vaginal wall. She bucked, the sharp novel sensation tearing his name from her throat. Dipping his head, he sucked her nipple into his mouth, lightly biting and licking the tender peak while he delivered measured strokes over the ultrasensitive gland inside her sheath, driving her straight to the edge of orgasm. Her legs squeezed around his waist. Her feminine walls quivered around his busy fingers. And he played with the pressure of his strokes, holding her at the precipice, her climax rushing forward, then receding.

"*Jules* . . ." It was a desperate plea. "I need to . . . I have to . . ." Her body was bathing his hand with more of her juices.

He released her nipple from his mouth. "Come? Not yet. Let it build. Hold it back. The longer you delay it, the more intense the release. Concentrate on the pleasure in the moment. Feel how good that is? It feels incredible, doesn't it?"

She threw her arms around his neck and pressed her cheek to his. Her quick erratic breaths tickled his neck.

He gave her two stronger strokes just to make her moan.

"You like that, don't you?"

She shuddered. He felt her nod.

Jules pulled his hand out. A soft sob escaped her. He walked over to the bed with her delectable form linked around him and sank his knee into the mattress. She let go and dropped onto the counterpane, her breasts giving a sweet little jiggle.

She came up onto her elbows.

Watching her pretty breasts rise and fall with each breath she took was driving him to distraction. He couldn't get enough of them. Of her. She was the only woman who'd ever challenged his self-control during sex. It was going to require a measure of restraint to hold himself in check while slowing down his fiery forest fairy.

Jules removed his doublet, then tossed it onto the upholstered chair. His purse followed. The item inside was something he'd show her later, when she'd be more receptive. Right now, she was watching him hungrily as he opened his breeches. He pulled his shirt loose and removed it.

She was up on her knees immediately and flattened her palms against his bare chest. Placing his hand at the back of her head, he pulled her close until her lips touched his.

Her palms slid downward. His muscles bunched. Jules pulled off the ribbon in her hair and ran his fingers through the silky pale locks, silently willing her onward.

She stopped at his waist.

"Ah, don't lose your nerve now," he urged, his eager cock craning out of his breeches. He took her hand and pressed it to his prick. "Touch me."

With only a moment's hesitation, she curled her slender fingers around the base of his erection, her touch soft, her grip maddeningly light, and yet it sent raw heat licking up his spine. Leaving his cock ecstatic and ravenous for more.

Clamping his hand over hers, he tightened her hold. "Like this." Resting his forehead against hers, he watched as he guided her hand up then back down his thick length, the sensations spine-melting. *Dieu*, he was actually throbbing in her hand. He released his hold. She caressed him all on her own. Emboldened, she found her rhythm soon after her initial awkward strokes.

The gentle friction was scintillating, sparks of pleasure streaking from his prick to the rest of his body. He closed his eyes and tilted his head back, battling with thoughts of tossing her down on the bed and claiming her perfect cunt with one solid thrust.

When he met her gaze again, a smile graced her lips. "You like this."

He returned her smile. "More than breathing."

"I like touching you this way, giving you pleasure."

"Good, because I want you to touch me whenever you like. Now take off your clothes."

He stripped away her clothing and his with practiced haste and in no time had her sitting with him in the middle of the bed, straddling his thighs. He thrust his tongue into her mouth, kissing her hard. Her heated response was immediate. Throwing her arms around him, she returned his kiss with equal fervor. Impatient, she squirmed.

He gripped her derrière and stilled her, her body visibly quaking with need. "Luxuriate in each sensation." He pressed her juicy sex tightly up against him. She gasped.

He groaned.

Cream from her core trickled down his cock to his sac, the sensation driving him wild. Thoughts of keeping her locked in their room, naked, until he got his fill of Elise Marquette ran rampant in his head.

"Up on your knees." His voice was gruff, desire sharpening his tone. Leaning back, he lowered her slowly onto him the moment she complied, watching his cock slip into her slit and disappear past her dark blond curls. She tried pushing down to take him all at once, but he easily arrested her attempt and kept to his slow ascent into her snug moist heat. "Oh no, you don't, *chère*. You're going to feel every inch as I feed you my prick." His blood pumped hot and fast.

Smoothly he glided deeper, her inner muscles drawing him in, until he butted up against the entrance to her womb. His growl melded with her soft cry.

A bead of sweat rolled down his back.

His cock firmly embedded, he fisted her hair and gently bent her backward over his arm, holding her immobile, and feasted on her breast. He had her pressing into him, rewarding him with throaty moans. Pleasure swept though her form in palpable waves, reverberating through him.

And nothing—absolutely nothing—in his life had ever felt more right, or perfect, than this moment. And this woman in his arms.

He released her hair, cradled her head in his palm, and turned to the other breast, lavishing it with the same carnal attention. Frenzied, she began thrusting her hips, desperate for the climax he withheld.

He released her nipple and pressed her back onto the bed, his weight stilling her. "Not yet."

"Now!"

Ever so slowly he withdrew and then tunneled back into her warm silky depth. "Soon." His body rioted for release. Raw desire burned in his blood. And the need to empty his cock was fierce. But he fought against it, basking in the stunning bliss. Each deep plunge and slow and steady drag was sublime.

Frustrated, she clenched her sex around him. The erotic sensation shot through him.

"Elise, don't do—" She did it again, giving him another jolting squeeze that snatched the words from his throat. *Jésus-Christ.* "All right." His heart pounded in his chest.

His control snapped.

He grabbed her hips and plunged his whole length into her. She whimpered her approval. He increased the speed and force of each downstroke until he was driving into her again and again with untamed intensity. "This is what you want, isn't it? You love being fucked hard like this, don't you?"

Her body convulsed. She vaulted into a climax so intense, she screamed out unabashed. The sound resonated in the room. Racing to a powerful release, he clenched his teeth, the walls of her sex contracting around him sending currents of hot pleasure pulsing through him. He rode through those wild uncontrollable clenches, unrelenting, reaming her down to the moment ecstasy slammed into him.

Come came barreling down his cock.

Rearing, he clutched her to him tightly and buried his face in her hair, semen shooting from his prick with unrestrainable force. A low groan surged up his throat as the magnificent rush went on and on, his prick pouring out everything he had until he was spent. Weak.

And awed.

Dieu, she was no one, born into a class that made her common, yet she was extraordinary. In a class all her own.

He heard her soft sigh, then felt the soft caress of her hand against the nape of his neck. This gesture should have become irritating by now, but instead, much to his surprise, he found it endearing.

Suddenly, her body stiffened under him.

He lifted his head and looked down at her.

Her delicate brow was furrowed. "Was I too loud?"

He smiled. "You were perfect."

"Do you think they heard us?"

"They?"

"The . . . ones downstairs," she explained.

He wanted to tease her and tell her that they'd likely heard *her* all the way to England, but thought better of it, given the uneasy look on her lovely face.

Her concern with those downstairs was slightly odd, but then, she didn't have enough experience to have developed a casual attitude toward sexual encounters. She shouldn't waste a moment's thought about what people of no account—whom she'd likely never see again—heard or thought.

"They're busy making our meal. Don't think more of it."

He gave her a quick kiss, rose from the bed, and walked over to the bowl and pitcher. He tossed the hand cloth into the bowl and poured water over it. Washing himself quickly, he rinsed the cloth clean and returned with it to the bed.

Smiling, he dropped down beside her and propped himself on his elbow. Softly, she laughed. Giving her one last light kiss, he then wiped her silky belly with the cloth.

She watched, chewing her bottom lip.

"What is it?" he asked.

"Nothing." It was a lie. He could tell there was something on her mind she was holding back.

Her stomach cleaned, he tossed the cloth in the general direction of the bowl, his focus on her. "Tell me what it is you wish to say," he insisted.

A blush stained her cheeks. "I . . . well . . . like it when you bathe me."

Jules smiled, lifted her chin up, and kissed the sensitive spot just under her ear. He wasn't surprised. A lover's bath was sensual. And so was she. "I have something else I think you'll like," he murmured against her neck. What he had in the velvet pouch for her would no doubt stir her further. He pulled away from the soft form.

Seeing she was about to protest, he placed his finger over her lips. "I want to show you something."

He retrieved the velvet pouch and returned to the bed and stretched out beside her. Dangling the pouch above her by its satin ties, he asked, "Can you guess what this is?"

She glanced at the pouch and then at him. "No."

With a lazy smile, he gave a shrug. "Then I suppose you'll have to open it and see inside." He placed it before her.

Bewildered, she sat up. Tucking her blond hair behind her ear, she picked up the pouch and opened it.

Her eyes widened as she pulled out the item.

"It's for you," he explained, lest there was any confusion.

"*Me?*" The word rushed past her lips in a breathy whisper.

"Yes, I sent Raymond to purchase it. I thought it was the

perfect gift for you." He touched the end of one of her long tresses and curled it around his finger. "A comb for your beautiful hair."

"But—But it's . . . made of *silver.*"

He hadn't purchased a gift for a woman in a long time. It felt good. Especially since the gift was for her.

"A silver comb for a silver-eyed beauty," he said.

The stunned look on her face was priceless. He knew she'd never owned anything so costly.

She placed it back in the pouch and held it out to him. "I cannot accept this."

It was his turn to be stunned. His brows shot up. "Pardon?"

"Please take this back." Her hand trembled.

His gifts had never been refused. Reaching for her, he pulled her back down onto the bed, partially covering her with his body, the pouch still in her hand.

"I want you to have it."

She shook her head. "No. I can't. It's too much." Her eyes filled with tears. "I don't deserve it, really."

He smiled down at her. "I'll not take no for an answer. Now then, tell me you'll accept the gift."

"No."

He dipped his head and brushed his lips just under her ear. She gasped. "Say yes," he murmured against her skin. "Tell me you'll accept it." He trailed his lips down her neck all the way to one pert pink nipple, then closed his mouth over it. She cried out and instinctively arched to him. He suckled her until he had her writhing beneath him and then released the hardened bud. She whimpered in protest. "Do you want more, *ma belle*?"

She was breathless again. "Yes."

"Then say it. Say you'll accept my silver gift."

It amazed him that she was actually hesitating. Someone of her station would normally leap at the opportunity to own such a luxurious item.

He lowered his head so that his mouth hovered over her other nipple. She arched to him, but he pulled back slightly.

He was not one to be denied or turned down. "Well?" he asked. "I can go no further until I have your acceptance."

"Jules . . . *please* . . ."

"Not the correct answer, *chère*." He gave her nipple a teasing lick. She shivered with pleasure. He waited, his cock growing stiffer by the moment. She panted, stubbornly trying to deny him while battling her own mounting arousal.

"Say it," he prompted.

She swallowed hard. "I'll accept your silver . . . gift."

12

Lying beneath him in the aftermath of yet another intense release, Sabine tightened her arms around Jules and returned each of his irresistible kisses. How did he do it? How did he make her so feverish? Wipe away everything with his magical touch?

His skillful mouth moved to her shoulder.

She closed her eyes, feeling wonderful. Years ago, when she still used to write, and would devote countless entries in her journal to speculating about how divine a single kiss from him would be, in her wildest dreams, she'd never envisioned anything like this. Being with him was far better than she'd ever envisioned.

She stretched an arm, her hand hitting something on the bed. Glancing at the item, she saw it was the velvet pouch.

His gift.

A stab of conscience speared her. Proficient at deferring pain and distress, she wrestled it down. Determined to stave off reality as long as she could, she fought to hold on to the final few moments before all this would end.

Who knew when she'd feel like this again? If she'd ever feel like this again?

There was a sharp knock at the door. She started, her head colliding with his nose.

He let out a grunt. *"Merde,"* he said, holding his nose.

"I'm sorry!" She tossed a quick glance at the door, her heart thudding wildly. "Are you all right?" Her family had arrived. The spell was shattered. Knowing them, they were likely to burst in. She prayed Jules had locked the door.

A second knock rapped against the door. Frantic, she turned to leap from the bed, but he caught her arm, keeping her from her flight.

"What is it?" he barked at those in the hall.

"Sir?" Sabine heard Louise say, her voice slightly muffled by the wooden barrier. "Your meal is ready."

"Not now. Return later."

"It's been prepared to perfection, for you and your lady." That was Agnes's distinct voice. "If left, it will get cold."

Jules softly swore. "Ten minutes. Return not a moment before," he ordered.

Sabine tensed, fully expecting Agnes to argue, as was her nature. To her relief and surprise, she heard Agnes respond, "As you wish."

Returning his attention to her, he said, "Relax, Elise. They won't set a foot in this room until I bid them enter."

Clearly, he knew little of her family's errant ways.

"Now then, where were we? Ah, yes. I believe I was about to kiss you." A smile teased the corners of his mouth. "We've enough time to make you come again."

Despite his delicious words, all she could think about was that her family would be returning in ten minutes. He leaned in. She rolled and jumped from the bed. He almost kissed the mattress.

"*Merde*. What are you doing?"

She raced about the room, trying to locate her clothing. "They'll be back soon."

"So?"

"So, we must dress." She scooped up her chemise, then her skirt. Her thoughts were frenzied. Her chest tight. There would be no more stalling. Reality had just knocked at the door. Spinning around, she sought her bodice and noticed that he was still on the bed on his side.

Arm bent, his cheek resting against his palm, he was grinning. With a wave of his hand, he said, "Continue. I'm enjoying the entertainment."

"Entertainment?"

"Mmm, yes. It's quite enthralling. The sweet jiggle of your pretty breasts, and of course, there's that perfectly gorgeous derrière of yours. It's inspiring a variety of lustful thoughts."

His words unbalanced her and warmed her body. "They'll return shortly," she forced herself to say. Picking up his breeches, she tossed them at him. "You should dress."

He caught the article but didn't look as though he was inclined to comply with her request. "Come here. I want a kiss."

Dear God, he had that look in his eyes. The one that told her he wouldn't proceed until she relented.

She wanted nothing more than to climb onto the bed and back into his arms, to hell with the world beyond their door, but she couldn't do that. Her problems wouldn't simply vanish on their own. To solve them required a serious amount of coin. And drastic action. The kind she was about to take.

She only prayed she had the strength to go through with it.

He was far too distracting at the best of times. In all his natural splendor, he was tempting beyond what she could resist. She simply had to have him clothed just so she could regain some semblance of her sanity.

"I'm waiting." He smiled.

With little choice, she walked over to the bed and leaned down to give him a kiss, pushing from her mind the painful thought that this was likely to be their last.

He grabbed her arm and yanked her down. She tumbled onto the bed with a surprised cry, falling across his lap.

Releasing the clothing she'd been clutching in her hands, she twisted around. "Jules, what are you doing? You said you wanted a kiss."

He sat up. "I do. I just never said where." He stroked a warm hand over her derrière, then leaned over her. He lightly bit her bottom. She yelped, the sensation both tickling and stirring. Then he pressed his lips to the same spot and kissed it.

"I think," he said, caressing where he'd just kissed, "that after our meal, I'll take you from behind, where I can admire this charming part of your anatomy—while you're tied and bound for my pleasure."

His words stopped her breathing for a moment, and sent her up in flames. Her sex responded with a hungry clench. What shocked and frightened her most was just how appealing she found the notion.

"But that's later," he added. "As for now, we have to dress." He gave her bottom a playful swat, moved her off his lap, and rose from the bed. With a wink, he put on his breeches.

It took her a moment to collect her wits. She sat up and slipped on her chemise. Rising from the bed, refusing to look at him, knowing it would only make it more difficult if she did, she hastily finished dressing. Just as she was tying the lacing on her bodice, there was a knock at the door.

Her heart lurched. Terror-struck, she looked at Jules. He wore his shirt untucked and stepped toward the door.

She turned away. Desperate to distract herself, fearing she'd do something to sabotage their well-laid plans, she began straightening and smoothing the counterpane on the bed.

"Elise, what are you doing?"

She froze mid-stroke and looked up at him. His hand on the door latch, looking perplexed, he awaited her answer.

Mentally she groaned. She was behaving bizarrely.

Forcing a smile, she straightened and smoothed her fidgety hands down her skirt. Sitting down on the edge of the bed, she folded them on her lap and answered, "Nothing. Aren't . . . you going to let them in?"

With a smile he shook his head—no doubt at her foolish antics—and unlocked the door.

"Sir," Louise and Agnes said with respectful nods, and entered balancing heavy trays of steaming food.

Vincent carried a tray of decanters, goblets, and dinnerware. "Sir, we have a fine meal for you and the lady," he said and placed his tray down on the side table near the window.

"We have pheasant and a wonderful stew I'm certain you'll enjoy," Louise added. "And, of course, you'll not find any mutton among the dishes." She smiled.

He gave a nod. "Be quick about your duty," Jules said, still near the door. He didn't care to have her family there any more than she did.

"Of course." Louise handed her tray to Vincent. "We'll allow you to enjoy your food momentarily."

Sabine struggled to keep her breathing normal, dreading the impending events. None of her family glanced her way. And she was grateful. Their presence unnerved her.

While Vincent lit the sconces to add to the dying light of day, Agnes and Louise worked diligently at covering the dining table with linen and setting down the ceramic service.

A clap of thunder startled Sabine. Rain began to strike the windowpane. Like tears, it ran down the glass.

Looking down at the counterpane, she blinked back her own tears and chastised herself for her emotional state. She was far better than this at keeping herself in check.

Needing something to keep herself busy, she took up the task of braiding her hair and securing it with her ribbon she'd spotted on the bed. Another clap of thunder boomed. She flinched.

Jules approached and stopped before her. She forced her gaze up his body to his face.

He slipped his fingers beneath her chin. "You don't like storms?" Clearly he'd been observing her and noted her distress.

"No." She uttered what felt like her thousandth lie.

He helped her to her feet, then whispered in her ear, "After our meal, I'll make you forget about whatever rages outside, Elise."

If only he could quell what was raging inside her right now. It would be as wonderful as hearing, just once, her real name from his lips.

"There we are," Louise announced. The table was set.

And so, too, was the stage for this foul undertaking.

Taking her elbow, he led her to the table; she forced each foot forward.

Only when Sabine was seated directly across from Jules did she glance at Louise, who returned her gaze ever so briefly before turning her attention to Jules. "Sir, I trust you'll find the food to your satisfaction. We've taken the liberty of bringing our finest burgundy and brandy for your pleasure. May we pour the wine?"

"You may," Jules responded.

Watching the burgundy filling his goblet, sensing it was laced, Sabine felt nauseous.

Agnes placed bowls of poached egg soup before them.

Turning to Sabine, Louise said, "Brandy and burgundy don't usually appeal to women. Do you wish some?"

By the look in her eyes and the statement, Sabine easily read that both wine and brandy had been tainted.

"No," she managed to force out, "thank you."

Vincent poured water into a goblet and set it before her.

"This burgundy has an odd taste to it," Jules said.

His statement grabbed everyone's attention. Seeing him holding the goblet up, frowning, knowing he'd just taken a sip, made her stomach drop.

"Why, it's our finest," Louise advised.

Setting the goblet on the table, Jules pushed it toward Louise. "I don't care for it. Take it away."

Sabine's heart missed a beat, uncertain whether she felt defeated or elated.

"As you wish." Louise picked up the goblet and the decanter of tainted wine. "Claire, rush downstairs and get another burgundy," she said to Agnes, handing her the items.

Without hesitation, Agnes hurried to do her bidding.

Vincent poured a goblet of the brandy and set it before Jules. "What about the brandy, sir? Would you care to try it?"

Sabine forced her gaze down to her soup, unable to watch Jules drink it. From the corner of her eye, she could see that Louise and Vincent were engrossed, eagerly anticipating Jules's sampling of the corrupted amber liquid. Sabine loathed every moment of this.

"It's good. The brandy may stay."

Sabine closed her eyes briefly before she shored up her nerve and returned her gaze to him.

He met her regard with those dark seductive eyes of his and a lopsided smile. He picked up his spoon. Sabine mimicked the gesture, schooling her expression, forcing a look of gladness she didn't feel.

He tasted his soup. Unable to bring herself to eat, she simply stirred hers. Given the state of her stomach, she feared she'd lose its contents if she dared try.

"Tell me about your cousin, Elise."

His voice yanked her out of her thoughts. "Cousin?"

"In Maillard. What sort of man is he?"

"Oh, him." She glanced at Vincent and Louise. Their expressions gave away nothing of the horrible scheme they were involved in. This had seemed like such a good idea once. But now, in the thick of it, it felt unscrupulous. Didn't any of this bother them? Even a little?

"He is a good man. I think I will enjoy living with him." What a consummate liar she'd become. She hated it. She hated it that

Louise and Vincent stood watching this wicked deception with morbid fascination. She hated it that she didn't despise Jules like before. Most of all, she hated it that she felt so corrupt and conflicted.

Jules reached for the brandy.

"Wait!" she exclaimed.

He lifted a brow, his hand around the goblet.

"Jules, do they"—she nodded at the familial spectators—"have to be here?"

"Why, we're here to serve your needs," Louise stated, obviously objecting to any sort of dismissal.

Before Jules could answer, Agnes rushed in.

"A different burgundy, sir." She gave him a ludicrous grin while holding a new decanter and goblet. Quickly, she poured the wine for him and set the items down on the table.

"Jules, I can serve us . . ." Sabine suggested, anxious to see her family leave the room.

"If they make you uncomfortable . . ." Jules turned to the threesome and said, "you may leave."

"But—" Louise began and was instantly silenced when Jules raised his hand.

"Without another word," he added with finality.

Sabine refused to look at her family, but sensed their piercing stares nonetheless. Having no choice, they left, closing the door behind them.

Sabine's small measure of relief was short-lived. Jules reached for the new burgundy that was undoubtedly as tainted as the first had been.

"Jules!" She stood up and walked around the table.

Slipping onto his lap, she wrapped her arms about him and buried her face in his neck. She drew in his scent and the warmth of his strong body, wanting, needing one final moment with him.

Think about what the Moutiers have done . . . But a voice inside her countered, *Think of the joy he's given you over the last day. More bliss than you've known in your entire existence.*

She gazed into his eyes.

"What is it, Elise?"

She wanted to blurt out the truth, but knew she couldn't. "I wish . . ." Her words caught against the lump in her throat.

"What?"

That I didn't have to do this. "That after we part, you'll think of me fondly." She was making a fool of herself. Jules de Moutier was accustomed to women who were more sophisticated about bed sport. What she'd just uttered amounted to no better than emotional gushing.

A smile formed on his lips. "I will think of you fondly." After what she was about to do to him, nothing could be further from the truth.

Despite her better judgment, she kissed him, savored his taste, the texture of his mouth, knowing that later she'd have to do everything in her power to forget everything about him.

He broke the kiss, and brushed his lips against hers. "*Chère*, as much as I'm enjoying having your bottom resting where it is, if it continues to remain there much longer, neither of us will be eating a warm meal." He rose with her in his arms, walked over to her chair, and set her down on it. Smiling into her face, he said, "I need sustenance. Sit and behave . . . *for now.*" The last two words were uttered with such heart-fluttering sensuality. She nodded and fisted her hands on her lap to keep from reaching for him and hauling him back.

Sitting across from her, looking better than any male ought to, he tasted his soup again.

"You know, Elise, once you've reached your cousin and have settled there, you must do right by your former lord. You owe him money."

Having just taken a drink of the water from her goblet, Sabine almost choked. *"Pardon?"*

"You need to attend to your debt."

She stiffened. "I did attend to my debt. I *left.*"

"That doesn't negate your obligation to him. You must pay it off. You lived on his land. He has every right to expect payment for it." He sampled the burgundy in his goblet. "At least this burgundy is better than the last."

She reeled from his statement.

"I've paid all that I can and will ever pay him. Thanks to his excessive taxes, he's stripped me of everything I hold dear."

"You lived under his protection, on his domain." He drained his goblet. "You received something in return for the taxes you paid. You were given the opportunity to flourish. If you didn't, it isn't his fault. He ought not to be denied what he's justly owed because of poor management of funds, or in many cases with the lower class, plain laziness." He sliced a piece of ham from the platter before them and placed it on her plate.

His words were like a fist to her belly.

Gone was Jules her lover. In his place was an Aristo, lacking in empathy for all those he considered a lesser breed of human.

"Laziness?" She could barely contain her ire. "*Opportunity to flourish?* How, pray tell, does one 'flourish' when the lower class must farm their lord's land before they're permitted to farm their own? When they aren't permitted to sell any produce until their lord's is sold? The lower class is made to use his mill and ovens and pay him for the 'privilege.' They cannot touch the forests or lakes on his lands, hunt or fish there, no matter how starved they are. And taxes are levied against them at his whim."

"It's his right," he said blandly. "He deserves what he's owed."

Her mouth fell agape, utterly incredulous. Quickly, she clamped it shut.

She was a fool! How many times did she have to be disillusioned by him before she finally accepted that there was no Dark Prince? Born of her imagination, he didn't really exist.

She'd seen signs of his arrogant noble airs again and again, yet still deluded herself into believing he was somehow different from his peers. Jules's disgrace hadn't humbled him at all. Not even a little.

"Elise, everyone bemoans the taxes," he said pouring more wine in his goblet and taking another drink. "But they are necessary and just." Setting his goblet down, he looked about the room, then rubbed his eyes with his thumb and finger.

Furious, she countered, "Just? If they're so *just*, then why doesn't the upper class pay any? They don't even pay taxes to the Crown. Those are paid by the lower class, as well!"

He shook his head. At first she thought he was protesting her statement, but then he dropped his head into his hands. Her tirade died in her throat. When at last he looked up, his face was pale, and his breathing quick. He blinked hard, as if he was trying to clear his vision. Glancing at her untouched meal, he demanded, "Why aren't you eating?"

Before she could think of an answer, he rose, his chair scraping against the wooden floor. He gripped the edge of the table and hung his head. "What's happening?"

With her heart pounding in her chest, she rose, too.

He met her gaze, his eyes narrowed, his expression fierce. "Tell me you haven't done anything. Tell me you haven't tainted the food." He was beginning to sway. "Tell me!" he bellowed.

She jumped.

"Come here," he ordered.

She couldn't speak and there was no way she was going to approach him. She took a step back.

"Damn you, I said come here!" He stepped away from the table. The sudden movement caused him to stumble back and knock over the chair. His large body collapsed, striking the chair, and landed on the floor with a hard thud.

13

Except for the uncontrollable quaking of her body, Sabine didn't move. Pieces of the broken chair around him, beneath him, Jules lay on his side, wisps of his dark hair on his cheek.

Her heart in her throat, she called out his name.

No response.

Cautiously, she approached him.

Lowering herself onto her knees, an arm's length away, she reached out a shaky hand and pushed at his shoulder. He rolled onto his back. His head lolled to the side, his hair falling away from his face. His eyes were closed and his chest rose and fell with every breath he took in his artificial slumber.

Her throat tightened. Such a beautiful face. Sadly, it belonged to a man who was so heedless of the suffering he and his class had caused.

Footsteps approached. She shot to her feet and stepped back. The door burst open. In rushed Vincent, Louise, Agnes, and Robert. Clearly, they'd heard the commotion.

They gathered near her and peered down at Jules.

"D-Did it truly work?" Robert asked, incredulous.

"It did," Sabine said.

A burst of joviality erupted from the foursome, startling her.

"She did it! We're rich!" Vincent embraced his sister, then Agnes.

Agnes giggled like a little girl. "We can buy whatever we want! We'll want for nothing ever again!"

Sabine didn't share in their gaiety. Her eyes were drawn back to Jules. Elise was gone. Sabine was back. And so was her empty reality. Yet she felt no sadness. No anger. Or even satisfaction over her deed. Only a dull familiar ache.

Standing behind her, Robert flung his arms about her waist, picked her up, and swung her around. "We are richer than the King, Sabine! Your plan worked!"

Sabine tried to smile. "Put me down, Robert."

The moment her feet touched the floor, Robert wrapped his arms around her shoulders, hugging her from behind, and pressed his cheek against hers. "We made them pay, Sabine. All of them. The men in the stables are down, as well. Gerard is there guarding the silver. There is so much silver!"

Agnes stepped forward and hugged her. "I had all the faith in the world in you." She gazed at Sabine and lovingly caressed her cheek. "You brought him down, just as the Moutier deserved."

Robert and Agnes stepped back when Vincent approached. For the first time in her life, she saw tears in Vincent's eyes. Giving her a fatherly embrace, he said softly near her ear, "What you have sacrificed for us, *tesora* . . ." using his native Italian.

She knew he referred to her innocence and should have been embarrassed by the comment, but the numbness had spread through her body. Being in a deadened state for so long, she hadn't known a day without it. Except during her time with Jules. Then and only then had it receded.

Now it was back, and like a shield, it protected her from heartache. And—she looked over at Jules—she was grateful.

Vincent placed an arm around Sabine's shoulders and led her toward the door. "Come, let us get you out of here. Everything will be fine. Wonderful, in fact." He kissed her temple. The others followed behind. "Agnes is right. The Aristo does not deserve regard or concern. If one of us were laid out on the floor, the only emotion he would feel would be annoyance because we were blocking his path." Sabine said nothing. Had nothing to say.

In the hallway Vincent joyfully shouted, "We can leave and return to Venice!"

That got rousing applause and hoots from the group behind her. Sabine stopped abruptly. "What do you mean, 'leave'?"

"We can start afresh," Louise spoke up. "Vincent and I can return to the Venetian stage. It's a beautiful city to live in. We certainly have enough to live well there. We can open our own theater." Born Louisa Carano, an Italian beauty, she'd been a star of the Venetian stage before becoming Sabine's father's premier actress and mistress. To her adopted nation, she and her brother were known as Louise and Vincent Caran. And she was still as attractive as ever.

"We cannot simply leave. Not until I know where Isabelle is," Sabine protested.

The pitying looks on her family's faces weren't a surprise. She didn't care what they thought. They'd no idea what it was like to live with half of yourself missing.

"Before we can do anything," she continued, "we must convert some of the silver into coins of the realm. Spanish coins are too distinct. It will make it easy for him to find us if we move from town to town using them."

"Sabine makes a good point," said Vincent. "I know someone in Paris. For a share, he'd quietly melt the silver. He can make a mold so the coins will resemble those of the realm."

"Excellent. Where is Joseph, the inn's owner?" Sabine asked.

"He and Anne are with his sister in the next town," Agnes advised. "It took some convincing before they agreed to our plan."

"Pay them generously for their sacrifice," Sabine told Vincent. "They won't be able to return again."

He nodded. "Especially when the Aristo and his men awaken."

"Precisely. We won't take any chances. Pay off anyone who needs to be silenced." The words tumbled from Sabine's mouth easily, with a detached authority she'd become skilled at. "We'll split up into two groups. Vincent, take a cart, two chests of silver, and go to the city with Gerard and Robert to convert the coins. While you're there, purchase fine fabrics—everything you can so we may dress the part. And look wealthy. We don't want to stir anyone's curiosity when spending silver coin. Louise, Agnes, and I will take our cart and the third chest and return home. We'll be safe there for the time being." She knew they'd have to leave the area. But that was different than abandoning Isabelle by leaving the realm altogether. "We'll divide their horses amongst us. Though they don't know our names, we don't want to leave them the means to follow us."

* * *

Jules groaned.

His body felt as heavy as his eyelids. Eyes shut, he didn't want to move.

But there was a stabbing sensation in his back, steadily growing more and more intense. He remained still, lethargic, until he couldn't stand it any longer.

Slowly, he forced his eyes open.

At first, he saw nothing but a blur of shadow and light.

It took several hard blinks before there was clarity. He realized he was alone in a room with bright sunlight streaming through the window. Confusion swamped him. Muddled fragmented thoughts seeped through the fog in his mind.

Elise on the bed . . . Kissing her . . . Taking her . . . Dining with her . . .

The tainted meal!

He sat bolt upright. A pain knifed him in the ribs. He fell back onto one elbow, clutching his side with a growl.

Damn the little witch to hell. The memory of her guilt-ridden face before he fell into darkness was forever seared into his brain.

She'd drugged him.

He could make no sense of it. He knew she was in dire straits, but the silver comb he'd given her was worth a tidy sum.

Holding his side, he forced himself onto his knees and then his feet, ignoring the searing pain. Something on the bed caught his eye.

The velvet pouch.

It rocked him. If robbery was her motive, why didn't she take the costly comb? Was he somehow mistaken? Or—his blood chilled—was she after a bigger prize?

MERDE!

He snatched the velvet pouch up and tore from the room, clutching his side. He raced down the stairs, sweat gathering on his brow. Fear and dread pushed him past the agony in his ribs. He sprinted through the common room, noting the eerie absence of life within, and flung open the front door.

Sunlight momentarily blinded him. He ran to the stables and stopped dead at the sight that greeted him inside. There'd been times in his life he was sure he'd fallen into hell. His first sea battle. His father's betrayal. But as he stared at his men sprawled on the hay, the vacant spot where the horses and cart—with the silver chests, with his future—once stood, he knew he'd walked into Hades.

And he'd let his fucking cock lead the way.

He drove his fist into the nearby wall. "NO!" And again and again, "NO! NO! *N-O-O-O-O-O!*" welcoming the brutal pain in his side with each punishing blow.

He didn't stop until his knuckles were raw, his lungs labored, and his side felt as though it was splitting in two.

Clutching his side, he marched to a barrel, scooped up water with the nearby bucket, and doused his men.

"Wake up!" he bellowed, dropping the bucket.

They began to cough, and were slow to move. Raymond was the first to finally sit up, looking sluggish and befuddled.

"Get up," Jules hissed out. "It was a trap. The silver is gone."

The word "gone" had a sobering effect on the men. They were on their feet in an instant, the empty stable confirming his words.

While expletives shot from the men's mouths, Raymond simply looked stunned. "How could this have happened?"

Jules clenched his teeth, the torture in his ribs and his volatile temper immense. He could hardly keep it in check when he said, "*Elise*. She fed us a tainted meal."

"But how? Wasn't she was with you the entire time?"

"Oh, indeed, she was with me," Jules said, contempt clawing at his vitals. "This was the work of a conspiracy—Gilbert, Bernadette, and Claire. The two young men from the forest are likely involved, as well."

"But, Commander, the item you had me purchase, did you not . . . give it to her?"

"Yes."

"Well then, why, with such a costly gift in her possession, would she feel the need to taint our food to steal from us?"

"Raymond, what you fail to understand is that she was after a much larger treasure all along. She knew about the silver from the beginning."

"But how?" one of the men, Fabrice, asked.

"Obviously, one of you had to have been careless," Jules growled. This entire episode had been nothing short of a comedy of errors and proved to him that his first instincts about her and her suspicious behavior had been justified. Bloody hell, why hadn't he heeded them!

"What are we to do now, Commander?" Daniel asked. "She's taken all the silver, including our share."

Jules grabbed a fistful of Daniel's shirt and yanked him close, butting noses. "I'm quite aware of what she's taken." The bulk of which was his. "Everyone will get their share of the silver once it's found." In a deadly tone he added, "And believe me, it *will* be found." Jules released the younger man abruptly, and flinched sharply.

"Commander, are you injured?" Raymond asked.

With an impatient hand, Jules waved off his concern. "It's nothing."

"The commander's correct." Marc, who'd been silent until now, spoke up. "The temptation to spend their newfound fortune will be too great. It will be easy to follow the trail of Spanish silver. Further, with the weighty cart—the chests, the supplies, and all those people—they cannot travel quickly. Even with the head start they have, we can catch up to them."

"We don't know which direction they're traveling in, and we don't have any horses," Fabrice said.

Clever though she was, she'd made one tiny misstep in her little plan.

Jules dangled the velvet pouch. "This will get us the horses and supplies we need." He tossed it to Daniel. "Attend to it. Fabrice and Marc, search the inn. I don't expect you to find anyone, but look for any clues that will aid in finding those we seek. Someone in this town knows who our conspirators are—or at least where we can find the real owner of the inn," Jules said. "He's clearly a part of this deception. Question the townspeople."

Jules watched as the men headed out of the stables, every fiber in his body seething over Elise's cunning duplicity. And his staggering stupidity.

Raymond walked on past. He clasped his hand on Raymond's shoulder, arresting his steps. "By the way, Raymond."

"Yes, my lord?"

"The next time you get the urge to convince me to fuck a woman for my own good, stop yourself."

"Yes, my lord."

Jules removed his hand from Raymond's shoulder. His servant

strode away but stopped just before the entrance. "My lord, I am truly sorry . . ." he said, looking sincerely contrite, then left.

Not nearly as sorry as Elise is going to be.

With the men out of sight, Jules approached a wooden bench, and clenching his teeth, he eased himself down onto it.

Lifting his shirt, he twisted to examine himself. A shot of agony tore up his side. He barely caught the groan that burned up his throat.

There, smeared across his skin as far back as he could see, was a massive bruise. A fresh wave of rage crested over him. Having seen enough injuries in his years of sea battle, he had a strong suspicion about what was wrong with his ribs.

It wasn't going to stop him from recovering his treasure.

Or getting his hands on Elise—or whatever her fucking name was—who'd played him so falsely.

She was going pay dearly for what she'd done.

* * *

Sabine walked through the fallow field toward her gray stone two-story home. Once an impressive structure, over the years it had fallen into disrepair, its loose shutters, its crumbling façade, lending to its dilapidated appearance. Its pretty gardens replaced by farmland for survival. Glancing at the angry sky, she sensed a terrific storm approaching.

She'd sent Olivier, her father's former music composer, to tend to the horses. It had become her daily routine to check on the spot where they'd buried the treasure. It remained safe and untouched. Raids by bands of criminals desperate and hungry made it too risky to keep that amount of wealth within their home.

Almost two weeks had passed since they'd returned to their dismal farm. However, this time the backbreaking work in the fields didn't bother Sabine as much as before. Her days here were numbered. Her life was going to change. She was going to spare no expense to locate her sister. And she *was* going to find her. Alive. And be made whole again.

She couldn't live without her.

Hadn't lived without her.

She was going to look into her cherished face once more. She was going to get the chance to tell her she loved her again. How much she'd missed her. Hear her laugh. Hug her tightly.

As soon as Vincent and her cousins returned, their new life would begin. And she'd go after the answers she needed to locate her sister—with a vengeance.

That cold detached note from the Marquis de Blainville, Jules's father, informing them of Isabelle's demise hadn't rung true in her heart. Isabelle was somewhere.

Not in that pauper's grave he'd said he'd placed her in.

Sabine squinted and shielded her eyes as the wind whipped up dirt from the unseeded plot. In no way did the land resemble the country estate it once was. Jules's father—the vulture—had been all too happy to swoop in and purchase it from her foolish father, for the Laurent property sat in the middle of the Moutiers' ancestral lands.

As tenants of the Moutiers, they quickly became overburdened with taxes owed to the Marquis when they were already struggling to pay the Crown taxes owed. Since the Moutiers had fallen from grace, the taxes had been rolled into one staggering sum.

Owed to the Crown.

Even if they had sold everything they owned, it would have put only a small dent in the debt.

But the silver changed everything. Their financial problems were at last over.

The wind picked up.

She heard the sounds of nickering horses. Many of them. Spinning around, she didn't see any. The stable was a distance away. The sounds couldn't be coming from there. She quickened her pace. Two hundred feet away from the house, she noticed hoof marks on the packed dirt. Several of them.

Vincent? It couldn't be. He couldn't have reached Paris and returned so quickly. Had something happened?

Her heart rapped wildly. She bolted for the house.

Reaching the door, she grabbed the latch, swung the door open, and rushed inside.

The sight that greeted her hit her like a fist in the belly.

Raymond and several well-muscled, well-armed men stood in the room, men she instantly recognized from Jules's camp. Agnes and Olivier sat at the table, abject terror etched across their faces. Louise's daughters stood near their mother in the corner, softly weeping with fright.

The door slammed shut behind her. Sabine jumped and spun around. Her knees all but buckled the moment she saw Jules leaning against the wall, his hand still flat against the door he'd just forcibly closed.

With the coldest, most menacing glint in his dark eyes, he said, "Hello. Remember me?"

14

Sabine stood perfectly still, her mind racing as fast as her heart.

Bearing the full weight of his regard, she watched him push himself from against the wall and thought she saw him wince. But her thoughts scattered as he approached. Like a predator. She, his prey. Caught in a trap. With her family.

She'd done everything in her power to save them.

And now they were hemmed in.

He stopped inches from her, his tall powerful form towering over her. She refused to step back. He was purposely using his physical advantage to unsettle her.

It was working.

Yet she wasn't about to let him know just how much.

Normally clean-shaven, his jaw was shadowed with at least a few days' growth, and his hair was mussed, likely from hours of hard riding. It made him look darkly dangerous. And, the devil take him, even better than in her recent dreams.

It was only there she couldn't shut him out. Where he would torment her with his touch, unchecked. Each morning she woke up cursing him, angry that he'd invaded the sanctity of her sleep, for he wasn't worth her time—day or night.

She returned his gaze unflinching, the silence between weighted with tension. His palpable fury lay just beneath the surface, waiting to be unleashed at any moment.

He raised his hand. Her heart lurched. She braced herself.

Show no fear.

Her family needed her to get them out of this predicament.

Don't faint!

To her surprise, he caressed his knuckles down the side of her cheek. His touch, though gentle, was not as it had been before—a lover's touch.

He'd never touched her while so enraged.

"Such creamy skin and brilliant eyes . . . She is beautiful, isn't she?" He spoke to his men without taking his gaze off her face, his every word rimmed with barely restrained anger.

Male murmurs swept around the room in concurrence.

He brushed his thumb across her bottom lip. "And she has a lovely mouth, wouldn't you say, Raymond?"

"She's definitely comely, Commander."

"Indeed." Jules nodded. "What a shame this exquisite mouth spouts nothing but lies. It's difficult to believe that a woman with such an angelic face is capable of such treachery. I bet you thought you'd never see me again."

Disdain and dread clashed inside her. "That was the plan," she managed to force out.

"Ah, yes. *The plan.* My compliments on your plan, and your acting. Both superb." His fingers slipped below her chin; he held both it and her full attention. "But one would expect a convincing performance from the daughter of a playwright, and his troupe of actors. Isn't that so, *Sabine Laurent*? Imagine my surprise when I learned Paul Laurent, a man whose theater I used to frequent, had twin daughters. One with dark hair and one with pale tresses.

Where are the others, *Sabine*? The actor Vincent Caran and the two other young men you had with you at my camp."

Full of contempt, and in defiance, she held her tongue.

His eyes narrowed. "Let me assure you, any sort of rebelliousness would be *most* unwise . . ."

His ominous words tightened her stomach. "How did you find us?" she asked.

"Your witch has quite a reputation." Jules threw Agnes a glare. "We found someone who remembered seeing her enter the inn and knew where to locate the inn's owners."

"I thought you said no one knew you in Delatour?" Louise snapped at the older woman.

"I've no idea what he's talking about." Agnes was quick to defend herself. "I told you, I spoke to no one other than Joseph and Anne in that town. Ever. If my popularity as an apothecary has grown, I can hardly help that. I am talented."

"You are a foolish—" At Jules's sharp look, Louise's words died on her tongue.

Josette buried her face in her mother's shoulder and continued to sob softly.

He returned his attention to Sabine, her chin still captive in his strong hand. Her heart still hammering so hard, she feared he could hear it.

"Does this appeal to you?" she demanded. "Do you derive some twisted pleasure out of intimidating women, a child, and an old man?"

"Well, *ma petite*, I wouldn't say I'm exactly *old* . . ." Olivier, her father's former composer, gently protested.

"Hush, you old fool." Agnes slapped his shoulder.

"Who are you calling old? You are older than I am!" Olivier countered.

"Silence!" Jules bellowed, then turning to Sabine, he said, "You knew about the silver from the start, didn't you?"

Despising him with all her being, hating the way he spoke to her family, she smugly answered, "Yes." Though the devil couldn't be wounded, for all the pain she had inside, she wanted to hurt him. She wanted him to know she'd used him, then discarded him. That he'd been treated with a level of callousness he'd shown others.

"And how exactly did you learn of it?" he demanded.

"I heard two of your men discussing your capture in Italian at the marketplace in Nadeau-Morel. I suppose they thought the peasants around them were too ignorant to know foreign languages. They thought wrong."

The muscle in his cheek twitched. "So you knew who I was all along."

She jerked her chin out of his grasp. "I know exactly who you are," she sneered. "Former Comte de Charbonneau. Former officer of the King's Navy. Self-indulgent firstborn son of Charles de Moutier, Marquis de Blainville. *Jules de Moutier.* A debauchee. Born into privilege and power, and like your father, abuser of both."

He hauled her up against him by her arms. She gasped. Her family gave a collective cry.

"I care nothing of what you have to say about me. But don't you *ever* speak of my father. I'll not hear his name from your lying lips. You aren't worthy to utter it. He was one of your father's patrons. And it was my family who purchased this meager parcel when your wastrel father squandered your family's fortune. You little ingrate, you've stolen from the hand that's fed you!"

"No. From the hand that's bled me. You drained us dry and reduced us to this state. I'm not sorry I stole from you. I lost my sister because of your corrupt family!"

By the fury in his eyes, she thought she'd gone too far. And she didn't care. She wouldn't take back a word. In fact, there was more she wanted to hurl at him.

"So you hate me," he said in a low snarl. "You've hated me

from the very beginning. Well, here is your chance. Don't miss the opportunity, *chère*. Look me in the eye and say it."

He taunted her. He thought she didn't possess the courage, for he was a man accustomed to being in authority. To being respected or feared. She'd show him she more than had it in her to say what others wouldn't dare. Straight to his face.

"I. Hate. You."

He lifted a brow. Dipping his head, he said near her ear. "Tell me, *Sabine*, how much did you hate me when you were begging me to fuck you? Or when you were screaming out orgasm after orgasm? How much did you hate me then?" He released her abruptly.

Torrid memories flooded her mind and heated her cheeks.

No matter how rattled he made her, she wasn't about to give him the upper hand.

Drawing on her acting experience, she took a deep breath and managed to reply coolly, "I never said your skills in the carnal arts were lacking. Due to your licentious lifestyle, you've had plenty of practice in the boudoir." She shrugged. "I enjoyed your expertise. However, it doesn't change the way I feel about you. Or did you think I'd fall madly in love with you over a few physical encounters? That's what you're accustomed to, isn't it? A steady stream of female adoration? Does it wound your overinflated male pride to know you don't have mine?"

"Don't flatter yourself. I've already told you, I care *nothing* about your feelings toward me. Why would I waste a moment's thought over a woman as base as you? Someone who is completely ruthless, willing to stoop to whatever it takes to accomplish her nefarious goals—even giving up her innocence. You are cold and calculating."

She gave a mirthless laugh. "Really. That's most amusing coming from you. A man without conscience. Someone completely unaffected by anyone outside the upper class."

He grasped her arm in an iron grip and jerked her close. "Well then, since I am, as you say, 'a man without conscience,' you and your band of no-accounts have cause for worry. I came here for my silver. I will get it back. *Every coin.* Whatever it takes."

He released her with a slight shove. She stumbled back.

"Marc," Jules said.

"Yes, Commander."

"You, Daniel, and Raymond search this floor. Bruno, watch them." Jules indicated Sabine and her frightened family with a motion of his chin. "Serge and Fabrice, search the upstairs. The silver is here somewhere. Find it. Leave nothing unturned. Take this hovel down stone by stone if you need to."

"No! You can't take the silver!" Pauline cried. "*Maman*, make him stop. We need the coin! You said we'd get pretty gowns. You said things were going to be better. You said!"

Bruno unsheathed his sword, the light from the fire blazing in the hearth reflecting on the blade with a deadly gleam.

"Hush up, Pauline!" Louise's sharp words silenced her hysterical daughter.

Without a backward glance, Jules walked out and slammed the door shut.

The men immediately began their search, pulling items down from shelves and discarding them onto the floor, breaking pottery and the few chipped ceramic plates they had left.

Agnes cried, burying her face in Olivier's shoulder. He placed an arm around her.

Watching the destruction of their modest possessions made Sabine feel sick. Yet with each object they shattered, her resolve and hatred intensified.

She'd outwitted him once. She'd somehow do it again. After all they'd been through, she'd *never* relinquish the silver.

* * *

Jules leaned back against the wall of the house and placed a hand on his side. The wind ruffled his shirt. He felt no different from the darkened clouds above. They, too, looked as though they could barely contain the tempest within.

Needing to calm down, he took in a careful breath—each one pure torture—and let it out slowly. His anger was only aggravating his injury, the tension in his body escalating the pain to unmanageable levels.

The only way to ease his discomfort was to remove himself from Sabine Laurent's presence. Just being in the same room with her made him want to do something he'd never considered doing before: thrash a woman.

During the hunt for her, his rage had acted as a balm, allowing him to push past the brutal punishment of his horse's every gallop. Yet seeing again the unscrupulous blonde who'd caused him such enormous grief, knowing she'd lied and schemed throughout their time together, vaulted him into levels of ire he hadn't known since he'd unjustly lost his father and family honor.

Jésus-Christ. He was a thousand times a fool.

He'd been duped by a group of actors, a witch, and some boys!

How laughable was that? Worse, he'd been captivated by a female of lowly origin and somehow touched by her false ways. He was a seasoned officer. A veteran in battle who'd survived based on his abilities, wits, and instincts, his very acumen responsible for his naval successes and survival. And yet he'd allowed a baseborn ingénue to do something no one else had managed to do—lower his guard.

Merde, how that seethed in his soul.

But it wasn't just her deception and his enormous stupidity that stirred his rancor. He actually mourned the loss of Elise Marquette, loathing that she was nothing more than a fabrication created to beguile and betray him.

Staring out past the fields to the forest, Jules gnashed his teeth.

The little fraud had awakened not only his body, with the stunning passion that burned between them—but also his spirit. She'd actually drawn out his former self, dissolving his anger and bitterness with her wit, her smiles.

Yet with her actions, she'd tainted the experience—just as she'd tainted his meal.

How could he have known such soul-satisfying sex with such a faithless woman? The little bitch had even taunted him about it and called him a debauchee. *Morally unrestrained*. Jules snorted.

That was laughable coming from a female who'd traded her virginity for silver.

Who the fuck was she to judge him?

He'd sooner cut out his tongue than tell her that something had happened during their time together, something that hadn't happened in years—he'd made a connection with a woman that wasn't strictly physical. She'd accused him of being unaffected by those outside the noble class. But she'd affected him.

He could just imagine the roars of laughter from his former peers if they were to learn that he'd been fascinated by someone so déclassé.

Merde, he'd even given her a lover's trinket. Was there a greater imbecile than he?

The door opened. Jules immediately released his side as sounds from the commotion of the search and protest of the thieves wafted out.

Raymond exited. "My lord, are you all right?"

"Yes. Fine."

"My lord, you must rest. You have ridden for days with broken—"

"Nonsense. The binding I have on is all I need. Return inside and—"

"Commander!" Marc shouted from within the house.

Jules and Raymond immediately reentered the stony abode.

Sabine and her lot stood near the corner of the room.

Standing before the table, broken pottery and flour at his feet, Marc poured at least fifty flour-dusted silver coins out of a cloth pouch and onto the wooden surface.

"Commander!" Daniel entered the kitchen with a similar pouch. Emptying it, he added to the silver coins on the table.

Serge descended the stairs holding four pouches and placed them next to the pile of silver. "These are filled with our coins, Commander. Fabrice and I have searched the rooms upstairs and have found two trunks. Both are locked. We couldn't locate the key."

"They hold some old books and clothes. Nothing that would interest you," Sabine said.

Jules ignored her. "Bring them down here."

"There isn't any silver in them. I assure you!" she argued.

"Yes, your assurances are ever so believable," Jules retorted dryly without looking at her. It only infuriated him more to have her in his sight. And his side was tormenting him enough.

Four men carried the two trunks down and set them before Jules.

"You have six pouches of silver. Take them and go." Her agitation was clearly mounting. "There isn't anything of value in the trunks," she insisted.

"If there isn't anything of value in the trunks, then why are they locked?" Jules tossed at her. She remained silent. "Break the locks off," he ordered his men.

"No, wait!" The witch rushed forward, but Raymond caught her arm, arresting her advance. "You don't need to break the locks," she said. "We have the key."

Jules wasn't about to give them any more opportunities for trickery. "Fabrice, I saw an axe outside. Get it," he ordered. The burly man left to do his bidding.

"She isn't lying, my lord," the old man stated. "There is nothing that will interest you in the trunks. You go to a lot of trouble for nothing."

Fabrice returned inside and approached the first trunk. When he raised the axe, Jules glanced at Sabine. She looked down at the floor.

One powerful downward stroke broke the lock off. Fabrice pulled open the lid. Colorful fabrics stared back at them.

Once again Jules glanced at Sabine. Her gaze was still cast downward, denying him the ability to see her face or read the look in her eyes. Not that it would make a difference. He didn't believe her expressions or words one whit. The savage pain permeating his side was a potent reminder of the consequences of trusting Sabine Laurent.

Fabrice sifted a hand through the fabrics. Gowns. Two of them. Fine ones for someone who could afford quality. As Fabrice tossed each one onto the floor, Jules watched his group of captives closely.

They'd all adopted stoic expressions, except the witch and the young girl. The witch looked horror-stricken and the girl silently wept into her hand.

"There are only ladies' things in here, Commander," Fabrice informed him once the trunk was empty and its contents strewn about. In addition to the gowns, two pairs of shoes and some stockings were on the ground.

"You see," the old man said. "Nothing of value."

"Open the other one," Jules commanded, his gaze on Sabine. Eyes still downcast, she remained quiet.

After breaking off the second lock, Fabrice pulled back the lid, revealing a number of books.

Fabrice began tossing out the leather-bound volumes, adding to the clutter on the threadbare rug. When he grabbed a larger book, the young girl gave a small muffled cry.

That spiked Jules's curiosity.

"Give me that," Jules said. Fabrice handed him the book. Opening it, Jules scanned the pages. Its author had a distinct flourish to his penmanship.

He held up the book before the band of delinquents, pushing aside the stabbing distress the movement cost him. "What is this?"

His question was met with silence.

"Answer me!" he barked.

Everyone lowered their gaze except the young girl. Her watery eyes, still leaking out tears, remained fixed on the book.

"Very well. Since you said the contents in the trunks are of no value—despite the costly gowns—we'll burn them. Starting with this book."

Sabine's chin shot up.

The young girl screeched, "NO!" then wept harder.

"Josette, compose yourself," Sabine scolded, then met his regard firmly. She was acting again, schooling her features, hoping he'd believe she wasn't as affected as the younger female.

Yet he'd noted that she'd paled slightly. And that she wouldn't look at the book in his hand.

He approached the sobbing girl, clenching his teeth against the brutal pain that tore up his side with each step.

"Tell me why I shouldn't toss this book into the fire, Josette."

"Josette is young, and you and your men are frightening her," Sabine said. "That is the way of it, isn't it, Aristo? Those with noble blood always prey on the powerless. Shame on you for tormenting a child. Why not question one of the adults in the room? Coward!"

The clever blond conniver was trying to goad him, trying to divert the conversation away from the young girl—and more particularly, the book. Trying to gain some control over the situation. And he wasn't going to let her.

Given how severe the pain in his ribs was, he didn't know how much longer he could maintain his ruse and not give away his injury. Though his men were well aware of it, he refused to give Sabine any advantage over him by letting her learn the extent of the damage she'd wreaked upon him.

He needed results. Fast. Though nothing would be sweeter than to force the information from Sabine, focusing on young Josette would bring about a much-needed rapid conclusion—whether the notion sat well with him or not.

"What is this book, Josette?" Jules pressed.

Cheeks dampened, the girl looked at Sabine. Jules placed a finger against her jaw and turned her face back to him. "Look at me.

Only at me. Answer my question, Josette." He kept his voice gentle yet firm, knowing that if he scared her too much, she'd be in hysterics and of no use to him.

Josette's eyes widened. "S-Sabine?" The name slipped past her trembling lips even though she couldn't see her while his hand restricted the movement of her head.

"Josette," Sabine warned sternly, yet he noted the slight panic in her tone. "You'll not answer any of his questions. We owe him nothing. And he'll get nothing from us except the few coins from the pouches and our scorn."

Jules gave the girl a look of darkening dismay. "It seems Sabine doesn't appreciate the danger she's placed all of you in, Josette, for that is foolish advice. Take a look at these men." He stepped aside to give her an unobstructed view. "Your family has stolen from them as well. Do we look as though we'll simply leave, content with a few pouches of *our* silver?"

The girl swallowed.

"Stop terrifying her," Sabine demanded.

"Be silent!" Raymond barked, clearly sensing Jules was running out of time. The pain in his side was mounting by the moment.

"Why don't you tell me where the silver is, Josette? I can tell you know," Jules urged. "If I don't get the answers to my questions"—he tossed a glance to each thief before returning his attention to the girl—"this book meets with a fiery end. And that will be just the beginning. You don't want to see that happen, do you, Josette?"

"No. Please don't, my lord," Josette pleaded. "Sabine, d-do something . . . You can't let him burn it. It's 'Sabelle's journal!"

Jules's brows shot up. " 'Sabelle? The sister who's passed away? Well now." He walked over to Sabine, miraculously maintaining a normal gait. The news gave him the burst of vigor he needed in order to break the woman who'd broken not only his ribs, but also his trust.

Oh, how delicious this was going to be . . .

"I believe this"—he held up the book in front of her—"would be something of great value to you, Sabine." To her credit, she didn't so much as flinch. Standing stock-still, she simply glared at him.

But her racing heart gave her away. It beat so violently, he could see her wild pulse in her slender neck, belying the mask of composure.

"I think this would be as valuable to you as my silver is to me," he continued. "I propose a swap. I give you your sister's journal and all her other items here on the floor, and you return to me the silver you stole."

She held her tongue.

"I'm going to need your decision. *Now.* Which do you value more?" He placed the book in front of her face so that there was no avoiding it. "The silver. Or your sister's journal?"

"Sabine?" the witch spoke up. "I think you should tell him where the silver is."

"Tell him, Sabine," the old man beseeched.

"Yes, Sabine, tell me, where is my silver?" Jules prompted. She stared at the book.

He had her. He'd cornered the little liar. And none too soon. Sweat beaded his brow. The longer he remained standing, the more uncomfortable the binding around his ribs became. He needed to loosen it. Quickly.

Pulling her gaze from the volume, she met his. Her cheeks were pink and her eyes blazed at him. He'd never had a woman look at him with such hatred. Good. The sentiment was mutual.

"Without the silver, we are done," she said softly.

He dug his fingers into the book cover, his patience and tolerance about at an end.

"We'll think of some other way to pay the taxes," the old man offered. "Don't let him burn 'Sabelle's things."

"*Choose!*" he commanded. "The book. Or the silver?"

She raised her chin slightly. "We'll split the silver. You get half. We keep the other half. Then you leave us alone."

The sheer audacity of her statement yanked a hollow laugh from his throat. "Did you hear that, Raymond?"

Raymond frowned. "I did, Commander."

"Why, how *magnanimous* of you, Sabine," Jules growled, "to allow me to have half of MY SILVER!" *Merde!* He'd never known anyone with such gall or who'd dare push him when he was clearly in an explosive state. It was his duty to fix what had happened to his family.

He owed it to his father. It was a matter of honor.

And nothing—absolutely *nothing*—more was going to be taken from him!

He stalked over to the hearth. It took all the self-discipline he possessed to keep himself erect and not double over in physical agony.

Holding the book near the fire, he said, "You have until the count of five to tell me where my silver is."

For an instant, her lips parted with a soft gasp and her eyes flashed fear.

Finally a crack in the brave façade.

It's what he needed. It's what he'd use, for he knew—no matter how much he wanted to, no matter how much she deserved it—he couldn't bring himself to beat her or any of her pathetic lot into submission. In battle he was capable of ferocity. But violence against this group—women, an old man, and a child—was another matter. It went against every fiber of his being.

Cursing his scruples, he barked out, "*One . . .*"

"Sabine!" the witch exclaimed. "*Tell him!*"

Her eyes glistened with tears. "He doesn't deserve to have the silver back!" she said, her soft breasts rising and falling with her rapid breaths. "It's ours. We need it more than he does!"

"*Two . . .*"

"Sabine, please," Josette urged. "I'm scared."

So was the blond bane of his existence. Her expression had changed to one of unadulterated heartbreak.

Seeing it struck him hard, momentarily unbalancing him from his intended course of action. He shoved aside his pang of pity with the same determination with which he fought against the physical hell in his side. A physical hell *she'd* caused.

"*Three . . .*" he said pointedly.

"Sabine, I'm begging you," the witch implored. "Isabelle's death was difficult enough for you. The loss of those journals—"

"Stop it. Stop badgering me!" Sabine rubbed her brow with a trembling hand. "I'm trying to think." Pure misery, the kind that consumed the spirit, reflected in the depths of her silver eyes—and resonated with him. At the moment she looked delicately feminine. Utterly vulnerable. Making the thought of setting the journal alight suddenly abhorrent.

Jésus-Christ! He wasn't going to be taken in by this act. She was nothing more than a corrupt pretender.

If she truly valued her sister's journal, she'd stop him.

He tightened his jaw with renewed resolve. "*Four!*"

One number left. *Dieu*, she had better break.

15

Sabine's entire world narrowed to Isabelle's beloved journal—perilously close to the fire.

Her chest was so tight, she could barely breathe. The thought of it being destroyed was tearing her apart.

On its pages were Isabelle's very heart and soul. She didn't want to lose any of her sister's belongings on the floor . . . but her journal. *Oh, God. Not the journal.* She couldn't lose that.

How could he be so heartless?

Because he's an Aristo. It was in his blood to be cruel.

Even if she did as he demanded, he might burn the journal out of spite. *Do something. Think!* There was no escaping suffering—with either choice. If she surrendered the silver, he'd win. She and her family would lose. Including Isabelle.

There was no doubt he was planning to use the wealth to ascend back into the aristocracy. And he'd likely succeed. Why should he get to rebuild his life when he'd leveled hers?

"You are the devil," she whispered, unable to command the full force of her voice as she tottered under the weight of her anguish.

"This is your final warning," he responded, unmoved by her plight, indifferent to her words. "WHERE IS MY FUCKING SILVER!"

A tear slipped down her cheek. Then another. Dear God, no. She dropped her chin and swallowed hard, horrified by the tears, fighting against the emotions that threatened to overtake her. She couldn't allow the wall she'd imprisoned her grief behind to fall. She'd never survive such emotional calamity.

"Very well," he ground out from between clenched teeth. "You leave me no choice."

Her gaze shot up to his. *Oh, no . . .*

"Fi-"

"STOOOOOOP!" The cry pierced the air, so loudly it ricocheted off the walls and left Sabine's ears ringing. Choking on a sob, she turned, confused, unsure where it came from.

Josette.

She was on her knees, one hand against her chest, the other extended toward Jules. "I'll tell you where the silver is! Please don't!"

"Bring her here," Jules ordered.

"Just a minute now!" Louise protested and stepped forward, only to be pushed back by one of Jules's men.

Two of his men caught Josette under each arm, easily lifted her to her feet, and brought her to stand before him. Josette wept so hard, she needed the men to hold her up.

"So you know where the silver is, Josette?" Jules asked.

Josette nodded her head vigorously. "Y-Yes. I'll tell you but . . . please . . . leave Isabelle's things be."

Sabine closed her eyes briefly. Normally bossy and petulant, Josette had never behaved this way. Never cared about anyone else's things but her own. She'd no idea what had gotten into her. And the girl was making a huge mistake. "Josette, you cannot trust him. You mustn't—"

"Quiet!" Jules cut her off.

It was as if she hadn't spoken at all; Josette blurted out, "Sabine made us each a pouch of silver coins for our own keeping and the rest—"

"Josette!" Sabine exclaimed.

"Was buried."

Louise stepped forward. "My lord, we'll return your silver, but please, once you have it, I beg of you, show mercy."

"Mercy? You want consideration?" Jules's voice was flat. "How about I show you the same consideration you showed me and my men?"

His forbidding words sent a cold streak down Sabine's spine.

Turning to Marc, Jules said, "Take Josette. She is going to show us where the silver is buried. Serge and Fabrice, you come as well. Bruno, you and Daniel watch the others. They are forbidden to speak. Not a word is to be exchanged among them." He walked past Sabine, though not with the angry strides she would have expected. Oddly his gait was slower, and she thought his breathing sounded quicker and shallower, too.

* * *

It's gone!

Leaning against a large oak tree, clutching his side, Jules could still hear the young girl's shriek echoing in his head. A bead of sweat trickled down his back. The pain in his side was so sharp it took concerted effort to keep his own howls contained.

Before him was the large rock his men had moved and the hole in the ground they had dug. But there was no trace of the chest. Or a single silver piece to be found.

He cursed both his weakness for women with blond hair and fate for pushing Sabine Laurent into his path.

Raymond, Marc, and Fabrice approached.

"We've interrogated each of them separately, as you ordered, Commander," Marc reported.

"And?" His voice was rough.

"And on comparing their stories, they each tell the same one—without any deviation whatsoever: Two chests are heading to Paris to be melted into coins resembling those of the realm, and the other was buried here under the rock. Each became distraught when they learned the chest was missing. In fact, all insisted we were lying about the missing chest."

"Do you think we can trust their answers, given that they are actors, Commander?" Fabrice asked.

"The two girls are not," Raymond said.

Marc nodded. "I questioned them personally. I think they're all telling the truth."

"Who could have taken the silver?" Fabrice inquired.

"No one had any idea." Marc looked dismayed. "As I said, they were quite incredulous and stunned over the fact that the silver is missing."

"Perhaps a band of wanderers saw them bury it and stole it?" Fabrice offered.

"Perhaps," Jules conceded. "But then again, it could have been someone known to them. It doesn't matter. The silver can be traced. It will be dark soon. At the first light, Serge and Bruno will begin with the closest town, making inquiries to see if anyone has spent even a coin. We'll find the treasure. As for the other chests, two of us will ride to Paris, while the other two stay here, just in case. I'll send Daniel to fetch Luc. My brother is waiting for me in the town of Clouquet. He'll have more men with him who can help search for the silver."

"Why not simply wait here for the group traveling to Paris to return? Sooner or later they'll come back for their family. No?" Fabrice asked.

"And leave our silver in the hands of an actor and two boys longer than necessary?" Jules shook his head. "Never. We ride in the morning."

"Commander, a private word with you, if I may?" Raymond requested. Jules nodded. The others stepped away.

Raymond lowered his voice. "My lord, you're in no shape to ride."

"I'm not staying here."

"I don't see that you have a choice. If you don't allow your ribs to heal, you run the risk of developing—"

"Enough, Raymond. I'll have a night's rest. I'll be fine in the morning." His body instantly balked at his words. He wasn't entirely certain he could even stand by morning, much less get on a horse.

"My lord, regaining the silver quickly is your goal. Order Marc and Fabrice to ride to Paris. They can travel faster than you, given your state. I'll stay here and attend to your needs. Forgive me, but it did take days longer to get here than it should have because of your injury."

"*Merde.*" Jules raked a hand through his hair. He hated it that Raymond was right. The frequent rests had eaten up time, though he'd pushed himself beyond what most men would have been able to endure suffering from a similar affliction.

Given the condition of his ribs, he couldn't ride as fast as Marc and Fabrice. And he knew the longer it took his ribs to heal, the greater his risk of developing lung fever.

But, *Jésus-Christ*, stay *here*?

Under the same roof as this corrupt lot?

He'd have to sleep with one eye open.

* * *

Jules insisted on walking into the house without assistance. Though by the time he'd crossed the field and the threshold, he could barely hold himself upright. Upon entering, he noted the home was still in disarray from the search and that the Laurent lot were seated near the hearth, looking stricken. Josette wept softly. Bruno, Serge, and Daniel stood guard.

Jules caught Sabine's gaze.

Her expression of distress quickly turned perplexed when she noted his irregular gait. He thought he saw concern flash in her eyes, but dismissed it as he concentrated on breathing and walking toward the room to the left off the common room as normally as possible. The bed inside beckoned him. Raymond directly behind him, Jules entered the bedchamber, grateful there was one on the main floor.

"Turn down the quilt. See if there are any fleas," Jules ordered. Though given his state, even if there was an infestation, he doubted he could have resisted the urge to lie down.

"It looks very clean," Raymond said, having pulled back the bedcovers.

Jules lowered himself onto the edge of the bed, refusing Raymond's help. He tried to pull off his shirt, but couldn't lift his arm without pain ripping across his side. He swore viciously. "Get this binding off me, Raymond. It feels like a vise!" He couldn't breathe, and the pain was making him impatient and irritable.

"Of course, my lord." Unfazed, Raymond removed Jules's shirt then undid the knot and deftly unraveled the binding from around his ribs. When it was off, Jules took in a breath and let it out slowly.

The door opened and slammed shut.

Furious that one of his men would dare intrude so rudely, Jules looked up to see who was about to receive the full brunt of his ire.

Sabine, balancing a tray with one hand, locked the door quickly with the other and turned to face him. Her eyes immediately narrowed on the massive discoloration across his ribs. Jerking her gaze up, she met his stunned regard with her own.

Rapid footsteps approached the door. Someone attempted to turn the locked latch, then pounded at the portal.

"Mademoiselle!" Marc called out. "Out of there!"

She glanced back toward the commotion. Raymond stepped toward her, the key visibly vulnerable in her hand. But she turned around before he could grab it and dropped the key down the front of her chemise, tossing him a "Don't you dare" look.

Raymond froze, then glanced at Jules for direction.

Jules placed a palm over his eyes, wrestling down the expletives bellowing in his brain. Clearly, he wasn't finished being tortured this night.

"Mademoiselle!" Marc continued to strike his fist against the door. "Commander?"

"Commander?" Raymond said. "What do you wish me to do? Um . . . fetch the key?"

Jules lowered his hand and slanted Raymond a look. Raymond had the good grace to blush.

"No," he managed to say calmly for the sake of his ribs, though it took considerable effort to tamp down the vexation boiling in his blood. "But you can tell Marc to cease his incessant pounding."

"Of course, Commander. MARC! ENOUGH!"

There was silence followed by footsteps retreating from the opposite side of the door.

Raymond smiled. "There you are, Commander."

Jules turned to the woman before him, astounded by her errant ways.

"Tell me, Sabine, when it's obvious I'd find nothing more enjoyable than to strangle you, why exactly would you lock yourself in a room with me?"

Sabine placed her tray on the table beside the bed, then smoothed her hands down the front of her skirt. "I don't know where the silver is. I wish to God I did. I know you don't believe me. However, that's not the reason I'm here. I'm here because I have a question."

"Ah, how wonderful. You have '*a question*.'" Jules formed a false smile, his tone caustic. "I can't wait to hear it. It must be one of utmost importance and urgency for you to sweep in here, without so much as seeking permission before entering."

She frowned. "I'm not a servant in this home. There is no reason for me to seek permission to enter here. This is my room. And that is my bed. What are you so concerned about? That I might happen upon you in your natural state? You haven't suddenly become bashful, have you?"

He dug his fingers into the mattress. *Calm* . . . "What is your question?" he responded through clenched teeth. "The one you risk life and limb for."

She glanced at Raymond. "My question is," her voice softened, "since it obvious that you are injured . . . Were you injured at the inn?"

"Why do you wish to know? So you can gloat? Rejoice with your criminal lot that your witch's brew had results greater than anticipated?"

"No. I don't wish to gloat. I am not as he says." She pointed to Raymond. "I *do* have a conscience." Jules glanced at Raymond, who immediately lowered his gaze, suddenly fascinated with a spot on his boot.

"I'll admit it; I have in the past and present wished every ill upon you," she continued. "I thought I'd find no greater joy than to see you suffer. But the reality is . . . seeing you hurt does not ease my pain. *I* am not indifferent to the suffering of others. If I were, it would make me like you and your class. And I am better than that."

He wasn't in any state to spar with her. Not when pain was knifing through him. Before he could order her out, she picked his binding up off the bed and threw it over a chair.

"That needs laundering."

Walking over to the pile of clothing his men had tossed out of her trunks and onto the floor, she picked up linen from the top of the heap.

"Take this." She handed it to Raymond. "It may be worn, but it's clean. Cut what he needs from it."

Surprised, he watched as she poured water into the water basin then soaked a cloth in it.

She knelt before him and stroked its cool wetness across his chest.

He seized her wrist. "What do you think you're doing?"

"I'm bathing you. I'll be gentle." She glanced at Raymond, who was busy tearing a strip off the linen she'd given him, then leaned toward Jules and whispered, "You've done it for me. I'm returning the favor."

Her words sent a rush of heated memories through his mind. A different kind of ache immediately rose up, this time from his stiffening prick. *Jésus-Christ*, the very last thing he needed was a hard cock to add to his physical torment. He couldn't believe his body was reacting to her—after all her transgressions.

"Heed this warning and heed it well." He gave her wrist a squeeze to punctuate his words. "Don't *ever* mention our time together again. Understood?" He released her.

"Jules—"

"And don't address me by my Christian name! That is to be used by friends. Lovers. Or those in my social class. You are none of those things. You will, whenever you speak to me, remember your place." He gave her a look daring her to mention his ignoble status. Regardless of how the court temporarily viewed him, he was still an Aristo by blood, untainted by a single commoner in his pedigree for more than five generations in all four of his bloodlines.

She returned his glare, then rose and tossed the cloth into the basin.

"Fine. Have it your way, *my lord*." She picked up the wooden goblet from the tray. "Agnes is known for her talents in healing. I convinced her to help you, even though you don't deserve it. This is a mixture of boiled poppy seed and herbs. It will aid with your pain and help you to sleep." She held the goblet out to him.

A mirthless laugh shot out of him. He snatched the goblet out of her hand, and peered at the brown liquid. "Raymond, the witch has prepared yet another elixir to induce sleep."

Frowning, Raymond shook his head.

Turning to Sabine, Jules said, "Why, thank you, Sabine. I so enjoyed the first one. Naturally I'd be interested in trying another.

Do tell, what sort of sleep will this one induce? *Eternal?*" He whipped it across the room, sending the contents spraying out. The goblet bounced off the wall and landed on the ground.

Grabbing his side, he growled, "You, your witch, and your potions can go to hell."

"I am trying to help you!"

"You want to help me? Then get out of my sight!"

"From your movements and your breathing, Agnes says it's likely you have broken ribs. Your bruising convinces me she's right. You wish to suffer pain, fine. But at least use this." She snatched up a small wooden bowl. "This is a balm. I've seen it work. It will heal your ribs quickly. It takes *two* days to prepare. Agnes made it for someone else, but I convinced her to allow you to have it instead. You merely spread it over the skin where the injury is—"

"Get out!"

"You're willing to risk *lung fever?*" She looked incredulous. "You won't even try it?"

"If it comes from you or your lot, NO!"

She slammed the bowl down on the tray and began unlacing her bodice.

His brows shot up. "What are you doing?"

"Proving a point to the most foolish mule-headed man in the realm." She tossed the bodice down on the bed and yanked on her chemise, pulling the knee-length garment out of her skirt. The key slipped out, landing on the floor. She scooped it up. Then, with her other hand, she gathered the fabric of her chemise and bunched it just under her breast.

Beautiful soft skin he knew all too intimately was exposed before him, snaring not only his attention but that of his hard straining cock.

Transferring the key to her opposite hand, she then dipped her fingers into the balm. "This is the approximate spot where your injury is," she said and smoothed the slick substance over her skin, making it glisten.

His mouth went dry.

She dipped into the salve again, then glided her moistened fingers along her side once more from the undercurve of her breast down to the waistband of her skirts. Then back up. And *Dieu*, back down. He watched, unable to tear his eyes away as she caressed herself, smoothing on the balm—her body now so sensuously glossy.

"There." She released the hem of her chemise. Like a curtain, it dropped down, covering the provocative sight, leaving him bereft and heated.

She tucked her undergarment back in her skirt. "You see? The balm is perfectly safe to use." She grabbed the bodice off the bed and laced it up. "If you're wise, you won't waste it like you did the pain tonic."

She marched over to the door, key in hand, unlocked it, and left with an abrupt slam.

Jules glanced at Raymond, who stared at the door, mouth agape.

"Are you done gawking, Raymond?"

His servant clamped his mouth shut. "Forgive me, my lord. The lady is, well, full of surprises."

"What the hell did you say to her?"

"Nothing! During my interrogation I merely mentioned that she shouldn't be so quick to judge others. She's rather an unpredictable woman. I certainly did not expected her to enter here and expose her—"

Jules lifted a brow.

"Um, may I help you lie down, my lord?"

"No. But you can go into the other room and tell Marc and Bruno to bring the sister's trunks. They'll be kept here near me. In fact, have all our supplies brought to this room. Also, I want you to explain to our band of thieves that they'll be having guests for a while and there will be new rules from now on. No one is permitted to leave this house without permission. No one is permitted to be out of plain sight. And for the love of God, get me that key *without* fishing your hand down the front of her bodice."

Raymond cleared his throat. "Of course, my lord."

The moment Raymond closed the door, Jules carefully placed his legs on the bed and slowly reclined, unable to hold down the fierce groan that quivered up his throat.

Once his back rested against the soft mattress, he closed his eyes. His chest hurt, his cock was still hard, and to add to his misery, Sabine's scent was emanating from her sheets, filling his senses with each and every breath he took.

Surely, no more havoc could be wreaked upon him.

The heavens responded with a thunderclap.

16

Sabine jerked the weeds out of the herb garden.

"Insufferable." Yank. "Overbearing." Yank, yank. "I curse the day I ever met him! Ever laid eyes on him!" She tossed the weeds toward the pile she'd made and jerked out more.

Agnes blinked as she watched Sabine, down on her knees, venting her fury on the vegetation.

"I don't believe I've ever seen you this incensed," Agnes remarked, holding a basket of carrots, radishes, and leeks.

Sabine shot to her feet. "I cannot believe our cursed luck! It's bad enough that the silver is missing—and I've been racking my mind trying to figure out when it was stolen and who could have taken it—and now we must deal with *him*!" Agnes knew full well she was talking about Jules. "He holds us prisoner and then acts as though he's our master, taking *our* eggs, cheese, all the best foods we have for himself! The very foods we use to sell for a few meager coins. What does he leave us? Some stale bread to dunk in soup made from that!" She pointed to Agnes's basket. "It's bad enough that Louise and her lazy daughters never do their share around here. Now we have His Majesty to contend with!" Sabine cleaned her hands on her apron with an angry swipe. "He even has Raymond pull furniture out of the house for his comfort outside. Awaiting the return of his silver, he sits on his throne. For *two* days he's dictated to us while you, Olivier, and I kill ourselves trying to scrape together enough to eat and toil in the fields!" So scorching was her fury, she was amazed her eyebrows hadn't been singed off.

Sabine curled her fingers into a fist. "I should march in there and break another of his ribs!"

"Sabine, he's injured, we took his treasure, and he's an Aristo by blood. You can hardly expect he'll help us in the fields," Agnes responded.

"His ignoble status makes him no more important in society than we are. I am sick and tired of this poverty. And his high-handedness. We're going to get our hands on his silver. We're going to climb out of this dark hole we have sunk into. I'm going to find my sister. And as for *the mighty* Jules de Moutier, he needs to be knocked off his perch. And I am just the woman to do it." She stalked toward the house, stopping abruptly when Agnes called out her name.

She turned back around, itching to give Jules a piece of her mind. "What is it?"

Agnes was smiling. "I do like one thing about the Aristo."

Sabine frowned. "What is that?"

"I like how he affects you. It's been five years since I've seen any sort of fire or life in you."

* * *

Jules leaned on the windowsill and gazed out at the summer day. *Merde*. He was climbing the walls. This horrible state of infirmity was so contrary to his active existence. Between the incessant agony in his side, the constant violin music from the music composer Olivier, and the actress Louise's loud spontaneous bursts into theatrical soliloquy, his sanity was being tested. The entire lot seemed to thrive on noise and theater. And despite the nerve-grating bickering that would ensue from time to time, they were constantly together, seemingly preferring it that way. Undercurrents of loyalty and affection coursed through the constant commotion.

He had far too much time on his hands. To think. To agonize for what surely had to be the millionth time over his father's betrayal. Over his missing silver. And then there was Sabine.

He spotted her just then standing in the distance with Agnes, engrossed in conversation. Sunlight shone on Sabine's pale hair, and it was bedazzling to behold. Even in her humble attire, she was lovely.

No woman who was as accomplished at deception as she was should be that beautiful.

Sleeping in her bed every night, with her scent all around him, he dreamed of her. Of fucking her. Of her gorgeous form, so sensuous and sensitive and responsive to his touch.

An instant feral need rolled through him. His groin tightened in response.

Jules clenched his teeth and swore softly.

Each morning he awoke with a stiff prick, battling back memories of tasting, caressing, and kissing those sweet spots on her body he knew undid her. Of being inside her climaxing core, so silken and snug, and feeling those decadent spasms as she came on his cock.

The pain in his ribs alone should have been enough to kill this ludicrous lust he had for her. But it wasn't. Nothing stopped the mental images of their time together in the forest and at the inn. Laughing and talking and feeling something he thought he'd forgotten how to feel.

Contentment.

She'd quieted his soul. Well, the bitterness and the anger were back. Full-blown.

And he hated it.

He hated it as much as the memories and this unbreakable pull. He wanted them dead and gone.

Jules turned away. The wooden plank beneath his hands creaked and lifted on one side. He pulled at it. It came away. Jules peered in the hole. Beneath the wooden sill were two books wedged between the inner and outer wall. Hidden as they were, they had to be important.

Removing one from its secret spot, he brushed the dust off and opened it to the first page. Across the top it said, *This is the very private journal of Sabine Laurent. Isabelle, put it down or I'll read yours!*

Yesterday, he'd glanced at the books in Isabelle's trunk, even thumbed through her journal. They hadn't captivated him. Yet the moment he turned the page and read the first line in Sabine's journal, he was ensnared.

I can think of no better way to begin a journal than to say, I am in love!

Glancing at the date of the entry, February 11, 1650, he made a quick calculation, realizing he was reading words written by a young Sabine just blooming into womanhood.

Oddly fascinated, he covered the second journal with the windowsill and made his way to the bed.

Jules tossed the volume down on the mattress. Gritting his teeth, he lowered himself onto the bed, his hand over the linen binding around his chest.

The wooden bowl on a small table near his bed caught his eye. It mocked him. And tempted him.

"It will heal your ribs quickly . . ."

He wasn't going to smear that concoction on any part of his body. Nor was he going to think about the arousing memory that was forevermore associated with it. *Damn her.*

Slowly he reclined, opened the journal, and began to read.

Oh, I have never felt this way. Not ever! But then I've never known anyone like my Dark Prince. I first beheld him when he attended Father's comedy two weeks ago. I haven't been able to stop thinking about him since. I will admit it here, on these pages alone, that I was completely aquiver and hopelessly enthralled by his every movement. He is so handsome and regal, with hair and eyes so dark. Oh, his eyes! I could stay immersed within their depths forever.

We haven't exchanged words or even looks, but we will. In time. When Father's not around, of course. It is inevitable. I know it. I feel a connection to my Dark Prince I cannot explain.

Jules turned the page to the next entry.

. . . Father demands that Isabelle and I remain unseen while at the theater. I would gladly break his foolish rule and approach my Dark Prince the next time he attends, but I haven't the courage to speak to him. I wish I had Isabelle's confidence. I know she would speak to the object of her affection—who is my Dark Prince's brother!—if it weren't for her fear of banishment from any more performances, as Father has so often threatened.

Jules's curiosity was more than piqued over the identity of the Dark Prince. Looking for more references to him, he came upon:

. . . He was here! My Dark Prince was at the theater tonight! It seems impossible, but he was even more beautiful than the first time I saw him. He looked so fine, so very princely. He draws a throng of adoring subjects to him. I loathe it that they are mostly of the female persuasion. They vie for his attention. I crave it, too . . .

Completely engrossed, Jules turned the page to the next entry.

. . . Father says Isabelle and I will marry men in the nobility. We will be great ladies one day. But there is only one man I want—the finest in the realm—my Dark Prince.

Jules gave a short harsh laugh. "The finest in the realm"? Shaking his head, he wondered how well he knew the poor Aristo she'd set her sights on.

He scanned more entries, looking for any clues to unravel the mystery of the Dark Prince once and for all.

. . . Louise noticed me watching my Dark Prince last night. She said he is far beyond my reach. That I dream too grand. But aren't dreams supposed to be grand? Alas, I am afflicted with a heart that won't be reined in. It reaches out to my Dark Prince and will be satisfied by no other. He is my destiny. I know it. I feel it.

He searched on.

. . . I saw my Dark Prince tonight! He was at the theater to see Father's newest comedy, "One Summer Night." The most magical nights are when my Dark Prince appears either in my dreams or before my longing eyes. How I adore his laugh. His smile shines brighter than the sun! Yet he looks through me, as one would the wind. I brush past, but he does not see or feel me. Nor does he sense the yearning in my heart. How I ache for a look, a touch. Oh, heaven would be a kiss from his lips! Nothing this side of the stars would be finer.

Who was the object of her romantic ramblings? Whom did she long to kiss?

. . . I've seen enough stolen kisses at the theater. I am confident I can do it well. When at last I kiss my Dark Prince, he won't want me to ever stop!

Frustrated, all he knew of the Dark Prince was that he had dark hair and a brother. That description matched many. *Dieu*, it even matched him.

Fast and furious footsteps approached his closed bedchamber door. *Merde*. He knew exactly who was about to burst in. Shutting the journal, he managed to stuff it under his pillow just as the door slammed open.

Sabine marched in, her skin flushed. Her breasts rose and fell with her rapid breaths.

Jésus-Christ. Stop looking at her breasts. So, she had the kind of tits a man could delight in for hours. There were plenty of other women. Plenty of other gorgeous breasts.

Briefly glancing at her lush mouth, he wondered if the Dark Prince ever got to taste those lips. She'd definitely done it so deliciously well, he hadn't wanted to stop.

"I have had enough of you," she stated. "You'll not take any more from us."

Jules lifted a brow. "I believe those should be my words."

Raymond rushed in and grasped her arm. "Come!"

She tried to pull her arm free and glared at Jules. "You need him because you're too much of a coward to face me alone."

"Really, Sabine. All your obvious baiting and carrying on about cowardliness is getting rather old, don't you think?"

"You are despicable!"

"Yes. And you're a lovely woman who gives her body to men, feeds them tainted food, and steals from them. Raymond, remind me to improve myself and adopt Sabine Laurent's high moral standards." His ire was mounting with every moment he looked into her deceitful face.

He resented this clash of disdain and desire that constantly warred inside him over this woman.

"Your father should have raised you with a firmer hand rather than to allow you and your sister to wander about the theater unchecked. You'd comport yourself better."

She stiffened. "How would you know anything about what my father allowed my sister and me to do at the theater?"

Merde. That was a slip. If he wasn't so incensed with her, if he didn't have pain shooting through his chest, he wouldn't have made the bloody blunder.

"It was a guess. Clearly he was lax in his parenting. He failed to teach you how to be a lady. How to speak to your betters."

In fact, he'd caught a couple of journal entries where she'd witnessed various explicit acts in dark corners of the theater and in the alley outside that most innocent young women didn't observe. Paul Laurent had been a fool to let his daughters roam so carelessly.

"My betters?" she exclaimed. "You are not my better. You are my equal. No, you are not even my equal. You are beneath me."

"I was. At the inn. And I think another time in the forest, no?"

A small gasp escaped her, completely taken aback by his words. And he delighted in it.

Quickly recovering, she said, "I thought you forbade the mention of our time together."

"I make the rules and I decide which, if any, apply to me."

"Why are you so angry?" she demanded. "Is it because you were duped? Or is it because you were outwitted by people you think of as less than you? You have only yourself to blame for being robbed. You've been to my father's theater many times. You've seen Louise and Vincent in his plays. Had you truly looked at them at the inn, you would have recognized them. But you didn't. You don't look at anyone who isn't part of the upper class. No one outside of it is worthy of your regard—unless you're interested in a tumble."

He tightened his jaw. "I've grown tired of our conversation." Jules waved her away. Raymond immediately began hauling Sabine from the room.

"I'm not finished yet!"

"Yes, you are," Jules responded calmly, though he seethed.

"You're not taking our best food any longer. Do you hear me?"

"*Chère*, they can hear you in England. And I'll take what I want until my silver is returned."

Raymond pushed her out and closed the door behind him, yet Jules could still hear her anger and frustration. Good. Why should he be the only one to feel that way?

He pulled the journal out and located the page where he'd left off. Several entries later Jules was stunned to read:

He kissed her! I saw him. My Dark Prince kissed Marie de Perron! Oh, how it makes me ache to see his lips touch another's.

Marie de Perron? A favorite courtesan among the male population of the aristocracy. An auburn-haired beauty whose charms Jules had personally sampled many times after his return from war in the summer of '50. In fact, they'd remained friends and lovers until his father's death years later.

Jules had definitely been to the theater during the time these journal entries were written. Could he be the Dark Prince? No. Marie had had many lovers. The Dark Prince could be anyone.

It wasn't him.

Was it?

17

"Good morning."

Without the courtesy of a knock, Claude Cyr and the large man he'd brought with him had opened the door and stepped into the Laurent home.

Their presence sent a chill through Sabine.

Almost twenty years her senior, Cyr smiled. The man looked like a rodent, inspiring the same feeling of revulsion.

Josette immediately inched away from Sabine and closer to her sister and mother, distress etched across their features. Agnes and Olivier were out in the fields, unaware they had unwanted visitors. And Raymond, well, Raymond was always somewhere attending to the needs of his master.

Knowing she'd have to deal with these men by herself, Sabine schooled her features. Cyr thrived on fear.

It would only encourage him to escalate his intimidation tactics if he saw any on her face. Sabine didn't have the luxury of expressing her own disquiet.

"It's not the end of the month." There was no need to pretend at pleasantries. She wanted them gone. The sooner the better.

"Now, is that any sort of a greeting?" Cyr said.

Sabine glanced at his companion. The scar on his left cheek added to his formidable look. "It's the kind the tax collector gets," she responded coolly, though her heart pounded.

"Such impertinence." Cyr brushed something off the sleeve of his costly doublet. "Your time is about done. If you don't pay *in full* this time, you will face the consequences."

"Yes. Well, thank you for the reminder. If you will see yourselves out . . ." Silently she willed them to leave. Cyr didn't bring the brute along for companionship. She feared what might happen the longer they lingered.

Cyr approached Sabine, stopping inches from her. Her heart lurched. A nauseating combination of sweat and perfume wafted off him. She fought the urge to step back and forced herself to maintain his gaze, his icy eyes vacant of empathy.

"I don't think you understand the gravity of the situation you're in."

She understood it all too well.

"A debtor's prison awaits you and your band of misfits if you don't make good on your debt this time. I don't think any of you will fare well there, especially you. Imagine how delighted the guards will be to see a woman like *you* . . ." He ran his knuckles down Sabine's cheek.

She slapped his hand away, the ring he wore stinging her palm. "Get out of our home!"

He grabbed her braid near her ear and yanked her to him, wresting a cry from her throat. And from Josette.

He brought Sabine's face close to his own. His vile breath assailed her nose and churned her stomach.

"Just who do you think you're talking to?" He tightened his cruel hold on her hair. Tears gathered in her eyes. She clutched his wrist, desperate to disengage.

"Let go!" she cried, then quickly added a softer "please" to appease him.

"That's a very pretty 'please.'" Another waft of his foul breath hit her in the face and roiled her stomach. "But I see defiance in your eyes." He gave her hair a vicious yank. She cried out. He was pulling so hard. The pain was unbelievable. Fearing he'd tear off her scalp, she savagely dug her nails into the flesh of his arm. He yelped in pain. She kicked him square on the shin with her wooden clog.

Cyr released her with a shout. She jumped out of his reach, her head throbbing.

A sword was suddenly thrust between them, its razor edge against Cyr's throat.

"Don't. Move," a familiar voice said.

Cyr froze. His brutish companion gripped the hilt of his sword. The ominous whisper of his rapier unsheathing sent a shiver of dread down Sabine's spine.

She looked from her assailants to her unexpected savior. Jules kept his focus on Cyr and the sword against his throat.

"Tell your man to put his weapon down or I'll open your throat here and now," Jules informed.

A bead of sweat appeared on Cyr's brow. He moved nothing but his eyes. Upon seeing exactly who was holding a weapon to him, he exclaimed, "My lord!"

Jules frowned. "Have your man drop his blade, then identify yourself and give me one good reason why I shouldn't run you through the gullet."

Raymond came rushing down the stairs. He immediately unsheathed his sword, poised to battle Cyr's giant companion. Louise and her daughters, who'd been cowering in the corner, took the standoff as their cue to run from the room.

"Raymond," Jules said. "It appears we have visitors."

Cyr swallowed. "Roland, drop your sword!"

Roland didn't move, sword still in hand.

"Do as I say, you fool!"

With an angry growl, the beast tossed his blade down. Raymond snatched it up and pointed both swords at Roland.

"My lord, it—it is I, Claude Cyr. I loyally worked for your family for years! Your faithful tax collector, my lord."

Jules raised his brows and lowered his weapon. "Cyr?"

"Yes! Yes, that's correct. Cyr." The rodent's smile was wary as he checked his fat neck for blood with a swipe of his hand. Looking relieved that none was present on his palm, his smile broadened. He gave Jules a low bow. "Your most humble servant."

His demonstration of "respect" irked Sabine. It was as insincere and corrupt as the rest of him.

Jules replaced the sword at the tax collector's throat.

"Taxes are collected monthly in the local parish. Why are you here and why would you attack this woman?"

He was defending her? *To his former tax collector?*

"My lord, if you would lower your sword, I could—"

"Answer me!" Jules barked.

Cyr started. He cleared his throat. "A-As you wish. I'm here on the King's business. Since your family lost . . . er . . . since the tragic *wrongful* charges against your father and the . . . change in ownership of these lands, I've been given the responsibility of collecting taxes for the Crown, an honor, I might add, as great as collecting for your prestigious family, my lord. I, for one, have never believed, even for an instant, that the charges against your family—"

"Enough gushing, Cyr. Get to the point."

"Of course. It is my responsibility to make certain that taxes are paid on a timely basis. Unfortunately, it is not easy to collect from degenerates who resort to avoidance, schemes—all manner of trickery to escape paying their share."

"So you collect taxes by brutalizing women?" Jules seethed. Though he'd been tempted to throttle Sabine several times, seeing the vicious assault shot hot rage through his veins.

"I collect by whatever means works. I must do my *duty*."

"Collection of taxes is one thing, your methods, completely another. They're *unacceptable*."

"Really? It never bothered you before. How else did you think taxes were collected?"

Cyr's words were jarring.

He lowered his sword and looked at Sabine. She stared back, indignation etched on her fine face. He realized he'd never wasted a moment's thought on it. Never imagined that excessive means were used, particularly on women.

"My lord, these people are a blemish on society. Lazy. Cheats."

Those were the very words he'd always used to describe the lower class, yet hearing them from Cyr's mouth made Jules mentally flinch. Though Sabine and her family were definitely the latter, they were certainly not the former. With the exception of Louise and her two daughters, these people were not lazy. He'd seen how Sabine, Olivier, and Agnes toiled daily.

"They're not inclined to pay unless one impresses upon them the importance of abiding by the law."

Sabine lifted her chin and responded softly, "We don't have enough to pay all the taxes owed to the Crown."

"You see what I must deal with, my lord?" Cyr said. "Such blatant disregard for the law and disrespect for authority. They live on someone else's land and yet don't feel obliged to pay for the privilege! I'm forced to make these home visits—visits I'd sooner forgo—when the debt is significant. As it is in this case."

"What is the debt?" Why the hell did he ask that? Why involve himself in matters that were none of his concern?

"Roland, bring the satchel."

The large man lumbered over to the table. Pulling off the satchel slung on his shoulder, he set it on the wooden surface.

Cyr pulled out the accounting ledger. "Here, my lord, is the exact figure and the date of their last payment, which, as you see was some time ago. I have lumped the entire debt here, but in actual fact, half this amount is for Crown taxes and half for what remains unpaid in local taxes."

Jules glanced at Sabine. "Is this the amount you owe?"

She moved to the table and glanced down at the figure on the open ledger. "Yes."

Dieu, it was considerable. He felt a stab of conscience—and it irked him. He wasn't the one who had mismanaged funds. The Laurents had.

This wasn't his problem, and he wouldn't be lured into it.

His physical pain tormented him. His mood was foul. And he decided to vent a little frustration and exact a small measure of retribution for his family.

God knows Cyr had it coming.

"Cyr, a payment is going to be made today," he announced.

Sabine's eyes widened.

"Really? Wonderful, my lord. How much?"

"All of it." Jules heard Sabine's soft gasp.

Cyr looked just as astonished. "Why, that's excellent! But bartering isn't permitted when paying the Crown's taxes, and since, in this case, it's the King who's owed the local taxes as well, I must insist the sum be paid in coin. Do they have the funds to pay in such a manner?"

"No. But you do."

Cyr raised his brows. "Me? Why on earth would I pay their taxes?"

Jules yanked Cyr to him by the hair, jerked his head back, and pressed the sword against his throat once more.

Raymond instantly stopped Roland's advance by placing the tip of one of his blades to the beating pulse at the side of the man's thick neck.

"For the endless skimming you did each time you collected taxes for my family. And don't"—Jules yanked the hair harder, enjoying the cry Cyr gave—"try to deny it." Cyr's eyes were wide, his breathing rapid. It gave Jules perverse pleasure to see the man so panicked, gripped with terror. He was one of many who would pay for betraying his father's trust. "Shortly before my father's arrest, he wrote to me and told me you were dipping your hand in deeper than was your due. He wanted to replace you. But he never got the chance. Me, I'm less merciful. I want to send you to hell."

"My lord, please . . ."

"Admit you stole from my family."

"I'll—I'll pay the debt! All of it! As you wish! In fact, I'll write it in the ledger right now!"

"Not good enough. I want the truth! I want to hear how you took a position of trust and twisted it into a self-enriching role, amassing sizable wealth, judging by the look of your clothes and rings. SAY IT!"

"I—I took only a little . . ."

Jules pressed the sword harder.

"Yes! All right! I admit it. I stole. I'll—I'll pay it all back."

Jules viciously tightened his grip on the man's hair. Cyr screamed out. "Oh, that you will. You'll leave your ledger here and I'll make some calculations to determine what you owe me. Make no mistake, Cyr, I will reclaim my birthright and you will never cross a Moutier again. Is that understood?"

"Absolutely." His profuse sweating added to his revolting smell.

Jules shoved him away, all too eager to distance himself from the man and his stench. Cyr stumbled back and clutched his throat as if to protect it.

"I'll be in contact with you soon, Cyr." He was going to keep the man unbalanced, hold the debt over his head. Cyr knew a lot of people and could be of use in Jules's quest for justice. "Don't try to avoid me, or I'll hunt you down like the dog you are, and you'll pay in more ways than one."

"No, my lord." Cyr said, visibly shaken. "I wouldn't do that."

"Before you go, mark down in the ledger that the debt has been cleared."

"Of course. But—But I don't have a quill or ink with me. I didn't expect . . . payment to be made."

"Get him what he needs," Jules said to Sabine. "And bring a parchment."

She didn't hesitate and rushed off. By the time she returned, Olivier and Agnes had torn into the house, clearly having recognized the horses outside, and now stood looking astonished by the scene before them—Cyr humbled and his henchman subdued by his own weapon.

Sabine set the items on the table.

Cyr wrote in the ledger. "There, my lord. Just as you willed."

"Now write on the parchment that the taxes are fully paid, sign it, and get out of my sight."

Cyr hastily obeyed, murmured a good day with a quick bow, and ran from the house with his giant plodding behind him.

The witch and Olivier exchanged looks.

Silence hung in the air . . .

A burst of laughter erupted from them.

"Have you ever seen Cyr so frightened? He practically pissed his breeches!" Olivier guffawed.

Incredulous, Sabine simply stared at Jules, her beautiful silver eyes holding his gaze. Her pretty lips were slightly parted; her breaths had quickened.

"I didn't know anyone's eyes could bulge like that," Agnes exclaimed. Another fit of mirth gripped the two.

A smile tugged at the corners of Jules's mouth as Cyr's distraught face came to mind. But he held it back. Though seeing Cyr's reaction was humorous, he wasn't going to celebrate with these people. He wasn't one of them.

They were as dishonest as Cyr.

He was determined to maintain distance, not to mention command with this lot.

The witch beamed. "You're definitely my least-despised Aristo!"

Olivier walked up to Jules and placed a hand on his shoulder.

"You've done a fine thing here today, son." He smiled warmly. "And since you're in a generous mood, I don't suppose you'd see fit to return my violin?"

He'd taken the damn thing away yesterday. The man's relentless playing drove him mad.

Jules glanced down at Olivier's hand on his person then met his gaze and lifted a brow.

Olivier's smile dissolved. He immediately removed his hand. "Sorry."

Jules sheathed his sword, his side feeling like it was ready to split in two. "No, I am not in a generous mood, and no, you may not have your violin. Your debt hasn't been canceled. It's been transferred. To me." His words vanquished the joviality of the group.

Jules turned and made his way to his room, feeling no satisfaction from killing the joy. In fact, to his surprise, he disliked the sudden sobering.

* * *

Sabine knocked on the door and entered her room.

She found Jules seated on the edge of the bed, baldric and shirt off. Down on his haunches before him, Raymond worked on the knot in the binding.

The sight of Jules's beautiful chest had its usual carnal impact on her senses. Her body warmed and she felt that familiar quickening low in her belly that he alone inspired. She missed having his solid strong body pressed against her, the feel of his skin.

She missed him, more than she could ever admit.

Jules met her gaze. His jaw tightened. "Well, at least you knocked this time. I suppose that's an improvement." He looked tired and no doubt his injury was causing him great discomfort. She should be rejoicing over his suffering.

But the truth was—her only joy had come from being in his arms. He'd surprised her on many levels during that time together. Just as he'd surprised her with Cyr.

She stopped before him and folded her hands. "May I have a private word with you?"

He studied her silently.

"Please," she added, her tone free of the sarcasm or biting edge she'd adopted around him. A tone she disliked. In fact, she was tired of the arguments altogether.

She didn't want to spar with him anymore.

Since returning to her staid existence, she found herself wishing more and more that she could recapture the bliss she'd known as Elise. In the dead of night, lying on her cot, knowing he was nearby, she couldn't seem to kill the longing. Or the memories of the time they shared. Day by day, the longing only got stronger. She ached to touch him. She ached for his kiss, his body inside hers.

She longed for the magic he possessed.

He was the only one who had the power to make the sorrow disappear and infuse her with joy.

As he gazed up at her, there was no trace of pleasure in his eyes over her presence—as there had been for Elise. She grieved the loss of that look, and his smile.

He gave Raymond a nod, dismissing him.

Raymond left and closed the door.

"All right. We are alone. What is it?" he said as he tried to untie the knot in his binding.

"I want to thank you for what you did. For stopping Cyr."

"I didn't do it for you. My motives were strictly personal. Damn this knot . . ."

She knelt before him, brushed his hands away, and went to work on the knot. "I know. But you have removed my family from imminent danger. And for that I am grateful." She untied the binding and unwound it.

Freed from the restraint around his chest, Jules took in breath and was instantly frustrated that it gave him only mild relief.

Slowly, he lay back and closed his eyes. "I've told you, you owe me now—the silver and the debt." His side throbbed painfully. He cursed his own stupidity at thinking with his cock. He'd never be suffering like this if he hadn't bedded Sabine Laurent.

Jules felt a gentle swipe and slick coolness against his skin. He snapped open his eyes. Looking down at his injured ribs, he saw that she'd applied the balm on it.

"Merde!" He grabbed her wrist, stopping her from dipping her fingers back into the bowl she held and applying more.

"This will help," she assured calmly.

"How? By killing me?"

"Don't be absurd. You saw me use it on myself. If you want, I can do so again—"

"No!" Good Lord. Anything but *that*.

"Then lie back and relax. It *will* begin to soothe and you'll feel better."

Dieu, she was right. Already the throbbing was easing and there was a warm tingling sensation where she'd spread the balm.

He reclined against the pillows, relishing the first moment of real relief he'd known in weeks. If the balm was truly tainted, he didn't care. Basking in its blessed effect, he released her wrist.

"It feels rather pleasant, doesn't it?" She smiled and lightly spread more over his tortured side.

The balm felt incredible, but so did the soft caressing strokes of her hand. Watching her at her task, he caught her eye. She blushed slightly and returned her focus to his ribs.

Her pulse was racing. He could see its rapid beat in her neck. Her breathing had quickened, too. He was affecting her. Touching him was inflaming her. The realization stiffened his cock. He closed his eyes briefly. *Jésus-Christ* . . . He was going to start panting like a dog if she kept this up. But what she was doing felt so good.

He didn't want her to stop. Ever.

"I'm . . . I'm sorry you were injured this way," she said. He was surprised by the apology and the tone. She spoke as sweetly as she had in bed, freshly sated from an intense release. Her cheeks were pink, and he watched as she bit down on that lush bottom lip. He was gripped with a powerful urge to pull her close and do the very same thing to that lush lip. "I only did what I did to help my family."

He wasn't going to fall for this again. Not the gentle tones. Or the empty amiable words. He'd heard them before. In the forest when she stirred his compassion and he'd agreed to take her to her "cousin."

This was merely a ploy to lower his guard.

"There," she said and placed the wooden bowl back on the nearby table. "Now we are even. Your actions allowed me to breathe easier, and I've returned the favor."

She rose with a small smile gracing her mouth. He caught her wrist and pulled her down, bringing her face close to his.

Intent on making matters very clear, he said, "We are not even. You *owe* me. And you'd better pray my men recover everything you took. I don't believe a thing that comes out of that pretty mouth. Nor do I think for a moment you've given up on stealing the silver," he growled. "That silver is going to aid my family. I won't permit anyone to come between me and my responsibility. My family's honor means everything. Your family means nothing." He released her wrist.

He was expecting the usual anger to flare in her eyes. Instead he saw something akin to hurt, and to his astonishment—*sadness*—in their silvery depths. She smoothed her hands down her apron, turned on her heel, and left the room, quietly closing the door behind her.

Worse, and even more maddening, she left him with an irritating sense of regret over his biting words.

* * *

Two days later, Jules felt better than ever, thanks to the balm. He could move about and even dress himself without the level of agony he'd suffered before.

Lying in bed, he was caught up in the vivid passages of Sabine's journal. He should stop reading the thing altogether but he couldn't seem to. Her writing was engaging. She was witty, intelligent, and her soulful thoughts often stirring. Definitely absorbing.

Little by little the entries became less whimsical, the ugly unrest of the *Fronde* slowly pervading the journal as she described the events that led to the downfall of the theater.

He read through more entries until at last he came to:

Father says we must leave Paris. I feared this day would come. Starvation on the streets is rampant. The people have stormed the King's palace. There is violence everywhere. As our beloved city is rocked by riots, as the number of patrons attending the performances has dwindled down to nothing, Father consoles himself with Madame de Riston. Louise weeps over it. Isabelle and I feel helpless. It is the worst feeling imaginable.

Do you know what it's like to lose everything you've ever identified with?

That last sentence resonated in his soul. He understood all too well the horror of it.

Will I ever see my Dark Prince again? How I wish he could save me from this fate. I don't wish to leave! Isabelle and I were to be introduced to society this year. I have dreamed of it for so long. The nobles have ruined everything! I hate them! I know my Dark Prince is different. He outshines them all. I must hold on to my belief, with the greatest of faith, that we will be together. Somehow, someway, fate will intervene and we will meet—just as we are meant to. And it will be no ordinary meeting. It will be unforgettable. It will be extraordinary . . .

The nickering of horses snared his attention. It was followed by a flurry of activity in the common room outside his door.

He sat up in bed with only moderate pain and stuffed the journal under his pillow.

"Sabine, the Baron de Lor is here!" he heard Louise exclaim. "Change into something more suitable. Hurry!"

The Baron de Lor? *Vit is here?* Why would Louise want Sabine to impress Vit? Jules hadn't seen him in five long years. Sébastien de Vittry was the last person Jules thought would have abandoned him. They'd been the closest of friends. But he had. Just like all the others.

Why on earth was he here?

Jules snatched open the door and stalked out of the house.

Leon de Vittry, Sébastien's younger brother, alighted from the carriage. Jules arrested his steps. Where was Sébastien?

The driver climbed down along with the servants he'd brought with him, but no one other than Leon had exited from the interior of the carriage.

If this was the Baron de Lor, then it meant Sébastien was . . . *dead*? Unlike his brother, who had only been an acquaintance of Paul Laurent, Leon had had a passion for the theater and a solid friendship with the playwright. For years.

Leon immediately moved past the small gathering, straight to Sabine and kissed her hand. The wind tousled his dark hair. His dark eyes fixed on the woman before him, to the exclusion of the others standing nearby.

Words from Sabine's journal suddenly raced though Jules's mind.

. . . with hair and eyes so dark . . .

Had the Dark Prince just arrived?

18

"I came as soon as I heard about your father," Leon said. "I simply cannot believe he's gone." Eyes glistening with sorrow, he drew Sabine gently into his arms. "My deepest condolences for your tragic loss."

"Thank you," she murmured.

Leon was the only one who'd continued to visit after they'd left Paris. And he was yet another man she was indebted to.

Thanks to her father's attempts to reclaim his prior fame.

She hadn't discovered the loan until after his death. He'd borrowed a staggering sum from Leon. And squandered it away during his many trips to Paris.

Leon stepped back. He was not as broad-shouldered, not as devastatingly handsome as Jules, but he did have features that were definitely appealing. Looking into his dark brown eyes, she was embarrassed by her inability to repay him; she had no idea when—or even how—she'd settle the sizable debt. It was this very reason she'd postponed advising Leon of her father's passing. It was this very reason she couldn't ask for more, despite their need.

Once, not long ago, she'd greeted Leon wearing lovely gowns, in her family's stately townhouse. Not in drab clothing and wooden clogs on a bleak farm.

Leon placed a soft kiss against her forehead. "Everything will be all right," he assured her in a whisper. "Louise." Leon turned to her and kissed her hand. "My heartfelt condolences to you as well. To you, too, Olivier." He placed a hand on the older man's shoulder. "Paul Laurent was a great man. I've come to pay him honor in a way that is befitting to his character. He always loved joviality. I've brought food and wine, and we will have a fête in his memory, just as he would have wanted!"

A delighted cry rose from her family. His gesture moved her. How she wished her heart held romantic feelings for this man. It would be far better than the sentiment and esteem she'd misplaced on her Dark Prince.

"Olivier," Leon said. "I expect to hear some music from his great composer. Now I know the pianoforte has been sold, but please tell me you still have your violin."

"No, he does not," Jules responded, Raymond at his side.

Leon's head snapped up. His eyes widened. "Jules de Moutier?" He approached and stopped before Jules's taller form. "Why, this is a surprise!" He smiled, and placed his hands on Jules's shoulders. "I'm overjoyed to see you alive and well!"

Grasping his wrists, Jules removed Leon's hands. "Where is your brother?"

Leon was clearly taken aback by Jules's action and curt tone. Having never witnessed Leon lose his temper, Sabine wasn't surprised when he responded calmly, "You haven't heard, then?"

"Heard what?"

"Sébastien died. Three years ago."

"*Died?* He was young. Strong. *Jésus-Christ*, my age. How did he die?"

"He'd been ill off and on for months. His stomach ailments worsened. Fever took him and . . . I lost my brother. For what it's worth, he was most distraught over what happened to you and your family. He tried to see you many times during your detainment in prison, but could not get past the guards. On his deathbed he asked for you. I had no idea where to search."

Grief tightened in Jules's chest. He was suddenly ashamed of the resentment he'd harbored. He'd felt betrayed and furious at Vit for turning his back on him. And he hadn't at all. He'd rather be angry with him still, than know Vit was gone for good. He hadn't even been there at his bedside when his closest friend was dying.

"I'm sorry . . ." Jules said, somehow managing to force the words up his constricted throat.

"Thank you. So am I. I miss him."

Jules looked across the field. "So do I."

"Well, then, why don't we have our fête in honor of Sébastien and Paul."

"Excellent idea!" Olivier rubbed his hands together as he watched the parade of food being brought into the house by the servants.

Leon smiled. "Now, where did you say your violin is, Olivier?"

Olivier's grin died and he glanced at Jules. "Monsieur de Moutier has it."

All eyes turned to Jules. He cleared his throat, hoping his voice didn't betray the depth of his devastation. "Raymond."

"Commander?"

"Get him his violin." Needing a moment, Jules turned and strode toward the house.

* * *

"What is it, Sabine?" Leon asked as they stood at the side of the house. In the distance, Olivier played with great fervor. The delicious smell of roasted meats sweetening the air seduced her stomach. Jules was still in the house, and Raymond had just returned inside. This was an opportune time for a private word with Leon.

Though this wasn't the sort of conversation she wanted to have, she'd no choice. She was obliged. "I wanted to talk to you about . . . the loan."

He looked down. "Oh. That."

"My father borrowed a vast sum, and I want you to know I will pay it back. Somehow, I'll find a way . . . It's just that things are rather difficult here—"

Leon placed his fingers over her lips to still them. "Sabine, it grieves me that you learned of it. I had no intention of ever bringing the matter up. As far as I'm concerned, the debt died with your father. I'll not take a single coin from you."

Her eyes widened. She removed his hand. "No, Leon, it's only right that I pay it back."

"No, it isn't. It was a matter between your father and me. The loan is forgiven."

Tears stung her eyes. "Leon, are you certain . . . ?"

"I am. I refuse to take any funds from you."

Feeling a tremendous weight lifted from her shoulders, she flung her arms around him. "Thank you!"

He chuckled. "I must say, I like your gratitude."

She gazed up at him, unable to stop smiling.

He glanced at her mouth, his smile slowly fading. "Sabine . . ." He lowered his head.

Her arms dropped from his shoulders, and she looked away, a purely reflexive reaction that stunned her. She'd never refused his kiss before.

Leon cupped her cheeks and turned her face to his. "I'm sorry. I shouldn't have done that. Especially under the circumstances. That was completely inappropriate. Please forgive me." He kissed the tip of her nose. This was exactly the sort of man she should *want* a kiss from—handsome, decent, and thoughtful. Why didn't he stir her as ardently as . . . She arrested that thought.

"Isn't this touching, Raymond?" Jules's voice startled her. She jumped back away from Leon and spun around.

Jules leaned casually against the wall, arms crossed. Ever-loyal Raymond flanked him.

"Very, Commander." Raymond's tone was flat.

Leon muttered an oath. "Moutier, your timing and manners leave something to be desired."

"Really?" Jules shrugged. "I thought they were perfect. Raymond, escort Sabine back to the celebration. I want a word with the Baron." Raymond moved toward her.

Leon stepped in front of her. "Sabine and I are in the middle of a conversation."

"A *conversation*? Interesting choice of words."

Sabine saw Leon's body stiffen. "I know your years in social exile have probably taken their toll on you, but you have been abrasive and rude. By what authority do you command anyone here? And what, for that matter, are you bloody well doing here in the first place?"

Sabine flinched at the fury in Leon's tone. Peeking around him, she saw Jules place a hand on the hilt of his sword. Her stomach dropped.

"This is my authority," Jules advised. "As to what I'm doing here, that is none of your concern. Don't inject yourself into what doesn't involve you."

Sabine's heart rapped wildly. Though dueling was illegal, that didn't stop men in the upper class. Certain as to who the victor would be, the last thing she wanted to see was Leon injured—mortally or otherwise.

She stepped around him. "It's all right, Leon."

"It is not all right. Why is he here, Sabine? Why does he order you about?"

"He does *not* order me about." She moved to Jules. Only when she stood close to him could she sense the full extent of his fury. Anger emanated from him in waves. Why was he *this* angry? "There will be no dueling," she said to Jules.

He dragged his gaze away from Leon. "If he does not provoke one, there'll be no trouble."

She turned to Leon. "Please, I ask you to keep your head, when he"—she glared at Jules—"cannot."

Leon gave a nod. "You have my word. I'll not cause you distress."

"Thank you. I know I can always count on you, dear Leon." She smiled.

Leon offered his smile in return.

Every soft sentence she uttered, every demonstration of affection exchanged, boiled Jules's blood. Feelings of possessiveness were foreign to him. It infuriated him further that not only was he feeling them now, but for a woman who was unworthy of any heightened interest.

The moment she rounded the corner with Raymond, Jules said, "You have an interesting way of offering your condolences, Baron."

"Sabine and I have known each other for many years. We have a deep affection for each other. I've watched her grow into the beautiful woman she is today. Don't tell me you haven't noticed her physical appeal?"

"I've noticed," Jules remarked, muscles taut.

"Yes, well there is more to her than just her comeliness. She also has wonderful wit and charm."

Other than her journal entries, Jules had never been exposed to either. *Elise* had delighted him with both. But she was a lie.

"But Sabine is an innocent," Leon said. "I've kept my distance."

Jules narrowed his eyes. He wanted to slam his fist into Leon's lying face. "Baron, I have over the 'years in social exile' developed a certain oversensitivity to lies. You have *not* kept your distance. There's been amorous contact between you in the past as well as the present. And, we both know you want more of the same."

"Sabine is aware of my attraction to her. What of it?"

"So you came to console her by coaxing her into your bed." It was a statement. Not a question.

"It isn't like that. My sympathies are genuine."

"So is your interest in fucking her."

It was Leon's turn to narrow his eyes. "Not that I owe you any explanations, but I sincerely want to save her from wasting away on this farm. She was born for greater things than this."

Jules crossed his arms. "You came to propose marriage?" His comment was purposely flippant.

"We both know that's impossible. Though a finer wife no man could have, no one in my family would ever sign a marriage contract between us. She's impoverished, with no noble blood to speak of."

"Then, you do intend to make her your mistress. Paul Laurent was indeed a fortunate man to have a friend like you. Here he's not yet cold in his grave and you're already sniffing around his daughter's skirts. Curious, did you make your intention to 'save her from wasting away on this farm' known to him when he was alive?"

"You are making me out to be some kind of roué. You know it's a far better option than what she faces here."

Jules hated it that Leon was right. It was an offer she might very well accept. Especially if, indeed, Leon was her precious Dark Prince.

"I'll ask her when the time is right," Leon said. "I'll ensure that she lives in a lifestyle befitting a lady. Why should any of this matter to you?" He studied Jules briefly. "You want her, don't you?" Leon sauntered over to him. "Leave her be. She wouldn't hold your interest for long. Your mistresses never do. She doesn't need a man who'll grow bored and discard her."

That was just it. She had held his interest from the moment he'd laid eyes on her. And he wanted it to end.

Jules stalked away.

He wanted to stop having erotic dreams of her every night as he slept in her bed. He wanted to forget the intensity of their past sexual encounters and the connection they'd made. *Merde*, he wanted to stop obsessing over her journal and snap this fascination he had with her and the identity of the Dark Prince.

He marched up to her as she stood listening to Olivier's music and clapping along with the rest of her family. Wrapping his fingers around her arm, he said in her ear, "We need to talk." Her soft blond hair tickled his nose.

Without giving her a chance to protest, he walked toward the house with purposeful strides, and her in tow.

He didn't stop until he reached his room. Shutting the door, he pressed her up against it. Her eyes widened.

He pressed his palms against the wooden barrier on either side of her head. "I'm going to ask you some questions, and I want the truth for a change. *Do you hear me?*"

She lifted her chin a notch. "Of course, *my lord*. Say it any louder and they'll hear you in England." She tossed his earlier words back at him.

He took a deep breath, striving for patience. Lord knows she tested it in the extreme.

"Who is the Dark Prince?" he asked.

Color infused her cheeks, and her breath caught in her throat. Her gaze darted to the windowsill then back to him. "You found my journals? And *read them*? How could you? They were private. You had no right!"

"Who is he?" he insisted.

"You have no decency?"

"Answer me."

"If you've read them, then you know the answer. Why ask?"

"I've read some, and I want to know here and now: Who is the Aristo? Who's the Dark Prince?"

He waited, willing her to say "Leon," praying it would kill his fascination for good.

She looked down. For a moment, he thought she'd refuse to answer. But then those gorgeous silvery eyes swept up and met his gaze.

"You."

He jerked back. *"Me?"*

"Don't let it swell your arrogant head. I was young. And I erred in the name. I shouldn't have called you 'the Dark Prince.' 'The Prince of Darkness' suits you better."

Jules was too stunned to be angered by her remark. "But . . . you wrote that we met once. Outside the theater. Something about *a glass slipper*?"

She laughed without mirth. "I'm not surprised you don't remember. Why would someone of your exalted station remember such an insignificant occurrence?"

But it hadn't been insignificant to her. It had been of great importance. A cherished moment she'd referred to repeatedly in her journal.

She often said he noticed no one outside his class. For the most part that was true. But *Dieu* . . . how could he have utterly missed a pretty girl who'd watched his every move with such touching adoration?

He scrubbed a hand over his face. "I don't know what to say." *Jésus-Christ*. It was truly him. This shed a whole new light on what had transpired between them. His thoughts were spinning.

"Don't say anything. Things are very different now. I don't feel that way about you any longer. I was mistaken about your character."

Oh, no. She wasn't going to resort to her usual ploys. She was trying to anger him. To distract him and distance herself from this revelation. He couldn't understand it, but knowing he was the Dark Prince actually . . . *pleased him*. His lips twitched as he fought back a smile. A lot.

His lovely little schemer was about to be deliciously cornered.

He wasn't going to let her squirm her way out of this one.

She was going to own up to some tantalizing truths. Those sweet caresses she gave him on the back of his neck every time he took her had just taken on a whole new meaning. Caresses he was sure she wasn't even aware she gave.

Sabine was mortified.

No one had ever read her journals. Not even Isabelle. He'd read her emotional outpouring. Knew how she'd felt about him. Her silly girlhood dreams.

Pressing his palms against the door again, he leaned his powerful body toward her.

Awareness rippled through her.

"Just because we had sex doesn't mean you know me or my character," he said.

She wished he'd step back. His proximity incited her senses. Just having him this near made her heart race and her nipples tighten. "I knew about your poor character long before that."

He lifted a skeptical brow. "Really? Isn't it interesting that you showed a man of 'poor character' such heated enthusiasm in bed?"

The heat in her cheeks crept down her neck. "It was all part of my plan to take the silver. I had to maintain your interest . . ."

He captured her chin and caressed her cheek lightly with his thumb. Hot tingles radiated from his touch. "I gave you a choice at the inn," he said. "We could have had our meal downstairs in the common room, which, given your plan, would have ended matters between us much sooner. But instead you chose to prolong our time together. You let me take you upstairs, strip the clothes off your body, and fuck you twice more."

Oh, God. "My family awaits me." She made to leave.

"Not so fast." He gripped her shoulders and held her in place. "Some honesty from you is long overdue."

"Don't let your arrogance delude your thinking," she said, hoping her voice sounded strong. "That you're the Dark Prince is irrelevant. I told you before—I enjoy your carnal talents. I decided to indulge."

He gave a short laugh. "You've not had enough sexual experience to be that nonchalant. I've read enough of your journal to know that, deep inside, you're a romantic."

She didn't know what she hated more, having her family accuse her of being too practical, or having Jules, privy to her fanciful ramblings, discover otherwise.

"I've changed," she insisted, desperate to regain the ground she'd lost. Though, even to her own ears, her remark lacked conviction.

"Is that so?" Resting a palm against the door, he slipped one of her tresses between the fingers of his other hand and played with a strand of her hair. "That first night in the forest, I asked you to name your pleasure, whatever sexual indulgence you wanted. Do you remember what you asked for?"

Yes. "No."

A devilish gleam entered his eyes. "A kiss . . . '*Oh, heaven would be a kiss from his lips*,' " he recited. " '*Nothing on this side of the stars would be finer.*' " Recognizing her words from her journal, she cringed. "You wrote that. You wanted that from the Dark Prince. I had you multiple times, Sabine. Each time you were keen, impassioned, highly responsive, and surrendered completely. You got caught up in your own game and fantasy." He dipped his head and whispered in her ear, "Admit it." Her belly fluttered.

She'd sooner cut out her own tongue before she'd admit to that.

He brushed his lips over that tantalizing spot under her ear. She gasped. Her sex answered with a warm gush. "I don't believe I've ever heard you this quiet." She could hear the smile in his tone. He was thoroughly enjoying this. Both the truth about the Dark Prince and her weakness for him. Damn her for the untamable desire she had for this man. "We both know you've kissed Leon, likely on more than one occasion. For a woman who claims she dislikes nobles, it's curious how you've only engaged in amorous encounters with highborn men."

He straightened. Softly panting, she forced herself to meet his eyes, so dark and devastating.

He smiled, looking smug.

She wanted to wipe that smile from his face, but couldn't muster a defense. She wasn't about to admit she'd only kissed Leon to forget "the Dark Prince."

He replaced both palms against the door and angled his head.

With his mouth so near, his breath warmed her lips. She felt its heat flow through her veins.

Caught between the wood door and his hard body, she was as trapped as she was transfixed, acutely aware of the mortifying hunger, all the signs of her feminine weakness to his masculine appeal.

"Poor *Leon*. He doesn't stand a chance at ever having you, does he?" Slowly, he lowered his mouth. Anticipating a kiss, her heart skipped a beat. But he stopped short. "And you are definitely worth having."

He skimmed his lips across hers, sending her thoughts scattering and her body rioting for more. His hot mouth was again pressed to the sensitive spot below her ear. Lightly, he drew on her neck. She closed her eyes and bit back her moan. Liquid heat pooled between her legs. *Damn him*. He had the upper hand and he knew it. She couldn't locate the will in her bereft body to stop him. Not when he was creating the most delicious sensations with his expert mouth. Not when she grew more and more desperate for him.

The pulsing between her legs was a terrible distraction, her body too attuned to this man, reacting to every little thing he did.

He burned a path to her jaw and up to the corner of her mouth. Her lips parted once more, needing to be kissed. Yet he still denied her.

"Did I fulfill your fantasy, *chère*? Did I live up to your expectations of the Dark Prince?"

More than she could ever comfortably admit.

"Tell me, pretty forest fairy, do you ever think about our time together? Do you ever lie in bed and remember the feel of my hands and mouth on your body? The feel of me inside you?"

Her breaths quick, ragged, shallow, she couldn't push words—another lie—up her throat.

One of his irresistible smiles appeared on his face, beautiful dimples and all. "This is a novelty. I don't think I've ever seen fiery

Sabine Laurent so quiet. Do I take your silence to mean you want me to answer for you?"

No, say something. But she couldn't think beyond the tormenting need throbbing through her feminine sex. She could barely contain the urge to reach for him.

"Very well, Sabine." He cupped her breast. His thumb was so close to her beaded nipple. Her body railed. She wanted him to stroke it with shocking desperation. "I believe you think about it, though you don't wish to. We made a strong carnal connection. The sex was intense and very good. You wanted me to fuck you. So much so, you kept coming back for more. In fact, you want to be taken right now, don't you, Sabine?"

He grazed his thumb across her nipple. She sucked in a sharp breath. But she didn't push his hand away. And he noted it.

"You don't despise me as much as you say you do, *chère.*" He repeated the stroke over the sensitive tip. A soft whimper quivered up her throat. "What you dislike is the desire you feel for me. You don't know what to do about it . . . Shall I refresh your memory?" He leaned in and licked her bottom lip. His thumb flicked her sensitized nipple. Her knees almost gave out. "Shall I give you what your body is begging for?"

Dear God . . .

He gently pinched her nipple. With a cry, she lurched forward, sealing her lips to his with a moan, long and low, a sound she couldn't hold back.

Snaking an arm around her waist, he hauled her up against him. Delving a hand into her hair at the back of her skull, he kissed her with savage hunger. She matched his fervor. She had no idea why she came to life whenever he touched her, but she reveled in it, in the feel of his beautiful body against hers, in his firm embrace, in his delectable taste.

She tangled her fingers in his hair and kissed him harder, vanquishing all reason, the kiss demanding, ravenous. Their tongues parried, the effect a heady rush.

She matched his intensity stroke for stroke. Her fever mounting by the moment. She feasted on his mouth as if he were her only nourishment in days. *Weeks* was more accurate. That's how long it had been since he'd fed her senses this way.

She arched into him, the pull so strong, pressing herself against his stiffened sex.

He growled with approval, slid his hands down her back, and gripping her bottom, ground her against him. Her delight erupted from her throat.

It wasn't enough. She needed more.

She needed skin—his against hers. She needed his hands touching her, touching all the places on her body that ached for him. She needed the fulfillment she knew he could give.

She needed *him*. Now.

Sliding her hands down his solid back to his waist, she fisted his shirt.

He stopped, his mouth suddenly gone.

Her eyes flew open. She was panting, bewildered. Her body beseeching.

He was frowning, staring at the door behind her. With a low growl, he let his arms drop, releasing her from his embrace.

No. *Why?*

Then she heard it. Pounding. Only it wasn't from her wild heart. It came from the other side of the wooden barrier.

"Commander?" It was Raymond.

Jules took in a deep breath and let it out slowly. "What is it?" he demanded.

"Your brother has arrived with a team of men."

* * *

"What the devil is going on?" Luc de Moutier asked, standing in the common room of the Laurent home. Though he was of similar build and height to Jules, that's where the similarities ended. Luc's blond hair and light green eyes were a sharp contrast to Jules's dark coloring.

Luc was damned sensitive about it, especially since he had a father he bore no physical resemblance to. Anyone who dared to mention it soon found himself at the sharp end of Luc's sword on a dueling field. Most treaded lightly around this hotheaded younger brother. Jules had defused many a situation. The irony was that it was now Jules who was quick to storm, and Luc who quelled him.

"What is this I hear about you being injured, about Paul Laurent's daughter—who the hell knew he had one—and a generous capture lost—"

"Paul Laurent had twin daughters, and I have men working on finding the silver. It will be recaptured soon. We will proceed as planned. This nightmare is going to end for us." The sooner the better.

Luc shook his head. "Well, at least you don't look terribly injured, so I'll take solace in that. I don't suppose you want to explain what Vittry is doing outside?"

"He and Laurent were friends. He's well acquainted with the theater troupe." *And he's eager to better acquaint himself with Sabine's lush form.* The possessive emotions that single thought incited stunned him. In fact, he couldn't stomach the notion of Vittry's hands on her. Especially now that he knew he was the Dark Prince. The endearing words from her journal had swirled through his head the entire time he'd been kissing her. And when she—unknowingly—began her usual tender caresses on the back of his neck, it inspired soft sentiments, the likes of which he'd never experienced during a carnal encounter. "He's the Baron de Lor now. Sébastien . . . died three years ago." It felt terrible to say. It felt even worse that Sébastien was gone for good.

"*Dieu*, I'm sorry, Jules." Luc placed his hand on his older brother's shoulder. "It's been one astonishing revelation after another. Nothing makes any sense."

"What are you rambling about?"

"I encountered Corrine d'Autmarre in Clouquet while I was waiting for you."

"Corrine? Your former favorite?"

"Yes. She insisted I return with her to her château. She said she had something she wanted to give me."

"No doubt."

A smile tugged at the corner of Luc's mouth. "*In addition* to several hours of erotic bliss, she gave me a letter." Luc pulled it out of his doublet. "It was inside a trunk of my personal belongings she'd been storing since the arrest years ago. The trunk came from my ship. It was sent to her by her brother, Thomas, Baron de Brimot. He was formally under my command. After the arrest, I was never able to return to the vessel to collect my things. Brimot sent the trunk to his sister knowing it would eventually be returned to me." He held out the letter. "Take a look."

Jules took it, noting it had their family seal pressed into the wax. "Is it from Father?"

"I thought so, too, when I first saw the seal. I thought perhaps it was something he'd written before his arrest, or soon after. It's undated, unsigned, and *not* from him."

Jules unfolded it.

Luc, Monsieur de Moutier,

What I am about to divulge is no hoax. Your father and your family are in great danger. You must take measures to protect the Marquis and yourselves. Trust no one. There is a conspiracy afoot. I will reveal more when I can. Until then, God be with you.

"What do you think, Jules? Who could have written it?"

Jules's heart raced. In his hands was tangible proof of what he'd believed for years: Someone had intended to do his family harm, resulting in his father being falsely and deliberately condemned because of it.

The author of the letter knew information—the author whose penmanship had a distinct flourish.

He'd seen this handwriting before. And he knew where.

19

Jules ran outside the moment he heard shouts from Raymond, Luc on his heels.

The sight before him arrested his steps.

A caravan of carts accompanied by thirty men on horseback neared. He spotted Marc and Fabrice, and then to his amazement, his commander, privateer Captain Simon Boulenger. Judging by the blood and dirt smearing their faces and encrusted in their garments, there had been trouble.

Out of the corner of his eye Jules saw Sabine gather together with her family and Vittry. The women's mounting anxiety was palpable as everyone scanned the men looking for Vincent the actor and Sabine's cousins, Robert and Gerard.

Jules spotted them just then, slumped in one of the carts, looking gray-faced and battle-sullied. Knowing Sabine and the others were likely to race toward the carts at any moment, Jules strode forward barking out orders. "Raymond, keep everyone back. Luc, order your men to help, then come with me."

When Jules reached the caravan, it halted.

"What happened?" Jules demanded the moment Simon, Marc, and Fabrice dismounted and approached.

"We had some trouble, Commander," Marc advised.

"And the silver?"

"Recaptured—with but a small portion missing. The majority of it remains intact in the two chests."

Relief rushed through Jules.

"Thank God," Luc murmured beside him.

"What sort of trouble did you meet?" Jules indicated the injured men with a nod of his head. "A band of vagabonds?"

Simon shook his head. "No. Not these men. They were well armed with quality weapons and horses."

"It was an ambush, Commander. Well planned," said Marc. "Had the captain not arrived when he did, it would have been an easy slaughter. We were outnumbered three to one. They specifically demanded you and the silver. They clearly knew we would be on the road from Paris with the chests."

"Merde, how?"

Marc smiled. "We don't know how, but we do know who."

"Go on," Jules pressed.

"Once the captain and his men arrived, we decimated the attackers. By the end, two were left barely clinging to life. They were questioned separately and both gave the same name before they died. The man who ordered the attack is the Archbishop de Divonne."

"The Archbishop de Divonne?" Luc repeated the name incredulously. "Our father considered him a friend."

Jésus-Christ. "I think we should consider him to be his betrayer. Who better than someone in his inner circle?" Jules said, his fury burbling in his blood.

Simon nodded. "With the wealth you've been amassing, he must have feared you'd soon regain your rank and title. His fear was strong enough to want you dead."

Jules had spent years racking his mind, agonizing over every possible traitor, considering everyone his father had ever known. During his months of incarceration it was all he had to occupy him, to torment him.

It had become his obsession.

His private torture.

Forbidden to reenter Paris once he'd been released, refused admittance to country châteaus he'd once been welcomed in, it had been impossible to learn the truth. The only one who'd been remotely willing to communicate with him was his father's friend Valentin, Marquis d'Argon. More out of a sense of obligation to Jules's father's memory than anything else, his notes were sparse, always apologetic for not being able to do more, and clearly unwilling to do anything to rectify Jules and Luc's situation. The Marquis was fearful of jeopardizing his privileged status. He didn't want to do anything that might inspire disfavor from the Crown.

Now Jules had the name—the Archbishop de Divonne—but not the reason. Luc's letter had mentioned a conspiracy. Who were his accomplices?

Hungry for revenge, every fiber in Jules being rioted for action, burning with the urge to ride out immediately and pay a long-overdue visit to the Archbishop.

"If he wants you dead, then he wants me dead, too," Luc surmised, frowning.

Jules turned to his younger brother. "You may have avoided an attack, as you and your men were not in Clouquet, as expected."

"True. My little detour may have spared us. I must remember to thank Corrine for more reasons than one."

"Commander, if the Archbishop knew our stolen silver would be returning from Paris, do you think he was the one who took the silver the mademoiselle buried?" Marc asked.

"I do." *Dieu*, Sabine could have been attacked and killed. His stomach tightened at the thought. He was thankful that she'd buried the treasure instead of keeping it in her home.

Luc's green eyes were aglow with lethal intent. "What do you wish to do?"

Jules smiled without mirth. "We will do what we are most proficient at. What we have spent years doing at sea. The Archbishop will have a visit like none he's ever known."

But first he was going to have a conversation with a spirited blond woman about the letter that was tucked inside his doublet.

* * *

Sabine fumed as she followed Raymond into the common room. Summoned by Jules and refused access to her cousins, she had a few choice words to direct at Raymond's master.

Raymond chose that moment to step aside, out of her line of sight.

It was then she saw that Jules was flanked by his brother and Simon. The angry words scorching her tongue dissolved when she found herself standing mere feet away from Luc de Moutier.

An ache welled up and pressed against her heart as thoughts of her sister rushed to mind. How utterly giddy Isabelle would have been to see the object of her long-held affection standing in her home.

Seeing Luc made her want to run back to her family all the more. She hadn't stopped reeling from her torrid encounter with Jules. Her anger at his highhanded ways combined with her unfed carnal hunger only made her more irritable and frustrated.

She donned a cool expression and gave him a mocking curtsy. "You've summoned me, *my lord-most-high*? Will *my lord* tell me what he wishes from me? Or shall I simply continue to bask in his exalted presence?"

Jules tightened his jaw.

Simon chuckled and sat down. "Oh, this is going to be entertaining."

"Naturally, I would rather be here than attend to my cousins' and Vincent's injuries," Sabine continued, "which is just as well since I have been forbidden to see them. Imagine my joy at having the privilege of breathing the same air as Jules de Moutier, noble-extraordinaire, charmer of women and wielder of a mighty sword." She thrust her fist straight up as if holding a blade.

Simon's mirth erupted from him.

"*This* is the thief?" Luc asked.

"Yes," Jules responded tightly.

Luc rolled his eyes. "I should have guessed she'd be blond."

Jules ignored the grating comment. "This woman's real name is Sabine, Paul Laurent's daughter," Jules continued. "You can ignore her theatrics. She has a flare for the dramatic."

"Really?" Simon grinned. "I think it sounds as though the lady has issue with your 'mighty sword,' Jules." He winked.

It was Luc's turn to laugh.

He placed his hand on Jules's shoulder. "I can assure you that no woman has ever complained about my brother's 'mighty sword,' or his skill at wielding it."

"Enough. Both of you," Jules snapped. "Lower your arm, Sabine, and sit down."

She crossed her arms. "Go to hell, Aristo."

Simon barked out a laugh. "Now those are words every commoner thinks, yet few have the courage to say." Simon stretched out his legs and crossed them at the ankle. "I like her."

Jules set his palms down on the table. "If you don't sit your derrière down on that chair, I'll place it there myself."

She glared at him.

He straightened and walked around the table.

Her heart lurched. She immediately sat, horrified that he'd make good on his threat.

He stopped behind her, and then pushed her chair up to the table. Leaning forward, he set his palms back down on its wooden surface. His body surrounding her caused her nerve endings to quiver with awareness.

"You are going to behave and be most cooperative," he told

her. "In essence, you are going to conduct yourself in a manner completely out of the norm for you." Clearly, at the moment, he was making it easy for her to cling to her ire. "As for your cousins and Vincent, their injuries are minor. My men are questioning them about their little adventure. Consider yourself lucky that I haven't had them flogged."

She gasped and shot him a look over her shoulder, her face now so close to his own. "If you are bent on revenge, then take it out on me. It was *my* idea to take your silver, not theirs."

"Of that I have no doubt. Right now, what I want from you is to look at this." He placed something on the table and straightened. "What do you see?"

She looked down at the creased parchment, the stunning sight hitting her like a physical blow.

Snatching up the letter, she shot to her feet, unable to tear her eyes off the familiar handwriting, its recognizable swirls and strokes. She spun around to face Jules. "This is Isabelle's handwriting! Where did you get this?"

He placed his hands on his hips. "It was sent to Luc."

"When?" Hope bloomed inside her, growing stronger with each hard beat of her heart.

"Years ago. It was sent to his ship, but he only just received it. It would seem Isabelle had learned some rather sinister information. Tell me, how is it possible that she managed to affix our family seal to the letter?" Jules demanded.

His words didn't shatter her optimism. In fact, upon turning the letter over and seeing the seal in question, gooseflesh raced up her arms. The feeling, the one that existed deep inside her heart, the one that told her that her sister was still alive, now roared. It was so strong, she felt giddy.

"My father sent Isabelle to work as one of your servants. She would have had access to the seal. She worked at your country estate Château Serein. It was there, we were told, she perished in a fire in one of the servants' outbuildings. But in my heart, I never believed it." Sabine turned to Luc. "Please, you must help me determine when she could have sent this letter."

Luc glanced at his brother. Jules gave him a nod.

"My ship came in for repairs and supplies in early May of '53. Then, because it would be at least a month before I could set sail again, I went to Clouquet to stay with a friend. I was arrested there in early June."

She spun back around to Jules. "They told us that she . . . that the fire occurred in the middle of May. She wrote this letter afterward. I just know it. I feel it. She's somewhere. Hiding. And I'm going to find her!" She marched up to him. "When you leave, I'm going with you. Together we'll locate her. For a third of the silver, I'll convince Isabelle to help you gain the information you want."

Jules's brows shot up. "A third of the silver?" He gave a harsh laugh. "A third of the silver remains missing, thanks to you. Besides, I already have the name of the man I seek."

"Isabelle has information you need. She can be of great help in clearing your family name. It would be foolish to dismiss the potential aid she might provide. One third of the silver for my sister's information. What say you?"

"I say you bargain without leverage. I don't need to pay you anything."

Raising her chin slightly, she held his gaze steadfast. "I will succeed in finding my sister and lifting my family out of poverty. You either work with me, or I work against you. Before you utter another word, consider this: The last time I was this determined, I lifted your entire capture right out from under your nose and the noses of all your men. What is it worth to you to keep me in your sight? To forge an alliance with me so that I don't interfere with your plans?"

He glowered at her. "I could have you and your lot kept here under guard."

She smiled. "I suppose that's an option. However, should you choose to leave some behind, make no mistake, Aristo, I will outsmart them."

Jules's expression hardened, her words clearly hitting their mark. "Gentlemen, I'd like a private word with Sabine."

Sabine's heart thumped madly as the men left. Anxiously, she awaited his reply. He was not going to deny her what she wanted. If he placed himself between her and her goals, she'd best him, or die trying.

Jules sat down on the edge of the table and returned her regard. Tension thickened the air.

"I admire your tenacity," he said at last. Gone was the tightness in his tone. His response took her by surprise. "You're the one who shoulders the responsibility for your family's well-being. That, *chère*, is something I understand. My *noblesse oblige* is no less burdensome. But we carry the weight of our familial obligations nonetheless. You and I are not so different."

She expected to have to argue, finagle. She hadn't expected to hear him express his understanding. Or . . . *admiration for her efforts?*

"You are struggling to regain your former life," he continued. "I understand that, too. I understand loss. The anguish of it. You lost a sister. I lost a father. Though you may not have cared for him, he was condemned for a crime he didn't commit. After being stripped of his rank and title, he was hanged on a public gibbet. Luc and I were arrested and left to languish in prison for months not knowing our fates. In the end, we lost everything we ever identified with."

Tears gathered in her eyes. Her chest tightened, his words twisting around her heart. Resonating in her soul. She could easily identify with his sense of injustice and depletion.

"I've come to understand why you despise nobles the way you do. Why the subject of taxes is so abhorrent to you. I don't condone Cyr's methods, but understand this: The lower class is made to pay in coin, but nobles are forced to pay in blood. In battle. The funds collected through taxes are used to raise and supply armies. We have a duty to the King." His tone hardened when he added, "A King who is young and foolishly swayed by lies, even though the Moutiers have loyally served the Crown—with swords and sons—for generations."

He rose and approached her. "You may not like nobles, but that is my world. It is everything I am. Where I belong. Where the Moutier name belongs. I will stop at nothing to restore its former prestige. Your loyalty to your family is just as zealous. For that reason, I don't trust you."

She looked up into his handsome face. They *were* alike. She couldn't deny it. They'd both experienced the same kind of pain and shared the same driving determination to reclaim what fate had snatched away.

At the moment, as she gazed into his fathomless eyes, she felt a deep connection with him. Greater than ever before.

Not since Isabelle had anyone understood how she felt inside. Not *truly*. Not unequivocally. Not the way he did. It made her want to sob. It made her want to put her arms around him.

It made her ache.

He'd been humbled. But it didn't break him. And he'd share the ordeal with *her*.

She was deeply moved. Tender emotions flooded her heart and she cautioned herself against them. She had every confidence he'd regain his former elevated status. Before her was the future Marquis de Blainville. Just as unattainable for her as he'd always been. Even when her father had planned to marry his daughters into nobility, he'd never set his aim as high as a Moutier. Much less Charles de Moutier's heir.

The lands and fortune he stood to reclaim would make him one of the richest, most prominent men in the realm. And it would be expected that his wife would have the same exalted pedigree.

"I understand your duty," she croaked, forcing the words past the knot in her throat. "Isabelle *is* alive. All I want is my sister back." Then she could live again. Get through the rest of her life, come what may. "I could help you. I can act, speak different languages, skills that could serve you in your mission. I must speak to the man who you think betrayed your father. I must question him about Isabelle. We can aid each other in fulfilling our goals."

He lifted a brow. "You'd wish to work together with someone who is a *dreaded Aristo*?" There was the barest hint of humor in his eyes and voice.

His gentle teasing drew a small smile from her. "Sometimes you are not so dreaded. Much of the time we spent together in the forest and at the inn, you were . . . charming. Quite wonderful, in fact," she said sincerely.

His brows shot up. "Good Lord, you weren't just speaking *the truth*, were you?" His words and gorgeous smile pulled a laugh out of her.

"Yes, you arrogant man . . . Don't get used to it," she teased back.

Jules caressed his thumb against her soft cheek. "I appreciate your honesty." Reluctantly he released her cheek. "I've decided to take you with me, after all."

Her eyes widened and filled with joy. "Thank you!" She smiled, brilliant and beautiful. Seeing it pleased him more than he ever expected.

He had no choice here really. She was as clever as she was lovely. Leaving her behind under guard definitely wouldn't do. Until he had a confession from the Archbishop and his life and silver back, he couldn't afford any additional complications. He had enough obstacles in his path without adding this sly sweet temptress.

It was best to keep her close and under his watchful eye.

Yet there was another reason for bringing Sabine along. Though he didn't believe Isabelle was still alive, she clearly needed closure. He knew from her journals just how close these twin sisters had been. How much Isabelle meant to Sabine.

It was likely Isabelle was killed in the fire on purpose because she knew too much.

He wanted to put the ghost of Isabelle Laurent to rest, for Sabine's sake.

"You will do as you're asked at all times, and if I think, or remotely suspect, that you're scheming in any way to take the silver . . ."

"I won't! I swear!" she declared.

"Good. Then we have an agreement."

"Not yet."

"Oh?"

"I'll help you gain back what you lost, and you will give back what I lost. You'll help me locate Isabelle, and once your heritage is restored, you'll return the Laurent lands. *All* of the lands that once belonged to my family. And I want you to forgive our debts and provide a modest sum to ease our burdens."

Jules scrutinized her comely face. He chose his words carefully. "I'll help you where your sister is concerned, and *if* you are instrumental in the return of my confiscated lands and title, then I'll return your lands, free and clear, with a sum as compensation for your assistance." That would hopefully keep her from plotting against him.

Her smile reappeared. "Agreed! I'll tell my family to pack—"

"Your *family*? Oh, no. Absolutely not."

"Only Agnes, Vincent, and Louise. I want them there when we find Isabelle. They'll be of great help to you, you'll see."

"I've already sampled their 'help.' "

Stubborn determination formed on her face. "You have your brother. I want some of my family with me. This is not negotiable."

Merde. He disliked *this* situation for its disagreeable familiarity. Moreover, he disliked any situation he was constrained to accept. He wasn't pleased to have any of his thieves accompanying him.

"Well, what is your answer, Aristo? Are we going to be allies or enemies?"

"The witch's potions stay here."

"Fine."

"And all personal effects will be searched before we leave tomorrow morning."

Elation lit her face. "Agreed."

She was looking far too confident for his liking. It was time to tip the scales back in his favor.

"Then I guess we have a bargain finally. My congratulations to you, Sabine. It would seem you've thought of everything. *Except* . . ."

Her delicate brows furrowed slightly. "Except what?"

He lowered his head, stopping just short of touching her enticing lips. "How will you keep your hands off me?"

* * *

Two weeks later, Leon de Vittry sat in the library of his château before the lambent flames crackling in the hearth, swirling his brandy in his goblet. The hour was late. The servants abed. The château was still. Tranquil. A sharp contrast to the storm that brewed inside him.

Tipping back his head, he downed the amber liquid.

Leon glanced up at his grandfather's portrait and took in the old man's pompous stance. The mockery etched across his arrogant features only spiked Leon's ire. He knew that look. Too well. He'd suffered it most of his life. From his kin. From his peers.

Nothing was more wretched than being born the second son.

Living in the shadow of the heir.

Living in the shadow of Sébastien de Vittry.

While the heir apparent had been doted upon and lavished with attention and the finest of everything, Leon had been treated as invisible. Sébastien had carried himself with a superiority and indifference that Leon admired. And despised.

The only thing his brother had ever done for him was to die. Leon smiled. The sounds of agony, the writhing, as Sébastien approached death's door had been as sweet as he'd always imagined they would be.

Sébastien may have had looks and brawn. But Leon had intellect.

And patience.

He'd learned to don a deceiving mask, a benign manner, and consequently had been underestimated—by everyone.

Now he had a title. Wealth. And an impending marriage to a woman he'd have never had as a wife if his brother hadn't been removed from his path.

It wasn't that Leon cared a whit about the stupid woman. What mattered was that he'd forged an alliance with one of the most prominent families in the realm. Even the terms of his marriage contract had been shrewdly negotiated, promising him a sizable dowry—the amount of which he gleefully intended to leak for the benefit of the gossipmongers who used to ridicule and dismiss him as insignificant.

After all he'd endured, he deserved *everything* he had. But there was one thing he still desired.

Leon rose, strode over to the decanter on the side table, and poured himself another ample goblet of his fine brandy.

One thing he'd wanted for a long time, but still didn't have.

Sabine Laurent—Paul Laurent's angelic blond daughter. How many years had he fantasized about having her naked, on her knees. About the brutal markings he'd leave on her flawless skin—his perfect canvas—as he forced her to succumb to the dark delights that pleased him. Nothing gave him more of a euphoric rush than to see the helplessness in a woman's eyes, the heady terror. He wanted Sabine that way, completely under his control.

How many nights had he taken himself in hand and drained his cock thinking about it?

He felt his cock thicken as the images swirled in his mind. He could already hear her delicious cries of agony.

Just when he'd grown tired of fantasizing, just when he thought he'd have to devise a plan to make it a reality, her father had fortuitously died.

And Leon had wasted no time rushing to her.

"Fucking little whore." He whipped his goblet at the wall, gaining little satisfaction when it shattered. All his patience and cajoling had been for naught.

Intending to pay her a visit to offer his "condolences," he'd spotted Sabine and her cousins on a cart that eve. Not knowing where they were heading in the middle of the night, his instincts had urged him to follow her discreetly. What he got in the end was a chest of silver and the shock of his life.

He never imagined he'd see her enter a camp of men. Or be witness to her deflowering.

He couldn't believe she'd tossed her virginity away on Jules de Moutier. A man who wasn't even a *noble* any longer. A man whom *he* outranked. And judging from her mewing and bucking, she loved every minute of it. He supposed he'd always sensed she had the soul of a harlot.

But she was supposed to be *his* personal harlot.

And she would be. He loathed being denied. She had no idea what he was capable of when he wanted something. She had no idea how elaborate and far-reaching his schemes had been.

"The Moutiers got what they deserved. Isabelle got what she deserved. And so, too, did Sébastien—everyone, in fact, who got in my way."

This was far from over. He wasn't through with Sabine Laurent. Or Jules de Moutier.

20

Jules, Luc, and their party of twenty men marched across the grounds. Dragged from the château with a sword to his back, Gaubert, the Archbishop's assistant, was reluctantly leading their party to the Archbishop's chapel. Focused on the ever-nearing stone structure located past the shrubs and statues in a remote corner of the gardens, Jules's dark mood was a sharp contrast to the bright early morning sun.

Only twenty feet away . . . Only a few heartbeats more . . . *Jésus-Christ*, after five years he'd have his confession, then revel in it.

Jules reached the door first and placed his hand on the latch.

"At last the time has come," Luc said at his side.

It had. Drawing his sword, Jules threw open the door and rushed inside. The heavy stench hit him hard and slid down his throat. He choked back a cough. The sight before him cleaved him where he stood.

He froze.

So did his blood.

While the men recoiled at the foul fetid air, he could do no more than to take in the Archbishop, quiet and still, his swollen head tilted to one side, a grotesque purplish blue, as he hung by a rope from one of the ceiling beams.

Jules lowered his sword slowly.

"NO-O-O-O-O!" The cry came from Gaubert but echoed in Jules's soul. The assistant pushed past the men and raced to his master. Dropping to his knees he wailed, the words "No!" and "Why?" his grief-stricken chant.

"Dieu . . ." Luc said.

Incredulous, Jules approached. The abominable odor increased the closer he got. The only man who could end Jules's turmoil was suspended off the floor. A noose around his neck.

"Commander." The urgency in the voice dragged Jules's attention to one of his men. He held a note. "This was on the ground."

Jules sheathed his sword and took the note.

I end my life with a clean conscience and the satisfaction in knowing that I sent Blainville where he belongs. To hell. I regret nothing I've done. Not to the man I loathed, nor with the woman I loved. It is far better to walk into death on my own than to be shoved into it by my enemies. In this way, I leave having denied them the satisfaction.

Barthélemy L. Bailloux

"Cut him down," Jules ordered, his heart heavy.

Merde. Was this nightmare ever to end? Was he ever to know why their lives had been destroyed?

As one man righted the chair that lay on its side under the Archbishop's dangling feet, Jules hauled Gaubert up.

"Explain this." Jules shoved the note at him.

The man was pale. The parchment quaked in Gaubert's hands as he read its contents.

"I—I can make no sense of it, monsieur, any more than I can make sense of—of—" Choking back an anguished sob, he glanced at the Archbishop, who was being freed from his noose.

"What woman does he speak of?" Jules demanded, his patience frayed to a mere thread—ready to snap. "Why did he turn against my father?"

"Your—Your father, monsieur? Who would that be?"

Jules snatched the note out of the assistant's hands and held it inches from his face. "The Marquis de Blainville!"

Gaubert's eyes widened. "Forgive me, my lord. I didn't know who you—"

"Answer. His. Questions," Luc ordered.

The older man swallowed. "I—I don't know anything. The monsignor was a private man. I do recall that your father and the Archbishop were at odds, but that was years ago, before the Marquis' arrest. I don't know the reason for their discord, I swear. As to the other matter, about the . . ." Gaubert lowered his voice when he said, "*Woman* . . . It's rather a delicate subject."

Jules released him abruptly. *Dieu.* Gaubert was making him pull information out of him an agonizing bit at a time.

Frustrated, Jules handed Luc the note and stalked away, toward the monsignor's body.

Jules gazed down at the Archbishop de Divonne, now on the marble floor, dressed in his costly red robes, death silencing his secrets.

The man had gone to great lengths to ensure that they would never have an encounter. First the ambush. Now this.

Why suicide? He could have devised another plan to gain the "satisfaction" he sought, without ending his own life. And *where* was the missing silver? Had the Archbishop been behind its disappearance from the Laurent land at all? Jules assumed that he and Luc were the "enemies" mentioned in his note. Or were there others?

Too many questions. No answers. Only gaping holes in the truth.

A morbid pull forced Jules down onto his haunches. With the rope removed from the Archbishop's neck, the wound was visible and raw, the beginnings of decay present. He'd been dead for a while.

Glancing at the Archbishop's arms, Jules noticed bruising peering out from beneath the man's long loose sleeve. Pushing up the sleeve, he revealed a long narrow contusion across the top of the right wrist.

Shoving the other sleeve up, Jules turned the stiffened arms to examine them thoroughly. The left had identical bruising, except it was across the inside of the wrist.

Luc crouched beside him. "What do you have there?"

"Peculiar markings." Jules showed him the bruises. "They're the kind of bruising a man might sustain if his wrists are bound together with a rope."

* * *

"Well? Out with it," Agnes demanded the moment Jules, Luc, and the men had returned to the camp. "I'm an old woman and this suspense isn't good for my health. Is the Archbishop ready to talk to Sabine? Did he have any information about Isabelle?"

"Yes, tell us," Louise pressed.

"The Archbishop is dead," Jules said.

Sabine's heart plummeted.

"Dead?" Vincent repeated, the word screaming inside Sabine.

Jules's jaw tightened. "We found him hanging by a rope, made to look like he took his own life."

"You don't believe he killed himself?" Sabine asked.

Jules cast a glance at his brother. "I don't."

"I do," Luc countered. "The Archbishop's assistant let you read the love letters between the Comtesse de Tonnere and the monsignor. And he told you how devastated the Archbishop was to learn of her death from smallpox. Gaubert and every servant we questioned confirmed the monsignor hadn't been himself since the

Comtesse's death. He killed himself. And with him died our chances of regaining favor."

"No," Jules said firmly. "It's not over. You saw the bruises on his wrists."

"The bruises prove nothing. We have no way of knowing how he got them. There's no real evidence, not even in his private documents, to indicate foul play. Why delude ourselves?"

"It's not a delusion. Whoever murdered the Archbishop also brought down our father, a man of good standing," Jules insisted. "We're dealing with someone clever enough to cover up his misdeeds."

"*Dieu*, Jules, I want my life back as much as you do, but you must face the truth. The Archbishop despised our father. Enough to betray him and have him hanged. He thought he could take your wealth and your life, too. When he failed, given his melancholy, he killed himself."

"No. It doesn't make sense. There are too many unanswered questions."

"Such as?"

"None of the Archbishop's men survived the attack. How, then, did he get word he'd failed? And so quickly? How did a man who'd become a virtual recluse and who was as forlorn as the monsignor had been over the death of the Comtesse pull himself together enough to arrange an ambush in the first place? I refuse to accept his 'suicide.' Someone has used the monsignor to make us believe he was involved. Whoever killed the Archbishop forced him to write the note and knows the truth of what happened to our father. We'll pursue this further. With the utmost caution."

Luc swore. "Fine. We'll do it your way. We'll ask Simon for more men. Amass armies to guard us." His tone was saturated with sarcasm. "We'll search for evidence that doesn't exist and entertain every possible theory of what led to our father's arrest, no matter how ridiculous. We'll lay blame at everyone's feet, except our most blameless, flawless father."

Jules's body tensed. "Careful . . ."

Luc gave a hollow laugh. "Why, for once, can't you admit that he wasn't perfect? That he may not have been as innocent in all this as you claim—"

Jules grabbed his brother's doublet with both fists. Sabine gasped.

"You dare call him a *traitor*?" Jules's voice was low and rimmed with rage.

Sabine's gaze darted to Raymond. He didn't look inclined to intervene.

Luc glowered at his older sibling. "I don't believe he was a traitor any more than I believe he was a saint. You, Jules, were his heir. I endured a side of him you did not."

Jules released Luc. "So you've said. If he treated me differently, it was because he knew I accepted my duty to my family while you would not."

"*Jésus-Christ*, I will *not* join the Knights of Malta. Can you imagine me taking a vow of *celibac*y—for the rest of my life?"

"You think sacrifices are not required of the firstborn son?"

Luc let out a sharp sigh and pulled out a folded parchment from inside his doublet. "I wasn't going to show you this, but I now believe you need to see it. When Gaubert wasn't looking, I took this from the Archbishop's private papers in his library."

Jules opened the letter and scanned its contents.

"It is written by our father's own hand," Luc said.

"It's meaningless." Jules tossed the letter with a flick of his wrist, sending it fluttering to the ground.

Luc's eyes widened. "You believe bruising on the Archbishop's wrists is proof of murder, yet a letter written by your own father's hand is *meaningless*?"

"That letter could be a forgery, regardless of the signature and penmanship."

"It even has our family seal on it," Luc exclaimed.

Jules lifted a brow. "So did Isabelle Laurent's letter and the letters that were used to condemn our father at his trial. Apparently *everyone* was using our seal."

Sabine snatched up the letter and opened it.

I grow weary with your reluctance. Need I remind you of Marie-Claire's perilous situation? If you don't do as I have asked of you, I'll expose your romantic involvement with the sweet vulnerable Comtesse de Tonnere to her volatile brutish husband. Do not make me wait any longer.

Charles de Moutier

"Jules, that *is* our father's writing. He was forcing the Archbishop to do something the monsignor didn't wish to involve himself in. It proves the Archbishop had good reason to do what he did to him. It proves that our father wasn't a man of impeccable character."

Jules pointed a finger at Luc. *"Enough."*

Sabine quickly interjected. "What about the silver? Did the Archbishop have it?"

Jules let out a sigh. "No. We searched. There was nothing. The servants claim that no one came to the château with a chest of any kind."

"What do we do now?" Sabine asked.

"I'd like to speak to Valentin, Marquis d'Argon. He was friends with my father and the Archbishop." Jules raked his hand through his hair. "There is also the late Comtesse's husband, the Comte de Tonnere, and the Comte de la Rocque—a recent visitor to the Archbishop's château. There was also an unknown visitor . . . Perhaps they're involved . . ."

"Then let us seek out these gentlemen!" she said with renewed hope.

"It is not that simple. Valentin and Tonnere and Rocque are in Paris, preferring the city to their country estates. Luc and I are forbidden to enter Paris. We'll be arrested on the spot and tossed back into prison."

"Valentin wasn't able to help our father, but did what he could to help Jules and me," Luc explained. "If it wasn't for him, we'd still be rotting in prison. The last time the Marquis was barely able to influence our release. This time, we may never get out."

"Which leads to the second problem," Jules said. "Even if we sent Valentin a note asking him to meet us outside of Paris, the Marquis is skittish. He would likely decline. Understandably, he fears that further involvement in any of this will result in his own family falling into disfavor. That's the last thing we'd want to do to Valentin."

Sabine felt a smile tug at the corners of her mouth. She glanced at Louise and Vincent and could tell by their smiles they were of like minds.

"No problem," Sabine assured. "We can get you into Paris and give you a way to move about undetected so that the risk to you and the Marquis d'Argon is minimal."

Sabine walked over to one of the carts, threw open the lid of one of the trunks, and shifted the clothing around until she found what she sought.

Holding up a worn sackcloth shirt and breeches, she said, "You'll have no trouble at all entering and exiting Paris in these."

Luc burst out laughing. "You jest."

Jules's brows shot up. "That's *peasant's* clothing."

"Correct. All the costly costumes were sold, but we have some peasants' attire left over from the theater."

"I'll not wear peasants' clothing," Jules said. "Nor will I act as one."

"I must agree with my brother here and decline," Luc concurred.

She responded, unfazed by the two stubborn Aristos in front of her. "As I see it, you don't have any other option—if you want to uncover the truth. Think of it as a role, with Paris as your stage.

You can either enter the city with a troupe of actors, dressed as peasants, or you can remain as you are. For another five years. Or *indefinitely.*" Sabine held the commoners' clothing up a little higher. "What say you, gentlemen? Shall we be donning these tomorrow?"

* * *

"Sabine." She started at the sound of Jules's voice.

Darkly beautiful, he held out his hand. Her heart danced. She recognized that look. It was the prelude to pleasure. All day she'd been anticipating nightfall. Her body hummed with desire.

She silenced all the sensible reasons to decline. Told herself she could give her body to Jules and withhold her heart.

Then she placed her hand in his, and rose.

He linked his fingers with hers, and led her away from the campfire and into the woods to a clearing, his touch sending tingles up her arm.

A small fire had been built, blankets spread close by.

She smiled up at him. "This looks familiar." She was so happy he'd done this. That he'd come to her first. It spoke of the extent of his own need for her. A need that equaled her own.

"It won't be like last time." Grasping one of the ties to her bodice, he pulled it loose. "This time there'll be no deceit. This time I'm having Sabine Laurent." A thrill quavered through her. His practiced fingers loosened her lacings. "And you're going to give yourself over to me. Completely, aren't you?" Her bodice dropped to the ground.

His scent, his proximity, bedazzled her. She could scarcely breathe. "Yes." She was so shamelessly eager. And she didn't care. She'd missed him. She'd missed this.

At the moment, she'd agree to just about anything.

"Good." His eyes took on that seductive glint that made her knees weak. He slipped his arm around her waist and pulled her to him, the press of his body, sheer rapture.

"Just for tonight," she said.

She simply had to have one more taste of bliss with this man.

"There you're wrong. We're going to have each other again and again until we're fully sated." Delving his fingers into her hair, he lowered his head until their mouths met. She fisted his shirt. His kiss was slow, delicious. He eased his tongue into her mouth, giving hers swirling caresses.

Hungry for more, she laced her arms around his neck and rubbed herself against the bulge in his breeches. His groan of approval reverberated in his chest, sending sensations rushing through her breasts. Her eager sex clenched.

He kissed along her jaw to her ear, teasing the lobe with his teeth. She shuddered.

She closed her eyes, keenly aware of the slick moistness between her legs. This time *would* be different. Elise was gone. She could enjoy this sensual man as herself, without pretense.

He stepped back. Her skirt ballooned down to her feet. She hadn't realized he'd undone the fastenings.

She was just about to reach for him when he removed his shirt and tossed it onto the ground. His skin was a warm hue from the firelight. His sculpted chest and powerful arms were breathtaking. And his magnificent erection, evident by the impressive bulge in his breeches—his body's reaction to *her, Sabine*—made her shudder. He knew exactly how to use that part of his male anatomy, with wicked mastery. He had such virile appeal. She was powerless to resist it. She always had been.

A slight smile teasing the corner of his mouth, he placed his hands on her hips and slid her chemise up her legs, to her waist, along the sides of her breasts, the tantalizing rise setting her on fire. She raised her arms. He slipped it off. A quick tug of the ties on her *caleçons* and they joined her skirts on the ground.

He gave her a seductive perusal. "In your bed, I've had more than a few dreams of you standing in all your naked glory before me, drenched in moonlight. My very own forest fairy, bound for my pleasure."

Her heart lost a beat. *Oh, God.* Did he say *bound*? A fresh wave of arousal hit her hard. The mere mention of it at the inn had had her undone.

His smile returned, with those disarming dimples. "What say you, Sabine?" He picked up a long sash she hadn't noticed before off the blanket. She recognized it from the trunk of costumes they'd brought.

He dipped his head until his lips hovered over hers, his breath heating her sensitized mouth. "Give me your wrists and I give you my word, you'll love every moment."

21

Sabine watched as he carefully bound her wrists together, nervous excitement mounting by the moment.

When he was done, he rubbed his thumb over the sash around her wrists. "Is it too tight?"

She shook her head, unable to muster words. *Don't think. Or be cautious. For once, just leap!*

"If at any time you wish to stop, you need only say so." He raised her bound wrists above her head and secured them to a branch above.

She tested the bindings with a tug. They held her soundly. Never had she allowed herself to be so vulnerable. Seized by anticipation, she didn't dwell on it. Delirious with desire, she didn't care.

She knew he wouldn't hurt her. Lord knows she'd made him angry enough in the past and never once had he done her any physical harm.

She wanted this.

She wanted to completely acquiesce and surrender to this delicious desire between them.

His gaze wandered over her once again. "*Dieu.* You look so good. Like every man's fantasy." He stroked the curve of her bottom. She jerked. Her body felt oversensitive.

She twisted around, the better to view him, but he placed his hands on her waist, halting her, and pulled her back against his chest. *Skin against skin.* She closed her eyes.

"Be still," he said against her ear. "Try not to move." He stepped away, leaving her bereft.

He reappeared before her, holding a smaller sash. "For your eyes," he explained.

It was maddening enough not to touch him. She wanted to see him at the very least. "Jules—"

"Shhh." He stepped closer and pressed his fingertips to her lips. "Trust me." He placed the sash over her eyes and tied it. "When your eyes are covered like this, your other senses heighten."

She hardly needed a sash to heighten her senses. They were heightened anytime she thought of him. Anytime he neared.

Her eyes covered, her world narrowed to the sound of the crackling of the fire, the night sounds of the forest. And him. She could sense him. Though he wasn't touching her, heat radiated from his body.

She heard movement to her left and then the snapping of a twig behind her.

She couldn't tell where he was, or what he was doing. Her pulse raced.

"Ju—" She was suddenly yanked forward, her breasts crushed against his chest. He claimed her mouth, sealing his name on her lips. His kiss was hot, demanding, taking her breath away, driving his tongue into her mouth on her gasp.

Oh, yes. Finally. And he was naked, too. She matched his heated intensity, rejoicing in the feel of his generous sex pressing against her belly.

Then his mouth was gone. Before she could protest, his lips burned a path down her neck. With a moan, she pressed her forehead against her arm, giving him better access. Being deprived of sight was doing exactly what he'd predicted it would do—heightening her fever. She was overly aware of the texture of his lips and tongue against her skin, the sound of her breathing. The slickness of her sex.

He moved lower still, down her breast—so tantalizingly close to her hardened nipple. Silently, she willed him to take her into his mouth. His tongue lashed across the sensitive tip. She shuddered.

"I've missed the taste of these pretty nipples," he said and sucked one into his hot mouth.

She cried out. He sucked on her greedily, his fingers capturing her other nipple, assailing it with perfect pinches and pulls. The double stimulation had her mewing and writhing as each muscle-melting sensation lanced to her core.

His hot mouth moved down her belly, lower and lower. Her body wept for more. Slowly he swirled his tongue around her navel, then released her.

Over her short sharp breaths she listened for sounds, movement.

He stroked his hands down the outside of her thighs. She jumped in surprise and delight. Sensing he was kneeling in front of her, she waited, gripped by anticipation. Her sex drenched. And aching for him.

"Come here," he growled, impatience tainting his tone. Her feet suddenly left the ground. She gave a startled gasp. He'd scooped her legs up and thrown one over each broad shoulder.

His strong hands gripped her bottom. She wiggled, realizing her intimate flesh was open and inches from his mouth.

"Don't move." He tightened his hold. His warm breath against her moistened folds was delicious torment.

She dug her heels into his back, bracing herself for the sensual siege. He stroked his tongue along her feminine folds. She lurched and whimpered.

"You like that, don't you, Sabine?"

She was breathing so hard, she felt light-headed. "*Yes . . .*"

"You want more?"

"Yes!"

His tongue grazed over her private flesh. She tossed her head back and arched to him, straining against the bindings on her wrists.

"Your responses are as delicious as you are." His voice was low and so seductive. "Cry out for me again." He gave her another luscious stroke of his tongue and she involuntarily complied.

He licked and sucked her juices, stopping every once in a while to torment her swollen clit. To drive her mad. Keeping her in sensuous agony, skillfully holding her on the edge of orgasm.

And wavering to and fro.

Just when she couldn't bear any more, his mouth swooped in on her clit and he gently bit down. She screamed, vaulting into ecstasy, euphoria flooding through her veins. Her body shuddered and convulsed. Gripped by powerful spasms, her feminine walls wildly clenched and released.

Jésus-Christ. Jules hadn't had this fiery woman in weeks. But it was worth enduring every agonizing moment that led to this. He had to fuck her. Feel her silky cunt gloved around his cock again. Or lose his mind.

Gently, he lifted her legs off his shoulders and set them back down on the ground. He was on his feet in an instant and caught her around the waist as her knees buckled. Holding her up, he moved around her and pulled her back against his front.

Standing on a slight incline, their bodies were perfectly aligned, his prick nestling along the seam of her luscious derrière.

He brushed her hair back to reveal her graceful neck. "I'm not done with you yet." He kissed the nape of her neck, drawing her soft skin between his lips.

And drove his cock into her quivering core.

Her sultry sound eclipsed his groan. Her sheath throbbed, drawing on his motionless shaft.

Clenching his teeth, he closed his eyes. She was so slick, so hot, so tight after her orgasm it was mind-numbing. "You have a cunt to die for."

He withdrew and slid back in with the most decadent glide. She moaned and squeezed around him. Any vague thoughts of moderation vanished. Tightening his hold on her hips, he began to thrust, hard, fast, pulling her to him each time he drove forward. Her legs grew steadier.

"Don't stop." He heard her soft tortured plea. There was no way he could. This was perfect passion. He'd found perfect bliss. She pressed hard against him, and arched her back. His cock wedged deeper. Guttural groans escaped him. He was hammering at her womb. He couldn't stop. She had him on fire. She gasped with each solid thrust, pushing back, meeting every one, matching his wild tempo.

"Jules, I'm going to . . . I'm . . . Oh!"

"Come," he growled. "*Dieu*, do it."

Rapture erupted from her throat. Her delicate muscles contracting around him, milking his thrusting cock, sent him over the edge.

He reared, tossed his head back, a long throaty groan roaring up his throat as come shot out of him with stunning force. Hot spurts of semen spewing to the ground until he'd purged his prick. The last dollop dragging a final feral sound up his throat.

Sabine's knees finally gave out. His arms were about her instantly. His strong arm around her waist to hold her up, he untied her wrists.

With infinite care he placed her down on the blankets and removed her blindfold. His handsome face was the first thing she saw. A slight smile graced his lips.

He massaged her wrists, her arms. "Are you all right?"

She nodded, her body still trembling in the aftermath.

His smile grew slightly. He stretched out on top of her and smoothed a lock of her hair off her cheek. "It was intense. And perfect." So was he. Softly, he kissed her. A knot formed in her throat. She slipped her arms around his neck, needing to hold him, to be held by him. Soft emotions she couldn't quell surged from her heart.

As she let his unhurried kisses soothe her, calm her, she made a startling discovery. "You're still . . ."

"Hard?" he supplied. Shifting his hips, he slid his shaft into her. She gasped, her sheath ultrasensitive from her recent releases. "I've waited a long time to have you again. One orgasm isn't going to be enough." His smile grew to a heart-fluttering grin.

Buried deep inside her, he remained still while he plied her with more gentle, stirring kisses.

"You are so very beautiful. And so desirable," he said in the softest voice. "I'm going to have you all night long. You're going to take my cock again and again. Get used to it, my beautiful forest fairy."

His words elated and scared her. What if she did get used to it? To him? What then?

* * *

Agnes snickered. With a stern look, Sabine lightly elbowed her in the ribs, but it didn't silence Agnes. As the older woman glanced at Jules, a louder giggle bubbled out of her. She'd been like this since they'd stopped just outside Paris not more than an hour ago to don their disguises.

Keenly aware of Jules's presence beside her, Sabine turned to Louise and Vincent—who sat across from her in the moving cart—looking to them for help. Sabine instantly saw she'd get none there. Vincent was doing a poor job at hiding his mirth behind his hand, and Louise, though biting her lip, was *blatantly* tittering.

And they called themselves actors.

Sabine glanced at Jules, dressed in his peasant garb, hoping somehow his and Luc's conversation about the Marquis d'Argon had been enough of a distraction, making them unaware of her family's amusement at their expense.

Jules's frown instantly told her not only that was he aware, but that he knew the cause of their hilarity.

"Don't be angry with them," Luc said, sitting across from Jules. "You do look ridiculous. And dirty."

Jules looked away, ignoring Luc's ribbing.

"You both look like peasants, which is how you want to look if you are to move about Paris without your peers recognizing you," Sabine reasoned. Their hair covered with powder and ash, their faces altered by makeup and smudged with dirt for good measure, they'd been made to appear older than their years and every bit the "dirty peasant" no Aristo would glance at.

If only she could do something about their physiques and comportment. Both screamed, *Nobility*.

Though Agnes had altered the commoners' clothing they wore to fit loose on purpose, their powerful bodies were still evident. Moreover, the Moutier men carried themselves with an inherent sense of authority that was difficult to hide.

Their peasant disguises, their cart, and the nag they'd obtained from a peasant en route, for Jules's carts and horses were too fine, all lent credence to the ruse. Everything that could be done had been done to make them unrecognizable to anyone acquainted with them in the grand city.

The clatter of hooves over cobblestone snatched Sabine from her thoughts.

Paris. She tensed.

Their cart moved into the chaos and confusion. The city streets were congested with Aristos and commoners, a clash of brilliant colors and the drab. Of luxurious carriages and humble carts. Of palaces known as *hôtels* for its exalted citizens, and barren alleys for its beggar-born.

Twisting and turning, she realized she was scouring the midafternoon crowds as if she'd spot Isabelle walking along the narrow store-lined streets, if she looked hard enough.

Warm fingers closed over her cold hand.

Jules brought her palm to his lips and kissed it. "If she's alive, we will find her."

"She's alive." Strangely, she felt it even stronger now that she was in Paris.

He wrapped an arm around her and pulled her close. Sabine rested her head on his shoulder and for a moment closed her eyes, savoring his warmth and strength. She floated through the noise of the city. Floated between worries and wonderment.

All those years ago, she'd vowed to return to Paris and win over her Dark Prince. And here she was, reentering the city with Jules de Moutier. Her most ardent, glorious lover.

Unlike before, she no longer dwelled on dreams, or the future. She was living in the moment, seizing fistfuls of bliss while she could.

The sounds of horses' hooves, several of them, a fast approach, grabbed her attention. A four-horse carriage thundered by.

"Raymond, turn the cart around and follow that carriage!" Jules ordered.

"Why? Who is it?" Luc asked, craning his neck.

Jules smiled. "It looks as though good fortune is with us today," he said as Raymond turned the cart, already in pursuit. "If that sorry excuse of a horse can keep up, we'll speak to Valentin shortly, for *that*, Luc, was his carriage. And I just spotted him in it. Alone."

22

Raymond drew the cart to a halt a discreet distance from where Valentin's carriage was parked.

"We'll walk from here," Jules said as he jumped down and quickly aided the women off. The thought of a meeting with the Marquis sooner rather than later made his heart race. "We must get into the Marquis' carriage. We need to distract the driver."

"We'll take care of the distraction." Louise smiled and glanced at Vincent.

* * *

"My ankle! *O-O-O-O-H-H-H . . .*" Vincent's cries and moans as he lay on the road in front of the Marquis' horse drifted to the back of the carriage where Jules and Luc hid. Waiting.

Vincent's feigned fall had been highly convincing. Louise, Sabine, and even Agnes supported the theatrics as they carried on distressed and distraught.

"Move him this instant," the driver demanded. "He is blocking the way. This carriage belongs to the Marquis d'Argon." With

Vincent on the ground in front and another carriage parked in back, the driver knew he was stuck.

"I don't care if it belongs to the King himself," Sabine shot back. "We cannot lift him! If you want him moved, then get down and help us."

A smile pulled at the corners of Jules's mouth. That was his feisty forest fairy. He'd reward her heroics later—in all her favorite amorous ways.

Spotting Raymond parked down the street, Jules gave him a nod. Without further ado, Raymond knew exactly what Jules required of him and rolled up alongside the Marquis' carriage.

"My dear husband . . . My poor, poor husband," Louise wailed.

"My friend, you'd better move that man," Raymond said to the driver. "It looks as though your master approaches." He indicated the Marquis with a jerk of his chin.

The moment the driver saw his employer descending the stairs, he jumped down with a curse to help move Vincent.

"Now," Jules said to Luc. They moved between the cart and the carriage and slipped inside the plush interior, unnoticed, quickly drawing the curtains shut.

With the dwindling light of day, inside the carriage it was dark.

"Monsieur le Marquis!" the driver exclaimed. The quick shuffle of feet told Jules the man was rushing to aid his master.

"Straight home," said a familiar voice, the same calm, even tone Jules remembered.

Poised, he waited.

The latch turned. The carriage door opened.

The moment the Marquis stepped up and leaned forward, Jules yanked him in and slammed the door shut. The Marquis landed on the seat opposite Jules and Luc.

His eyes widened. "Who—Who are you? What—What do you think you're doing?"

"Valentin, it's Jules de Moutier and my brother, Luc."

"Monsieur!" The driver pounded on the door, unable to open

it while Jules held it shut. It had been jerked from his hands, alerting the man that something was amiss. "Monsieur le Marquis, are you all right?"

Speechless, Valentin stared back at his unexpected guests. He sat up and peered closer, his gaze traveling from Jules to Luc and back again. His expression changed from surprise to shock.

"My God," he breathed. Reaching out, he grasped both Jules's and Luc's hands and squeezed. "What has become of you?" His voice quavered with emotion.

"Monsieur!" The pounding persisted. "Please, are you all right!"

Valentin cleared his throat. "Yes. Yes, I'm fine."

"Valentin," Jules said. "We must speak to you. Somewhere private."

* * *

In the Hôtel d'Argon, in the Marquis' private apartments, the distinguished Aristo took in the trio before him, his expression aggrieved.

Light from the flickering flames in the hearth, the silver wall sconces and torchères revealed the extent of Jules, Luc, and Sabine's beggared appearance.

But Jules wasn't embarrassed. The importance of this meeting blanketed whatever personal discomfort Jules might derive dressed as a pauper before Valentin.

Sabine shifted her weight from one foot to the other. At Jules's behest, she'd been admitted in the Marquis' carriage.

Surrounded by lavishness, she stood between Jules and his brother, her eyes uncharacteristically downcast. Every so often she touched her frayed skirts. Clearly, she didn't share his indifference to their appearance, but was embarrassed by her mode of dress and diminished status, especially since she'd learned in the carriage that Valentin had been an acquaintance of her father's.

"Disguises or not, you are of noble birth, of superior bloodlines. It grieves me to see you like *this*," Valentin said, the sincerity of his words reflecting in his benevolent eyes. "You wouldn't have gone to such lengths unless you were in dire straits." He moved to his writing desk, stacks of his beloved books covering most of its surface. "I'll advance you funds."

"Valentin—" Jules began but the Marquis held up his hand to stop the flow of his words.

"I insist. Think nothing of it, son. Now then, how much will you need?" He picked up his quill and glanced at Jules, then Luc.

"We didn't come here for money," Luc said.

Valentin dropped the quill back into the crystal inkwell. He stepped around his desk, concern etched on his visage. "Then why do you risk your freedom? Your *life*? You know the consequences you face if either of you is caught in Paris. What has happened?"

"Valentin." Jules paused, grappling with his words. The Archbishop had been the Marquis' friend. He hated being the bearer of bad news, being the one to cause the tenderhearted man distress.

So different from the other Aristos Jules knew, the Marquis d'Argon, who disliked darts and dice. Who preferred prose over promiscuity—it was common knowledge he'd never been unfaithful to his wife. Even Jules's father, who'd held himself to a higher standard of conduct than most of his peers, had had mistresses—though he never flaunted them.

"Five years ago you took a great risk to help us," Jules began. "You were the only one who didn't believe my father was a traitor to the Crown. It's something my brother and I will never forget. We are forever in your debt."

Valentin waved off Jules's words, looking embarrassed by them. "I simply did what was right." The man was as modest as he was decent. "I couldn't sit back and watch you and Luc meet with the same fate as your father. There had been enough injustice already. I'm sorry you lost everything," he said, rueful. "I'm sorry I couldn't do more."

"There is something more you can do," Luc injected, his impatience showing. "We need information."

"Information?"

"Yes, Valentin, my brother is correct." Jules briefly tossed Luc a stern look, cautioning him to watch his outbursts. They had to broach this gently. "I loathe to ask for more of you, but you're the only one we can turn to."

"But I have told you all that I know," the Marquis assured them. "Making inquiries is difficult and dangerous. Even now. Your father hasn't been forgotten or forgiven. I want to see your lands and title restored. But there is nothing more I can do. Especially now. I'm in negotiations with the Duc de Talon over the marriage contract between his son and my Marguerite. I cannot jeopardize her future—"

Jules approached. "We don't wish to place you in peril or risk disgracing your family . . . We came here looking for information regarding your friend, the Archbishop of Divonne."

"Bailloux? What about him?"

Jules's silence was saturated with reluctance.

"I'm afraid I have some bad news," he said at last. "I'm sorry, but he is . . . dead."

"Dead?" Ashen, Valentin simply stared back at him in stunned disbelief. "H-How . . . do you know this?"

"We found him in his chapel, hanging from a rope." Jules pulled out the Archbishop's letter from inside his doublet and handed it to him. "We found this near his body."

The older Aristo's hands slightly trembled as he read the contents. When he finally met Jules's gaze, his eyes glistened with tears. "I—I cannot believe it . . ."

With care, Jules explained the events that led to the discovery of the Archbishop's body and the scene in the chapel.

The Marquis slowly sank into a nearby chair as though the weight of the news was too great for his legs to bear.

Jules placed his hand on the Marquis' shoulder. "Are you all right?"

"Yes . . . No . . . I—I don't know . . ." His anguish resonated with Jules. He'd been no less grief-stricken when he'd learned his father had lost his life swinging from a rope.

He hated pressing Valentin when he looked so shaken, but had no choice. "Valentin, I must ask you: Did you know he was in love with the Comtesse de Tonnere?"

The older man's gaze dropped back down to the note. "Yes . . . He is"—Valentin swallowed—"*was* a good friend and confided as such . . ."

"Were you aware of the animosity the Archbishop felt toward my father?" Jules asked.

Valentin remained silent, blankly staring at the note. Jules thought he hadn't heard the question, but then he answered, "I knew Bailloux was angry and upset with him . . . but I never knew why. Neither of them would say. They didn't wish to place me in the middle of their dispute."

"Then you never heard anything about my father blackmailing the Archbishop?" Jules asked, tossing a glance at Luc.

"Blackmailing Bailloux?" Valentin scrubbed a hand over his face, his other hand still clutching the note. "No."

"Nothing about my father threatening to expose the Archbishop's affair with the Comtesse?" Luc pressed.

"No. Why would you say such a thing?"

"My brother found a letter in the Archbishop's study," Jules explained. "He's convinced it's authentic. Signed with my father's name, its contents threaten to reveal the Comtesse's adultery to her husband."

"Good Lord. That would have devastated Ballioux—and incensed him. He was highly protective of her."

"Then it's possible that the Archbishop could have been my father's traitor, no?" Luc asked.

The Marquis dropped his forehead into his palm. "I don't know . . . I honestly don't know what to think. I'd planned on visiting Ballioux after I'd settled matters with the Duc. I know he was distraught over the Comtesse's death. The tone of his letters concerned me. If only I'd been able to get away . . . If only I'd been there . . . He might still be alive . . ."

Still with a hand on the man's shoulder, Jules lowered himself onto one knee. "Valentin, you knew my father. He would *not* blackmail a friend. Or anyone. He wasn't that kind of man."

The Marquis looked at Jules. "Your father was a proud man. At times too proud. Easily offended. This note you speak of could have been written by him in a moment of anger. Something he didn't mean, yet Bailloux took profoundly to heart. Bailloux was normally a placid man, and prior to his involvement with the Comtesse, pious, too. Under the right circumstances, any man can behave as he never has before. Bailloux may have been the traitor you seek. Or not. Now that he is dead, we may never know the truth."

Jules shook his head. "I will learn the truth. I must. I owe my father as much."

Valentin placed his hand on Jules's shoulder. "Your father is not here to give you his counsel. Allow me to give you fatherly advice, Jules."

"Of course, Valentin. I value your opinion."

"Let this go. Concentrate your efforts on reclaiming your lands and status. On gaining the King's forgiveness. Perhaps in a year or two we can begin to reacquaint you with old friends who may be able to bend the King's ear in your favor. Leave the ghosts of the past behind."

"I can't. I don't believe the letter found in the Archbishop's study bearing my father's name is authentic—it's a disparaging portrayal of him, utter nonsense." Jules rose and took the letter from Valentin's hand. "And I don't believe the Archbishop killed himself. However, I do think there's a connection with the Archbishop's death and my father's betrayal."

If he was correct, than there was still someone out there who wanted Jules dead. The same someone who had attacked his men.

Valentin's eyes widened. "A connection? But . . . who would harm *Bailloux*? Why? And why would someone want both your father and Bailloux dead?"

"I don't know. What about the Comtesse's husband? He was always known to have a temper. To be 'offended easily.' Perhaps he, too, was at odds with my father? Perhaps he recently learned of the affair—"

Valentin shook his head. "Impossible. He died in a duel two months ago. His temper being what it was, if he were at odds with anyone, everyone would know about it. He wasn't one to rein in his ire."

Jules raked his hand through his hair. "What about the letters? The ones used to condemn my father at his trial. Do you have any idea how the letters ended up in the satchel of his personal couriers? Have you heard any whispers—any information at all—as to who could have been the true authors of those letters?" Desperate, he was grasping and he knew it.

"Had I learned more, Jules, I would have informed you straightaway." What few communiqués Valentin dared to send were delivered to a tavern owner outside the city whom Jules paid and trusted.

"Anyone who was connected—either by kinship or friendship—to men condemned as traitors to the Crown were, and still are, under scrutiny," Valentin said. "No one wishes to suffer the fate your father suffered. It's unlikely anyone would be so reckless as to discuss such a nefarious plot openly."

Frustration crushing down on him, Jules knew Valentin was right.

The older Aristo looked heavy-hearted and weary. Jules reined in his questions. "The hour is late," he conceded reluctantly.

Valentin nodded and rose to his feet. "I can offer you a night's stay, but until the matter of the marriage contract is settled, I can do no more. I'm sorry, Jules."

* * *

In their private opulent chambers at the Hotel d'Argon, Jules pulled Sabine to him tightly, sending bathwater spilling over the side of the tub.

In the circle of his strong arms, his solid chest against her back, her fears ebbed, but didn't vanquish. She tried not to think of the peril they were in. The peril Isabelle was in. The thought of a possible attack, of someone seeking to kill Jules, sent waves of terror through her.

He kissed her neck, a languorous meeting of his mouth and her skin, sending stirring sensations swirling through her body. Briefly she closed her eyes, relishing the sublime distraction from her distress.

"You're pensive tonight. I know you're concerned," he said. "My men and I are no strangers to attack. We're experienced in battle. I won't let anything happen to you. Or your family," he said with such confidence, it was difficult to doubt him. He tucked her hair behind her ear.

His touching statement stirred up the usual tender emotions. Emotions she needed to quash, but couldn't wrestle down. This was a temporary affair. Nothing more. "I don't want anything to happen to *you*."

"I'll be fine." Capturing her chin, he lowered his mouth onto hers, the texture and heat of his lips enthralling. Liquid heat pooled in her belly. There was more she needed to say. She broke the kiss before she lost her wits.

"The Marquis is afraid." Already she was breathless.

"He is."

"What will we do if we can't get him to help? How will we find out the truth about your father? The missing silver? Isabelle?"

"We will succeed. We won't relent until we do. As for your sister, our servants were scattered to the winds when the Crown confiscated our lands. Raymond remembers them better than I. He is making discreet inquiries. It's likely someone from our hôtel still lives in the city. We'll hunt down servant by servant until we find one who knew Isabelle and can tell us more."

A knot clogged her throat, choking off words of gratitude.

He kissed her wet shoulder.

He rose and stepped out of the tub, his wet skin glistening in the firelight. He dried himself with a towel, the muscles in his arms flexing with his movements. Absorbed in the masculine grace of his large powerful body, she was captivated by the stirring sight. She could watch him perform the simplest task for hours. Stare at him a lifetime.

Her gaze dropped to his shaft, fully erect, long and thick. Fire shot through her veins. He'd kept her up most of last night, that magnificent part of his male anatomy inside her, driving her to rapture and back again and again.

She licked her dry lips and met his gaze. Amusement glinted in his wickedly sensuous eyes; he'd noted her ogling him.

He held out his hand. "Come here." His tone spiked her pulse.

She rose, and he helped her out of the tub.

Slipping an arm around her waist, he pulled her to him and trailed the towel over her shoulder and then along the curve of her breast—the softest caress—wiping away water droplets, sending inflaming sensations swirling through her.

"We make perfect bliss together," he said. She couldn't argue with that. His touch alone was heaven.

Tossing the towel away, he dipped his head and swirled his tongue around her nipple, licking the droplets off her skin. She closed her eyes.

He brushed his lips over her nipple before he drew the sensitive tip into his moist mouth.

Her head fell back with a whimper. Juices wept from her sex as he skillfully sucked at her breast.

Ceasing his sensual torture, he swept her off her feet, marched into the bedchamber, and dropped her in the middle of the bed. She landed with a small bounce, sprawled out, her legs open. Keenly aware of the cool air against her slick folds.

He sank one knee on the mattress between her thighs and then the other. Leaning over her, his palms down on the bed above her shoulders, he cupped the drenched curls between her legs. "You want to come for me, Sabine." It was more of a statement than a question.

Urgency pounded in her veins. "Yes!" She answered just the same.

He slid two fingers into her moist slit. Her breathing hitched.

"You're so wet. And perfect." Curling his buried fingers, he stroked over the ultrasensitive spot inside her sheath. A sharp stab of pleasure sent her arching off the bed with a cry.

Pressing the heel of his hand against her throbbing clit, he repeated the stunning stimulation and lowered himself onto the bed beside her without missing a stroke or relenting the scintillating pressure on her needy clit. She fisted the bed linens, grinding herself against his hand. A shattering release was fast approaching.

"I enjoy seeing you like this . . . so wildly aroused," he murmured against her ear, easing the pressure of his fingers, pumping them in and out of her more slowly.

His light strokes were maddening. Her clitoris pulsed unbearably. "No . . . Don't slow down . . ." She arched again, desperate for more friction. "Harder . . ." she panted. "*Now.*"

He chuckled softly, his warm breath tickling her skin. "Ask nicely and I might let you come."

"Hurry!"

"*Nicely* . . ." Slightly he increased the pressure of his fingers. Pleasure shot up her spine—a sampling of what was to come.

She wrapped her arms around him tightly. Her cheek against his, she said in desperation, "*Please* . . ."

"How can I resist such a pretty plea?" She heard the smile in his voice, too fevered with passion to be irked by his teasing.

He shoved his fingers in hard, striking the spot with glorious accuracy.

Her hips flew up. She screamed with rapture, her vaginal walls contracting around his unrelenting fingers. He continued to pump his fingers in and out of her until the last spasm ebbed. She collapsed on the bed. Boneless.

It took time before her breathing and heart calmed. His fingers eased out of her, his stiff shaft against her hip.

Resting his cheek against his palm, a slight smile gracing lips, he sported the look of a man sure of his mastery of the carnal arts.

"Don't look so smug," she said, yet couldn't help smiling. She felt wonderful. He was the only one who could inspire amorous fever one moment and blessed contentment the next.

He pulled her up against him. Her nerve endings sparked to life once more.

She sealed her lips to his and deepened her kiss. The press of his body was glorious, stoking her desire, renewing her hunger.

Jules rolled with her onto his back, her soft form on top of his body, his cock pressing into her belly. As usual, his fingers were drawn to her silky hair. He toyed with one of her blond locks. She sat up, a gleam of mischief in her eyes.

Resting her pert derrière on his thighs, she gripped the base of his cock. "This certain part of your anatomy has been neglected long enough, wouldn't you say?" She stroked her hand up to the engorged head of his shaft and back down, the sensation exquisite.

She leaned over him, her pale hair cascading around them. "I want to taste you."

His prick gave an eager jerk. His gaze dropped to her lips. He couldn't wait for his cock to be enveloped in that hot sweet mouth. The very thought sent heat scorching through his groin.

He tucked an errant tress behind her ear. "By all means. I have no objections." His sac was drawn so tight. His body screaming for release. For the first time in his life he could barely contain himself, all because of one virginal little mouth. And he was going to show her how to use it on his greedy cock.

She grasped his wrists and pinned them down on the mattress near his head. "Good. You'll be at my mercy just as I was at yours last night. Since I have nothing to tie you with, you'll keep your hands here. And you will not move them." She released his wrists.

Despite the amorous agony he was in, he felt a smile tug at the corners of his mouth.

"I won't move a muscle." He slipped his hands under his head, a small act of defiance to playfully goad her.

An adorable frown briefly eclipsed her features. "You move and I'll stop," she warned.

Little liar. Her interest in tasting him had been building with each amorous encounter. She wouldn't stop.

"Make certain your beautiful hair is pulled to one side. I want to watch you," he said.

She tilted her head. "You're always commenting on my hair. Always touching it. You really like it that much?"

"It's but one of your many fine features."

A wily smile formed on her lips. She leaned into him and gave him a slow, unhurried kiss. He savored her mouth, soft and warm, using the time to steel his control, determined to allow her to dictate the pace, at least initially.

She trailed kisses to his jaw, down his throat and chest. Gathering her hair to one side, she worked her way down his abdomen. His muscles tightened in anticipation. He closed his eyes.

He felt her grip his shaft, then something soft envelop it. Something that was definitely not her mouth. Snapping his eyes open, he was stunned by the sight before him.

She'd wrapped her silky hair around his cock.

"Sabine, what are you—"

With a naughty glint in her eyes, she gave her hair a little tug. It swirled around his shaft in a feather-like caress, sending a jolt of sensation coursing along his length, snatching the breath from his lungs.

Clenching his teeth, he softly swore, his heart pounding. "*Dieu*, where did you learn that?" His will to moderate himself in serious jeopardy.

"Nowhere. I thought it was something you might enjoy—since you like my hair so much."

He laughed. "I've never liked it more."

"Really?" She grinned with genuine pleasure and coiled her lustrous locks around his cock again.

His heart lurched, unsure he could withstand more of this exquisite torment. "Wait—" But his willful forest fairy did no such thing. This time the decadent caress tore a groan from his throat.

Before he could recover, she flicked her hair to one side and brought her mouth down on his cock.

With a primal growl, he fisted his hair at the back of his head. It took everything he had to keep from gripping her head and thrusting vigorously into her mouth.

Unsure, she drew on him, a gentle suck. His sex in her mouth, she gazed up at him, looking for direction.

"In and out . . . No teeth," he explained, his voice hoarse.

She began to move her mouth up and down his length, in a slow and steady tempo. "That's it. Just like that." He had no idea what about her novice mouth had him so enthralled, but the pleasure was bone-melting, his cock basking in glory, celebrating each delicious sensation.

Suddenly emboldened, she took him deeper, faster, surprising him with her unexpected fervor.

"Sabine . . . slow down . . ." His control was rapidly unraveling with each hungry suck.

Defiantly, she tightened her grip on the base of his shaft, refusing to relent on her ardent pace.

His blood thundered in his ears. His control snapped. He felt the beginnings of his orgasm racing over him.

"*Dieu*. I'm going to come," he warned. But his words didn't faze her. She neither stopped nor slowed down. Semen rushed out his cock. His hips jerked as he poured out his prick, giving her all he had. She didn't stop, gluttonous for more until she'd drained him dry.

His muscles lax, he lay on the bed, his ragged breaths slowly returning to normal.

She crawled up his body and smiled up at him. "I like the way you taste."

Dieu. There was so much about her that he liked. This beautiful, unique woman affected him on so many disquieting levels. She was the only woman he knew who could stir his heart as strongly as his body.

* * *

Leon watched with amusement as the tall burly man before him kept his gaze straight ahead, avoiding the body of the bound woman on the floor in Leon's antechamber.

It was a shame Hubert wouldn't look at her. With clean precise slices patterning her naked body, she was a masterpiece to behold. Lying in a heap on the floor, her dark hair covering her face, soaking in blood that pooled in a puddle around her, she'd been thoroughly enjoyable.

Every cut he'd made on her satiny skin as she screamed helplessly behind her gag had been sheer rapture. Had made him harder. Thicker. He'd come inside her with a glorious rush. And then snapped her neck.

Fresh from his bath, standing in his night wrap, Leon had cleansed her blood and scent from his body, but the memory of their encounter still hummed in his veins.

He was in a fine mood.

Leon dragged his gaze back to his most trusted man. Hubert had done his share of killing, for a sizable purse. He'd had no qualms about hoisting the Archbishop off the ground with a rope around his neck as he kicked and thrashed. Yet whenever a woman was involved, he became amusingly squeamish.

A smirk tugged at the corner of Leon's mouth. For this reason, Leon had Hubert meet with him in the antechamber—where the woman was. Seeing the ruffian squirm was highly entertaining.

"You have news to report?" Leon asked.

"I do. The Moutier brothers, the woman Laurent, and members of the troupe are en route to Paris."

"Paris? Really. Whatever for?"

"I don't know. Moutier keeps his camp heavily guarded. We can't get close enough to learn anything. The men sent to the Laurent farm have informed me that it, too, is guarded, with additional men having recently arrived as further reinforcement. The young cousins cannot be questioned without a battle."

"Leave them. I'll take care of them later. Besides, the last time your fools attacked, they did so when Moutier wasn't even there to be slaughtered. I lost out on two chests of silver, and they got themselves killed."

"We did manage to recover the chest buried on the farm," Hubert was quick to point out.

"Yes," Leon replied dryly. Lifting off the table the bloodied dagger he'd used on the whore, he casually studied it. "But I'm never satisfied with less than everything." He pressed the sharp tip against the brute's thick neck.

Hubert froze.

His Adam's apple bobbed as he swallowed hard. Leon lightly scored the skin along the jugular, scraping but not piercing the flesh.

"Monsieur . . . ?" The tinge of desperation in his tone pleased Leon immensely. He reveled in the quickening pulse beneath the blade. The bead of sweat suddenly on Hubert's brow. And best of all, the tangy scent of terror that emanated from him.

The smell of fear. There was nothing like it. He couldn't get enough of it.

"I want it *all*, Hubert," he told him. "The silver. The Moutier brothers dead. The blonde to myself. And you are going to help me achieve my goals—without further mistakes."

"Yes . . . of course. I am at your service, as always." Hubert's face was flushed.

Most reluctantly, Leon lowered the blade. "Excellent." Hubert was still needed.

Relief was evident in the large man's eyes. Hubert was wise enough to compose himself quickly. His thick black brows drew together. "Why do you hate the Moutiers?"

Why indeed. "Jules is no different than Sébastien was. The Marquis de Blainville was no less a bastard than my father was. They represent everything I hate about Aristos, and yet they were stupid enough, arrogant enough, to believe they were untouchable." Leon smiled. "There is tremendous satisfaction in unseating the mighty."

He stepped away from Hubert. "Tell me, are the mademoiselle and Moutier . . ." The words caught in his throat.

"*Fucking?*" Hubert supplied, then gave a snort. "He had her last night. No need to get close to the camp to hear her enjoying every moment of it."

Leon's smile died. "I see." His good humor was immediately scorched away by ire.

"B-But she'll be yours soon," Hubert promised promptly, "to do with as you wish."

Not soon enough. He'd already waited far too long to have a woman of such low rank. He'd suffered the chaste kisses, restricted himself to the occasional touch—the caress of her hand when Laurent wasn't looking, the *accidental* brush against her breast. She'd always been hesitant when it came to his advances. He'd always believed it was due to her innocence.

And yet she'd eagerly spread her legs for Jules de Moutier. Without qualm.

Leon approached Hubert, took a corner of the man's shirt, and wiped the whore's blood off the dagger with it. Hubert stiffened but said nothing.

"Clean up this mess," Leon ordered, indicating the woman on the floor. "Toss her body outside in the privy with the others. The natural odors there will, as usual, mask any smells of decay."

Leon stalked into his bedchamber and slammed the door shut. He flopped down onto the bed, still clutching the dagger. Slipping a hand under his head, he watched as the candlelight from the nearby torchère gleamed on the blade.

"You've disappointed me, Sabine. You've chosen to behave like a dirty little whore. And I'm going to have to treat you like one." The blade caught another beam of light. "I *will* have you. Sooner or later, I always get what I want. As for Jules, he'll finally get what he had coming to him five years ago. How fortuitous that he's placed himself right in the perils of Paris." First thing in the morning, Leon was going to leave for the grand city. He had a feeling he'd find there the underhanded tax collector, Claude Cyr. The fool thought to elude Leon since the botched visit to Sabine's home.

A visit where Jules wasn't to be in attendance and had meddled in Leon's affairs once again.

His plan had gone off course, but he'd remedy that soon enough.

"Moutier may have been your first lover, sweet Sabine, but I shall be your last."

23

Flanked by Louise and Agnes, Sabine sat perched on the settee. They were in the home of the most sought-after woman in Paris, Marie de Perron—the queen of enchantment. Whose charms her own father had enjoyed. Sabine glanced at the clock on the mantel for what surely must have been the hundredth time.

Last night Raymond had located the whereabouts of one of the servants who'd worked with Isabelle at the Moutiers' château. Ninette. And the popular courtesan was her employer.

Louise plucked at a thread on her peasant skirt, her fidgeting fingers abrading Sabine's frayed nerves.

"Let her look old and wrinkled," Louise muttered. She knew Louise was referring to Marie.

They'd gained instant admittance into the courtesan's stylish townhouse once she'd learned that Jules de Moutier wished to see her. Twenty minutes ago he'd been escorted to Marie's private apartments—while the rest of them were shown to the *Room of Inspiration*.

With its erotic mural spanning the ceiling—images of men and women engaged in various sex acts—there was no doubt what the *Room of Inspiration* was meant to inspire.

She refused to contemplate what the ceilings in Marie's private apartments depicted. Or how *inspiring* they were.

Sabine looked at the clock. Again. Restless, she tapped her foot on the colorful silk carpet. How much longer before she knew whether or not Ninette had answers to questions about Isabelle?

Raymond and Luc stood near the entrance of the room talking. Makeup removed, like the rest of them, they, too, wore their peasant costume. Luc looked perfectly at ease in his surroundings—despite his attire.

"*Will you look at that . . .*" Vincent said in awe from a nearby chair, his head tilted back, staring at the images above. "I don't think it's physically possible for a woman to bend like that."

"Vincent, will you stop looking at that ceiling!" Louise snapped.

Unheeding, head tilted back in similar fashion, Agnes's mouth was agape as she studied the ceiling's intricate decadent design. "*Yes . . . Fascinating . . .*" Agnes remarked.

Louise huffed in disgust and leaned into Sabine.

Agnes let out a loud cackle. Sabine jumped and cursed her frayed nerves.

"Look at *that*." Agnes pointed to the ceiling. "Look at the size of that man's—"

"Agnes, please." Sabine gave the older woman's knee a gentle squeeze. "Do behave yourself."

Agnes affected a serious expression. "Yes. Yes. Of course." Then grinned. "It's a good thing he's naked." A giggle bubbled out of her. "How would he ever fit that into his breeches? It looks like a third leg!" She burst out laughing.

Vincent joined in.

Louise threw up her hands. "Dear God, we are in the very Den of Iniquity. This place is evil. It corrupts everyone who enters here. Marie has made certain of it. Only she would commission such a mural." She turned to Sabine. "I don't like the woman. I never have. And will you look at how I'm dressed?"

"Oh, Louise, stop carrying on," Agnes scolded. "Stare at the ceiling. That will keep you entertained."

The ornate doors opened.

Sabine twisted around.

Jules entered the room with Marie de Perron, who held on to his arm with a distressing level of familiarity. Dressed in a rich green gown, her auburn hair arranged in perfect, fashionable curls, Marie looked stunning.

Sabine rose.

Louise and Agnes quickly stood.

Sabine smoothed her hand down her drab skirt, so sharp a contrast to Marie's elegant attire. Sadly, nowadays her normal mode of dress wasn't much better than the costume she wore.

Jules and Marie stopped before her with Luc and Raymond a few steps behind them.

"This, Marie, is Sabine Laurent, the late Paul Laurent's daughter," Jules introduced.

A light scent of jasmine rose from the beautiful auburn-haired woman before her. Dear God, she smelled as wonderful as she looked. In fact, Marie was even more bedazzling up close. It was no wonder that she was a prize coveted among the male aristocracy.

"Mademoiselle Laurent." Marie grasped both of Sabine's hands. "I am sorry to hear of your father's death. My deepest condolences."

"Thank you," she murmured.

"He was a lovely man," Marie continued. "I enjoyed his plays very much. He was very talented."

Louise snorted.

Releasing Sabine's hands, Marie turned. "My dear Louise . . ." she said warmly. "How glad I am to see you."

Louise smoothed a hand over her hair. "Marie." Her tone was taut.

"And you, too, Vincent." Marie reached out a hand to him.

Vincent immediately took it and pressed a kiss to her knuckle. "It is a great pleasure to see you again, Madame de Perron." He grinned.

She returned his smile, her ruby lips no doubt the object of desire and delight for her multitude of lovers and admirers.

"When Jules told me you were both here, I couldn't believe it. Why, this is an evening full of truly wonderful surprises. I'm delighted to have you all in my home."

Marie's jewel green eyes moved from Jules, to Luc, to Louise and Vincent. "I have thought of each of you often since you left the city. I cannot adequately express my joy at seeing firsthand that you are all well."

"Yes, we are fine," Louise said, her words curtly dealt. "And this"—she touched her skirt—"is not my normal mode of dress, by the way. It's a costume. As you can see, we are all in costume. We did not go to this trouble for a social call, Marie."

Sabine mentally flinched. That was no way to talk to someone they needed help from.

"Yes, I know, my dear," Marie said graciously. "Jules has informed me of the reason why you're here." She turned to Sabine. "Mademoiselle Laurent, I've summoned Ninette. She'll be here shortly to answer any questions you have of her. I pray she has the answers you seek."

Sabine managed another "Thank you." Her heart pounded nervously as she prayed that Ninette indeed could be of help.

There was a light rap at the door.

Upon hearing Marie's bidding, a woman about the same age as Sabine entered the room. Her brown eyes were wide as she approached.

"Madame." She gave her mistress a quick curtsy. "You—You wish to see me?"

"Yes, Ninette. Do sit down."

Ninette lowered herself onto a chair. Her gaze moved from person to person in the group surrounding her. "H-Have I done something wrong, madame?"

"No, Ninette. I need you to answer some questions. Do you recognize these men?" Marie indicated Jules and Luc.

"Yes, madame. They're the sons of the late Marquis de Blainville. I—I worked for Monsieur le Marquis until his"—she lowered her eyes—"until the servants were let go."

"This"—she indicated Sabine—"is Mademoiselle Laurent. She has questions for you about the late Marquis' household. The Marquis' sons want you to answer her questions. Therefore, you'll respond truthfully to her every inquiry. Understood?"

"Yes, madame."

"Did you know Isabelle Laurent?" Sabine asked.

"Yes, mademoiselle. She, too, worked for the Marquis."

"Isabelle is my sister," she told Ninette.

"*Is*, mademoiselle?" Ninette cast an uneasy glance at her mistress before returning her gaze to Sabine. "Did they not tell you? Isabelle is . . ." Ninette twisted the fabric of her apron around her finger. "She . . . d-died. In a fire. In the servants' outbuildings. Some years ago."

"Yes. I was informed. I want you to tell me everything you can remember about her during her employ with the Marquis de Blainville—all the events leading to the fire."

"I'll do my best. What do you wish to know?"

"What was it like for her there?" Isabelle's letters were cheerful without much detail. Sabine often wondered what her sister's days were really like.

Ninette unraveled the apron from around her finger and shrugged. "Same as the rest of us. She had chores to do. She liked to do them quickly."

"Quickly? Why quickly?"

Ninette glanced nervously at Jules and then to her employer before she turned her gaze back to Sabine. "Isabelle loved to read and write. She'd rush through her chores so she could do both."

Sabine frowned. "I helped her pack. She brought no books or writing materials with her." In a heated moment, just before she left, Isabelle had proclaimed that she wanted nothing more to do with writing or the things that reminded her of the theater she missed so much. She intended to start life afresh at the de Moutiers' château. Knowing what writing meant to sister, Sabine hadn't believed her. Isabelle often let her emotions rule her tongue. She'd worried how Isabelle had managed without it. "What did she read? What did she write? What supplies did she use? She was only given enough ink and parchment to write one letter per month."

Once again Ninette cast a wary glance at Jules and Luc and then at her mistress.

"Answer her." Marie's order was gentle but firm. She was a woman who could command compliance with but a whisper.

"She . . . took books and extra writing materials from the Marquis' library and study."

Sabine sensed Jules stiffen.

"But—But she always returned the books!" Ninette was quick to add. "She missed you, mademoiselle. Very much. Spoke of you often. She told me that reading and writing gave her joy in your absence because it made her think of you."

The lump in Sabine's throat swelled as tears rushed to her eyes. God, how she missed her sister.

"What exactly did Isabelle take?" Jules asked.

"A few parchments. Some ink."

"How did you learn of it?" Jules continued.

"Perhaps Ninette is simply unaware that she was given permission by your father to have the items," Sabine was quick to point out in defense of her sister.

Lowering her head, Ninette fidgeted with her apron again.

"What say you, Ninette?" Jules said. "Is it possible you are just unaware that she had permission to enter my father's private study and take his things?"

"No, monsieur," she murmured to her lap. "She admitted to

borrowing the books and taking the parchments and ink when I caught her in the library. I begged her not to touch the Marquis' things again. I didn't want her to get into trouble." She gazed up at Sabine. "I'm sorry, mademoiselle. I don't mean to cast a shadow on your sister's memory. I liked Isabelle. She was funny and very smart, too. Then there was a change. Toward the end, she was not herself at all."

"How so?"

"Sh-She was withdrawn," the servant responded, "and short-tempered with the other servants when questioned about it. A few days before the fire, she misplaced her writings. She insisted that she kept the parchments hidden in her room. She searched everywhere. She became very upset when she couldn't find them."

"Perhaps someone took them," Sabine said.

"Why would anyone want them, mademoiselle? The servants couldn't read. We had no idea what she wrote."

"Could someone have taken them out of spite?" she asked.

"I don't think so, mademoiselle. Your sister was well liked among the staff. I can't think of anyone who'd want to do that to her. Some of us helped her search."

"Did you ever see her with her hands in the couriers' satchels?" Jules asked.

Sabine shot Jules a glare. "What are you suggesting?"

Jules placed a hand on her shoulder. "Easy."

"Sabine, let the girl answer the question," Vincent urged. "We seek the truth."

"Did you ever see Isabelle opening or placing anything in the couriers' satchels?" Jules repeated to Ninette.

She looked at Sabine, then at her hands on her lap. "Yes."

Sabine's gaze darted to Jules and then Luc. Both men's faces were taut. "Of course Isabelle was seen with her hand in the satchels. She wrote letters to her family—*with* your father's permission. And there was the letter she wrote to Luc. How else was she to have Luc's letter delivered?"

Jules stepped closer to Ninette. "How often did you see her do this?"

"Twice." Ninette glanced briefly at Marie.

"Did you ask her about her actions?" Jules questioned.

"Yes, monsieur. I asked her about it both times. Both times she said that the Marquis had ordered her to place some letters in the satchels for him."

"You didn't believe her, did you?" Jules said.

Ninette shook her head.

Jules lowered himself onto his haunches. "Why didn't you believe her?"

"No one was permitted to touch the satchels, except the Marquis' personal secretary. All letters were to be given to Monsieur Bedeau. Besides, the second time I saw her adding letters to the satchels, she was weeping. She wouldn't tell me why. That was days before she died. As I said before, she wasn't at all herself toward the end. She wept often, all her gaiety gone."

Sabine's heart gave a painful throb. Isabelle was not easily moved to tears. How she hated the thought that her sister had been in such distress without her there to comfort her.

What was the reason she was so overwrought?

"Can you venture a guess as to why she was so distraught that day?" Sabine asked.

"I thought it was because—" Ninette's brown eyes slid over to Luc and then back to Sabine. Ninette's cheeks warmed.

"Go on." Jules rose.

Ninette wrung her hands. "The Marquis had a gathering a few nights before. Isabelle anxiously awaited the arrival of a certain guest. She'd confessed to me that she had a *tendre* for this man. She'd asked me many questions about him. She was crushed when he didn't attend. In fact, she'd confided once that she was disappointed that this man didn't visit the Marquis as she'd hoped."

Jules's gaze darted to Sabine and then his brother. Sabine's eyes were drawn to Luc, too, knowing, like Jules, exactly whom Ninette was referring to.

Luc lifted his brows. "What?" he said to his sibling and Sabine. To Ninette he asked, "What man do you speak of?"

Ninette exchanged glances with Sabine, then softly replied, "You, monsieur."

"Me?" Luc was stunned. "A *tendre*?" He turned to Sabine. "How is that possible? I've never met the woman."

"She saw you many times at her father's theater," Jules answered for her.

Eager to continue her questioning, Sabine asked Ninette, "You said you thought the reason Isabelle wept in the library was because Monsieur Luc de Moutier didn't attend the gathering. Do you now believe differently?"

"I don't know what to believe. She was more upset than usual. Even more than when she couldn't find her writings. Something was terribly wrong. I don't know what."

"Did something happen at the gathering that would have upset Isabelle?" Sabine knew she was grasping.

"I don't think so, mademoiselle. I know of no such occurrence."

"Who was in attendance?" Jules asked.

"I don't remember. It was years ago, monsieur."

Frustrated, Jules rubbed his neck. "What about the Archbishop of Divonne? Was he there?"

"I can't recall."

"Did he visit often?" Jules's patience was quickly leaking out of his tone.

Ninette shifted in her chair, looking uncomfortable with Jules's changing disposition. "I—I don't know. I don't mind such things. It isn't my place to notice."

"Do you recall my father being at odds with anyone?" Clearly, it was Jules's turn to grasp. "Do you remember any arguments . . . ? Ever?"

Her brows drew together. "Arguments?" She thought for a moment, then her eyes widened. "Yes! There was an argument—of sorts—at that gathering, actually. The Marquis de la Rocque arrived late and was well into his cups. There was some commotion. Your father immediately took him into his study. Sometime later, Yves was summoned to escort the Marquis de la Rocque back to his carriage."

Luc snorted. "That's hardly an odd occurrence. The Marquis de la Rocque is always well into his cups and causing a disturbance."

Eyes downcast, Ninette twisted her apron again. "I'm sorry. That's all I remember."

"What about the events leading to the fire?" Sabine spoke up. "What transpired the day of the fire?" she asked, needing to know the details of that horrible day.

"Isabelle finished her chores early, as usual, and returned to the servants' outbuildings. A fire started. She perished."

Sabine blinked. "That's it? You have no other details?"

"No, mademoiselle. That's all I know."

"Was she alone?" Sabine could feel her heart racing, terrified that her feeling about her sister still being alive would evaporate like the morning mist if she didn't hear something, anything, that gave her a bit of hope to hold on to—something more than just a feeling.

"She was alone. We rushed outside and tried to douse the flames. By the time the fire was extinguished, it was too late. I'm sorry," Ninette said sadly. "I wish I knew more."

Sabine choked back a sob, trying to contain the tide of emotions welling inside her. *Nothing*. She'd learned *nothing* to help her find her sister. And what little she'd learned only distressed her more.

She felt a masculine arm around her waist. Looking up, she found Jules staring back at her. She buried her face in his chest, laced her arms around him, and held on, battling the anguish shredding her heart.

"I'm sorry you didn't get the answers you wanted," he said softly near her ear.

So was she.

And yet, despite the emotional pain, she realized that the feeling, that incessant tormenting feeling, hadn't died. She still felt Isabelle was alive. That somehow she hadn't perished in that fire. That the badly burned body found in the aftermath wasn't her sister.

"Mademoiselle Laurent?"

Sabine turned, the beautiful courtesan's face blurred by her unshed tears. She felt weary. Her limbs leaden.

"Why don't you lie down for a while?" Marie said. "Ninette, show the mademoiselle to one of the rooms upstairs so that she may rest."

Sabine shook her head and was about to decline when Agnes and Louise pulled her away from Jules and urged her to follow Ninette. The servant was already halfway to the doors.

Mutely, she let them escort her across the room. Just as she reached the doors, she glanced back at Jules.

The look in his eyes told her he understood how she felt. Her kindred spirit. His touching compassion swirled around her heart.

The doors closed. He disappeared from sight.

* * *

Jésus-Christ. It killed Jules to see the pain and sorrow in Sabine's beautiful eyes.

"Well, Brother, what do you think now?" Luc asked before the small group remaining in the *Room of Inspiration*.

Jules had to clear his throat before he could speak. "Isabelle Laurent is dead." He'd never met the woman and yet the words were piercing his heart. He'd so wanted a better outcome for Sabine.

Vincent hung his head.

"Do you think she is guilty of wrongdoings against your father?" Marie asked.

That brought him back to his initial gut suspicion. "I think Isabelle had been used as a pawn. She'd stumbled into something that led to her demise." He didn't believe the fire was an accident.

But the all-too-elusive "who" remained disturbingly, infuriatingly unanswered.

When he found this "who" who'd leveled his life, and the lives of so many others, how dearly he would pay.

He reached into his shirt and pulled out from the inner pocket the Archbishop's letter.

Opening it, he studied it. He'd read it so many times, its contents were branded into his mind. Every taut muscle in his body screamed for action, yet what action could he take?

Marie drew closer. Glancing down at the parchment in his hands, she said, "Darling, is that Bailloux's letter? The one you said you found near his body?"

"Yes."

"May I?" She held out her hand and he placed the letter on her palm. She immediately engrossed herself in it.

"Marie, men confide in you," Luc said. "You're privy to information others are not. Have you heard anything that can help us?"

Marie's delicate brows drew together as she slowly pulled her gaze off the page in her hand. "Men confide in me *because* I never betray their confidence."

"What about—" Luc began when Jules interrupted him.

"Luc, I have already asked her every question conceivable. She doesn't have any information that will shed light on the situation."

"I want to help. Truly I do. But I honestly have no information to offer." She looked at Luc. "After the arrest of the *Frondeurs*, everyone connected to them was under intense scrutiny. Our letters were read. We were often followed. No one talked. No one dared. Everyone was afraid they'd suffer what your father and your family suffered. I couldn't help you as I would have wanted."

"I understand," Jules said, though he did not. He knew with every fiber of his being that Sabine would have done more, risked more, to help a friend. A lover.

Her eyes returned to the letter. "This is odd."

"What is?" Jules asked, looking down at the parchment.

"Look at the signature. It's signed, *Barthélemy L. Bailloux.*"

"So?"

"The Archbishop's name was Barthélemy Thomas Bailloux. Why did he place an 'L' in his name?"

Jules snatched the letter out of her hand and looked closely. Bailloux had definitely, distinctly, written an "L."

Luc drew closer and peered over Jules's shoulder at the letter. "His personal secretary assured us that this was the Archbishop's handwriting. Are you certain about his name?"

"Absolutely," she said with utmost confidence. "I'm surprised his secretary missed it."

"Gaubert was distraught. Wept heavily," Jules reasoned. He couldn't keep the smile off his face. It was a small clue but it was something tangible to hold on to. Hope shot through him like an invigorating jolt. "Perhaps the Archbishop was trying to give us a clue as to who his murderer was."

"I have pleased you then? Helped in some way?" Marie returned his smile.

"You have."

"Good. It's the least I can offer—especially after you saved me this evening from my guests."

"You have guests? Here and now?" Jules asked.

Marie nodded. "I'm quite annoyed with them and left them to amuse themselves. They thought it humorous to bring along an uninvited guest. I was getting ready to have the individual, in fact the lot of them for their annoying prank, removed from my home when I was notified that you were here."

"Who is this guest?" Jules couldn't help but ask.

"Claude Cyr," she said. "A repulsive man and social climber of the worst order."

"Cyr? The tax collector?"

"Yes, Cyr. The tax collector. His fat derrière is on one of my silk settees at this very moment." She crossed her arms, vexed.

Jules smiled and glanced at Raymond. His loyal servant smirked. He knew him well enough to know what he was thinking.

"There's a small matter between Cyr and I that remains unsettled. Send him in, Marie, and don't tell him I'm here."

Marie smiled. "With pleasure."

Minutes later, spotting Marie elegantly seated on a chair in the middle of the *Room of Inspiration,* the rat scurried in. Yet what he got was a rude welcome as the door was slammed behind him and his body slammed against it.

Cyr gasped in fright the moment he recognized the man pinning him against the wooden portal by the throat.

"M-My lord! How—How good to see you." His breath gave off a horrid stench.

"Yes, I'm sure you're thrilled we've crossed paths again."

"Oh—Oh, definitely. I'm always delighted to see you, my lord." He gave him a miserable smile.

"You do recall I told you to make yourself available to me, don't you? And that I would pay you a visit shortly to settle the score?"

"I believe I remember you saying something like that."

"I sent a man to your home, Cyr. He was informed you weren't there. In fact, you've made yourself quite scarce. You wouldn't be hiding from me, now would you? You aren't trying to avoid paying your debt, are you?"

"N-No!" Cyr squeaked. "Absolutely not!"

"Then what are you doing in Paris? The place, you well know, I'm not permitted to enter. Did you think you'd be safe from me here?"

"No, no. It—It isn't like that. I—I have important business. The King's business," he stammered.

"Really? The King's business is conducted in Marie de Perron's home?" Jules squeezed Cyr's sweaty neck a little tighter. A strangled sound instantly emitted from the vermin's throat. "You're here for self-promotion. Hoping to elevate your social worth. But you see, the lady isn't interested."

"I most certainly am not," Marie confirmed.

"I should kill you here and now for your lies," Jules growled at Cyr.

"Please, my lord, I—I have a proposition for you! I give you something you want and you—you reduce the debt I owe you. Th-That sounds fair, no?"

"What could you have that I would possibly want?"

"Information. Perhaps it may help remove the stain that has tarnished your family's name."

That grabbed his curiosity. Cyr was a serpent. Completely untrustworthy. Yet still, Jules couldn't help asking, "What information?"

"F-First the debt. I tell you the information and you cut it by half."

"You tell me the information and I *may* let you live to see tomorrow. But I'll not take a coin"—he pulled him from the door and slammed him against it again—"off the debt you owe my family. Is that clear?"

Wide-eyed, Cyr shook. "V-Very clear. I—I see your point, my lord. I truly do . . ."

"Out with it," Jules demanded.

Cyr swallowed hard. "L-Last week I heard while playing dice with some fine gentlemen, like yourself, my lord, the Marquis de la Rocque, say—mind you, he was quite drunk at the time—that he'd lost his entire fortune to your father in a game of Basset. He said, 'The problem'—by problem, I believe he meant your father—'was taken care of.' Then he fell facedown, senseless."

Marquis de la Rocque. Why did this man's name keep resurfacing? Hadn't Ninette mentioned him as being at his father's last gathering? Didn't the Archbishop's secretary, Gaubert, say that Rocque was one of the last visitors Bailloux had before his death?

Rocque's name was . . . *Leopold. Jésus-Christ.*

"I've made a decision, Cyr. I'll reduce your debt to me."

"Really? How much?"

"The amount will depend on how well you serve me. From now on, you're in my employ."

"What? But—But, my lord, I cannot. I have responsibilities. You cannot force me to—" Tightening his fingers around Cyr's neck choked off his words.

Jules eased his grip on the man's throat to allow him to breathe. "I'll allow you to choose. Should you decide to accept my offer, you'll be under guard day and night, your every move watched. Your freedom restricted. Or die here and now." Jules squeezed Cyr's throat a fraction. "Which is your choice?"

Beads of sweat rolled down Cyr's read face. He lifted the corners of his mouth in what was a semblance of a smile. "I'm delighted to be back in your employ, my lord."

24

Leon strutted into the antechamber. "You wished to see me?" His comment was purposely flippant, annoyed that he'd only just arrived in the city, and barely settled into his townhouse, when he was summoned.

How he hated being ordered about. Loathed it with every fiber of his being.

He was immediately taken aback by the haggard appearance of the Aristo before him.

Dark circles below his eyes, his complexion gray, he looked older than his fifty-six years. True, Leon hadn't seen his friend the Marquis for many months, but even at his worst, he hadn't looked like this.

The Marquis rose unsteadily from his chair. "What have you done?" he asked.

Glancing down at the table that separated him from the older Aristo, Leon cocked a brow. A decanter mostly empty. A crystal goblet mostly full of amber liquid. The Marquis' most excellent brandy.

Leon smiled. "It's only ten o'clock in the morning and you're already into your cups. Tsk, tsk."

"It is the only thing that calms my frazzled nerves. I haven't been able to sleep since I heard the news about the Archbishop of Divonne. Rumors about his death are rampant in the city."

Leon pulled out a chair and sat. "Why, thank you. I would love to sit down. You are most gracious." Each word was edged with sarcasm. Reaching for the decanter and a clean goblet, Leon poured himself a healthy portion. He swirled the brandy in the glass. "You don't mind, do you?" He brought the goblet to his lips, not caring a whit if the Aristo objected. Tipping it, he let the fiery liquid flow smoothly down his throat. The sweet burn was a pleasure unto itself.

"Do you know what they are saying about the Archbishop's death?" the Marquis sputtered, still standing on his unstable feet.

"I believe I heard something along the lines that he had a *tendre* for his mistress and killed himself because he couldn't cope with her loss. Most tragic," he added blandly before enjoying another taste from his goblet. "I suppose some might think it terribly romantic—together in death and all that."

The Marquis slammed his fist down on the table, practically upsetting his goblet. "Don't play me for a fool! The rumors range from suicide to murder. *Murder*, Leon! Anyone who knew the Archbishop longer than an hour knows he wasn't capable of suicide. It goes against the Church and his personal beliefs." He raked both hands through his hair. "We were finished with this. Blainville was dead. It was behind us. You did this! You killed Bailloux. And you have stirred a hornets' nest. When you kill a man of the Archbishop's standing, there are questions. There will be inquiries. We'll be caught for our misdeeds."

Leon narrowed his eyes. "We will not be caught if you hold your tongue, which would be easier to accomplish if you stayed sober."

"I thought you restricted your killing to local whores." His wits dulled by drink, the Marquis prattled on, uncensored. "Why did you do this, Leon? Bailloux helped us. He'd been loyal and silent all this time."

Rage smoldered in Leon's gut as he stared at the ingrate before him. The fool would have nothing if it weren't for him! How dare he have the gall to question him.

Leon placed his goblet down on the table and slowly rose.

The Marquis' anger dissipated from his eyes, only to be replaced by an emotion much more pleasing.

Fear. He felt an inebriating surge of power flood through his veins.

"I had a loose end that needed attending. Bailloux's demise couldn't be helped." His voice was low. Indicative of his simmering ire.

"Wh-What do you mean, 'loose end'? Bailloux was not a loose end. He was a man of rank and morals."

A laugh erupted from Leon. "He was a man who was fucking a married woman and helped most willingly in a conspiracy against an equally despicable character who was hated by just about everyone—the Marquis de Blainville. Or have you forgotten?" Leon stepped closer, his intent intimidation. His intent worked, evident by the blanching of the older man's visage. "Have you forgotten what Blainville intended to do to you and your family? How he tried to prey on your weakness? Have you forgotten who helped you stop him? Who saved you and your family from ruin? IT WAS I!" he barked in the Marquis' face, making him jump. "I kept my end of the bargain by ridding you and your friends of Blainville," he said with a slow and deliberate tone. "And you kept yours, by killing my loathsome brother for me. Do not speak to me about morals. You and your lot have none."

Leon fisted the Marquis' shirt and yanked him close, the older man almost butting noses with him—his red-rimmed eyes widened—fumes from the brandy the Aristo had consumed emanating from him. "I saw both you and the *scrupulous* Archbishop in the crowd during Blainville's execution. After what he was going to do to you, you liked seeing his feet and hands bound, that noose placed around his neck. The jerk of his body when his neck broke. Don't bother to lie. I saw the satisfaction in your eyes as well as the Archbishop's."

"What—What are you planning next?" The man's brandy-soaked breath wafted him in the face.

Leon abruptly released him, sending the Marquis staggering back. "I have a personal matter to attend to." He smoothed out his doublet, not caring for the newly formed crinkles. "I intend to rid the world of two more Moutiers."

"Blainville's sons?" the Marquis choked out, horrified.

"Precisely. You can blame Jules de Moutier for the Archbishop's death. If he hadn't been poaching where he shouldn't have been, it wouldn't have been necessary to kill Bailloux. If he'd simply faded away, left well enough alone, and not been so bent on regaining status and avenging his family's honor—he and his brother might have lived to a ripe old age."

The Marquis shook his head and sank into a nearby chair. "You cannot do this. You cannot keep killing men of consequence. You must stop."

"Nonsense. The Moutiers are of no consequence. And I can do as I please. I'm far cleverer than the 'men of consequence,'" he responded smugly. He approached, leaned into the Aristo's ear. "Including you. You will keep silent, or pay dearly," he promised.

The Marquis looked away, his shoulders slumped in defeat. "You are Satan. You're killing people senselessly," he whispered.

Leon chuckled and sauntered to the door.

Since he was a boy, his governesses had made similar comments, mostly for his penchant for torturing and killing small animals for fun. He didn't mind being referred to as Lucifer, for he was a figure that invoked terror. Leon liked that comparison very much.

"You will surely damn us," the Marquis bemoaned.

A smile lifted the corners of Leon's mouth. "Sir, you've made a pact with the devil. You are already damned."

* * *

Jules strode into the bedchamber in Marie de Perron's home. Sabine rose from her chair.

"I have news," he said. "It would seem we may have some answers yet." He explained about Claude Cyr and the Marquis de la Rocque.

"That snake, Cyr, is under the same roof?" She shuddered at the thought.

"Don't worry. He's tied up and under Raymond's guard. In fact, Louise, Vincent, and Agnes all gleefully volunteered to help watch him. He'll not get away."

"But what do you plan to do with him?"

"I don't know yet, but I have a feeling that that ambitious vermin has been privy to his share of secrets and gossip. Raymond will interrogate him thoroughly. In the meantime, I intend to get de la Rocque good and drunk. His tongue loosens up considerably when he's into his cups."

"How will you do that?"

He smiled broadly. "Marie is having a masquerade ball tomorrow evening. He's invited."

"A masquerade? Really? Oh, that's perfect." With the anonymity of a mask, they could move around freely.

She looked down at her humble garb. That is, if she had something to wear. She couldn't very well attend a ball dressed as she was.

Before she could mention her dilemma, he walked up to her and cupped her cheeks.

"Are you all right?" His concern moved her.

"Yes, I've been thinking. If you are looking for a possible culprit, why not look to your father's secretary, Monsieur Bedeau? He had access to the satchels. He could have easily added any and all damning letters."

"Monsieur Bedeau served my father for three and a half decades, and even insisted on going to prison to serve him while incarcerated, fully expecting him to be exonerated swiftly. Unfortunately, it was not a brief detainment. Bedeau took ill while in the Bastille. Advanced in years, he never recovered and died before my father was hanged. He was loyal until his very last."

"Then perhaps it was one of your other servants. You had many that could have—"

"I finished Isabelle's journal last night while you slept," he injected.

That froze her words on her tongue.

She'd given him permission to read both hers and her sister's journals.

"I finished yours, as well," he said. "I've learned a great deal from reading them."

"Oh?" was all she could muster.

"For instance, I know that your sister loved you very, very much." Lightly he brushed his knuckles down her cheek.

"She still does, Jules," she countered. "She is not dead."

His eyes were soulful and sad, but he did not argue the point. "I also know that Ninette spoke the truth when she said Isabelle stole parchments and ink. Her passion for writing was indeed strong. That said, my father's arrest and false charges couldn't have been the result of a disgruntled servant or even a group of servants. It would take someone of high rank to topple a man of my father's standing."

He tucked an errant tress behind her ear. "I read about your experiences during the *Fronde*. The horror. The terror you felt. If I could, I'd erase them from your heart and soul."

His words slipped inside her heart.

"I am sorry for the added hardship my family placed on yours," he said. "The restrictions we put on the mill, the forests and rivers, the constant raising of taxes, each constraint increasing the risk of starvation. I am sorry you suffered through such things.

"My father's laws were not ideal. I see that now. They were heavy-handed and should have been tempered."

Her defenses were crumbling. She felt the pieces give way with each soft sentiment he spoke. Tender feelings she'd tried to contain flooded through her.

"Your journals only further enforced what I already know about you," he continued. "How strong you are. How brave. How compassionate and caring. A woman who longs to live and love passionately. Freely. You don't need Isabelle to be whole. The woman before me is in no way lacking or incomplete. I see you as you are. And I very much like what I see."

A single tear slipped out of the corner of her eye.

There was no point even trying to ignore, deny, or fight the truth any longer—she was deeply in love with him. She'd always been in love with him. She'd always had a connection to him. From the moment she first saw his beautiful face.

"You are not 'Sensible Sabine,'" he quoted. How she hated it every time her father had called her that. "You are so much more. And you should continue to dream grand."

Another tear slipped down her cheek. She couldn't do that. He was her dream. Beyond grand. He was too far out of her reach. It didn't escape her notice that neither of them talked about the future.

Jules wanted to soothe her. He wanted to erase her pain. *Dieu*, he just plain wanted her. In his arms. In his life. And he couldn't. Not the way he wanted. His familial obligations were a barrier. One that couldn't be overcome. He couldn't even ask her to be his mistress. She'd never agree. Too many journal entries were dedicated to her father's many mistresses and Louise's suffering because of them.

He slipped an arm around her waist. Her soft form against his body felt so good. And so right.

He nuzzled her neck and pressed a light kiss against the downy skin just below her ear. Her response was immediate. She laced her arms around his neck. His cock hardened.

Jules swept her up in his arms, then placing her down on the bed, he lowered himself onto her soft body and claimed her soft mouth, eager to pull them into the magic that was their very own.

How on earth was he going to have his fill of this woman?

For a man who always had a plan, he had no idea how to sate this untamable desire she inspired or how to conquer what he felt for her.

* * *

Leon slammed open the door to his study. Hubert scrambled to his feet.

Leon stalked over to the side table and snatched up the decanter of brandy. "I warn you, Hubert, I am in a foul mood. You'd better have news that pleases me." He filled a goblet with the amber liquid and downed it with a toss of his head.

"As a matter of fact—"

Leon spun around to face the burly brute. "Do you know where I have been all night?" he injected.

"N-No."

"With my future bride and her boorish father." He slammed the goblet down. "Who does he think he is, speaking to me that way, the condescending pompous ass. I'm not some common riff-raff. He should be grateful to me. He should get down on his knees before me and thank me for agreeing to take that ugly sow he calls his offspring as my wife!"

Seething, he walked over to his desk and flopped down onto his chair. "He'll pay for this offense," he swore with clenched teeth. "And so will his daughter." He conjured up deliciously violent images of their mangled bodies to assuage his rage. "I'll keep her only until she provides an heir, then the fucking bitch dies. Of course, her father's demise will follow close behind. And I'll move on to a wife that isn't quite so vomitous."

He returned his attention to Hubert and found the man standing in the middle of the room, nervously shifting his weight from one foot to the other. There it was. Fear. Each time he invoked it, it was a heady rush. It was power.

Leon rose. "Well? Tell me you found the Moutiers. Tell me you found that snake Cyr." He smashed his fist down on the desk. "Tell me you bloody well found *someone*."

"All of them. We found them all."

His fury ebbed instantly. "Oh? Where?"

Hubert smiled, flashing a display of rotten teeth. "At the home of that courtesan—Marie de Perron. The Moutiers weren't easy to follow, especially in the large crowds of Paris. They were cautious and clever. We lost them for a short time. But then, Victor caught sight of Cyr. He was entering Perron's townhouse."

"So Cyr is busy social climbing. Why on earth would Marie de Perron entertain his company?"

"Don't know. But that was yesterday, and she's still entertaining it today. He's still there."

Leon cocked a brow. "Really?"

"Yes," he responded smugly. "And so are both Moutiers."

Leon stepped out from around his desk. "Go on."

"We were outside her townhouse waiting for Cyr when the brothers arrived with the acting troupe and your mademoiselle. We didn't recognize them at first. They are wearing peasant disguises and they arrived in separate groups and entered using the servants' entrance."

"Interesting. Moutier brings his present mistress to the home of his former one. Is he fucking both of them under the same roof?" A fresh wave of rage crested over him. He paced. "He thinks he's going to regain his rank and lands by using Perron's social clout, doesn't he?"

"I don't know, but you can ask him tomorrow, if you want," Hubert said.

Leon arrested his steps. "Tomorrow? Why tomorrow?"

"I heard it on good authority that Madame de Perron is having a masquerade ball tomorrow night."

It was Leon's turn to smile. "A masquerade, you say? Well, well."

He strode up to Hubert. "Bring enough men and make certain they don't fail this time. Slaughter the Moutiers and that band of no-account actors they're with."

"Yes, monsieur."

"As for Cyr, he'd sell his own mother for coin. Question him first. Learn how loose his tongue has been, then kill him as well."

"As you wish."

Leon crossed his arms, feeling much more content than when he'd walked into the room. "The mademoiselle is all mine." He'd secure an invitation to the ball.

Tomorrow, Sabine would finally be his.

And she had some major penance to pay.

25

"You look like an angel . . ." Agnes dabbed her teary eyes with a handkerchief and then blew her nose in it.

Standing in the long corridor, she and Sabine could hear noise from the masquerade, the mingling of music and chatter rising up the distant stairwell.

"Thank you." Sabine's stomach was in knots.

It was incredible. Magnificent. Nerve-wracking. She hadn't worn a gown like this in years. Her silver and blue gown was so luxurious. So sumptuous. She couldn't help touching her skirts every so often.

She couldn't help noticing the startling similarity between this evening and one she'd dreamed about many years ago.

Strange, how destiny had arranged the stars. How fate had aligned the events that led to this night. Sabine Laurent dressed in such elegance. Jules de Moutier waiting for her downstairs. A masquerade. Music. Dance. Perhaps even magic and a miracle or two.

"You look so lovely." Agnes smiled. "I am grateful to Marie for her generosity."

Marie had lent Sabine not only her gown, but also the staff to make any necessary alterations. She'd even sent maids to help with Sabine's hair, now in perfect fashionable curls—and of course, there was the gilded demi-mask with colorful silver plumes.

Best of all, Agnes, who had managed to keep her silver coins hidden, had purchased her the most beautiful slippers. Silver with tiny glass beading. So reminiscent of her former pair.

"You're all set to go the ball." Agnes kissed Sabine's cheek. In her ear she whispered, "You will take his breath away. Do not neglect to enjoy yourself, for a night like this does not come around often." She pulled back and gazed into Sabine's eyes. "I have a feeling this night will change everything between you."

Sabine hadn't been able to shake that same feeling. Something was going to happen tonight. Something monumental.

Excited and nervous, she was breathless by the time they reached the top of the stairwell. A dozen steps down to the landing, then a turn to the left, and she'd see Jules.

She couldn't wait for him to see her in something that was not old and worn. She gathered her skirts and began her descent, her pulse beating in double time.

Reaching the landing, she took a deep breath and turned the corner.

She captured Jules's attention in an instant. Standing at the bottom of the stairs, he smiled. Her gaze was riveted to him. His tall muscled form, his broad shoulders were accentuated by his silver doublet and breeches.

He looked utterly regal and just like in her dreams.

Her insides quavering, she made her way down the last six steps with all the elegance and poise befitting her attire.

His smile deepened, bringing out his heart-fluttering dimples. "You are a ravishing beauty."

She looked up at his handsome face, letting her gaze caress his beloved visage. "So are you," she said.

He chuckled. Taking her hand, he pressed a kiss to it. "I can safely say no one has ever said that to me before," he gently teased, then held out his hand and said, "Will you dance with me?"

Her cheeks hurt from the sheer size of her grin. She placed her hand in his. "I will."

* * *

He was a dead man.

His nervous breathing audible, Cyr peered into the corridor. The commotion from the masquerade was a distant din.

He had to get out of here. Fast.

Behind him were the unconscious bodies of the old actor and the witch. After two intolerable days, he seized the first opportunity to escape.

He had no idea how long they'd remain senseless. Physical violence was not his forte.

Slipping into the empty hallway, heart pounding, he rushed along the shadows, steering away from the wall sconces. Up ahead was the door that led to the servants' passageways and stairwell. Cursing the slowness of his rounded form, he pushed himself, forcing his leaden legs to eat up the distance.

He'd been in binds before. But this was by far the worst. If he was caught . . . Sweat rolled down his face. He raced on. Ten more feet. His lungs laboring, he sucked in air hard and fast. Eight feet. He'd make it. He'd make it. Five.

Rocque was sure to be here tonight. Moutier, either brother or both, would question him. Cyr had to be long gone before they came looking for him.

Move!

Perspiration stung his eyes.

He practically fell against the door when he reached it. His fingers fumbled. The latch opened.

He shoved the door open, quickly shut it behind him, and slumped against the wooden barrier to catch his breath and wipe the sweat from his eyes. The servants' passageway was darker.

And quiet. Most of the servants would be downstairs during the masquerade.

With a huff, he pushed himself off the door and waddled to the stairs, his legs aching. Cautiously, he made his way down the steps, reaching the main floor unchallenged. Unobserved. Panting.

He found himself in another corridor. Scanning the doors to the left and right, he tried to orient himself. Left. Yes, that would lead him to the vestibule and out the door.

He took a step and stopped dead. There would be crowds of people at the main entrance. What if someone recognized him? He had no mask to hide behind. No. The servants' entrance was better. But which way was that?

To the right. That was the direction. He hoped. Cyr turned and moved along the hallway, passing a number of doors, hoping he'd intuitively know which one was the correct one.

Female laughter reverberated up the corridor. He stopped. Hearing footsteps approaching, he knew it was only moments before someone turned the corner. Panicked, he grabbed the closest latch, opened the door, and rushed out.

Right into the vestibule. Filled with a crush of people. Brilliant colors and plumes everywhere.

The throng was so large, he was instantly pressed against the wall. It wasn't where he intended to exit, but it *was* an exit. Mere feet away was the main entrance. All he had to do was keep his head down and move against the direction of the entering mass. Feigning a forehead itch, he used his hand to shield his face as he moved through the horde, the bedlam drowning out his hard, heavy breaths.

He was close. Making good his escape was all but clinched.

Peeking up, Cyr saw a large man before him shift to the side. He caught sight of the door once more. And the figure entering it.

He froze. So did his blood. Though the man wore a mask, Cyr recognized that chin. That seemingly innocuous manner. That rather average form. For those who didn't really know him, they would think he was a regular man.

But there was nothing regular or harmless about him.

Depraved. Malicious. Deceptively disarming, insidiously placid—blocking the entrance was the Baron de Lor, Leon de Vittry.

Cyr had known cutthroats and thieves. He understood greed and ambition. But he had no understanding of the evil that dwelled in Vittry. Worse still, the demon was looking for him.

His heart thundering in his ears, Cyr twisted around in the crush and scrambled for the door he'd just used.

He'd take his chances in the servants' hallway.

* * *

The last notes faded, ending their second dance. Jules bowed to her. Sabine smiled at her Dark Prince and curtsied. She'd remembered all the steps to not only the *menuet*, but also the *allemande.*

She caught sight of Raymond standing in the crowd, looking anxious for a word. Clearly, Jules had seen him, too. He led her off the dance floor, and headed straight in his direction.

"My lord, your brother is with . . . his *friend*," Raymond said the moment they reached him. There were too many ears about. Sabine knew the "friend" Raymond was referring to was the Marquis de la Rocque.

"Good." Sotto voce, Jules asked, "Where are they?"

"In the library. They have been enjoying some excellent brandy. Your brother thought you might like to join them?"

Jules turned to her.

"Go," Sabine insisted, heartened by the look of regret in his eyes. "You don't want to miss an opportunity to spend time with your brother and his *friend*."

"Raymond, escort Sabine back to her rooms."

"Raymond should be with you in case you or Luc needs him," Sabine said. "I'll go to my chambers straightaway. I promise. I'll be fine." Sabine couldn't stop smiling and stepped closer to him. "I'll remember this night forever."

His eyes softened. "So will I." He caressed her cheek tenderly with his knuckles.

This night had been perfect. A fantasy come to life. A dream come true.

"Good luck," she added. He gave her a quick hard kiss and disappeared with Raymond in the crowd.

* * *

The merrymakers were loud and rambunctious, jostling Sabine about as she tried to make her way through the crowd. Like a strong current, the multitude swept her up. By the time she finally managed to disengage from the throng, she found herself in the courtyard.

The night was warm, strains of music from the harpsichord and violins floating on the gentle breeze. She looked about. The stone benches were occupied by elegantly clad guests, their masks as rich as their attire. Groups were scattered about, engaged in conversation and laughter.

She was nowhere near the servants' door. There had to be another entrance into the passageways used by the hired help.

Briskly, she strode back into the Grand Salon and reentered the conflux. Moving along the perimeter of the room, she searched for an exit, receiving an unavoidable bump time and again.

Upon reaching the corner, she paused. The overcrowded salon was warm. Too warm. It didn't help that she stood near a large wall sconce and its many burning candles, but at least there was a bit of breathing room here. God, how she wanted to reach her chamber and remove the mask. It was starting to get hot and uncomfortable.

Rising onto the balls of her feet, she tried to peer over the heads of the people in front of her, but couldn't see over the wall of elaborate coiffures and decorative plumes.

She lowered herself back onto her heels and was about to continue on when the man next to her caught her eye. Only a short distance away, she saw him lift his hand. Candlelight from the wall sconce flashed onto his large gold ring. He removed it from his finger and slipped it into his pocket. Then he slipped into the crowd.

She'd seen that ring before. It was a nobleman's family emblem—an olive branch and lion. And it belonged to Valentin, the kindly Marquis d'Argon.

Odd that he was here. He didn't strike her as the sort of man who enjoyed such distractions. Odder still was his removal of his ring. He didn't want anyone to recognize it. He didn't want anyone to know he was present.

Why?

Someone grabbed her arm. Startled, she snapped her head around. A man in a gold-colored mask dressed in pale blue held her firmly.

"Sabine?" said a familiar voice.

Furrowing her brow, she gazed into the brown eyes behind the mask. "Leon?" Could it be?

"Yes, my darling. It is I. This is a huge surprise."

Relief flooded through her, bringing a smile back onto her face. "Leon, I'm so very glad to see you. I've gotten myself hopelessly lost. Perhaps you would escort me to my room?"

"My darling, I'd do anything you ask, you know that, but . . . what are you doing here? Dressed this way?"

She tossed a quick glance about to make certain that no one was listening. "I'm searching for Isabelle."

"Isabelle?" he repeated, astonished.

"I know it sounds mad, but I *know* she's alive. I feel it. I won't stop until I find her." Her smile returned. "And I will find her, Leon. I'm in search of servants who worked with Isabelle. As it turns out, Marie de Perron employs one. She allowed me to question her."

"And? Did you find anything out?"

"No, regrettably. I intend to find all the Marquis de Blainville's former servants, and question them one by one until I know the truth about what happened to my sister."

He shook his head. "Why didn't you tell me this before? I could have helped. Had you confided this in me, I would have told you that I employ two of the late Marquis' servants."

"*Two?*" Dear God, this evening was too perfect. "Oh, Leon, that's wonderful! I want to question them."

"Absolutely . . . but there is a problem."

"Oh?"

"Viviane and Nicolas are elderly. They're leaving my employ to live out the remainder of their days with their son. I'm afraid I don't know where he lives. Or even his name. Their final day is tomorrow."

"Tomorrow? Where are they now? Are they in Paris?"

"No, darling. They are at my château."

She felt crestfallen. "Perhaps the other servants can tell us where their son lives? We can go to his home later . . ."

"Quite honestly, given their age, I wonder if they will even make it to the closest town. It would be a miracle if they reach their son at all."

Crushed, she looked down. It seemed too cruel to learn about these servants when it was too late. What if these people could have made a difference?

"I have an idea," he said. "If we leave right now, we can travel through the night and, weather permitting, arrive at my château by midmorning." He smiled. "They're old and slow. Chances are good they will still be there, or at least in the near vicinity."

"Oh, Leon, do you really think it's not too late?" she asked, hope swelling inside her.

"If we leave now, I believe we'll catch them."

"Then we'll leave now." She looked about at the crowd. She'd take Agnes, Louise, and Vincent and leave a note with one of the servants for Jules to inform him of her whereabouts. He could join her when he was through. She simply couldn't afford to pass on this opportunity. "Why don't you see to the carriage. I'll get my family and meet you out front." She stepped away.

He caught her arm. "No time for that. In this crowd, darling, who knows how long it will take to reach them. Besides, I've only just arrived. My carriage is likely still out front. I'll settle you in the carriage and then leave a note with one of the servants for our hostess. She'll see that Louise and the rest are informed, no?"

An uneasy feeling rushed over her. "I suppose . . ." Was she willing to travel with Leon alone? Be alone with him until the rest joined her?

He took her hand and gave it a gentle squeeze. "I'm sorry. I fear I've made you uncomfortable. Of course you are right. It's only proper that Agnes or Louise come with us. Perhaps when the rest join us on the morrow, we can finish the fête we never got to have in your father's memory. I'll attend to the carriage as you request. Or would it be better if I helped you search?"

She was being foolish. This was Leon. Her father's loyal friend. Always kind. Obliging. Giving. He was generously offering to leave the party and travel hours for her. She quashed her apprehension.

"No, Leon. You're the one who's correct. If we dally any longer, we may miss Viviane and Nicolas. We'll leave straightaway, as you suggest." She hugged the man she'd known since childhood. "Thank you for helping me. How can I possibly repay you for all you've done?"

* * *

Jules walked into the library with a decanter of Marie's quality brandy in hand, his mask offering him the anonymity he needed. A roar of drunken laughter rushed up to greet him. He found his brother and Leopold, Marquis de la Rocque, seated together on a settee near the hearth.

The Marquis, obviously well into his cups, had tossed off his mask. Luc, however, was still masked—and convincingly inebriated. Jules watched him empty the decanter of brandy into Rocque's goblet without adding to his own. Being around Sabine's family was having an effect on his brother. He was putting on a fine performance.

Jules closed the door behind him and held up the brandy. "May I join you?"

The older Aristo peered at him, his face lighting up the moment he recognized the fresh supply of his favorite spirit.

"Come, come." He waved Jules over. "Join us, friend." He elbowed Luc. "I don't know about you, but anyone who has brandy is a friend of mine." He let out a boisterous laugh. Jules and Luc joined in as Jules sat down across from them.

Luc had done an admirable job of intoxicating the Marquis. The fool had no idea who Jules and Luc were. Didn't even seem to care. Then again, he hadn't much cared about conspiring against an innocent man and sending him to his death either.

Luc slapped Rocque on the back. "I agree with my friend here. You are most welcome, sir," he said to Jules, slurring his words a little. "And so is your brandy." He fell back howling, Rocque joining in, sending some of the brandy sloshing out of his goblet and onto himself.

Sobering slightly, Luc turned to Rocque, and asked, "Now that we have more brandy, wh-what shall we drink to?"

Jules held up the decanter. "To friendship!"

The Marquis shot his arm straight up in the air. "To friendship!" He tossed back a mouthful of the amber liquid.

"Friendship," Luc concurred and brought his goblet to his lips, but he didn't drink any.

"To parties!" Jules toasted and took a small swig from the decanter.

The Marquis and Luc joined in chorus, "To parties!" Rocque happily took another healthy gulp from his goblet.

Luc raised his goblet, his hand unsteady. "How about to pleasurable distractions—lusty women, strong drink, and a good game of *Basset.*"

Rocque gave a hearty full-bellied laugh. "Oh, friend, I do like those distractions." He consumed the brandy in his goblet and then thrust it out toward Jules, a silent command for more.

Laughing along with Luc and Rocque, Jules refilled it. "I don't mind telling you I have lost a fortune in that game of chance," Jules lied.

Luc nodded. "Me, too."

Rocque drained his goblet, then wiped his mouth with his sleeve. "You know," he began, swaying a little in his seat. "I sh-shouldn't tell you this, but . . . since we're gentlemen . . . an-and friends who share the same interests . . . Once"—he held up a finger—"I lost my entire fortune"—he gave a broad swipe of his arm—"in a game of cards."

"Really?" Jules acted astonished. "You don't seem impoverished. What did you do? Win it back?"

Grinning like an imbecile, Rocque responded, "No. I waited until they hanged the bastard who won it." He snorted. "Never paid him a single coin."

A dark deep rage crept over Jules. Mastering his fury by sheer force of will, he kept his features carefully schooled. "How did you manage that?"

The Marquis guzzled down more brandy, then let out a belch. "Manage it? I'd like to say I was responsible for the bastard's demise, but . . . truth is, his misdeeds got the better of him. Perhaps you've heard of Charles, the former Marquis de Blainville?"

"I know him!" Luc exclaimed. "I don't come to Paris often . . . b-but I played cards with him, too. Lost a goodly sum to the man."

Rocque placed his arm around Luc's shoulder. "So sorry to hear that, my friend," he commiserated. "I don't suppose you know he cheated?"

Jules clenched his teeth. "Cheated, did he?"

"Yes, he cheated. He was a dirty cheater," Rocque practically spit out the last word. "N-Naaawt only did he h-h-habitually cheat, but . . . no one dared call him on it. He had the reputation of being vicious . . . retaliatory. Took offense . . . Made you pay for all perceived transgressions. *Underhanded* is what they called him."

"Who called him that?" Jules squeezed the decanter.

The older Aristo removed his arm from around Luc and held out his goblet for more brandy. Reluctantly, Jules obliged and poured.

Rocque swallowed some of the fiery fluid, then said, "Everyone said it. It's common knowledge." His swaying was more pronounced.

"If you thought him to be so ruthless, why play cards with him at all?" Jules asked, his tone tight as he watched Rocque drain yet another goblet. The man was drinking the brandy as if it were water.

Rocque let out another loud belch and slumped against the back of the settee. "Blainville goaded me . . . Had to play him. You want me to lose face? Then he took me for everything." His grasp on the goblet was loosening and tipping to one side. A few drops spilled out onto his lap without any reaction from the Marquis.

"I heard it rumored that someone set Blainville up," Jules said. "That he wasn't really a *Frondeur*."

Rocque waved his hand dismissively. "That rumor's been 'round for years. I wish it were true. Poetic justice for a man who brought misery to many. In . . . fact, gentle—men, I wish I'd been the one who'd done it . . ." Rocque's eyes began to close.

Luc gave him a sharp shake, startling the man awake. "I heard the Archbishop of Divonne had something to do with it."

"Arch-bishop of Div . . . onne? Don't know anything . . . 'bout that."

"Aren't you friends with the Archbishop?" Jules said, despising the disparaging comments about the man he respected and honored.

Rocque shrugged. "I suppose . . . Went to visit him recently. Just before he died. Lovesick fool was mourning the death of his favorite." Sleepy, Rocque smiled. "Thought I might coax him into a game of cards. In his depleted state . . . I'd win some coin, for certain." His eyes fell shut, his head fell back, and his body was suddenly lax. The goblet in his hand dropped onto the carpet with a muffled thud.

Jules shot to his feet, murderous furor flooding his body. Luc was there to hold him back in a heartbeat.

"Jules, no," Luc said. "You don't have social standing to protect you. You do anything to a man of the aristocracy, and you will hang for it."

Gazing down at the unconscious Marquis, Jules fisted his hands, nostrils flared, his anger escalating with each hard breath he took. But it wasn't just ire that gripped him. A sinking feeling of doubt had taken hold, corroding his theory. The man before him was detestable. No doubt about that. Dishonorable and opportunistic, too. But Jules was having some serious doubts about Rocque's culpability in his family's disgrace.

"I don't think he's responsible." Luc spoke the very words resonating in Jules's head, for Rocque wasn't smart enough to hold his tongue. Moreover, the opportunity to brag about unseating the Marquis de Blainville would have proved too tempting for him.

Merde. Merde. "Merde!" He wanted him to be guilty. He hated the man. "Why couldn't he be the one?"

Before Luc could respond, there was a knock at the door.

Vincent staggered in, holding his neck, Louise beside him looking pale.

"What's happened?" Jules demanded.

"Cyr," was all Vincent said.

"That's not all. I can't find Sabine," Louise said.

That dissolved Jules's ire. "What do you mean you can't find her?"

"I looked for her in her chambers and throughout the townhouse. I located Raymond and together we searched. That's when we came upon Cyr in the servants' stairwell. Raymond dragged him back to his chambers, where we found Vincent and Agnes on the ground injured. Cyr is weeping. Says he thinks he knows where Sabine is. He won't tell us. He says he'll strike a bargain with you. He'll only speak to you."

Jules was out the door in an instant, his heart pounding in his throat. He shoved his way through the crowd, terror tightening his stomach. He had a bad feeling in his gut he couldn't shake. The throng was but a blur of colors. A fusion of noise. A barrier that was keeping him from finding Sabine. The moment he reached the closest stairwell, he grabbed the banister and took the stairs two at a time, his anxiety mounting by the moment.

He burst into Cyr's rooms. Tied to a chair in the middle of the antechamber, pleading and sobbing with Raymond to be released, was the rodent. Jules ripped off his mask and tossed it to the floor.

"My lord!" Cyr exclaimed. "My lord, I—I—I need your protection. I—I only tried to escape because I'm in a bit of trouble, you see. I—I can help you. I might know where the mademoiselle is. In return you—you help me." Cyr gave him a feeble smile.

"Untie him," Jules ordered, ignoring the surprised look on his man's face. Raymond quickly loosened the knots in the rope that held Cyr.

Looking relieved, Cyr rose as soon as he was freed. "I thank you—"

Jules shoved Cyr against the wall.

His eyes widened. "M-My lord, what are you do—"

Jules pulled out his dagger from inside his sleeve, pinned Cyr to the wall by the throat, and drove it into Cyr's thigh. Cyr let out a shrill cry in agony.

Slowly, Jules twisted the knife. "Where is she!"

Cyr shrieked and squirmed, his sweaty fingers clutching Jules's wrist, but he couldn't free himself from Jules's hold any more than he could evade the blade slicing open his flesh.

Jules yanked the dagger out. Cyr's knees weakened and he was back to blubbering.

"Where. Is. She?" Jules repeated, fear tearing him apart. "Who has her?"

"My lord . . . pl-please . . ." Cyr whimpered between pants, assailing Jules with wafts of his foul breath.

Jules raised his arm, poised to strike again.

"All right! All right! I—I'll tell you!" Cyr cried.

"*Everything!*"

"Yes. Yes. I—I—I won't leave any-anything out. I swear!"

Jules lowered his arm. "Speak. *The truth.*"

"I—I—I think Mademoiselle Laurent is with that devil, Vittry. I saw him here tonight. He has been on a quest to have her. He approached me some time ago. Told me he'd help me gain the position of tax collector for the King—s-s-said he had influential friends who'd see to it. In return I was to help him."

"Help him how?"

"Once I had the appointment, Vittry told me I was to put pressure on the Laurent family—compound the interest on the taxes and raise it exponentially so—so that they couldn't meet it. He wanted them in a desperate state. Vulnerable for him to sweep in and have your mademoiselle. Monsieur Laurent had sent one daughter to work for your father. Vittry wanted Sabine Laurent sent to him. It was all he talked about. Having her. Then when Monsieur Laurent died, he became most impatient for the girl. I was to have broken her that day I came to her home. But—But you were there. You weren't supposed to be there. Monsieur de Vittry doesn't like failure. He's been looking for me ever since." Cyr sobbed harder.

"You—You don't know what he's capable of, my lord. I believe he had his own brother killed . . . for the title, and was involved in the conspiracy against your father. He'd hinted at these things m-many times. M-My lord, Vittry is dangerous. Cold. Mad. He has this room . . . I—I—I've seen it. He does things to people in there. To women. Your mademoiselle is in great peril. An-And so am I. You—You've got to help me!"

Jules's head was spinning. Terror had him in a vise. He couldn't breathe. Vittry. Leon de Vittry. A name that began with "L." *Killed Sébastien. Brought down your father.*

Dieu, he has Sabine!

Vaguely he heard Louise crying. Tears of fear.

Jules slammed the blunt end of the dagger against Cyr's skull, and the whimpering man collapsed to the ground, unconscious.

"Vincent, tie him up!" Jules commanded and bolted for the hallway, his brother and Raymond on his heels. They raced down the servants' stairs and through the kitchens all the way to the servants' entrance. His sole thought was to get to Sabine. Save Sabine. He prayed she was all right. He prayed Leon had taken her to his townhouse in Paris. He prayed he wouldn't get there too late.

They sped out the door, toward the stable, and made it halfway down the darkened alley when Jules abruptly stopped. Half a dozen men had stepped out of the shadows into the moonlight. They were a menacing bunch. Formidable. And fully armed.

Jules shot a glance behind him. Another group just as large in size and number had removed the possibility of retreat.

They had them surrounded.

Jesus-Christ, they'd walked into an ambush. They were three against twelve. Cold sweat rolled down Jules's face. He drew his sword. Luc and Raymond did the same.

If he didn't make it out alive, Sabine would die.

26

Sabine heard her own soft moan.

Her lids were too heavy to open.

It was too soon to wake up.

Cocooned in blackness, she slipped back into sleep. Jules was there to greet her. Smiling, looking so handsome, he held out his hand to her.

"Come now, Sabine," he said, his voice different, but his form and face the same.

Eager, she tried to reach for him, but her arms wouldn't move.

He lowered his arm. "Wake up."

Wake up? Why? This dream was perfect. Why couldn't they stay exactly as they were forever?

Why couldn't she move her arms?

"Sabine . . . Wake up. I'm tired of waiting." Again he spoke. But again it wasn't Jules's voice, and to her dismay, he was quickly fading from sight.

"*Jules?*" she murmured, her tongue feeling thick and foreign in her mouth.

"Not quite. Open your eyes." The disembodied voice was sharp and pulled her out of the dream realm.

Her eyes fluttered before she finally managed to open them. Objects were blurred. Indistinguishable.

"There. That's right." A hand stroked her hair. "Wake up now."

She blinked. And blinked again. Slowly, shadow and dark took on recognizable shapes. A simple wooden table across the room. A darkened room. Not much light. And she was lying on her side on what felt like a bed.

Where was she? Her thoughts as sluggish as her body, she struggled with her last memories. The masquerade ball. Dancing with Jules. The crowd. And . . . there was more. But with her mind so muddled, she couldn't remember what.

She felt someone rise from the edge of the bed and then heard the sound of a chair being dragged. Suddenly there he was, seated before her, leaning his elbows on his thighs.

"Leon?"

His face close to her own, he caressed her cheek. "Yes, darling. Now you have it right. It's Leon."

"What's happening?" The fog in her head was so thick, she couldn't think clearly at all. What was wrong with her? "Am I sick?" She'd never felt so sapped of strength.

He chuckled. "No. Perhaps a bit sleepy. You'll feel better soon. We've arrived at my château."

Arrived? Yes . . . now she remembered. They were traveling to Leon's château to speak to his servants. Briefly, she closed her eyes. A fresh wave of fatigue threatened to pull her back under. She forced her eyes open. "Are Viviane and Nicolas here?"

"No."

Oh, no . . . "Have we missed them?" *Get up.* She had to find the elderly servants.

"No. We haven't missed them, darling." He grazed his finger over her bottom lip. "They don't exist."

It was as though someone had just splashed her in the face with cold water. “Pardon?” She tried to sit up but immediately fell back onto the mattress, realizing at that moment that her wrists were bound behind her back. “What—What is this?” She twisted and tried to pull her hands free, but the knots wouldn’t give. “Untie me,” she demanded. “I don’t know what game you’re playing, Leon, but it isn’t amusing.”

“No game. This is real. A dream come true for me, actually. I’ve waited a very long time to have you all alone. And here you are . . .” He brushed a lock of hair from her cheek. “All mine.”

If his words weren’t frightening enough, the soft ominous tone of his voice was chilling. The memory of being in his carriage and drinking the wine he’d offered flooded her mind. Her stomach roiled.

He’d laced the wine.

It was then that the magnitude of the situation hit her like a physical blow. *No one knows where you are.* She was at his mercy. He could do whatever he wanted to her. The man before her in no way resembled the Leon she knew. She had no idea who this terrifying stranger was. Or what he was capable of.

What was he going to do to her? Rape? More? *Don’t ask. Think!*

He gripped her arm and hauled her up to a sitting position. Dizziness speared her right between the eyes. She squeezed them shut.

He dragged her lethargic legs off the makeshift bed. Her feet hit the stone floor. One foot was colder than the other. She was missing a slipper.

“Look at me, Sabine.”

Praying this was a bad dream, she reluctantly opened her eyes. Her vitals clenched. It was still Leon. She was still bound in the darkened room.

And no one is coming to your rescue. Stay calm. Don’t panic.

He was watching her intently. His thighs were on either side of hers. They all but touched. She wanted to pull away, but didn’t, afraid it would raise his ire. He’d never lost his temper before.

Then again, he'd never given any indication he'd do anything like this.

Carefully her fingers tested the knots. They were tight, secure, and impossible to undo on her own. She scanned the room. No windows. Two doors. The bed. One chair and the table. Two torchères were the only sources of light.

"Leon," she began. *Show no fear.* But her heart pounded so hard, she worried he'd hear it. *Reason with him. Bargain. Dupe him. Do whatever is necessary to escape what he's got planned for you. Put on a performance.* It was her only chance. It had to work. "We've known each other a long time. You were one of my father's dearest fr—"

"Your father was an ass. I found it appalling that a man without a drop of noble blood considered himself so important. And was even treated as such. But the Aristos liked his ridiculous plays. I"—he jabbed his finger into his chest—"am of elevated birth. And yet a fool with a quill was extended invitations to the finest salons in Paris. Salons *I* couldn't gain admittance to until I befriended him."

"You used him, then," she said, managing to keep her disgust from her tone. Keep him talking. She needed time to clear her head of the effects of the wine. She needed to quell her breathing. Did he notice it was more rapid than normal? Was it giving away the extent of her terror?

"Elevating my status has always been paramount. Befriending a playwright brought me in contact with powerful men who would never rub elbows with me before. Men with secrets and schemes. I'd no intention of living my life dismissed by my class or overshadowed by my brother. I loathed being the invisible second son."

"How fortunate your brother died." With this newly revealed aspect of Leon's personality, she now had serious doubts that Sébastien de Vittry's death was from natural causes.

The malevolent smirk that formed on his face confirmed her suspicions before his words did. "I make my own good fortune, Sabine. I had Sébastien killed. Does that shock you?"

There was something in his eyes she'd never seen before. No

longer guarded, a savageness glowed within their depths. Goose-flesh prickled her skin. She suppressed a shiver and weighed her words before responding. "No. It doesn't." It was no lie. Clearly, he was capable of *anything*. "I always thought you to be a very clever man. Now you have title and the respect you deserve. I'm glad. And I'm glad you used Father. I loathe him for sending Isabelle away. I've told you that before." She'd repeated the sentiment on several occasions, but inside she no longer denied the truth. Isabelle had wanted to leave. No one forced her.

Leon cocked his head to one side. Slipping his fingers beneath her chin, he caressed his thumb against her face. "Hmmm . . . so you have."

She suffered his touch, concealing her aversion. "There's no need for the ropes, Leon. Why don't you untie me? I won't run away from you. You know how I feel about you." She managed a smile. If she could at least coax him to unbind her wrists . . .

He returned her smile, then cracked the back of his hand against her jaw so hard she saw sparks of white light before slamming onto the mattress. An explosion of pain tore through her skull. She lay on the bed, stunned, her ear ringing.

"Don't try to be clever. You're not as clever as I," he said. Viciously, he jerked her up by the arm. Tears burned in her eyes. Her face and head were in agony. Grabbing a fistful of her hair, he hauled her to him. She gave a strangled cry. Their noses all but touched. "You chose a worthless Moutier over *me*. You've been whoring. Admit it."

The terror was suffocating. Her breaths were ragged. It took everything she had to tamp down the hysteria rushing up her throat. *Stay calm. Stay calm. Stay calm.* "Leon—"

"Don't deny it," he warned. "I saw you enter Moutier's camp with your cousins that night. I saw you spread your legs for him." Tightening his hold on her hair, he gave her head a fierce shake. She choked back a whimper. "I watched Moutier claim your maidenhead. You enjoyed every moment of it, too. Later, I had you followed. You let him have you again and again and you begged for more. You gave him what was mine to claim. After all the time I spent on you, you let *him* fuck you? All I got was a handful of chaste kisses!" he bellowed. She flinched.

Oh, God. Say something to quell his vexation. Was it possible to garner empathy from a madman? Did he possess *any*? "Leon . . . I am truly sorry. I would never want to offend you. Or hurt you in any way. You and I are alike, don't you see? We both had to do things . . . things that were necessary to improve our circumstances. I, too, was forced to make my own good fortune. I was in dire straits. Jules had a wealth of silver. With it I could pay my debts—my father's debt to you. I struck a bargain with him. I simply wanted to escape poverty."

"Don't you dare compare yourself to someone like me," he growled.

"Forgive me! I misspoke. I wasn't suggesting that you and I are in any way equal. I'm not as clever as you. I lost the silver." She knew exactly where the silver went now. "You have the chest I buried, don't you?"

He released her hair. Her scalp throbbed. "I do," he said with a good dose of boastfulness. He rested his elbows on his knees again. "You've no idea of the lengths I have gone to for you. To have you." She didn't like where this was going. "You were supposed to come *to me*."

"My father had already borrowed a substantial sum from you. I couldn't ask for more when there was no way for me to repay the original amount." She took in a fortifying breath and let it out slowly. "I want you to know that I have always considered myself fortunate to have a man of your superior worth show interest in me . . ."

"Interested in you?" He laughed. "I don't think you understand. The privileged treatment your father received was intolerable. I so despised his lofty airs and his unjust popularity that I decided soiling one of his precious daughters, whom he boasted would marry into the nobility, was not only a perfect idea, but just. I find it offensive that someone as common as you might outrank me through marriage. I thought being the whore of a nobleman was as high as you should rank. Sadly, you've already given your innocence to another. Whatever shall I do with you?" Though posed as a question, it wasn't. He'd planned out exactly what he was going to do to her.

He moved his gaze down the length of her body, a nauseating leer. "You know, I'd forgotten how good you look in finery. I haven't seen you dressed this way for some time." He ran his finger along the top curve of her breasts, tracing the low neckline. "You have such pretty skin . . ."

She didn't dare move. Barely breathed. *Deter him from whatever path he's heading down.* "There's more silver to be had, Leon," she blurted. Appealing to his greed might distract him. "There are two more chests."

"I know." He didn't so much as glance at her as he dragged his knuckles back the other way over her skin. "I intend to have it all. By now your lover is dead, as are his brother and everyone you were with at the courtesan's home. I knew that once they noticed you were missing, they'd come looking for you. I had men waiting for them outside for their slaughter."

"*What* . . ." It was a breathy sound, his words knocking the air from her lungs.

He met her gaze, his expression both malicious and smug. "They're all dead. Every last one of them," he assured, "even the men at the Moutier camp outside Paris who were guarding the two chests. The silver should be arriving soon. You see, when I want something, I get it."

No. No. No! Jules was not dead. He wasn't! And neither were Luc, Raymond, her family. She didn't believe it. She couldn't believe it. It would be too much to bear. She needed all her strength to get out of this. Leon was a liar. There was no reason to believe anything he said. He was saying these things to break her spirit.

"Are you sad, Sabine?" he taunted. "How do you feel about me now?"

She loathed him. She loathed herself for being duped. For not seeing what he was sooner. For putting herself and everyone who mattered to her in such danger. "I am in awe of your accomplishments." Careful not to move her arms and give herself away, she worked at the knots behind her back with determination.

"Really?" He looked suspicious. "What about the demise of your lover and family? No sense of loss there?"

Jules was a master swordsman and accurate shot, she reminded herself. He was all right. Everyone was all right. She was going to be all right, too. She'd see Jules again, her family and her sister. Stay strong.

She schooled her features and shrugged. "He was a means to an end. And Louise, Vincent, and Agnes are not my family. By ridding me of them, you've eased my burden." She despised what she was forced to say. "Thank you, Leon. I've not sufficiently appreciated your many talents. I hope you'll forgive me. You are truly a brilliant man." Her fingertips burned as they abraded against the rope, desperate to loosen the knots. Time was of the essence. If she was to have a fighting chance, she needed her hands.

He grabbed her aching face. She froze. His fingers gouged into her cheeks. "I don't believe your lies for a moment, but I will tell you about my *many talents* and just how great my achievements have been."

"Please do," she said, unflinching despite his severe grip. Painfully pulsing, her face felt bruised and swollen.

He released her abruptly and sat back, the corner of his mouth lifting. She braced herself, unsure of the extent of his misdeeds.

"I was behind the Marquis de Blainville's arrest and ultimate execution. The man was despised by everyone. Yet none had the courage to do anything about him. Except me," he proclaimed proudly.

She stiffened and thought of Jules. "Oh? How did you manage such a feat?"

"The aristocracy are by and large a corrupt lot. I knew sooner or later I'd discover some tantalizing bit of information that could be exploited. And I did. Blainville was plotting against the Marquis d'Argon. I told d'Argon and convinced him to turn the tables on Blainville."

Marquis d'Argon? Kindhearted Valentin? The memory of seeing him at the masquerade flashed in her mind.

"You look incredulous, Sabine. I take it you've met d'Argon?"

"Yes. He seems too—"

"Weak to carry out such a scheme? I assure you, he went along with the plan willingly. He was dedicated to the end. It was an ingenious plan, really. Blainville hanged for the very same fraudulent crimes he was going to have laid against d'Argon. Poetic justice, don't you think?" He laughed.

She reeled. Jules trusted Valentin. She didn't know what to say. What to do. What to think.

"I even ensnared your very own sister into our plot."

"Isabelle?"

"Yes. I had her routine observed. From the woods near the servants' outbuildings, she was seen smuggling items to her room. One afternoon, knowing she was alone, as usual, I paid her a visit. I told her that certain powerful men were intent on seeing Blainville fall. I told her I was being forced into the scheme, and if she didn't use her skills in thieving to aid these men, terrible things would befall her, me, and you."

She clenched her jaw to keep from screaming the hot words burning in her mouth. She had to swallow twice before she could speak. "You got her to put the letters in the couriers' satchels?"

"Not only place them there, but press Blainville's crest on each one."

She quaked harder. "*Why?* Why did you pull her in? To get back at Father?"

He sat back in his chair. "Partially. Also, I needed someone within the household to take part in the plan. I knew I'd have to kill whomever I chose once they were of no use. She was the one I selected.

When your bitch of a sister realized it was d'Argon and I behind it all, she tried to send letters warning you and Luc de Moutier. Fortunately, I interceded them. That was the day I decided she had to die."

"No!"

He grinned. "Yes. Give up your delusions, Sabine. I locked her in her room myself and watched as my men set the outbuilding ablaze. She's quite dead."

She clenched her teeth. "You. *Lie.*"

He stood up abruptly, his chair scraping backward against the stone floor, and grabbed her arm, hauling her to her feet with a furious yank.

He stalked to one of the doors, his fingers cruelly biting into her flesh, opened it, and shoved her inside. She stumbled to the middle of the room and frantically looked around. The blood drained from her limbs, the shocking sight all but buckling her knees. Covering the walls were countless locks of hair. Various colors. From various people. Long tables along the perimeter of the room had various trinkets on display—bracelets, pins, combs.

Stock-still, she stood trapped in the horror of it, for it dawned on her immediately what the gruesome display depicted.

"This is my treasure room. There"—he pointed to the chest in the corner of the room under a table—"is the silver. These"—he gestured to the walls—"are from the whores who went before you."

Among the items, a stack of parchments stood out. A morbid fascination gripped her. The lure was irresistible. She moved toward it despite the foreboding that darkened around her and the inner voice that warned her to stop.

The closer she got, the clearer the handwriting became, and the distinctive penmanship took on an undeniable, devastating familiarity.

Isabelle's handwriting. The sight knifed into her. She'd been wrong about everyone. Everything. Her instincts had failed her at every turn. She was wrong about Isabelle, too.

Isabelle was dead. She'd never see her sister again.

Her heart shattered. *"NO-O-O-O-O-O-O-O-O-O-O-O-O-O!"* she screamed, doubling over in agony.

He bent and said near her ear, "At last you believe me. Your sister is gone."

Tears flooded down her face. *"Isabel-l-l-l-le . . ."* Her knees collapsed under the weight of her misery. She pressed her forehead against the cold floor, wailing her grief.

"There's no need to carry on. You'll be dead soon, too. You'll be joining her." He dragged her to her feet and spun her around. Her vision obscured by tears, she didn't know what he was about until he grabbed one of her long locks and sliced it off with the dagger she now realized he held. "A keepsake," he said. "I've left a spot for you. I'll put it beside your sister's. I cut hers off her just before she died. She cried and screamed, like you. I liked it when she screamed." He dragged the tip of the cold blade over the tops of her breasts. "All this pretty flesh . . . I intend to make you my greatest masterpiece, Sabine. Perfect markings and carvings . . . you'll be my finest work. What a delicious encounter this will be. You'll be in excruciating pain until I fuck you to death."

She was already in excruciating pain. There was nothing he could do to her to hurt her more. Rage singed her skin from the inside out. Alone and bound, she knew he thought he'd rendered her helpless. He thought he'd won.

You can die. Or you can die fighting. She'd be damned if she'd simply surrender her life. For all his wickedness and depravity—for what he'd done to Isabelle and Jules—the very least she could do was inflict some pain.

In one fluid motion she jumped back, leaned against the table behind her, and kneed him in the groin with all she had.

He howled, grabbing himself as he fell to one knee, the dagger dropping out of his hand. She kicked it away and bolted for the door. She made it only a few steps when he caught her gown and violently jerked her backward. Without her hands to break the fall, she hit the floor, her head slamming against it in a jarring collision.

She lay on her side, dazed, vaguely aware of him standing over her. He raged—but his voice was distant. His words, indecipherable.

She was going to die. At least then the emotional pain would end. *She'd be with 'Sabelle.* Her vision was slowly narrowing. She wondered if the encroaching blackness would mercifully claim her before Leon pierced her with the dagger.

Waiting for death, an odd calm washed through her until Jules's face flashed in her mind. A single tear slipped out of the corner of her eye. "Jules . . ." She'd love him in this world and the next. Always . . . But she was wrong about him, too. He wasn't her destiny. That was clear to her now. She was going to die.

An explosion suddenly reverberated in the room, then a heavy weight crushed down on her.

Something warm oozed over her belly. *Blood?* She'd been shot . . .

It was her final coherent thought.

The blackness pulled her under.

27

Jules threw Leon's lifeless body off Sabine, and dropped to his knees. "Get him out of here!" Leon's dead eyes stared vacantly at the ceiling. His abdomen was covered in blood.

Luc and Raymond dragged the corpse away, leaving a dark red smear across the floor.

Sabine's face was battered. Her belly blood-soaked. A pool of blood near her side. So much blood. All around. Its very scent permeated the air. As did the smoky smell of gunpowder. Terror iced in his veins.

Quickly, he cut the rope around her wrists and gently rolled her onto her back. With a fervent prayer, he pressed his ear to her chest. The moment he heard the steady thumps of her heart, he all but wept with joy. Sweeping her up into his arms, he rushed into the other room and placed her with infinite care on the pallet. Sitting on the makeshift bed by her side, terrified she'd suffered a belly wound, which was almost always fatal, he used his dagger to slice open the front of her gown. Frantic, he peeled each sodden crimson-stained layer away until at last he saw her unmarred flesh. Weak with relief, he tossed his head back, closed his eyes, and let the air rush out of his lungs, realizing at that moment he'd been holding his breath. He looked at his bloody hands. It was all Leon's blood—the blood on her dress and on the ground. Thank God.

Now all he had to worry about was what horrors the bastard had put her through.

She groaned, but didn't awake. He wiped his hands clean on his breeches, ripped off his doublet and dressed her in it, then wrapped her with the blanket on the bed.

Slowly he laid her back down and carefully slid his hand from beneath her head. Across his palm were fresh streaks of blood. His heart lurched. Immediately he pulled her up to examine the back of her head and found her beautiful blond hair was matted and caked with blood. Touching the visible cut, he noted the large lump that had formed at the side of her skull.

"Jésus-Christ," he growled. He drew her closer and pressed his cheek against the downy hair at her crown. "What did he do to you?" He wanted to know as intensely as he didn't.

Torturous images of Sabine and what Leon might do to her had consumed him as he'd raced to Leon's château. He'd agonized about the amount of time she'd been in Leon's clutches and the hours still to go before Jules could reach her, praying all the while that he'd find her alive. Safe. Thinking up ways of torturing de Vittry, forcing a confession out him with as much bodily pain as possible for all his misdeeds, did little to alleviate his anxiety. The physical force he'd used on Leon's man, Hubert, to gain information of Sabine's whereabouts hadn't satisfied Jules's bloodlust. Nor had killing the attackers Leon sent to ambush him.

By the time they'd reached his château and found the secret rooms at the back of the stables, someone had already shot Leon dead.

Who? Why? *Merde.* He felt cheated. Enraged. Terrified.

Had Sabine seen the shooter? The gunman could have easily

killed her regardless—yet spared her. This was obviously someone who was only after Leon.

A soft sound from Sabine drew his gaze to her face, covered in contusions and distorted by the swelling. For every bruise on her sweet form, he would have dealt twenty on Leon. Now he had no choice but to save his wrath, for there were others involved in this foul plot.

Simon Boulenger and Luc lowered themselves onto their haunches beside him.

"How is she?" Luc asked.

"She's fine." Though it was more a desperate wish than a certainty.

Simon indicated the other room with a jerk of his chin. "*Dieu* . . . I've never seen anything like it. What sort of madness is that?" Jules hadn't even noticed when Simon entered the room or that he'd seen the other chamber and its disturbing items.

"I don't know, but it looks like de Vittry was about to add to his morbid collection." Luc touched one of Sabine's tresses that had been clearly cropped.

"Indeed," Raymond said from the doorway, holding up a lock of Sabine's blond hair.

Profanity shot out of Jules. "We should have been here sooner!" He glared at Simon.

Simon raised his brows. "I reached Paris as soon as I received your letter requesting aid. And, I might point out, this is the *second* time I've saved your aristocratic ass. Without me and my men there tonight, the three of you would be dead."

Jules sighed. "I'm sorry, Simon." He shook his head. It was midday and he had yet to sleep. He was exhausted and overwrought. "You are right, of course. I thank you for everything you've done. For the employ. For the loyal friendship. And for saving my *aristocratic ass* two too many times."

Simon smiled. "Apology accepted."

"My lord," Raymond said. Jules looked over at him. "If I may say . . . I found the missing chest of silver." Still standing at the doorway between the two chambers, he indicated behind him. "And parchments. I believe they belonged to Isabelle Laurent."

Jules was about to respond when something glinted on the ground near Raymond's boots. "What is that at your feet?"

Raymond looked down, picked up the item, and brought it over to where the three men stood.

A ring.

Carefully easing Sabine down onto the bed, Jules then stood and took the ring from Raymond's open palm.

"That's Valentin's ring." Luc was incredulous.

The d'Argon family crest glared back at Jules. The significance of it being in this particular room came down on him with crushing force. He wanted to believe there was an innocent explanation—but couldn't vanquish the sense of unutterable betrayal surging inside him. Valentin? Involved in all this? Not *him*.

"He couldn't be part of all this, surely . . ." Apparently Luc warred with the notion, too.

Bile churned in Jules's stomach. He felt ill.

He'd seen Valentin wearing the ring only days before. The discovery of the ring in this room meant that Valentin had been here recently.

Worse, it meant that he was privy to Leon's gruesome practices, for he doubted Leon would admit a casual visitor or mere acquaintance into these hidden chambers.

Jules fisted his hand, squeezing the ring. "Question the servants. Find out if he was here last night. Who was here last night or recently."

He opened his hand. The ring left indentations on his palm. How many times had Valentin told him what had been done to his father was unjust? Pretended to care? "Look over the parchments. See if they say anything that's of use." He handed the ring to Raymond. It felt heavy in his hand. In his heart. He couldn't stand to hold it any longer. "But first, get Sabine a change of clothing.

Anything the servants can offer is better than her bloodied gown." Raymond turned to do as bidden.

Sabine stirred again, this time with a murmur. She was waking at last.

"I'll have some of the men gather the servants." Simon walked out.

"I'll look over the parchments and together with Raymond interrogate everyone at the château," Luc said. "Vittry's body is in the stables."

"Leave him there. I'll get a confession out of Valentin first before notifying anyone."

He'd get a confession before nightfall by whatever means necessary.

The moment they left, Sabine's lids fluttered. Jules sat down on the edge of the bed and took her in his arms. Her lovely visage marred black and blue and swollen, she'd never looked so vulnerable. So delicate. *Dieu*, he should have never allowed her to return to her chamber unescorted.

At last she opened her eyes and met his gaze. Then she did something he'd never seen her do before: She burst into tears.

"Jules . . . He—He said he killed you . . ."

Lightly, he caressed her bruised face and pressed a soft kiss to her brow. "He didn't kill me. We are both very much alive."

She gulped hard but could not stop her weeping. "My—My family—"

"Everyone is all right. And safe. You're safe, too. I have you. Vittry is dead. He'll not hurt you ever again." He cupped her uninjured cheek. "Are you all right?"

She shook her head. "She . . . she's dead," she stammered, copious tears flooding from her eyes.

"Who is?"

"Is-Is . . . sabelle. My 'Sabelle. He—He . . . *killed her.*" She sat up, flung her arms around him. Burying her face in his shoulder, she sobbed aloud.

He wrapped his arms about her. "I'm so sorry." The words

seemed insignificant given the enormity of her anguish. But what could anyone say that would lessen the pain or the loss she felt? Seeing her so racked by grief made him feel helpless and renewed his anger. Someone else had had the pleasure of sending Leon to hell. That there were others involved in this plot still to vent his wrath upon offered a small conciliation.

He gently rocked her while she cried, soaking his shirt with her sorrow. A lump formed in his throat. How he wished there had been another outcome. What he wouldn't have given to find Isabelle still alive. To see the joy that would have brought Sabine.

He lost track of time, unsure how long she'd wept in his arms. When finally her crying ebbed, she gazed up at him with the most tortured look in those captivating eyes. Not since the day he'd watched his father's execution had he felt this heartsick. "Leon said . . . that he was responsible for what happened to your father."

Jules remained silent, allowing her to speak, determined not to add to her grief by letting her see the varying emotions raging inside him.

"He—He said . . . he was in partnership with Valentin, Marquis d'Argon." Fresh tears welled forth. "He—He said . . . that they forced Isabelle to participate in the plot. They made her . . . They made her . . ." She broke down again.

He cupped her face. "Shhhhhh . . . I know Isabelle was not the sort of woman to harm anyone."

"I—I love her . . ."

"And she knew it well."

"I miss her so much . . . I—I must live the rest of my life without her." She closed her eyes and softly cried.

"She'll always be with you, Sabine. She lives in your memories and in your heart."

She opened her eyes again, but a knock at the door stopped her from responding.

"Enter," he bid. Two matronly servants bearing clothing, pails of water, and a washbasin stepped into the room. He considered having Sabine brought to the château to change, but doubted she'd want to be in Vittry's home any more than she wanted to be in the stables. The best thing was to get her dressed and away from Vittry's home altogether. As quickly as possible.

He coaxed her into letting the servants help her and promised to take her away from Leon's château as soon as she was ready.

Outside the stables, Jules wasted no time, immediately joining in on the questioning of the servants—who'd been filed outside—by Luc and Raymond. Simon and the men stood nearby.

It quickly became apparent that Vittry's hired help was very much afraid of him and that when he ordered that no one approach the stables—as he had last night—no one dared defy him. No one saw a thing.

"Leon's only visitors were women. They came but never left," Luc said, revulsion and disgust in his tone.

Jules had learned the same thing by those he'd questioned. "What about Isabelle's writings? What did they contain?"

"Some poetry, a short story—lovely stuff, but nothing in connection to Valentin or Leon."

Sabine's blond hair caught the corner of Jules's eye. Pale, except for the black and blue contusions, she approached, somber, her hair in a simple braid. Back in humble clothing. He hated to see it.

She stopped before him. He was about to ask Luc to give them some privacy but realized Luc had already stepped away and was talking with Simon.

Her eyes glistened with unshed tears. He could tell she was fighting to maintain her composure. She swallowed and he wondered if, like he, she had a knot in her throat. "I want to go home. Be with my family. See my cousins again." Two tears spilled down her cheeks.

"Of course. I'll have Raymond and a small party escort you back to Marie's townhouse to fetch Agnes, Louise, and Vincent, then to the farm. I'll meet you there after I settle the matter with

Valentin. He'll pay for what he's done to both of us. I swear it." He cupped her cheeks.

Grasping his wrists, she pulled his hands from her face. "Jules, what we've shared . . . we knew was temporary. You will have your justice. And I have my answers. It's . . . over now."

"Sabine," he began, his heart rate quickening. "You are upset and understandably so. This is not the time to discuss this."

"What future is there for us? You are about reclaim your birthright. Live the life you were born to live—have a wife with exalted bloodlines. We both know you have a duty to your family. That you are honor-bound."

He felt as though he'd been cleaved in the heart. "We can be together in other ways."

She shook her head. "I want the grand dream, though I know it's impossible. I can live with nothing less."

Not this. Not now. Exhausted as he was from his mad ride to Vittry's château, he feared he didn't have the fortitude to do what was expected of him.

He forced himself to remember his responsibilities.

But words welled from his heart. Words he couldn't utter. Wasn't free to say. You can't. You *can't*. He forced himself to remember his father. The injustice of his senseless death. The horrific writhing at the end of the hangman's noose while the mobs cheered and jeered as the rope choked the air from his lungs and slowly strangled the life out of him.

"Will you have Raymond escort me back now?"

The knot in his throat was so large, it took him a moment before he could speak. "Of course."

She turned to walk away. The next thing he knew he had her wrist in his hand and had pulled her back. "Don't go," was already out of his mouth. His arm was already around her waist, holding her soft form against him. His hand touched her uninjured cheek. "Stay with me, Sabine. Don't leave. Not like this."

Tears streamed from her eyes. He knew that when she was out

of sight, she'd collapse into total discomposure. As it was, he had but a fragile grip on his own composure.

She didn't want to be a mere mistress and exist on the fringes of his life. She wasn't going to change her mind. He sensed it. Knew it down to his marrow.

She was about to speak. He sealed his lips to hers, needing her kiss. Needing her. Just when he'd found her, he was going to lose her. For good.

His kiss was anguished. His heart felt it was rending in two. Being pulled apart in opposite directions.

She trembled against him. He trembled, too, but she didn't push him away. He reveled in it. Maybe if he kissed her long enough, held her long enough, she'd reconsider. He deepened the kiss. She broke away from him and choked on a sob, leaving him bereft, her tears on his lips.

"I have to go," she said, looking as shaken as he felt. She managed a small smile through her tears. "I know you will regain your position and lands now, and you'll have the life you've wanted back."

It didn't sound as wonderful as it used to.

She stepped back. He caught her hand. "I'll fulfill my promise. You'll have a share of the silver and the Laurent lands will revert back to you," he said, instead of those three words burning in his throat.

She nodded and slipped her hand from his grasp. He held his arms at his sides, though he wanted nothing more than to reach for her again.

"I wish you much happiness." She turned on her heel and walked away, her hand covering her mouth. It was her only way to hold back her sobs.

Jules turned away, the pain inside him excruciating, unable to watch her leaving his life.

"Raymond!" he barked.

His man was by his side immediately. "My lord?"

Curtly, he dealt out the order to take ten of the men and escort Sabine back to Paris and then home.

"Yes, my lord."

"I'll be going with Luc, Simon, and the remaining men to see Valentin." He was on the precipice. All that he wanted was within his reach. So why did he feel like he'd lost . . .. everything.

The misery inside him was suffocating. His only foreseeable joy was what he would do to Valentin when he got his hands on him. Beyond that, he wouldn't think about the future. A future without his beautiful forest fairy.

28

Jules and his party of twenty thundered into the courtyard of d'Argon's country estate two days later. Much to his amazement, a somber majordomo immediately opened the door upon hearing the horses' hooves. It was as though he'd been waiting in the vestibule the entire time to bid them entrance.

Prepared for anything, Jules followed the man into the Marquis' home with Luc, Simon, and the men on his heels. Crossing the foyer, he heard weeping. Women's tears. How many women, he couldn't guess, but the sound came from behind one of the many closed doors.

Stopping before one of the wooden portals, the servant rapped lightly on it and, upon hearing the gentle command from within, opened the door and allowed them admittance into Valentin's study.

He found Valentin seated at his large wooden desk, slumped in his chair, his appearance haggard, looking as though he'd been drinking and perhaps even crying for hours. Maybe days. Valentin lifted his red-rimmed eyes, met Jules's gaze, and immediately began to weep.

Jules exchanged glances with Luc, his brother looking no less surprised. Vengeance had burbled in Jules's veins over the last couple of days. The pity that the sight before him stirred was unexpected. Unwelcome. Anger was easier to deal with—and all that kept his pain of losing Sabine at bay.

Jules turned to the men crowding the room. "Out," he ordered everyone but Luc and Simon. It wasn't until they'd left that Jules approached the older Aristo, stopping before the desk.

Valentin wiped the tears with his hand and sniffled. "How is Mademoiselle Laurent?"

Yet another surprise. Jules hadn't expected that question. Nor the sharp stab in the heart at the mere mention of Sabine.

With three quick strides he reached Valentin, grabbed him by his doublet, and yanked him up off the chair. "What is it you're asking, Valentin? How badly Vittry hurt her? How destroyed she is over the death of her sister?"

Valentin didn't so much as flinch but remained woeful. "I didn't want her hurt or to have her sister involved. Or killed. It was Leon who did that."

"No? You just wanted my father *executed*, is that it?" He gave Valentin a fierce shake. "You pretended to be his friend. I thought you were mine."

Valentin didn't try to extricate himself from Jules's hold. "What would you do, Jules, if your family were faced with ruin? If someone was threatening your good name? Your very existence."

"What are you talking about? I don't want riddles. I want you to admit what you did! Admit you destroyed an innocent man."

"He may not have been a *Frondeur*. But he was not an innocent man."

Jules slammed him down on the desk, pulled out his dagger from inside his sleeve, and pressed it to Valentin's throat. "I should kill you right now. You deserve to die. Do you know how many lives you have ruined? How many people have suffered because of what you've done. *Jésus-Christ*, you even killed your own minion,

Vittry. Don't bother to deny it. You dropped your ring in his den of horror."

Valentin broke into sobs. "I'll not deny it . . . An-Any of it . . . I have lived with this on my conscience for years. I can do it no longer. That is why I shot Leon. He was mad . . . out of control. He was going to kill you and Luc. I couldn't allow that to happen. I c-couldn't . . ."

Jules hauled Valentin upright, but kept the blade at his throat. "Why do Luc and I matter to you?"

"Because this was between Charles and me. I didn't want the matter to spill over onto you, or anyone else. I did my best to lessen the impact on both of you. I got you out of the Bastille. I couldn't have you to languish there . . . I'm sorry for what I have done to your lives. I'm sorry I struck a bargain with that devil, de Vittry. He killed the mademoiselle in that fire . . . He killed Bailloux—his twisted way to thwart you from regaining your previous prominence . . ." He covered his face with his hands, his shoulders hunched, his posture that of a broken man.

Jules looked at Luc. He simply shook his head.

"Why, Valentin?" Jules asked. "What is this matter between you and my father? What made you do this?"

"I turned down your father's offer to marry my Caroline to you. He became incensed. Threatened I'd rue the day I refused to join our houses and that he would never forget the insult. I had no objections to you as a husband for my daughter. It was your father that gave me pause. I know you loved him . . . but he was a different man when he wasn't around you. Caroline is such a delicate flower." He hung his head, softly crying.

"So you had him arrested on false charges because of an empty threat? A meaningless utterance said in a moment of anger?"

"No. I did nothing. I wanted to forget his words and desperately prayed that he had, too. Two months later, Leon approached me. He'd learned Charles was plotting to have me arrested as a *Frondeur.* My loyalties have *always* been with the Crown. He said he'd help rid me of Charles if I gave him what he wanted . . ." He choked out a sob. "He wanted . . . his brother dead . . . for the lands and title he held."

Disgusted, Jules released Valentin with a shove and stepped away. "You killed Sébastien? Why would you believe that serpent? He was nothing but a lying, opportunistic—"

"I didn't believe him! Not at first. I refused to strike such a malevolent bargain. But then he told me Charles was blackmailing the Archbishop de Divonne to turn against me. I went to see Bailloux. He broke down and admitted that your father was threatening to expose his illicit affair with the Comtesse de Tonnere if he didn't conspire against me. He was most enamored with her and feared what her husband would do to her if he found out. That was the moment I knew I had no choice. I couldn't expose Charles's fiendish plan against me. It would be my word against his. Likely, we'd both be hanged in the end, for there was such scrutiny and chaos after the *Fronde*. Any whispered connection to the *Frondeurs* and you could be arrested and detained in prison indefinitely. My future and that of my family hung in the balance. Either I sat back and let him destroy me, or I took action and stopped him." He quietly cried. "I—I am not a violent man . . ." he bemoaned. "The night I agreed to Leon's conditions, I wept till dawn . . . couldn't eat or sleep for almost a week. I couldn't kill Sébastien . . . I convinced Bailloux to help me and . . . together we poisoned him. Leon took care of fabricating letters to use against Charles."

Jules seethed. "You expect me to believe this story? That all this was because of a mere insult over a betrothal?"

"It is true! Every word. I—I have proof!" He twisted around and picked up a stack of parchments, his hands atremble.

Jules snatched them from his hand. Staring back at him was a very familiar penmanship. *Isabelle*. Luc was immediately at his side, peering down at the writing.

"Where did you get these?" Luc demanded.

Valentin dropped back into his chair and wept and wept and wept.

"Answer!" Jules shouted.

"L-Leon gave them to me. He said it would help remind me what kind of man Charles was . . ."

Jules's gaze darted to the parchments, scanning Isabelle's daily accounts of her employment.

. . . How I miss Sabine. I think of her each night as I fall asleep and each morning when I awake.

Jules closed his eyes briefly. God help him, so did he, no matter how hard he tried not to.

I remember everything we've shared. Every dream we've had. Every secret we've exchanged. I think about the theater. And the dismal days at the farm. The countless plays we wrote and performed for our only audience there, the chickens . . .

A rueful smile tugged at his lips. The very same silly chicken story that Sabine had recounted. There was no denying these parchments were authentic. These were Isabelle's writings.

. . . poor Sofie was beaten simply for dropping a tray. An empty tray. No damage. No harm done. Monsieur le Marquis ordered her to be lashed until she bled, her backside horribly torn by the whip. In her battered state, he made her work through the night, without any rest, her every movement reopening her wounds. By morning, her clothing was blood-soaked. Some of the other servants and I washed the blood off the floor, for if the Marquis saw it, he's likely order more lashes . . . He is a horrible man . . .

Jules's stomach fisted.

. . . Bernadette is ill. She has worked for the Marquis for decades. He has tossed her out as soon as he returned from Paris, saying she was too old to be of use. It's winter. She has nowhere to go . . .

Jules wanted to stop reading, gripped by the feeling that what he was about to read, he didn't want to know. His instincts told him that his doubts, the suspicions he was having about the authenticity of his father's character, were about to be realized.

. . . Marquis de la Rocque left raging and weeping. I have never seen a member of the nobility in the throes of such despair. It took but a few inquiries of the other servants to learn that the Monsieur de la Rocque lost everything he owned to the Marquis in a game of cards two nights prior. He begged Monsieur de Blainville not to take everything all at once, to wait until after the marriage of de la Rocque's daughter, but was scoffed at and tossed out of the château bemoaning and bewailing. I can't imagine what the Monsieur de la Rocque and his family will do now. Sofie told me Monsieur de Blainville always wins at cards because he cheats.

His stomach clenched tighter. Stop reading . . . *now.*

. . . The Archbishop de Divonne was here today. The Marquis would not grant him a meeting. He was escorted out, literally dragged across the foyer as he shouted to the Marquis to have mercy. That a woman's life was at stake. I don't know what woman he speaks of but I do know that Monsieur de Blainville is compassionless and would never be swayed by such pleas. In fact, he laughed from the

threshold of his study, turned, and closed the door. He delights in his cruelty.

Jules clutched the parchments in a white-knuckle grip. Page after page he read. Instant after instant of abhorrent behavior. Ruthlessness. Viciousness. Where was his honor? *A man must live honorably.* How many times had his father told him that? *Jésus-Christ*, where was his decency?

... The Marquis is going to do something horrible ... I heard him speaking to Monsieur Bedeau. An innocent man is going to be accused of being a Frondeur ... Something about an insult. This man will be executed falsely! I hate him. I hate it here. Why did I leave my home! My Sabine ...

Jules's heart and head reeled in turmoil.

... Leon came to me ... I don't want to do what he asks ... He won't tell me who these men are who ask this of me ... Leon says they will hurt the Marquis and his sons ... Monsieur de Blainville is away ... I care not if he suffers, but I must find a way to warn Luc ... He has suffered enough simply by having a man like the Marquis as his father ...

Jules reached the final pages. The shakiness of the handwriting, the water stains on the pages—likely from tears—hit him hard. He knew at a glance, Isabelle was distressed.

... Leon struck me ... He's never behaved this way before ... He terrified me. I must leave here ... I must warn my family, Luc ... Leon and the Marquis d'Argon are the ones behind this plot!

"Jules?" Luc placed his hand on Jules's arm. "Are you all right? You're . . . pale."

His heart pounding, Jules looked up and realized he was sweating profusely, yet his limbs felt chilled. He felt hot. Cold. Sick.

Heartsick.

His head was spinning with memories, of Luc as a boy, and the many times he'd found him crying over the ill-treatment received by their father. Then there was the weeping . . . that terrible sorrowful weeping he'd often heard coming from his mother's chambers, now echoed in his ears. Moments in his life he'd dismissed, drowned beneath his adoration for a man who never deserved his respect, reverberated inside him, leaving him quaking and out of breath.

He sucked in a ragged breath, trying to sufficiently fill his lungs, struggling to quell his rapid breathing and maintain some semblance of composure. But then his gaze fell on the parchments once more. A bellow shot up his throat and out his mouth as he smashed his fist against the wall.

Valentin jumped. "I—I intend to do the right thing, Jules. I'll speak to the First Minister and even the King himself and admit what I have done. I've already admitted everything to my wife. I'm prepared to face the consequences of my actions."

Jules pressed his palm against the wall and leaned his weight forward. He hung his head. "Please get him out of here," he croaked out, Isabelle's parchments burning in his other palm.

He heard the shuffle of feet and then quiet.

Luc approached. "Jules . . ."

Jules placed his hand on his brother's shoulder. "You were right. I didn't want to believe you. I didn't want to see the truth about him. I ignored everything, including your pain. I'm so very sorry, Luc. I've not been a fool. I've been the greatest of fools."

The corner of Luc's mouth lifted in a rueful smile. "It is difficult to see the truth when he concealed it from you. If it is any conciliation, you were the only one he treated with any decency. You, my brother, brought out the best in him."

Jules shook his head. "It was only an act. All this was his doing, Luc. *He* brought this misery down upon us. He went after a good man, Valentin, and completely corrupted him. His wickedness infested many lives, causing unspeakable agony, leaving four bodies in its wake. Valentin will be added to the death count. He'll be executed for his crimes against his peers. A man who, if not for our father, would have led a quiet decent life, never harming a soul. He was right when he said Charles de Moutier, Marquis de Blainville, may not have been a traitor to the Crown, but he was a traitor to everyone around him." Jules clenched his teeth. His sense of obligation toward the man dissolved. "He got what he deserves."

"And now you will have what you deserve." Luc squeezed his shoulder, his smile brightening. "You will have title, lands. And you will do things differently than Charles de Moutier."

He finally had his answers. Yet he didn't feel any of the satisfaction he'd imagined. In fact, he felt disgust. Distaste for the prominence he'd sought.

Everything he'd chased after, now meaningless. Empty.

"I *do* intend to do things very differently, Luc." He knew exactly what he wanted in his future. And how he wanted it to be.

* * *

Sabine heard the horses' hooves before she saw them.

Her family instantly stopped their work in the fields.

Josette rushed forward and shielded her eyes from the sun. "Sabine, it's your Aristo!"

Sabine's heart lurched. *Jules is here! He only came to deliver the silver*, she reminded herself. Yet her insides danced at the thought of seeing him one more time.

Robert and Gerard ran up to stand near Josette. Sabine tried not to run but walk around to the front of the cart, where half a dozen men on horseback now patiently waited. She saw Raymond, then a smiling Luc.

Her pulse quickened the moment she spotted Jules. All masculine grace, he dismounted and approached, the wind caressing his dark hair. In his costly clothing, he looked every bit the regal prince. She clasped her hands, the urge to throw her arms around him unbearably keen.

He stopped before her, scrutinizing her face. "You look well. How are you?" he inquired, his soft voice rippling through her heart.

She still had nightmares of her time in Leon's chambers. "I'm well," she said instead.

"Valentin confessed. It would seem that my father was as dishonorable as they come. But he was not a traitor to the Crown. Valentin told them as much and pleaded for the reinstatement of our land and status."

"And did they grant you that?"

"They did." He glanced around at the curious onlookers. The rest of her family had gathered close. Jules nodded to Raymond. He stepped forward and handed Jules a scroll. "By royal decree"—Jules handed her the scroll—"the land that once belonged to the Laurent family has reverted to them, including the village and surrounding property."

Agnes let out a jubilant squeal.

Jules stepped closer. "I have your silver with me," he said.

"Thank you . . ." She clutched the scroll to her heart, wishing it were he that she held close.

"There is more."

"Oh?"

"A townhouse has been purchased for you and your family, fully staffed and furnished. I know how much you, Louise, and Vincent love Paris."

She was moved and overwhelmed by his touching gesture. Tears filled her eyes. Yet she wouldn't cry as she'd done the last time he'd seen her. "That is most generous of you . . ."

"It's my way of thanking you and your family for all you have done for me and Luc."

A single tear slipped down her cheek. "I'm happy for you, Marquis de Blainville." She smiled.

A slight frown furrowed his brow. "I want nothing to do with that title. A new title was created by the Crown, since the other was dissolved. Luc is the Marquis de Fontenay."

"But . . . what about you?"

"I am sick of France. I'm leaving for the West Indies." Her stomach dropped.

"The West Indies?" She'd never see him again. Not even a chanced glance. Nothing at all.

"Yes. I'm told it's quite beautiful there."

She looked down at the scroll in her hands. "Well, then . . ." *Don't go.* "Have a safe journey . . ."

Footsteps approached. "Sabine?" She looked up at the sound of Luc's voice.

"I wanted you to know I received your sister's journals. I've started reading them. She was an extraordinary woman. I'm honored to have them. Thank you for giving them to me." He smiled then kissed her hand and returned to where her family had gathered a short distance away. Isabelle would never get to learn more about Luc, but Luc could learn about the woman who'd adored him from afar. She felt it was right for him to have them.

"One last thing," Jules said. "There is the matter of an item you stole from me."

Perplexed, she said, "I have nothing of yours."

"Not true." He lowered himself onto one knee. She lost her breath. Her family collectively gasped. "You have my heart. And it is yours. I love you," he said. "And I wish to have children and grow old with you. Will you marry me?"

She covered her mouth with trembling fingertips. Two tears spilled down her cheeks. She couldn't believe her eyes. Her ears.

A dream come true . . . She laughed, cried, and shook.

"Sabine, what say you?" he asked, looking anxious for a response and utterly adorable kneeling on the packed dirt.

She dropped to her knees and flung her arms around his neck, raining kisses on his face. "YES!" His lips . . . "YES!" His face and lips . . . "YES! YES!"

She was going to be his wife. He'd be all hers.

Her family erupted in boisterous hoots and cheers. Jules laughed, caught her cheeks between his palms, and gazed into her eyes. "You'll come with me to the West Indies?"

"Yes!"

"You'd want an Aristo as a husband?" He was grinning. "I'm now recognized as one and can purchase a title at any time."

"I want you, Aristo or not. Here or at the ends of the earth."

He nuzzled her neck and said softly in her ear, "I have one more thing for you." He rose, helped her to her feet, and motioned Raymond over.

Raymond stopped before her, holding a yellow box tied with a rich purple bow.

Jules untied the bow and opened the lid. The contents made her gasp.

Jules was smiling, "Your new lucky glass slippers."

She had to swallow hard before she could speak. Having read her journals, he got the slippers just right. A perfect replica of the ones she'd once owned all those years ago. And lost.

Returned to her by her Dark Prince.

She threw her arms around Jules. "I love them! I love you. I always have . . ."

Angling her head, he brushed his lips against hers. "Forever."

"Forever," she concurred before he possessed her mouth in a long searing kiss, sealing the pledge.

Epilogue

And so the cinder-girl married her Dark Prince wearing a golden-colored gown, and glass slippers, just as she'd dreamed all those years ago . . . Their story quickly spread. Their romantic tale soon became a legendary love story that rippled though the realm. And time. A love, they say, that was written in the stars. A tale destined to be adored by generations to come.

So, what became of the beauty and her prince, you ask? Well . . .

Marguerite Island, West Indies

The balmy evening breeze swept into the room, fluttering the white bed curtains. Jules climbed into bed with a smile, noting that his beautiful wife had doffed her night chemise. Sabine returned his smile and snuggled her warm lush form against him, his cock stiffening by the second. After a year and a half of marital accord, he still couldn't get enough of her. And he knew he never would.

"Is your daughter asleep?" Sabine murmured, her hot mouth grazing his neck, a tantalizing trail.

He'd carried their ebony-haired baby to the nursery and laid her down in her cradle, amazed at the amount of love such a tiny child could inspire. But like her mother, she'd captured his heart. "Mmmm . . . yes, Isabelle is fast asleep with a gluttonous smile, most content after her nursing." He cupped Sabine's breasts and gently thumbed her nipples, delighting in her gasp. "Now these are all mine."

"Until the next nursing." Her silver eyes shone with mischief. "You'd better hurry."

He could smell her arousal. She was already wet for him.

He pressed her down on the bed, pinning her under him, and lodged the head of his shaft at her opening, but didn't penetrate her despite the alluring wet heat. "We have a lifetime. No need to hurry," he teased, knowing it would rile his impatient wife and make her hungrier.

She thrust her hips upward, trying to draw him in, but he easily evaded her, countering her movement with a tilt of his hips.

She sighed, adorably frustrated. "You wouldn't want to be remiss in your conjugal duties, would you? I may despair that you don't want me," she baited. How he loved matching wits and wiles with her.

Stroking the length of his hard cock along her slick folds, he said, "I think you know very well how much I want you."

She caressed the nape of his neck. "Maybe you only want me for my silver?" A smile graced her sweet lips.

He plunged inside her, making her gasp. "I don't need the silver. I'm already a rich man, thanks to my very beautiful, all-too-spirited, silver-eyed wife."

. . . they lived happily ever after . . . of course.

In France . . .

Seated at her writing table, a dark-haired woman stared at the journal entry before her. One she'd written mere months ago.

Near fields of swaying cornstalks,
The sun shines upon a sister's grave.
Yet, there is more to this humble place of repose,
And there are truths that must be staved.
There is a person who keeps secrets.
The world does not see,
That this grave is not what it appears.
And the woman buried there is not me . . . Isabelle.

Isabelle's heart constricted, tears gathering in her eyes. News had just reached her of her sister's marriage—and to whom. It left her reeling. And overjoyed. Sabine had made her dream come true.

It was time to put an end to their separation. Now that Leon was dead, it was time to come out of hiding. Closing the journal, Isabelle placed it back inside her desk. She had a letter to write. A sister she desperately missed to reunite with.

Dipping her quill into the crystal inkwell, she wrote:

My dearest Sabine . . .

Glossary

Antechamber—The sitting room in a lord's or lady's private apartments (chambers).

Caleçons—Drawers/underwear.

Chambers—Another word for private apartments. A lord's or lady's chambers consisted of a bedroom, a sitting room, a bathroom, and a *cabinet* (office). Some chambers were bigger and more elaborate than others. Some *cabinets* were so large, they were used for private meetings.

Chère—Dear one. Endearment for a woman (*cher* for a man).

Chérie—Darling or cherished one. Endearment for a woman (*chéri* for a man).

Comte—Count.

Comtesse—Countess.

Dieu—God.

Fronde, the—A civil uprising that started in 1648 and ended in 1653. Incited by power-hungry nobles, they almost dethroned their boy King. (Louis XIV was only ten years old when it began.) Louis was forced to flee Paris in the night with his mother and live in exile for a while. He never forgot what he and his mother endured during this tense, tumultuous time. He developed a lifelong dislike and mistrust for the aristocracy. Intent on being absolute ruler, he spent his reign intimidating them.

Frondeur—Someone who is a traitor to the Crown, having been part of the uprising against the young King Louis XIV.

Hôtel—A mansion located in the city. The upper class and the wealthy bourgeois (middle class) often had a mansion in Paris (*hôtel*) in addition to their palatial country estates (*château*).

Lettre de Cachet—Order/letter of confinement—without trial—signed by the King with the royal seal (*cachet*).

Ma belle—My beauty. Endearment for a woman.

Merde—Shit.

Seigneur Dieu—Lord God.

Tesora (Italian)—Darling.